THIS TIME NEXT DOOR

(OAKLAND HILLS #2)

GRETCHEN GALWAY

ETON FIELD

THIS TIME NEXT DOOR

(Previously published as *The Geek Who Loved Me.*)
Copyright © 2012 by Gretchen Galway

Eton Field, Publisher
www.gretchengalway.com

eBook ISBN: 978-1-939872-03-6
Trade Paperback ISBN: 978-1-939872-04-3

IT WAS THE FIRST TIME Rose had ever been asked to take off her clothes for a job interview.

"You want me to strip?" Rose asked, surprised. "All the way?"

The woman in front of her wore a measuring tape around her neck and had hair like a snowball, white and round. *Like me*, Rose thought.

"What kind of bra are you wearing?" Snowball asked, looking her over.

Rose glanced down at her chest, unusually compressed for the occasion. "It's a sports bra. Brand-new. I thought, since you're looking for a model for workout clothes, I should—"

"Panties?"

Rose paused. "What about them?"

"What kind of underpants?"

This is a very odd conversation. The receptionist had sent her up to the engineering floor for her appointment, and Snowball had ushered her down a hallway without any preamble, not even a quick exchange of names.

"They're just... regular," Rose replied. "Not a thong or anything."

"Control-top?"

"No."

The woman nodded. "Good. We'll need to know your real numbers. We'll add on a little for the bust. Just strip down to your underwear and let me know when you're ready." She nudged Rose deeper into the storage closet and pulled the door shut between them.

Rose looked around. She'd imagined something a little more glamorous than a dim closet overstuffed with clothes on racks and sagging shipping boxes. Maybe the fashion industry in San Francisco was as casual as everything else on the West Coast. And of course, Fite Fitness was just a fitnesswear company, not couture or anything.

She unzipped her knee-high leather boots and pulled them off, unwound her favorite silk scarf, then stripped off her low-rise black pants and magenta wrap sweater, and folded it all into a neat pile. Wearing only her underwear and jewelry—a trio of long silver necklaces and assorted bangles—she peered into the small mirror on the wall to check her lipstick.

Satisfied, she pulled open the door and strode out into the workroom.

It was drafty. She hoped she didn't have to wait out here like this for very long. Snowball was nowhere in sight, so she walked down the hallway and past a row of long, flat tables covered with patterns, bolts of fabric, piles of clothes. "Hello?"

A bald man in his fifties with purple reading glasses glanced up from a table. With a start, he dropped his pencil and stared. "Plus-sized fit model on the loose!" he called out.

"Where is she?" Snowball asked from behind her. Then, "Oh!"

The man picked up his pencil and went back to work.

Another head popped up from another table off to the side. The young woman's dark eyes went wide.

Rose turned to Snowball. "Sorry. Was I supposed to stay in the closet?"

There was a snort from the man at the table.

"Most girls prefer a little privacy," Snowball said.

Shrugging, Rose walked back to the closet, head high. "I've never done this before."

The woman joined her in the closet and shut them inside. "Have you done any kind of modeling?"

Oh, sure. Whenever I'm not selling used paperbacks on Amazon to pay off my college loans. Keeping a straight face, Rose said, "It's been a few years."

"You've got the hair for it. And the skin." Her gaze dropped down over Rose's exposed, pale form.

"Thanks." Rose was used to people complimenting her Barbie-like blonde hair and peaches-and-cream complexion. Right before they suggested how lovely she *could* have been if she'd just stop eating. "By the way, what's your name? I like to know the names of people I get naked with."

The woman glanced up at her over her bifocals. "Meryl." She peeled off one of the measuring tapes dangling around her neck and moved closer, her arms extended in front of her like a cartoon zombie. "Hands up. And don't suck anything in, please."

Rose did as she was told, feeling the brush of Meryl's fingers against the sensitive flesh of her waist, the small of her back, her abdomen. The tape met over her tummy in the woman's small hands.

Don't suck it in. What did that mean? It was impossible not to tense a little bit under the circumstances. Taking a shallow breath, Rose looked over the woman's fluffy white head and focused on a very slim pair of black running pants hanging on the back of the door. "You're just starting a plus-sized line?"

"Mmm," Meryl said. "Waist, thirty-five and a quarter." She let one end of the tape fall to the floor as she jotted a note in a yellow pad balanced on top of one of the lopsided boxes. "That might be a problem. We're looking for thirty-six."

Rose smiled. "I'm too small? That's a first."

"In the waist, anyway," Meryl said, staring at her chest.

"I told Blair I didn't know what my measurements were, but she said you guys wanted to meet me anyway."

"Let's see what else you've got."

"Plenty, as it happens," Rose said.

Meryl leaned in to measure her bust. "Arms up again, please." She slid the tape back and forth, paused. "Forty-five and three-quarters. But I'll have to add on an inch to allow for the bra."

Rose stared at the ceiling as Meryl went back to her notebook, muttering, "Forty-six and three-quarters."

This was unexpectedly awkward. When Rose's roommate had told her about a job that paid seventy dollars an hour just to try on clothes, she'd been happy to hop on the first BART train to San Francisco. She hadn't considered how being poked and prodded might make her feel like a twelve-year-old undressing in the school locker room for the first time.

Meryl wrapped the tape around her again. She wiggled it down to Rose's hips, holding on with one hand as if she were lassoing a calf—

Don't go there, girl, Rose told herself. *Chin up. Big and beautiful.*

"Forty-eight and a quarter," Meryl said, draping the tape around her neck. "Well, that one's a deal-breaker."

"I really do wear an 18. Often," she said. "Well, sometimes."

Moving to the door, Meryl tucked her yellow pad into her pocket. "You can get dressed. I won't need the rest of your numbers."

Rose propped her hands on her hips. "Too big?"

"A little bit. Thanks for coming in… uh…" She stared.

"Rose."

"Right," Meryl said. "Rose. Thanks for making the trip. You can bill us for the full hour."

Rose let out the breath she'd been holding. So much for that. For a few days she'd enjoyed a little fantasy about making some easy money. It would've been fun to tell people she was a model.

Without lying.

"If you lose a few pounds," Meryl said, "call us. We could measure you again."

Rose flashed a half-smile. "Don't count on it."

With a shrug, Meryl said, "Best of luck to you," and closed the door.

While she got dressed, Rose faced the hard facts. She was unemployed and thousands of miles from home. Her monthly college loan payments were killing her. The glamorous world of plus-size fashion didn't want her.

She draped her scarf around her neck, combed and fluffed her hair, looked around the dingy closet.

Just as well. She was twenty-six, long past time for her to find a real job.

Preferably one that didn't involve taking her clothes off.

&

"Mom, it's no big deal. I just didn't have the measurements they were looking for," Rose said.

She heard her mother's answering sigh through the phone.

"Just think—my kid, a *model*," her mom said.

"It wasn't real modeling. Just trying on clothes. Like sweatpants and stuff. I had to get naked in a closet."

"How about other companies? Isn't the Gap in San Francisco?"

"As if the Gap needs a plus-size fit model, Mom. They'd take one look at me and laugh."

"They wouldn't. You're gorgeous."

Rose ducked into the drugstore on Market Street and bent over to grab a basket. "You're right. And I get my looks from you. So how come you're always putting yourself down?"

"You get your brains from me. Which I'm happy to take credit for."

Rose shook her head as she made her way past makeup and moisturizers to the shelf of nail polish removers. She had to put the basket on the floor to free up a hand to claim the biggest bottle. "You should look in a mirror sometime, Mom. You look just like me." She found a bag of cotton squares. "Just a little older. A *very* little bit older."

Her mother sighed. "Nobody ever thought we were sisters, honey. Big women always look older than they are, even at eighteen."

"I thought you were seventeen."

"Rosalind..."

Rose laughed. "Oh, right. That was just the conception."

"You promised you weren't going to joke about that anymore."

"Only around Slug. Or do you think he's listening on the other line?" Her mother's new husband was not her favorite person.

"I'm serious. Perhaps I should hang up."

"No, don't. I'm sorry," Rose said. "Look, I'm in a CVS in downtown San Francisco getting the supplies for a manicure. I'm just… I guess I was feeling homesick. I miss you. I'm *thousands* of miles away. I know other people live like this, but I didn't think we would. We're close."

"Enjoy your freedom. You're young, you're single, and you're doing something wonderful for a friend."

Rose could hear the longing in her mother's voice. Becoming a single mom at eighteen had changed everything, even with a supportive family. She'd had no opportunity to be young and free.

"It's weird thinking I can't just drop by and paint your nails tonight," Rose said.

"You always pick colors that are too loud for me."

"You look great in brights. No point trying to hide if you're three hundred pounds, might as well—"

"You do *not* weigh that much," her mother said.

"Not me. You."

Her mother fell silent for a moment while Rose studied a bottle of iridescent dark purple. "You enjoy yourself out there in California. I can get my nails done at the salon."

"I miss you," Rose said. "That's all I'm saying."

"It's only until the baby's born. Or Blair changes her mind about living with the father's family. How's she doing?"

"Better. Though she throws up a lot." Her roommate and best friend, Blair, was unexpectedly pregnant. The charming, handsome sperm donor hadn't wanted her to keep the baby, but his mother had. Desperately. The woman offered Blair a house, financial support, family—three things Blair lacked. She only had to move across the country to California to get them.

Rose had joined her to offer her support. In exchange,

Rose would finally get to spread her wings, grow up a little. Except for three years of college, she'd lived at home her entire life. And since her mother had remarried, home wasn't as homey as it used to be.

"The worst thing is," Rose said, "she's still hoping John changes his mind."

"Maybe he will."

"You'd forgive him for abandoning her to this? You? Ms. Teenage Single Mom?"

"Don't interfere," her mother said. "They need to figure this out on their own."

"Blair can be such a wimp. If John can't man up now, why expect him to later?"

"It's not your place."

"Sure it is. I'm her best friend."

"He's the father of her baby. Stay out of it."

"How can I?" Rose asked. "I moved to the other side of the country to live with her while she figures this out. I'm not allowed to give my opinion?"

"Since when does sharing living quarters give you the right to make the biggest decision of her life?"

"Like Grandmother did with you? Or me?"

"Exactly," her mother said. "That's exactly right."

"I'm not her mother. I'm her friend."

"Right again."

Rose dropped the dark purple nail polish into her basket, then added a glittery crimson. "I'm taking her out clubbing. Finding her a new guy. To hell with John."

"Good idea. There's no harm in her proclaiming her independence."

Rose strode toward the register at the front of the store. "You give such great advice. How come you can't ever apply any of it to yourself?"

"You went with the red again, didn't you?"

"You know it."

"Good choice."

Unloading her basket on the belt, Rose nodded hello to the cashier and readjusted the phone at her ear. "I'm mailing you the purple."

"I'll never use it."

"Maybe Grandmother will."

Laughing, her mom said goodbye. Rose swiped her debit card, hoping she had more than twenty bucks in her account. That modeling job would've made her life a lot easier. She was signed up with a temp agency, but nothing had come through yet.

Secretarial work. How depressing. Premed wasn't much use if you didn't follow through on the "med" part after graduation. Unfortunately, she knew now she didn't want to be a doctor, or a vet, or a nurse, or a psychiatrist, or a long list of things. What she *did* want to be was an elusive, invisible cloud of mystery.

The cashier, a thirty-something woman with hair like a brown pyramid and thin, heavily lined lips, handed her the bag. Rose studied her while she worked.

At least she knew she didn't want to work behind a cash register. She'd worked retail through high school and college, enough for a lifetime. Unfortunately, retail didn't do much for her résumé, any more than selling used books, baby clothes, or antiques on the Internet did.

She checked the time on her phone. She'd agreed to meet Blair at Bloomingdale's. As if she could afford to buy anything right now. It was masochistic to get within fifty feet of a department store.

Besides, Blair was a size 4, at least for another month or two; shopping with her was a spectator sport. The plus sizes were kept far away from the skinny stuff, in quarantine on another floor, as though the extra inches were contagious. Which is why, since they were teenagers, Rose and Blair met in the sock department. Socks were cheap and they fit. Though everything seemed expensive these days.

"Oh my God, look at you," Blair said ten minutes later when Rose waved at her across a display of terrycloth slippers. She dropped the package she was holding and stared. "You're a vision. Where did you get that sweater?"

Rose looked down at herself, stroked the vivid pink knit hugging her curves. "This old thing?" She smiled. "I made it."

"Really? Oh my God, it's so beautiful. I didn't realize you could knit that well. I knew you could make scarves and things, but—" Blair stopped abruptly, her eyes narrowing. "You're teasing me again, aren't you?"

Rose grinned. "Sucker."

"How can you lie to me? I told you I don't like it."

"How can you believe me? I told you I can't help it."

Blair shook her head. "It's amazing I ever believe anything you say."

"Isn't it?"

"It is. It really is," Blair said, picking up the package she'd dropped. Then her eyes widened. "Hey, how'd it go? I wasn't sure we wanted to trust Ellen about the modeling job, but John said she'd never do anything to hurt Fite Fitness. He said she's given her life to that place." Fite Fitness belonged to John's family.

"Well, they don't want me. Said I'm too fat."

Blair froze. "I'm sorry. God. I shouldn't have—"

"What are you apologizing for? It would've been great if I'd been right for them, but I wasn't, so there you go. Nothing for you to feel bad about."

"It was my idea. Did you have to… never mind. I'm sorry.

I should've asked for more information before you had to expose yourself like that."

Rose smiled, reached for a package of lacy red thigh-highs. "You know me. I like the attention." She held the package out to Blair. "Speaking of which, I think that's just what you need. Pregnant chicks are sexy. Show it off, baby."

Rolling her eyes at the red tights, Blair said, "Don't change the subject."

"Blair, it was no big deal. Years of telling off my anorexic grandmother have made me invincible."

Blair snorted. "You're not as tough as you seem."

"I am about this." She patted Blair on the shoulder. "Really. I'm fine."

"Yeah? Why'd you suddenly need to go to CVS? Which made you late to meet me?"

"Tampons."

In a flash, Blair snatched the bag away, pulled it open. "Just what I thought. You always go for manicure therapy when you're upset."

"I was missing my mother, that's all. I was talking to her on the phone and got homesick."

Blair's triumphant smile faded. "That's my fault. You being here."

"No moping. Let's go upstairs and get your eyebrows sculpted."

"Right. As if that's my top budget priority right now."

"Come on." Rose reclaimed her bag, tucked it under her arm. "It's twenty bucks. You've got gorgeous eyebrows. Dark, arched, dramatic—give them a little love."

"You can. I'll watch."

"There's no point doing mine. They're invisible. I could shave them off and nobody would notice the difference."

Blair licked her lips. "I shouldn't. What if I have to raise this baby alone? I'll need every penny I've got, and I don't even have a job. Who's going to hire a pregnant English major?"

"They aren't hiring English majors who *aren't* pregnant, so there's no point dwelling on that. Besides, maybe they'll be afraid of looking like they're violating your rights and hire you because of it. Not that you look pregnant."

"I'm totally poufing out. Look at his." Blair put her hands on her hips and arched her back. "I can barely button my jeans."

Rose glanced at her concave abdomen. "Must be twins."

"Shut up."

"I should give you that phone number at Fite Fitness. I hear they're looking for a plus-size fit model."

Blair shoved her in the arm, biting back a smile. "All right. I won't do eyebrows, but we can check out the dresses. Something stretchy and cheap."

"Just like your roommate sophomore year. What was her name, the gymnast?"

With a laugh, Blair took off for the elevator. "Come on, let's do it. If just to get you to shut up."

"Dream on," Rose said.

&

"Damn, Mark," Jared's voice said in his ear, "I've been trying to fix that bug for seven months. You do it in a week and now I look like an idiot."

Mark Johnson tore open a bag of Flamin' Hot Cheetos while he stared at the computer screen in his bedroom. His new job writing code was going pretty well. He was making four times what he'd made as a teacher, and he didn't even have to leave home. Or put on pants.

"No problem," he told Jared, glad he hadn't let on that the

chore had only taken him a few hours. Best not to show off. "What else you got for me?"

While Jared launched into a description of another project, Mark covered the mic of his phone's headset with one hand so he could politely munch on his Cheetos.

"So what do you think?" Jared asked after a few minutes.

Mark mulled it over. "Two weeks?"

"Really? You think you can get it done that fast? QA wants a full month to test it before the release."

"I think so," Mark said. "I'll have to look at it for a couple days to be sure."

"That would be awesome," Jared said. "I'll tell the big guy, okay?"

Mark swallowed another mouthful of Cheetos. "Okay."

"Awesome. You sure?"

"No problem," Mark said.

When Jared finally hung up, Mark peeled off the headset, careful not to get Cheeto dust on his keyboard, and got to his feet.

What time was it, anyway? He glanced at his monitor and recoiled. Already 5:24 p.m. and he hadn't even gotten dressed yet. With blackout shades on his windows to reduce the glare on the trio of monitors on his desk, sometimes he lost track of the world outside.

Sometimes? More like always. Was this what he wanted when he quit teaching? Living with his mother at twenty-nine years of age, never leaving the house, never seeing a soul who wasn't related to him?

He went over and flipped up the shade. Bright sun shining over the Golden Gate made him squint.

What a waste. He had a million-dollar view from his own bedroom and he didn't even look at it. His mother's house in the hills of Oakland, the one he'd grown up in, had most of its windows facing west to enjoy the panorama of San Francisco to Marin spreading out from left to right. The sky was clear, the fog blanket only beginning its creep over San Francisco.

It was September now; days were getting shorter.

Practically thirty. How was that possible? He still got carded when he bought beer. How could he be so old?

He leaned his forehead against the window and peered at the house to the left, telling himself he was just enjoying the way the sun was lighting up the modern windows with platinum streaks.

Was *she* home? He flattened his cheek against the glass to get a better look. The house looked quiet, but she seemed like the quiet type.

Quiet was good.

Indulging in a memory of the new neighbor waving at him over the bushes in the front yard, Mark closed his eyes and conjured her up in his mind.

He pushed away from the window. Of all the women to fixate on, he picked one who's involved with a future in-law of his. His brother was finally getting married, which was great, but his fiancée, Bev, had not-so-great relatives. Like the dude who knocked up his neighbor.

Groaning, he strode across the room. He had to get out. Just a walk, a run, maybe shoot some hoops in the driveway, anything to remind him of the real world.

His clothes were in a pile on the floor where he'd dumped them from the dryer, but at least they were clean. Except for the stains. And the jeans were too short because he'd been too cheap to pass up the five-dollar Levi's on the clearance rack.

He pulled them on anyway and looked in the mirror. A thirty-two-inch inseam wasn't what it used to be. With a shrug, he turned away from the mirror and jogged downstairs.

Maybe it was time to take some of the money he'd squirreled away to buy some new clothes.

One of these days.

He walked past the old upright piano and the dining room table into the kitchen. His mother, Trixie, was using the old avocado-green rotary phone that had hung on the wall since Mark was born.

"That's terrible," his mother said into the receiver, twisting the cord between her fingers. "Which houses were hit?"

Mark paused in the doorway.

"Oh, no, I understand that would be confidential," his mother continued. "So little privacy these days."

An alarm bell went off in Mark's head. "Mom, who's on the phone?"

She waved at him, smiling, but then turned and addressed whoever was on the line. "Oh, but you see, I don't live alone," she said. "My son is here. Mark, my middle child. He's better than any alarm system, I'm sure."

"Mom," Mark repeated. "Who are you talking to?"

Her smile faltered. "Yes, I suppose he will be moving along someday."

Mark strode over, reached for the phone.

"Soon, yes," she said. "Probably soon."

He took the receiver just as a man's voice was saying, "Ma'am, that's precisely the type of home these criminals are targeting—women living alone. Especially in such a large house as yours. How many square feet did you say it was?"

"A lot bigger than the prison cell you'll be living in if you call here again," Mark said.

He heard a grunt before the line went dead.

With a sigh, he turned to his mother. "You're on the sucker list, Mom. Don't let them start in on you. Just hang up."

"Really? Again? He sounded so real."

"Real?"

"I always hang up on the robot people," she said. "Even if it's Diane Feinstein."

Mark put an arm around her. Barely sixty, his mother was too young to be so gullible, but when it came to predatory telemarketers, she was as vulnerable as an elderly shut-in. Part of it was her natural friendliness, her joy in a good chat, her excessive free time. "What did he offer you?"

"It's not like I would've taken it," she said with a sniff.

He looked down at her. That was probably true, but you never knew. Ever since she'd taken in more than a dozen Chihuahuas last year as part of a rescue operation, she'd been the object of a series of charity scams. She'd rather get cheated, she'd say, than fail to help a person—or animal—in need.

"I'll answer the phone from now on," Mark said.

Rolling her eyes, she patted him on the chest. "If it makes you feel better."

"And I'm going to put in a real phone with an ID screen," he added.

"As long as you leave Old Greenie where it is, you can do whatever you want." She cocked her head. "Is that the doorbell?"

Hearing the distant chime, he groaned. It seemed like an hour didn't go by without somebody harassing them. Phone, door, mail, Internet. He'd put his mother on all the do-not-call lists, added a No Solicitors sign to the door, unsubscribed her from online spam and corporate mailing lists, but it took time for the word to get out.

And possibly a court order.

"I'll get it," he said.

"Good," his mother said. "As long as you're wearing pants."

Putting on his most manly, hostile expression, he strode

through the house to the front door and jerked it open. "Whatever you're selling—"

His voice went dry in his throat. It wasn't a solicitor; it was a woman.

His neighbor.

2

CALM DOWN, HE TOLD HIMSELF. His heart was beating too hard. *It's the other one. Her roommate.*

"Sorry to bother you," she said. "I live next door. I'm on a mission to find some jumper cables."

He tried to fix his gaze above her neck, but there was a lot to look at below it. She was a big woman, not tall, but easily two hundred pounds. Young, twenty-something. She wore a black tank top that didn't quite cover the expanse of her chest, a pair of men's shiny basketball shorts with a white stripe down the side, and black high-tops. Her hair was pulled back under a backward-facing, rainbow-emblazoned baseball cap, exposing a round face that was shiny with sweat and devoid of makeup. Hands propped on her hips, she stared at him, hurried and businesslike.

Men's clothes, no makeup, rainbow.

Lesbian, he thought, relaxing.

"You can borrow mine." He reached for his keys. "They're in my car. Need help?"

"That's all right. I've already got my roommate's hood up. Such bad luck. Bad day."

He smiled. "At least you had one. I've been staring at a computer all day. Totally lost track of time."

"You get paid to do that?"

"Well, yeah."

"Lucky you."

He closed the front door behind him, agreeing with her. Some of his friends, old classmates and fellow teachers, had been without a real job for months, even years. "I'll get the cables."

She followed him out to his car in the short driveway next to hers. The houses were perched on the steep hillside to enjoy the view, leaving little room for yards or parking. "What's your name?" He untangled the cables from the blankets in the back of his old Jetta and handed them to her. "I'm Mark."

"Rose." She flashed a quick smile before sinking back into her funk. "The dome light must've been on all day. Didn't close the door all the way."

"Bad luck."

"Yeah. Well, thanks."

A gust of wind blew between the houses and whipped her blonde ponytail off her shoulder. He took a deep breath, realizing how reviving it was to suck in some fresh air. He *really* needed to get out more. "Do you play basketball?" he asked abruptly.

She had already turned to walk away. "Excuse me?"

"Sorry. You look like you were—forget it. I have a hoop, see? On the side of the house? I just wanted you to know you could use it if you wanted."

With a glance down at her outfit, her face turned pink. "God, I forgot what I was wearing. No, I lift. Weights. I was just working out. My roommate needs to run an errand, but my car is dead behind hers, blocking her in." She smoothed her shirt over her hips.

"Sorry." He ran his hand over his face. "I don't get out much and I forget how to talk to people. What you just had the pleasure of witnessing was my feeble attempt at socializing."

"It was pretty good." She smiled briefly. "Sorry I didn't play along."

"No problem. I'll warn you next time when I'm about to make another effort."

With a smile that finally reached her eyes—stunningly blue, almost the same color as his car—she said, "Looking forward to it."

He looked down at his bare feet. Pebbles from the cracked driveway were biting into his skin. "Let me grab my shoes and I'll help you. It's easier with two people."

"You really don't have to—"

"Warning—this is another attempt."

She laughed. "Busted again. All right. That would be nice. Blair, my roommate, isn't very butch."

He stared at her. Were they both gay? That didn't make sense. Blair was pregnant. Then again, Mark had heard the pregnancy was unplanned; and John, his ex-neighbor and future relation by marriage, was still in New York.

"Just a second." He jogged back to the house and shoved his bare feet into his Birkenstocks. Maybe the quiet brunette was bisexual. Or hadn't decided yet. Which was why she couldn't agree to marry…

"Chill, dude," he muttered to himself. Countless hours in his programming Man Cave had decimated what few social skills he'd had to begin with.

Rose already had the hoods propped up when he returned. Her car, the one in back, was a silver Corolla. Blair's was a white Corolla, same model year.

Hers and hers cars?

More confused than ever, he joined her under the hood of the dead one to help her with the cables.

"I really appreciate this," she said, squeezing the red clamp and bending over the battery. "Since we just moved out here, I don't have anyone I could call." She connected the clamp to the positive terminal.

"You came from New York, right?"

She nodded. "Upstate. Never thought I'd live in California."

"What'd'ya think?"

"Until today, it was fine."

He walked over to her roommate's car, ready to help, but she strode past him and attached the other clamps to the good battery without hesitating.

She certainly was capable around an engine. Why was it most women never learned anything about cars? Then again, most men didn't seem to know much either. He was a software guy, but at least he knew the basics. Modern humans completely relied on machines they knew nothing about, depending on the few who did to keep them working. Cars, computers, electricity.

"So, Mark, what do you do?"

With a start, he realized she'd already started up her roommate's car and was standing right next to him. It wasn't like him to forget a woman was nearby—one of his most limiting hang-ups.

"I'm a software engineer." He watched her face, waiting for the knowing-but-not-knowing nod. It wasn't like saying *brain surgeon*, which conjured up the concrete image of latex fingers holding a scalpel as it sliced through delicate gray matter. *Software engineer* made people think not of the action but of confusing, opaque technicalities. Computers, code, whatever. Fascinating, wonderful stuff most people thought was as thrilling as lint.

"Right," she said, sighing. "I forgot everyone in the Bay Area is a software engineer."

"Hardly."

She gave him a sour glance. "Everyone with a job."

"Not even them."

"Everyone under thirty." She climbed into her car, and in a moment it started. "Yes!"

Mark gave the Toyota an encouraging pat before disconnecting the cables from both engines. When he climbed into Blair's car to turn it off, he noticed how clean it was, with a little silk daisy on the dash. He smiled, inhaled the faint scent of perfume.

Rose tapped him on the shoulder. "I'll tell Blair she's been liberated."

His heart gave a thud as he realized he was going to meet the quiet brunette face-to-face. So far he'd had to admire her from across the property line. "You'll want to drive around for a while to keep the battery going," he said, swallowing hard. "Thirty minutes or so."

"Yeah, I know. Should be fun."

"Could be worse."

"Tell me about it. I spent a week in this car driving across the country without anyone to talk to, since Blair drove out hers, too. I wish I'd left it at my mom's, but everyone said you can't live in California without your own car."

"Hey! You got it going!"

There she was, jogging over from the house. Blair. She was wearing jeans and a T-shirt, understated but pretty. Her hair was down, all wavy and long and soft-looking around her shoulders, and a purse bobbed on her shoulder.

"Thanks to Neighbor Guy," Rose said as he got out of the car.

His mouth went dry. His mantra, *Don't be a dork*, blared in his mind.

"Oh," Blair said, freezing in place. Eyes wide, she stared at him, obviously shy. After a moment, she laughed awkwardly and waved. "Hi. I'm Blair."

"I know," he said, then cringed. "I mean, hi. Mark is me. I mean, I am Mark." He closed his eyes. *Kill me now.*

"You're making another one of those efforts, aren't you?" Rose asked him.

Teeth clenched, he turned to glare at her, then saw the warm humor in her face. "Always risky," he said.

"Nice to meet you," Blair said.

Silence stretched between them. How did he acknowledge the potential connection between them without being rude? *By the way, my brother is marrying the cousin of the father of your unborn baby…*

"We're practically family," he blurted.

Smile falling, Blair glanced at Rose.

"Sorry, sorry," he said, waving the cables. "I'll go back into my cave now."

He got as far as his mother's rosebushes before Blair called out after him. "Thanks for your help."

He turned, a familiar mortification seeping into his veins, and waved again. *Way to go, Casanova.*

Luckily the nice brunette didn't seem to hold a grudge; she smiled and waved back at him as she got into her car.

She was prettier than he'd imagined, and he'd imagined a lot. Like a little fairy. If lacy wings suddenly appeared between her shoulder blades, flapping dreamily and bearing her away, he wouldn't be surprised.

Were her eyes brown or green? He'd been too stressed to get a good look.

His gaze drifted over to Rose, whose bright blue eyes were fixed on him, a single mocking eyebrow cocked high. She'd seen right through him, of course. If he were a cartoon, little hearts would be swirling around his head.

"Better get a move on," Rose said, getting in the car.

He flinched. He was willing to embarrass himself, but he hated to offend anybody. Especially a neighbor. Still clutching the jumper cables, he strode back over the creeping rosemary between the two driveways to Rose's car and pulled open the passenger door just as she was revving the engine into reverse.

"Hey," he said quickly, "Want me to ride shotgun?"

ROSE FROWNED AT HER TALL NEIGHBOR, SURPRISED. DID he think Blair was going to be coming with them? "You don't have to do that. I'm fine."

He climbed in anyway and grabbed the seat belt. "You'd be doing me a favor. I'll just spend the next half hour worrying about you getting stranded."

She put the car in park and gave the car more gas as it idled. "No, really, I'm fine."

"Please. You never know what might happen. Lots of steep hills up here. Bad spot to get stuck."

Biting her lip, she stared at him. Blair was obviously in her own car waiting to drive somewhere else. "Is this another one of your efforts?"

"Is it that obvious?"

She glanced at the other car. "I'm not going where Blair is going, you know."

"I didn't think you were," he said. And then, "Why would you say that?"

She just laughed and backed up into the street. "So, Mark, where should we go?"

"Do you get carsick easily?"

"Yes."

"Oh, good. Me too. That rules out the scenic drive through Tilden," he said. "You could get on 580, drive for fifteen minutes, turn around."

"Get on the freeway during rush hour? Kind of risky, don't you think? Stop-and-go traffic with a dead battery?"

"Right. Well, where do you want to go?"

"I don't want to go anywhere. That's why I'm annoyed," she said. "Think of something else."

"Why should I think of something else?"

"You're the one who jumped in."

"Well, where would you have gone if I hadn't jumped in?"

"I have no idea, but you did, so make yourself useful and tell me where to go." They pulled up to a stop sign at a steeply angled intersection.

"Turn left."

"Where are we going?" she asked.

"No way. If you're going to make me navigate, you can't ask so many questions."

Her face broke into a grin. "Fair enough," she said, gunning the engine and turning left. "Should I close my eyes, too? Make it a little more exciting?"

He gripped the dash. "That won't be necessary," he said. "Turn right."

"What, here?"

"Are you going to listen to me or not?"

"Fine!" She braked and turned, screeching the tires.

"Will you slow down? Little kids live around here."

"Little kids can't afford to live around here, from what I've seen. The average age in this neighborhood seems to be about eighty-nine."

"There are kids, believe me, so slow down."

"Man, what a baby," she said, but she did as he asked. The winding road came to an empty six-way intersection. She braked, but the car was on an incline and the idle sounded a bit weak. Paranoid about the battery, she hit the gas.

A large male hand grabbed her thigh. "Wait! Uphill traffic doesn't stop."

She braked abruptly just as a Prius popped over the hill and flew past her front bumper with only a foot to spare.

After a long second, her heart pounding in her ears, Rose looked at him. "Thanks."

He opened his eyes. "That car was going at least twenty over the limit."

"Hybrids are way too quiet." Paranoid now, with her eyes fixed on the downhill road, she puttered across the intersection.

Mark's hand was still on her thigh. Her sweaty, exposed thigh, barely covered by the sleek polyester fabric of her shorts.

Not that he looked like he was getting turned on by the experience. Probably because of the trauma of a near collision, he seemed to have forgotten where his hand was. From the way his fingers pressed into her flesh, mapping tiny circles with his thumb, she wondered if he was finding some comfort in the contact, like a kid with a blankie.

"Mark?"

Then he realized. With a start, he jerked his hand away. "Sorry."

"No, I'm sorry. I scared you."

He shook his head, looking angry. "I'm fine. I really need to get out more. It's making me jumpy."

"Well, that was really close. It made me jump, too." She put a hand on her chest. Sure enough, her heart was still racing. The last thing she needed was car repair, let alone a trip to the hospital without health insurance.

His eyes followed her hand and lingered there. If he hadn't been so obviously smitten with Blair, she would've thought he was checking out her breasts.

Looking back at the road, he said, "I recognized the guy, too. Lives around here. Smug prick. Always speeding."

She drove on, winding past modern homes hanging on the steep hillsides. "Now where, Captain?"

He looked at the dash. "How much more time do we have?"

"Counting the minutes, are you? You know, I didn't ask you to come."

"Take it easy. I'm just calculating our options. I figure we can drive down to El Cerrito and back along the frontage road. Have you been to the Berkeley marina yet?"

"I went to a used bookstore on Telegraph, but that's about it for my sightseeing."

"Then turn left here and take it all the way down to San Pablo. It's not a tourist destination by any means, but you might as well learn how to get around."

They drove down the windy, leafy streets in silence for ten minutes until they'd left the residential neighborhoods and were creeping through the congestion of the gourmet ghetto of boutiques and restaurants between Oakland and Berkeley.

"What do you read?" he asked.

"Excuse me?"

"At the bookstore. You said that was the only sightseeing you did. Were you looking for anything in particular?"

Her poor job prospects had made her desperate enough to think, with a little hard work and self-directed reading, she could go to graduate school in a field that might employ her. But she didn't want to talk about that with a computer geek who probably couldn't relate to being unemployable. "Not really."

"Turn right at the light," he said. After a few minutes, he looked at her again. "How do you and… your roommate… like living in California so far?"

"Too soon to tell," she said. "And Blair has other things on her mind."

To her surprise, he said, "The baby."

"You know about that?"

"My brother is engaged to John's cousin. His mother, Ellen, used to live in that house. Before my time, but our families have known each other for years."

"Lucky you."

"You know them, then?"

When a bus stopped in front of her, she looked over her shoulder to pull into the other lane. They'd left the retail strip and were now passing small bungalows and concrete apartment blocks huddled right up against the busy divided street, fronted with patchy brown lawns and low iron fences. "Not that I like Ellen, but at least she's interested in the baby. Offering Blair the house was quite a gesture. Paying her doctor bills clinched it. No way Blair could turn her down."

"I haven't seen John in years," Mark said.

Rose glanced at him, wondering what gossip had reached him. "He's a selfish jerk."

The car was silent for a few moments. "Does Blair agree?"

"She's beginning to notice. Breaking up with her when she told him she was pregnant was her first clue."

He let out a long breath. "But she's here with his family."

Rose heard more than casual interest in his voice. She braked at the light and looked at him. "She didn't have anyone else. Her mother died in a car accident—she was an alcoholic—and her dad's super religious, wants her to marry the first guy he can line up. Ellen is Mary Poppins in comparison."

His face clouded. "Man."

"Yeah."

When the light turned green, she asked him, "Should I stay on this road?"

"Yeah. Turn right on San Pablo. You've still got a ways to go." He rolled the window down, then up, then down, making a little tapping sound with his finger on the plastic. "How could John just leave her out here to face his mother alone?"

Rose appreciated his indignation but didn't like the way he was playing with the window controls. "I don't know. Could you please stop doing that? It might mess up the wiring."

"It won't."

"How can you know? I've had enough trouble with my car, and I don't want any more."

"The switch is designed to raise and lower the window. How is using it going to break anything?"

"I don't know," she said, "but it's driving me crazy."

"That, I'll accept. Not some uninformed claim that I'm inflicting mechanical damage."

"You know," she said, flicking the turn signal, "I think the battery will be fine after I drive you back up the hill."

"What's your problem?"

"Dude, you invited yourself along on this journey, and quite frankly, I'm not enjoying your company."

"It would be stupid to turn back now," he said. "You'll have to borrow the cables again tomorrow, which will make my mother think you're trying to be friendly, and believe me, that's not a risk you want to take."

She pulled over next to a white curb in front of a liquor store. "Why are you tormenting me?"

"I told you."

"Socializing is not tormenting."

"It is to me. That's why I avoid it."

She slapped her hands on the steering wheel before pulling back out into the road. "To heck with it. I'm going home. If the battery dies in the driveway, I'll borrow Blair's car."

"You really don't have to. I'll be quiet."

"Too late." She took the corner without braking, turned again. Soon they were heading back the way they'd come.

He started rolling the window up and down again. "It'll probably be fine. Leave it idling in the driveway for ten minutes after we get back."

She didn't reply. The fog had rolled in, bringing early gloom to the evening and a chill that was creeping across her bare arms and legs. Her clothes were still damp from her workout, and an icy current of air was whipping in through Mark's open window.

Why was she so annoyed with him? He was just some geeky guy next door. So what if he'd drooled over Blair? Rose didn't want a guy—she was off the market. Moving to California was her fresh start. The day she'd found out about Blair's pregnancy, Rose had made a solemn oath to herself: no more casual sex. Poor Blair got unlucky the first time she tried it. Rose had escaped serious consequences for years.

She stopped herself from mentally reviewing her own life, uncomfortable with the train of meaningless guys that chugged through her past. Another fling was the last thing she needed.

Blair, however, had always been alone, and if anyone needed a good guy in her life, it was her. She'd always been so shy, so understated, she'd never had much luck with men. One reason John had blinded her so easily.

Mark was just the kind of man Blair needed. He seemed sweet. A little awkward, but funny, self-deprecating, kind. The opposite of John Babydaddy Larkin.

She glanced at him. Not completely the opposite. There was a hint of a young Harrison Ford about him—brown hair, unassuming good looks. A young, nerdy swashbuckler in disguise. Although she'd had to crane her neck up to see all six-plus feet of him at his front door, she hadn't noticed his handsome profile or long, athletic build until he'd grabbed her thigh in a panic.

That ratty T-shirt and jeans didn't do anything for him. Frayed and tight, they made him look like a gawky teenager. And his hair was shaggy and uncombed.

"You need to get out more," she said.

"No kidding," he replied.

Smiling, she decided she'd been rude. His obvious preference for Blair had wounded her pride, and that was silly. She'd never had any trouble finding men who were interested in her. Blair, quiet and mousy in her black sweatshirts and jeans, did.

"Tell you what," she said. "Come over for dinner tomorrow night. Blair's been craving pasta like you wouldn't believe. I was going to make something a little better than the fluorescent mac and cheese she's been snarfing down. Some linguini, maybe a cream sauce, chicken, peas, something like that. Interested?"

He didn't reply immediately. "Really?" he said finally. "Do you want to check with her first?"

"Why would I need to do that?"

"It's her house too."

"Technically, it's neither of ours. I think she'd be glad to have company. She's not much of a social butterfly, but even she needs to be with people sometimes."

"Like me," he said softly.

Oh, boy, he was a goner. She wasn't jealous, she was happy for Blair. Of course she was. "Exactly," she said, smiling brightly.

"Okay, yes," he said. "I'll come. Great. Thanks."

3

THE NEXT MORNING, FRESH OUT of the shower after a fitful night, Mark waited until he saw Blair's car drive away before striding over to knock at the house next door.

"I can't come," he said quickly.

Rose, looking very different from the afternoon before in a filmy blue robe with her blonde hair long and loose, squinted at him over a steaming mug of coffee. "Excuse me?"

He told himself to look at her face, not the body beneath it. He almost preferred the weightlifting clothes. "Tonight. Dinner. Can't do it."

"Why not?" Holding her mug to her chest, she opened the door wider. "Hold on, Mark. Come in. It's chilly out there and we haven't figured out how to run the furnace yet."

"It's only September."

"I don't care. We're freezing."

He looked around, not surprised they'd made old Mr. Roche's house feel feminine somehow. Flowers on the table in the hall, colorful pillows on the sofa, some delicious smell coming from the kitchen.

"Nice," he said, but it did seem cold. "What's the problem with the furnace?"

"I have no idea, but when we turn up the thermostat, not much happens. We got nervous about gas so we turned it off."

"Was there a clicking sound or anything?"

She shrugged. "Maybe. I'm not sure. If we didn't run the risk of getting Ellen involved, we'd call somebody in to look at it."

He took a few steps deeper into the house, scanning the walls of the living room for the thermostat. "Want me to check it out?"

She studied him with a combination of amusement and impatience. "Blair and I would appreciate that, but it's not necessary. We'll have to deal with Ellen sometime."

"Still, it would be easier not to, right?"

Nodding, she said, "Well, yeah. That lady is way too into being a grandmother. Just this morning we found out she set up a baby registry at a boutique in San Francisco and emailed a copy to everyone she knew. Without ever asking Blair what she wanted." She rolled her eyes. "Though it was nice she CC'd her."

"Ellen terrifies me. She even terrifies Liam, my brother, not that he'd admit it. They worked at Fite together for years. And he's plenty scary himself." He found the thermostat along the back wall of the living room and flipped open the casing. "The battery seems fine."

"I checked that already. But thanks."

She peered over his shoulder, distracting him with the smell of coffee and perfume. Something sweet and flowery, very girly, which surprised him. He tapped and fiddled with the switches inside the thermostat, wishing he understood her relationship with Blair. "Did you check the furnace itself? In the basement?"

"You don't need to help us with another one of our mechanical failures," she said. "Are you hungry? I just plated an omelet."

"I'm fine. I can't." He looked around for the door down to the basement. He'd been in it once, years ago, helping old Mr. Roche carry some boxes.

"You can't come to dinner and you can't eat an omelet. Why?"

He strode back into the foyer, testing doors. He frowned into a closet. "I'll just go down and check it out."

"Mark." She touched his arm. "Was yesterday too much socializing for you? Was that it? Because I promise, we'll respect your space. We like our space, too."

He didn't know what the relationship was between Rose and Blair, if there was a tragic love triangle brewing, but he knew he didn't have the social stamina to get involved. "I'm really sorry. I was thinking—maybe another man is the last thing you need."

Her eyes went wide. "Me?" Then some mischief came into her expression. "Or Blair?"

"Either of you," he said. "I mean, you've got enough problems without me adding to them."

"How could *you* add to them?"

"No need to get nasty."

She laughed. "Come in, have some breakfast. No strings. I was making it for Blair, but she was afraid of being late for work. No appetite, anyway. Poor thing."

"She's got a job?"

"Temping. This is her first day of a two-week assignment. I'm signed up with them too, but they don't have anything for me yet."

Curiosity piqued, he followed her into the kitchen and accepted the plate she pushed at him. "Thanks."

"Ellen's going to pry when she finds out Blair's working, but Blair needs whatever independence she can get. She can't be that woman's bitch."

He nodded. "Good for her."

"Ellen wants to go to all the prenatal appointments. She showed up in her Lexus an hour before the one last week and was furious when Blair said no."

He imagined shy, sweet Blair staring down the imperious Ellen. "Good for her," he said again.

"Here's a fork. Coffee?"

What the heck? Stomach growling, he took the plate over to the small table by the window with its panoramic view of the bay and sat down. "Thanks."

She brought over a mug and joined him.

"Aren't you going to eat?" he asked.

"Already did," she said, sipping her coffee, watching him.

He took a bite, realized he was starving, took another. It was cold but tasty. "Wow. This is good. And I know good food, living with my mother."

"Thanks."

He stared down at his plate. "That seems really pathetic, doesn't it? Living with my mother."

"Not these days," she said. "I was living with mine until six weeks ago."

He swallowed another savory mouthful. "Really?" Smiling, he reached for the coffee. "That does make me feel a little better."

"I'm surprised you can't afford your own place, though, being an engineer."

"Oh, I can afford it. I just like living at home." Then he saw the way her eyebrows shot up on her forehead. "It's just for a little while," he added, but the damage was done.

Loser alert, her face said.

A very pretty face, though the blue robe was making it impossible to keep his gaze above her chin. Her breasts were a wonder of nature. They'd impressed him yesterday in the tank top, but now, full and lively and barely covered by the thin robe she wore, they struck him with awe. The nipples—lord, the nipples. He slathered butter onto a piece of toast and relived the sight from moments ago when she'd been chilled in the doorway.

"I just moved back from Milwaukee, you see," he said. "I haven't had time to get my own place."

"Sure," she said.

Who was he kidding? He liked living at home. And Rose probably saw right through him anyway. "I lived by myself in Wisconsin and barely survived." He smiled at her over his coffee. "I live with my mother because she adores me and feeds me fantastic meals and tells me I'm awesome."

"I completely understand." Her face broke into a grin. "I've got one of those myself. If she hadn't married Slug, I might still be at home myself."

"Not his real name, I gather?"

"It is to me." She lifted her shoulders in a mock shudder, drawing his gaze down to her chest again. "It's just you and your mom at the house?"

That was one hell of a robe. She didn't seem uncomfortable with him seeing her in it, which amazed him. Even if she didn't like men, an assumption he was beginning to question, she was awfully relaxed about letting a near-stranger see her hard nipples poking through thin, shimmery bedroom material.

"Mark?"

Pretending to cough on his eggs, he lifted a napkin to his mouth and stared at his plate.

"Sorry, I shouldn't pry," Rose said. "Would you like another piece of toast?"

"It's fine," he said. "Just went down the wrong pipe. What was the question?"

"Nothing, really. I was being nosy."

Enough of him had been paying attention to rewind what she'd said in his mind. "Ah, yes, we do live alone. Yes, though my brother and baby sister are nearby. Liam has a condo in San Francisco, and until recently, April was crashing at his place. Now he's engaged and April's finally got her own apartment." He poured himself more of the excellent coffee from the carafe on the table. "She'll probably move back home when she feels like being an adult is too much work."

"Ouch."

He grinned. "Liam's the only ambitious one in the family, I'm afraid."

"But you're an engineer. That's a great career."

"I could do better," he said softly, and felt the truth of it to his bones. Ages ago, he'd been a prodigy. The kind of kid that taught himself calculus in junior high. Won chess tournaments. Went to MIT before his seventeenth birthday.

"Couldn't we all?" Rose replied, a lopsided smile on her face. She held up her mug. "Here's to untapped potential."

Her gown gaped open. A rounded curve of pale, soft breast appeared, and his breath caught. Making a show of lifting his own mug to hers, he gritted his teeth, smiled tightly, and willed his lungs to draw air.

I need to get out more.

"Did I gather from what you said that you're having job troubles?" he asked.

"Can you call it that even if you don't have one?"

"Ah."

"Yeah."

"What would you like to do?" he asked.

"That's the problem." She stood up and yanked her belt tightly around her waist. He gazed at her, stricken again by the view. Now he could see part of her upper thigh, right above the knee, peeking out from under the fabric.

Her skin looked impossibly soft. He'd had acne as a teenager and was in awe of anyone with a perfect complexion like hers. Smooth as white chocolate. Unreal, not found in nature. Supernatural.

He forced his gaze upward. "Is what you want to do illegal?"

"There's an idea." She put her hands on her hips. Curves, curves, everywhere. "Maybe I need to think bigger."

I know what you mean. Nodding, he gulped down a last mouthful of coffee and wiped his lips with a napkin. Time to get out of here. He was feeling light-headed. "I'll see what I can do with your furnace." He pushed away from the table.

"You don't have to do that," she said with a sigh. "We need to learn how to deal with Ellen. She's not going anywhere."

"Neither am I until I find that furnace," he said. "I need to earn my breakfast."

"Cold eggs?"

He shrugged. "The burden will haunt me."

She laughed again. "Okay, okay." She pointed at a door in the hallway. "I'll be sure to tell Blair who came to our rescue."

That made him glance up at her as he walked past, but she didn't look annoyed. Not entirely sincere, though. That mocking blonde eyebrow was raised.

"I like fixing things," he muttered, and strode into the hallway.

"Me too," she said behind him. "That's why I invited you to dinner."

He stopped and turned around. "You felt sorry for me?"

"Don't look like that. I'm not a social worker. I was just being nice."

"I don't need you to be nice."

"Says the guy who wants to fix our furnace for no reason," she said.

"I don't think it's good for a pregnant woman to be freezing to death."

"There's your reason—you feel sorry for Blair. How do you think that would make her feel?"

Did he feel sorry for the quiet brunette? "It's not pity. It's concern."

"Which is more than I feel for you, and yet you feel oppressed with the burden of my invitation."

"Fine, I'll eat your stupid dinner," he said. "Satisfied?"

"As long as you fix our stupid furnace," she said, walking past him. She was grinning again. "I'm getting dressed. I'll meet you down there."

He watched her retreating form swish and bounce away with a sinking feeling. He'd come over to wiggle out of the dinner invitation but instead he'd eaten her breakfast, was about to work on their furnace, and was more stuck than ever on the dinner.

Well, what did he expect? His social muscles had atrophied from years of disuse. He didn't want to get too involved with these women, given the complexities of their problems, but he could be casually social in a neighborly way. He would just come over, eat, chat, go. No big deal.

He pulled open the door down to the basement. The stairs, very steep and narrow, reeked of mold and decay, and the light didn't respond to the switch. He made his way down carefully in the dark, his hand gripping the banister.

He was surprised, since Mr. Roche had been a very rich man, that the house wasn't better maintained. Maybe it was because the old grouch had been a widower and a workaholic who never spent much time at home. Since he died earlier that year, the house had bounced between his two adult daughters and their offspring, but nobody had made a home of it.

"Careful," Rose said from the landing above him. "The light doesn't work."

"I noticed."

"Hold on, I've got a flashlight."

He heard her come down the stairs, felt her hand on his shoulder, and took the heavy metal cylinder she handed him.

And now it was Mark, the neighbor, and Rose, a complete stranger from the other side of the country, who were stumbling through the dark depths of the house to fix its furnace.

As his foot hit flat concrete, he reached out for the wall for balance, flicking on the flashlight. It was bright and cast a wide beam. "Nice flashlight, anyway."

"I brought it from home," she said.

He wondered about that. "So, I kind of understand why Blair is here. But… you…" He trailed off.

She didn't answer right away, and when she did it was with a light, dismissive laugh. "Are you kidding? Free rent. I only need to find a job to cover food and nail polish."

"What if you don't find one?"

"I'll find something."

He pointed the flashlight at the floor, scanning the wide, empty space. Emboldened by the darkness, he asked, "And if that something is back in New York?"

"I'm staying. Blair loaded up her car and drove thousands of miles, alone, trusting John to change his mind and follow her, and he didn't." She stepped past him into the shadows. "No matter what, she'll have somebody to lean on, somebody who loves her. Nobody should go through this by herself."

Mark appreciated her loyalty. "You'd think John would feel that way."

She turned to him, nodding, her eyes reflecting the light. "How can he sleep at night?"

He pressed the knuckles of his free hand into his temple. "I've only met Blair once, and I'm already having trouble."

"She's so nice, too. Totally doesn't deserve this." She lowered her voice. "Or him."

"I've never liked the guy," he said, though he barely remembered him.

"If he ever visits, I'm going to beat the shit out of him."

"I'll hold him down while you swing."

She laughed. "Thanks." Then, "Hey. It's hot down here."

"You're right." He swung the flashlight around the low-ceilinged space, found the furnace, which was humming, then followed the ducts out of it up to the ceiling. "Well, looks like this won't be too hard. Look at that."

One of the ducts affixed to the ceiling was cracked wide open at a sharp bend in the corner. "Huh. No wonder."

He turned toward her and accidentally shone the light in her face. She flung up her hands and he lowered the flashlight, at first grateful she'd changed out of the distracting gown, then freshly struck by her new getup.

Every time he saw her she looked like a different person. Now she was wearing a form-fitting jogging suit, sporty but heavily embroidered with sequins that reflected the light in abstract geometric patterns. As she lowered her hands, he saw the zipper was only halfway up, showcasing her cleavage and a shining necklace that disappeared into it depths of her warm, lush body.

"Mark?"

"It's hot down here," he said.

"Hey, you're good at this. If that computer thing doesn't work out, you can pursue heating and cooling repair."

He'd ignore that. "Do you have any duct tape?"

"Funny—the one time I'd actually be using it for its intended purpose," she said. "I don't think so. Not unless it was left behind, but they cleaned the place out pretty well. Even down here."

He swung the flashlight around the bare floors. "You're right. The family seemed happy to bury the guy and move on."

"Blair says Ellen talks about him like some great fashion business mastermind, and yet, I don't know, we both get the impression it wasn't a happy relationship."

He shrugged. "They weren't here much, which was fine with me. My brother, Liam, was close to him after our father died, which is how he started working at Fite." He moved closer to the gaping duct and wiped away the beads of sweat building on his forehead. "Liam was an Olympic swimmer."

"I heard about that. I'm an only child, so I wouldn't know, but is it hard to have such a successful sibling?"

"Not the way you'd think." He aimed the flashlight at the stairs. "Let's go up and turn it off. I'm melting down here."

She followed him silently upstairs. Sucking in the cool air with relief, he strode over to the thermostat to switch it off.

"Well, thanks," she said. "Guess I'll be making a trip to the hardware store."

"You don't have to do that. I've got loads of duct tape at our house." He wiggled his foot. "How else would I repair my favorite footwear?"

She looked down and her mouth dropped open. Pointing a red fingernail at the silver tape wrapped around the beige suede strap of his Birkenstock Arizonas, she said, "Right there, on your foot—that's a crime against civilization."

He laughed, only just then noticing the girly pink-and-purple polka-dotted slippers she had on her own feet. "You're one to talk. What the hell are those?"

Not smiling, she squatted down and grabbed his ankle. "My God, they're even worse close up. How many layers of this crap are on there? Why wear shoes at all? Just put plastic bags on your feet and be done with it."

"Tried that," he said, looking down her shirt from above. "No arch support."

Her fingers wrapped around the heel and tugged. "Take them off. I'm doing an intervention."

He tried to hop away, but she held on too tightly. If he didn't stop struggling, he'd end up kicking her in the face or falling down. "Stop. Really, stop. Leave me alone."

"How can your mother let you wear these? How can she even let them in the house?"

Annoyed, he pulled his leg free, but the shoe didn't come with it. In fact, his mother made him leave them on the porch, but he wasn't going to tell Nosy Rosie that. He put his bare foot on the floor and bent over to retrieve his shoe from her snobby, pointy-fingered clutches.

Shaking her head, she stared him in the eye as she chucked the shoe behind her, then scrambled up to her feet to reach it before he did.

Her round bottom, jiggling as it scurried away, distracted him for a moment. "I saved you a visit with Ellen, and this is how you repay me?"

She swung around, shoe in hand again, cheeks pink, eyes shining. "Yes! Exactly. I am *so* doing you a favor by taking these away from you." She pointed at his other foot. "Give me that one too."

"Are you crazy? Give me the one you stole," he said. "Yes, *stole*."

"It's not stealing if I burn it."

"No, that would be arson."

She stared at him in amazement. "You're really upset. I took away this nasty, stinking piece of garbage that was clinging to your foot and you're *upset*."

"They're comfortable." He took a long step toward her. "They have sentimental value." Another step. "And they're *mine*." He backed her up into the corner of the front doorway, looming down at her, glaring, before he forcibly retrieved the offending item.

She stayed there with her back against the door while he strode away and shoved it back onto his foot.

After a moment she said to his back, "Give me the shoes and I won't make you come to dinner."

"You can't make me do anything."

"Sure I can. For instance, I can ask Blair to invite you. Somehow I don't think you'd be able to disappoint her if she batted those big brown eyes at you."

So they *were* brown. He turned around. "She's at work."

"I'll send her over right when she gets home. I'll tell her that I've made way too much pasta and how you fixed our furnace today, et cetera." She flashed an evil grin. "Imagine how grateful she'll be. She won't take no for an answer."

He ran a hand through his hair. "You play dirty."

"Sweetheart, you have no idea."

"What's it to you, anyway? Maybe you're projecting your own feelings for her onto me."

Her eyes went wide. "Excuse me?"

"Just because you've got the hots for her doesn't mean I do," he said.

A long, gaping silence ensued, leading Mark to wish, fervently, that Undo buttons worked in real life. So maybe he'd been wrong about the lesbian thing. He shifted his gaze to the door. Unfortunately, she stood in his way.

"You think I'm gay?"

"None of my business. You do need some duct tape, though, so I'm going to go get that for you." He kicked off both of his shoes, nudging them toward her like a zookeeper offering steak to a lion. "You'll need a ladder, too, and maybe a shop light. If you plan on staying here very long, you'll want to fix the wiring down there. Not that I know how long you're staying."

"Well, if my dream comes true, I'll be staying here forever, feathering my gay love nest."

"I wish you all the happiness in the world," he said, stepping around her.

"No, no, don't look so worried. It's a relief, actually, that you guessed."

He paused, eyeing her.

"You saw right through me. You're very sophisticated to have caught on so quickly. But I guess you've figured out that all confident women are actually lesbians."

His face was burning hot enough to melt butter.

Unlike her mouth, obviously, the sarcastic vixen.

"That's not what—never mind." He put an arm around her waist and swiveled her out of the way. She was big, but he had an orange belt in judo. And laughing so hard made her weak. "Just for that, you can get your own duct tape."

She was still laughing when he jerked the door open.

"When you're at the hardware store, buy yourself some jumper cables," he said.

She followed him out onto the porch. "Dinner's at seven," she called after him. "Tonight!"

4

To ROSE'S DEEP ANNOYANCE, BLAIR thought it was hilarious.

"You! Gay!" she cried, clutching her stomach. "Pining over me. I love it!"

"No, it's me who loves you, darling," Rose said, pouring cheap white wine into a glass. It was only six, but she wanted time to prepare a staggeringly excellent meal for His Geekiness next door. "Remind me to spit on his pasta. Since I can't spew semen on it anymore."

"What's your problem? You don't usually have trouble laughing at yourself."

"Me? How does this have anything to do with me?"

"Okay, fine," Blair said. "The situation, then. It's just too funny."

"To you, apparently."

Blair came around the counter to stand behind her at the stove. "Are you really bothered by this?"

"Why should I be? He's obviously a socially stunted recluse. He wouldn't recognize a lesbian if he saw her go down on Ellen Degeneres on national TV."

Biting her lip, Blair filled a mug with water from the pitcher and stuck it in the microwave. "Socially stunted, huh?"

"He said so himself."

"He didn't seem very reclusive to me," she said, smiling at Rose over her shoulder as she punched the buttons. "Didn't he jump into your car when you were recharging the battery?"

"Just to get closer to you."

"Well, you'd know how that feels, wouldn't you?" Blair came over and put a hand on her shoulder. "Dreaming of me all these years."

Rose glared at her little hand. "Do you want this dinner or not?"

"If you think you're up to it, of course. It might help you work through your frustrations."

"I'm frustrated all right."

Blair laughed. "You know what I think?"

"Yes, and you're wrong."

"What?"

Rose got out the old plastic cutting board her mother had let her have when she'd packed up the car the month before. Along with one dented pot and a nonstick frying pan that was probably carcinogenic because of all the scratches on its surface. "He's not that cute. It has nothing to do with me being jealous."

Tilting her head, Blair batted her eyelashes at her. "I didn't say anything about that, but if it crossed your mind…"

Rose banged a bowl of white mushrooms down onto the cutting board and gave Blair a tight smile. "You're right. It is funny." She grabbed a chef's knife and a sharpening steel out of the wood block and sliced them together. The knives had been her first real purchase in California. Not necessarily a good omen, but she couldn't survive without a decent set of knives.

"Don't hurt him," Blair said. "He probably feels really bad."

"No wonder the guy's single. If he assumes every woman in shorts and a tank top is gay, he's really limiting the dating pool."

Heated water in hand, Blair joined her at the counter, dunking her tea bag up and down. "I think it was the way you jumped the car. All that confidence with the cables. Very macho."

"Exactly," Rose said. "He's probably never met a woman without a father or brother to rely on for that sort of thing. You should have seen him tinkering with our thermostat, assuming it was just needing batteries. As if we were too stupid to check that first."

"I was," Blair said.

"Yeah, well, you straight chicks are too afraid of getting your hands dirty."

Smiling, Blair sipped her tea. "There you go. I knew you could laugh at this."

"I thought it was hilarious."

Blair laughed loudly. "Sure you did," she said, giving Rose a squeeze before pulling out her phone.

Her smile fell.

"I wish you could give up on him," Rose said softly, slicing the ends off the mushroom stems.

After a long period of silence, Rose stopped chopping to glance at Blair. She'd turned the same cadaverous gray as the mushrooms.

"He's here," Blair said numbly. "Just landed in San Francisco."

Rose felt the breath catch in her chest, her throat tighten. "Who?"

Blair stared at her phone. "Sorry. He says he's sorry."

Oh, God.

"He's coming. Right now," Blair said.

Rose looked down at the cutting board. She'd planned on a tarragon cream sauce, heavy on the cream. "I wonder if the prick's still a vegan."

Blair leaned against the counter. "Oh. I feel sick."

This wasn't an abstract threat coming from a pregnant person. Rose wiped her hands and herded her out of the kitchen. "Deep breaths. I'll get you a cool washcloth."

Blair stumbled, eyes wild. "I haven't shaved in a week."

"Please. If he wants a landscaped woman, he needs to give the crew notice." Flicking the light on, Rose nudged her into the bathroom, grabbed a clean cloth off the shelf.

"I'm going to puke." With a surprising burst of energy, Blair shoved Rose out of the bathroom and slammed the door.

"Save some for Mr. Sperm's shoes," Rose called out. "A homecoming present."

Blair's voice was high, panicked, confused. "How can he do this to me?"

Then the retching started. Powerless, Rose leaned against the door, hands bunched into fists, and plotted.

If John thought he was going to waltz into the house like he owned it (which he didn't, damn it, that was his aunt) and have Blair smile and fawn over him as if she hadn't been crying alone every night, he'd be too dead to have another think coming.

"Well, at least you'll be hungry for dinner," Rose said when the vomiting finally stopped.

The door creaked open. Wiping her hair off her forehead, Blair leaned into the door frame. "Now I'm all sweaty."

"Tell him you were having hot sex with the neighbor," Rose said. "No, don't worry. I'll tell him."

"He just landed. If traffic's light, he could be here in an

hour. Or less." She rubbed her eyes. "My God, I have to shower. I'm ripe as a banana."

"It's past time he sniffed a real woman. The man needs to face up to reality."

"I can't risk it," Blair said. "I can't do this by myself. I just can't."

"First of all, better to know now what he can handle than later, when you're really dependent on him. And second, you can handle it. Whatever it is, you can. You're tougher than you think. Don't let him get away with being horrible just because you think you need him so much."

"I do need him. The baby needs a father. How can I ever afford college tuition by myself? Have you seen the annual growth rate of educational expenses?"

"While I'm sure your kid is a genius, even he or she won't be going to college in the next two hours." Rose pushed her back into the bathroom. "Go ahead, take your shower. It'll make you feel better. I'll see if I can come up with a vegan alternative to the cream sauce."

"Oh, dinner. Rose, I'm so sorry, but I don't think I can do it."

Rose started to protest but thought better of it. Blair was right. As much as she hated to admit it, she couldn't mediate this one. "Maybe tomorrow, then," she said.

Blair peeked her head out, managed a weak smile. "You're the best."

Rose went back into the kitchen and decided she should let Mark off the hook. Too bad; she'd looked forward to making him squirm.

Not having his phone number, she slipped on her shoes and walked over to knock on the door.

A woman answered. "Oh, thank God. I thought you might be those curb painters coming back," she said, holding out her hand. "I keep meaning to come over and introduce myself. Trixie Johnson."

A smiling, tall woman, Mark's mother looked like a throwback hippie to Rose's eastern eyes: naturally gray hair cut short, tie-dyed T-shirt, baggy jeans and Birkenstocks. Her sandals, however, sported a floral purple pattern and were not held together with duct tape. Nevertheless, compared to Rose's preppy mother, who ironed her pajamas and wouldn't step out of the bathroom in the morning without her makeup on, Trixie seemed very au naturel. In a nice way. Relaxed, friendly, low-maintenance.

Rose shook her hand. "Rose Devlin."

"Trouble with your car again?" Trixie asked.

"Oh, no. Nothing like that. I just needed to talk to Mark. It's kind of embarrassing. You see, we invited him to dinner but…" Rose stopped herself, not sure how much she should say. Blair liked her privacy, and Trixie, though she appeared very sweet, didn't look like the type to embrace polite ignorance. Her eyes were bright and sharp, scanning Rose's body like somebody eager to help. "Blair has had a sudden change of plans. I wanted to ask if Mark might be able to join us another night. Is he here?"

Glancing behind her, Trixie reached into her pocket, took out a tube of pink lip balm, popped off the cap.

"What a shame." Trixie slid the balm along her upper lip. "I hope she's feeling all right? I always felt the first trimester was the hardest."

"She's hanging in there. Thanks." Rose glanced across the driveway, wondering how many minutes they had until John got there. The nerve of him. Just showing up. Not even bothering to call before he got on the plane. "Will you tell Mark how sorry we are? We'd love to have him over another night. And you, too, of course, Mrs. Johnson. Listen to me, my mother would kill me for my bad manners. Will you join us for dinner another night? Both of you?"

Trixie smiled. "That's very sweet of you. Yes, of course. If you promise to come over here first. Anytime. And you don't need to come as a set—if your friend isn't up to it, don't let that stop you. I can see you're the social type, probably going stir crazy all alone in that empty old house up here in the hills with nobody to talk to."

Rose suspected Trixie knew a lot about that. "I'd like that. Well, thank you. Tell Mark I'm sorry about tonight."

With a wave and a smile, Trixie nodded and shut the door so quickly, Rose flinched. Trixie's warmth was sincere, but Rose got the feeling she was missing something.

Like that Trixie was trying to get rid of her.

Ah, well, who knew? Maybe she was in the middle of a TV show or something. Turning her attention back to her friend, Rose returned to her house.

ꝼ

MARK CAME DOWNSTAIRS AT 6:55 P.M. WEARING A PAIR OF tailored pants he'd acquired just that afternoon. Wondering where his mother had disappeared to, he found some scissors in the kitchen junk drawer and cut off the tags.

There was no sticker down the rear leg to remove—a step he'd forgotten, to his lasting embarrassment, on his first day teaching eighth grade algebra in Wisconsin years earlier.

This pair was a lot classier than the other had been. No stickers. They even reached all the way to the ground. At twenty-two, he'd been clueless. Now he wasn't any more fashionable, but he had the sense to go to Nordstrom's, where an older dude in a purple shirt had been very happy to protect him from his own tasteless default settings.

After a long afternoon, Mark had driven home from Walnut Creek with two pairs of perfectly tailored pants, three pairs of designer jeans, five polo shirts in assorted colors, five button-down casual shirts that cost more than a year's rent on his first apartment, and yes, one pair of new Birkenstocks.

He'd also stopped at the hardware store for new duct tape, whether Rose wanted it or not. As a housewarming present.

"Mom?" He walked through the house to the back porch, where she kept the dogs. There were only a few Chihuahuas living with them these days, unlike a month earlier when the herd had grown to alarming proportions. Finally admitting she'd overextended herself as a rescue operation, Trixie had found homes and other shelters, though parting with all of them would've been too much of a loss to endure.

When Mark had returned from Wisconsin, he'd planned to get his own place within a month or two, but she was so happy to have him around. He'd lived thousands of miles away for over a decade—why not keep her company for a while? It wouldn't kill him. He might even learn how to cook.

Seeing the porch was empty, Mark concluded she'd taken the three remaining animals out for another walk.

Hopefully, Liam and Bev would have kids right away, give her something to do, bodies to hug. Maybe that's why she'd been willing to part with so many of her dogs, hoping babies weren't too far off. He wouldn't be surprised if she converted the dog porch into a playroom and then invited Liam and Bev over for dinner to prompt them to visualize a day care center.

Dinner. It was 6:59. Breathing onto his palm one last time, Mark squared his shoulders and headed out the front door, duct tape slipped over the neck of a bottle of Shiraz. He felt good. The clothes made a difference, he realized, indulging in a grin as he tapped on Rose and Blair's front door.

The wait was longer than he expected, and after a long

minute he heard the women arguing with each other inside.

Maybe they were still getting dressed. That reminded him of Rose's slinky robe from that morning.

He tapped again. "I can come back later," he called out.

The door flew open. Rose frowned at him. "Mark?"

He glanced at his wrist, forgetting he never wore a watch anymore. "You said seven, right?"

"I told your mom we… there was a problem about tonight." Then her gaze raked him head to toe and she flushed a remarkable shade of pink. Almost like a highlighter pen. "Oh, Mark. Look at you. I'm so sorry."

Her long, tight sweater was pink, too. Even the belt cinched tightly around her waist, under her… pink… breasts.

Not the hair, though. That was pale gold.

Blair appeared at her side. "Mark? Oh, Mark." She let out a deep breath. "Good to see you."

He took a step back. He hadn't even noticed she was there. Not wanting his sweaty palms to drop the wine, he thrust it at her. "But not expected. I'm sorry my mom and I screwed up. I'll go. No problem."

"No, don't," Blair said quickly, reaching forward to clasp his arm. "We invited you."

"No, it was Rose, and it's obviously a bad time, and really, it's no problem." He tried to take another step back, but he was paralyzed by the feel of Blair's fingers wrapped around his bicep. Should he flex? Do a little muscle demo?

"It's a perfect time," Blair said, dragging him inside. He did his best to flex and follow at the same time without stumbling.

"John will be here any minute." Rose caught Mark's alarmed glance and nodded. "Just called from the airport."

A righteous anger flooded through him. "Really. With no warning?"

"None," Rose said.

They shared a look of barely contained condemnation.

"Which is why you have to stay." Blair kicked the door shut and tugged him into the living room. "Rose has made this fantastic meal, and there won't be anyone here to eat it."

"You won't let him eat your food?" Mark asked Rose.

Her lips pursed. "He's a vegan."

"And I'm not feeling well," Blair said, resting a hand on her stomach, looking down. "Besides, we'll probably go out."

Rose took the bottle of wine from her. "She only got sick when she heard John had landed in San Francisco." She plucked off the roll of duct tape and offered Mark a small smile. "Thanks. I never did make it to the hardware store."

"I'll go downstairs and put it on if you like."

Rose frowned at him for a moment, glanced at Blair. "That's nice of you, really, but—it wouldn't be fair." Her look sharpened. "To you."

Mark knew what she was saying, that with John in the picture, there was no reason for Mark to be. "Sure. I understand." He moved toward the door. "I'll go. This is obviously a bad time."

"No, don't go," Blair said. "Please. I'll bring you a glass of wine." She went into the kitchen.

Rose put a hand on his arm. "She's right, Mark. Have a seat." She fluffed a pillow on the couch, stared until he sat down. "I hope you like cheese," she added.

"I like cheese."

"Pasta?"

"That too."

"Asparagus?"

"Sure."

Rose tucked an errant strand of golden hair behind her ear. "Blair is right. It might make it easier, having you here." She gave him an intense once-over that made him shift in his seat. "You clean up good."

He leaned back, crossed an ankle over his knee, trying to ignore the way his pulse raced when she looked at him like that. "Am I supposed to hold him down while you swing?"

"Tempting, but not tonight," she said.

"When do you think he'll get here?"

Rose made a face. "Who knows? Maybe he'll catch a movie on his way over. Do a little shopping. Have his hair trimmed," she said. "Selfish pig. I promised Blair I'll be polite, but it'll be hard. She's probably counting on your being here to keep me from killing him."

He dropped his foot to the floor, crossed his other leg, and wondered what his father would've done in Mark's shoes. (The new ones, not the ones with duct tape.)

Never a good idea to think of the big man. His father had died before he'd graduated from high school, but that had been long enough to leave scars. Still… would he have stood guard at the front door and told John to get a motel? His father had had the bravado to pull it off and the physique of a linebacker. He'd scare John shitless, and Blair would see what a real man looked like. Like his mother, she'd swoon and never recover, no matter how cruel and hard that kind of man would be as a father.

Blair came back into the room with a glass of wine. "Sorry again about the mix-up." She handed it to him and settled on the couch across from him.

"No, I'm sorry, not your mistake," Mark said, taking a sip.

His father wouldn't be here at all, he realized. Two women alone, one pregnant and unmarried, the other large and sarcastic; he wouldn't even have lent them his jumper cables. His father's weak powers of empathy would've been reserved for the man in the story, and never, not even for Mark's mother, would he give his heart to a woman who bore another man's child.

Unfortunately this didn't make Mark feel better. Only raw and vulnerable.

"If you're uncomfortable sticking around, I totally understand," Rose said quietly. She stood next to the couch, a plate of cheese in hand. "It might get ugly."

"No, it won't," Blair said. "We're not like that. We can handle this."

Rose set the plate down on the coffee table. "I'm not good at hiding my feelings."

"You won't have to. John and I will go out," Blair said. She twisted her hands together in her lap. "What do you do, Mark?"

"I'm a computer programmer at the moment. Software engineering. Geek stuff."

"At the moment? What did you used to be?" Blair asked.

Her eyes were light caramel brown, very gentle, but her gaze made him uncomfortable. "Oh. More geek stuff. Math teacher." He sipped his wine and forced it down his throat.

"You didn't mention you were a teacher," Rose said. "What age did you teach?"

"I'm sure there's tons about Mike we don't know," Blair said, staring at Rose with a look he couldn't read.

Rose tapped him on the head again. "I know enough to bet Mike here is too polite to tell you his name is Mark."

"Mark! Jeez. I'm so sorry. I'm such a mess," Blair said, standing up. "They say it only gets worse. When the baby gets here I won't remember my *own* name."

He smiled. "It's okay. Call me whatever you want."

"Will you go lie down like I told you?" Rose said to Blair. "I'll let you know when he's here. You'll make yourself sick again."

"I'm fine. I like talking to Mike. Mark."

"It is such a shame you can't drink," Rose said with a sigh, and went into the kitchen.

"Why can't you drink?" he asked.

"Bad for the baby," Blair said.

"Really? Just a little wine?"

"Oh, yeah. My book is really firm on that."

"I had no idea." He sipped his own wine and then, feeling guilty, set it down next to the cheese. It looked good, but it might make her turn green to watch him eat it, so he passed. He'd gone to extensive trouble today to prevent girls from vomiting at the sight of him.

"None of your friends have had babies yet?" she asked.

"No." He folded his hands in his lap. "Though my brother is engaged. Of course you knew that. My mom can't wait for them to push out a few puppies. Human ones this time."

"Human this time?"

His internal dork alarm was buzzing. Hard to go up against so many years of conditioning. "I mean, of course humans are babies. I mean, babies are human." Oh, he was sinking. *Press on, man, there's still time to recover.* He forced a laugh. "My mother loves dogs. She does Chihuahua rescue. Or she did. That's what I was trying to say—since she used to call her puppies her babies, I wonder if she'll call the actual babies her puppies."

Oh, give it up. He sank down into the sofa. Why was it always so hard for him to talk to women? He could feel his muscles growing fatigued from the excessive tension throughout his body. He'd be sore tomorrow.

"That's cute," Blair said. "I like puppies."

"Me too," he said. So lame.

"Hey, you're not eating the cheese," Rose said, coming into the room. "You assured me you were pro-cheese."

Mark turned to her in relief. "I am definitely pro-cheese. Some might even say I'm cheesy."

"Then get to work, mister. Blair, could you help me with something in the kitchen?"

Sensing a life raft, Mark clambered to his feet. "I'll help."

Rose stared at him. "Are you sure?"

"Why? Is it hard?"

"No, but you're a guest."

"Let me work for my keep. That was part of my rationale for living with my mother—picking up a few much-needed domestic skills." He smiled at Blair as he bolted, hoping she was too distracted with her own problems to notice his discomfort.

Stepping into the kitchen, he felt his tension drain away. Rose was already back at work at the counter with her back to him; a row of spice jars, a head of garlic, onions, and a bunch of fresh basil arrayed on the counter in front of her. Her hair was pulled up on top of her head, exposing the back of her neck. Pale, smooth skin peeked out under tendrils of blonde hair, making her look surprisingly vulnerable.

She swung around with a knife raised. "Can you mince garlic?"

"Sure."

When he was set up at a cutting board next to her, she said, "I was trying to get Blair away so you'd eat some of the cheese. You were trying to be polite, weren't you? Not eating or drinking?"

"Whenever she looked down, she made this face." He demonstrated a grimace.

"Morning sickness is such a bullshit term. It's all day long."

"I'm so glad I'm not a woman." He whacked the garlic clove with the flat of the knife. "Begging your pardon. You must've felt differently."

She glanced at him.

"Before you got the operation," he added.

Her laughter almost made him forget about the agonizing conversation in the other room.

"Ten points." She bumped her hip against his. "Shall we call it even?"

"No, not yet. Though I did warn you I don't get out much, so your expectations should've been low enough to prevent taking serious offense."

She handed him the basil. "I wasn't offended."

"Mmm," he said.

"Don't 'mmm' me." After a moment snapping asparagus stems, she added, "What would you say was the major factor in your faulty first impression of me? Because if you tell me it was jumping my car, I'll be disappointed. For one thing, I won't be able to let you fix our furnace because I'll have to represent heterosexual womanhood."

"I was impressed with your confidence around an engine, I've got to admit."

She sighed. "Shoot. I really wasn't looking forward to getting up on a ladder to fix the ducts, but it looks like you need another demo."

"I'll do it. I really don't mind."

"No, I can't let you, not now. You need proof women like me exist."

"No, I don't. My mother is proof enough."

"I'm like your mother?"

"My mom is very handy," he said.

"But single. For all you know…"

It took him a second to understand what she was saying. "Are you suggesting my mother is a lesbian?"

"Oh, sure. Now *you're* offended."

"You don't know her at all. Have you ever even talked

to her?"

"Sure. When I told her dinner was off," she said. "Don't look like that. I'm just kidding. Of course I don't know anything about your mother. And if she were gay, she would've hooked up with a woman by now, right? Half of the Bay Area is gay from what I can tell. Either that or married with kids. Or both. If she wanted to snuggle with Jane Doe from the Chihuahua Club, she would."

Mark put down his knife.

Studying his face, she laughed. "Now who has morning sickness?"

"I told you I was sorry I thought you might be gay," he said. "I didn't give it much thought, honestly, and we hardly know each other. As you say, half the Bay Area is gay, so you should expect your neighbors to be open to the idea. Without prejudice. So can we drop it?"

She bit her lip and went back to the asparagus. Chop, snap, chop. He turned his attention back to the garlic, which was now minced into infinitesimal pieces, mere molecules of garlickness on the cutting board.

"Mark, I'm sorry. I'm a little tense about John surprising us tonight."

"Maybe I should go home."

She put a hand on his arm and gazed up at him with those stunning blue eyes. "No, please don't. I'm glad Blair asked you to stay. I'd just be storming around here making her feel worse if you weren't here. I promise I'll tone down my annoying personality. Okay?" She squeezed his bicep, face smiling, eyelashes flapping.

"You're not annoying."

Her smile faltered a little. "Thanks." She ducked her head, went back to work.

Like with the car, she was quick and efficient in the

kitchen. Her air of confidence suited a more mature woman. Looking at her face up close, however, he guessed she was still a few years from thirty.

Unlike himself. "How old are you?" He peered over the edge of his wine glass.

"Twelve going on fifty. You?"

"Can't you answer a simple question?"

"No." She grinned. "Whoops. Just did."

"I'm twenty-nine, in case you were wondering."

"Really?"

"You thought I was younger, didn't you?"

Shaking her head, she poured steaming pasta into a bowl, drizzled olive oil over it. "Older."

"You're lying."

"Though I give you credit for picking up on my unfortunate habit for falsehoods, no. I really did." She lifted a lid to stir something.

"I don't believe it. I'm still living with my mother."

"So? You're not twelve or anything, right? What's the difference between twenty-nine and thirty-nine?"

The wine seemed to hit him all at once. He leaned against the counter for support. "You didn't think I was thirty-nine."

"I didn't say I did."

"But—"

She held up a hand. "Shh. Did you hear that?"

He paused, still shaken by the idea of him a decade older and still living at home. That he looked the part. "You think he's here?"

"I swear, it's like waiting for a car accident. Drain the asparagus, will you? I'm going to go look."

She returned a moment later, rubbing her hands on a dish towel, her full lips pressed into a tight, flat line. "Let's get this party started."

5

ROSE LEFT MARK IN THE kitchen and jogged down the hall to tell Blair her prince had arrived. She was sitting cross-legged on the end of her bed, her back perfectly straight, eyes closed. An iPod rested in her hands; the white earbud cord snaking down her torso was in stark contrast to her black clothes.

Her eyes popped open the second Rose tapped on the door frame. When she saw Rose's face, she bolted off the bed and yanked the cord out of her ears.

"Deep breath," Rose said, grabbing her by the shoulders in the doorway. "Stay here. Look cool. Let him stew a little."

Blair froze, nodded. "Cool. Right."

"I'll tell him you'll be out in a few minutes."

"No, you shouldn't rush to him either," Blair said.

"Don't worry, I'll take my time."

"You haven't seen him since…"

"I'm just going to let him in. Relax. I won't start anything," Rose said, adding to herself, *Not now, anyway.*

She strode back down the hall to answer the front door, then paused, more than a little annoyed when she heard he was already inside. Two male voices rumbled through the house, one too quiet to make out the words, one very clear.

"Mark Johnson," she heard John say. "My mom told me you were back home."

Rose put a hand on the wall and drew in a breath, telling herself to calm down. She'd promised Blair she would stay out of it, but as she stood there, knowing she'd have to listen to John's cheerful, arrogant charm in person, she wondered if that was going to be possible.

Mark said something in reply she couldn't make out. Then John's infectious laugh rippled through the air, setting Rose's teeth on edge.

"Don't put yourself down," John said. "You're a genius, always were. Maybe we can go into business together someday. Cash in on some of those brains."

Greedy bastard. He thought everything and everyone was ripe for the picking—all of humanity a buffet, with him holding the plate. Lifting her chin, she strode around the corner into the foyer.

"Perhaps we could sell them on eBay," Mark said, then glanced at Rose. He had his hands stuffed into his pockets and his voice was quiet, but he'd placed himself directly in front of John, blocking his way into the living room.

Following Mark's gaze, John turned and saw her.

For a moment they just stared at each other. Rose knew her face was probably as red as her manicure, but she finally managed to smile, barely, and say, "Hello, John," without spitting.

He, of course, had no trouble at all. Gorgeous as always, charming as always. "Rosie Posey," he said softly. "Nice to see you."

Out of the corner of her eye, she saw Mark frown.

Typical of John. After everything he'd done, he thought he

could get out of trouble by being cute and reminding her of better times.

Big mistake. "Blair will be out in a few minutes. She's not feeling well."

His brow creased in concern that—damn him—looked sincere. "Was she sleeping? I hope you didn't wake her up. She doesn't have to get up for my sake."

"*Now* you care," Rose said.

"I deserve that. Do your worst." John sighed, ran a hand through his mussed hair. "Do you mind if I use the bathroom? I was in such a hurry to get here, I didn't use the one at the airport."

For a second Mark stayed where he was. Then he nodded and stepped aside. After John patted him on the arm and strode past him into the house, Mark raised his eyebrow at Rose.

"Rosie Posey?" he asked.

"I liked your blocking action. Didn't have a maneuver for the Bathroom Trick, though, did you?" Making jokes helped her keep from screaming. Seeing John again was harder than she'd expected. Her hands were shaking. "Let's eat. The pasta's cold and mushy by now, but I don't want him to think we're going to rearrange our lives for his unannounced visit."

He followed her into the kitchen and took the plate she handed him. "Rosie Posey?" he repeated.

"Do you mind if we just load our plates as it is? Normally I'd stir the sauce and penne together for a moment to finish it off, but—no, you're right, I should. Why skip it just because he's here? Hand me the pasta." She reached out for the bowl behind him.

"It's fine. Let's just eat it as is."

"The asparagus is cold."

"I'll nuke it. Can I pour you some wine?" He took the bowl of asparagus from her and put it in the microwave.

"I'd rather have a martini." The mushroom sauce was lumpy. She'd forgotten to cook the chicken. Or was it prawns?

How could he just swagger in here and smile at her like that?

"Start with this. I'll look for the booze." Mark put a glass of wine in her hands.

What a fool she'd been, thinking she could joke and tough it out. Assuming he'd never visit, let alone stay.

She'd been wrong. Not that she knew why he was there, but she feared—and hoped—

Oh, she didn't know what she feared and hoped.

Closing her eyes, she reminded herself he was Blair's problem, not hers.

Blair touched her shoulder, making her jump. She was wearing her coat. "We're going to go out for a drink. Sorry about skipping dinner." Her eyes were bright, her cheeks pink.

"It smells incredible," John added. He stood behind Blair with his hand on her shoulder. Blair didn't shake it off.

"She can't drink," Mark said to John.

"Just alcohol, dude. I think other liquids are encouraged," he said with a grin.

Rose turned back to the stove, pretending to adjust the burners. "See you later." When, after a long minute, she finally heard the door slam, she put a hand on the counter and closed her eyes.

"Drink." Mark had an arm around her, his free hand guiding the wine to her lips. "Then we'll sit down and talk."

She gulped it without tasting. "I need to grate the Parmesan."

"I hate cheese. Let's just eat the pasta with your awesome sauce."

She let him guide her to the kitchen table, but as she took the fork he handed her, she shook her head. "I set the table in the dining room."

"I hate dining rooms. It's better in here." He shoved the newspapers to the side and put both plates on the table. "Eat while I look for the hard stuff."

"I'm not hungry." She finished her wine, gazed into the bottom of the empty glass.

"Sit." Two firm hands on her shoulders pressed her down into a chair. The pasta was as pale as the sauce. The basil was still sitting on the counter. And the asparagus was in the microwave. "This is the worst dinner I've ever made in my life."

A martini appeared on the table in front of her. "Now you're just bragging." He sat down next to her and made a show of unfurling a paper napkin in the air. "I hope you don't mind if I start eating. I'm starving."

She sipped her drink, heart still in her throat, head spinning.

When the alcohol began to take the edge off, she let herself settle back into her chair, regained some of her earlier calm, fantasy though it was, and watched him dig in. He managed to consume an impressive mound of penne with each forkful.

"Did you learn to shovel like that in Wisconsin?" she asked. "All that snow?"

He grinned, cheeks bulging, and saluted her with his wine. "She's back."

She took a bite. "It's not terrible, is it?"

They ate in silence for several minutes. When she saw he was slowing down, she shoved her plate away to focus on the martini. "Imagine how good it would've been with the other half of the ingredients."

"I hate ingredients," he said.

She laughed. Held up her glass. "Here's to hate."

He tapped his glass against hers. "To hate."

They drank. She took another bite. Not as bad as she'd expected.

"So," Mark said, pushing away his empty plate. "What the hell just happened?"

"Guess I can't cook under stress."

"That's not what I meant."

She glanced at him, then back at her plate. "She thinks she has to give him another chance."

"If you don't want to explain, you can say it's none of my business."

Empty stomach, wine, martini. Putting her hands on the table, she tested her leg stability before standing up all the way. "Let's fix the furnace. I could use a distraction."

He shook his head but followed her out of the kitchen and down the hall. She grabbed the duct tape and flashlight from the hall table before making her way to the basement stairs.

"You aren't as steady on your feet as you were earlier," he said. "Why don't you hold the light while I get up on the ladder?"

Halfway down the stairs into the gloom, she turned the beam of light on him. "You brought a ladder?"

Squinting into the light, he said, "Rose."

"What?"

He turned around and went back up the stairs to the house.

"Where are you going?" she asked.

"To get a ladder. Why don't you come with me?"

The darkness was soothing. She sat down on the steps and clicked the flashlight on and off. It wasn't that she was jealous, not the way they thought. How could she be jealous of an unplanned pregnancy, a relationship without love, and no time to sort it out properly?

"What happened, Rose?"

And she wasn't dying to have a baby. Someday, probably, but she was only twenty-six, and her mom had been warning her since puberty about the price of growing up *with* your babies instead of *before*.

"I really didn't expect it to hit me this hard," she said. "I'm sorry. Very embarrassing."

The stairs creaked as he came down to join her, sitting one step above hers, his legs stretching down alongside her raised knees. He didn't say anything, which was nice. Just waited.

"You're not going to believe this," she finally said.

THE BEAM OF THE FLASHLIGHT LIT UP THE DUST MOTES in the dark basement like fireflies.

"A long way back, ages and ages ago," she said, "so long ago I can hardly remember it, John and I had a little thing going."

Mark let out an audible breath. "Rosie Posey."

Hearing that nickname on his lips in the darkness gave her an odd shock. She stifled a shiver. "I didn't blame Blair. Well, I did at first. The baby changed everything, of course."

"She's only, what, a few months pregnant?"

"Not even. She tested positive at only eleven days."

"So, how long ago was this long-ago, ancient relationship?"

This was what she didn't want to get into. It gave the wrong impression—of Blair, of herself, even of John. Flicking the flashlight back off, she stood up. "It ended the night the baby was conceived. Let's go upstairs, shall we? You're right, the furnace can wait."

He didn't get up. "Jesus," he said. "Why did you move out here? Are you a masochist?"

"Not at all." She nudged his knee with her foot. "Cashing in on my victimhood. Since she got herself knocked up by my boyfriend, Blair has to let me live here rent-free. See? I'm actually quite mercenary."

"I don't believe you."

"Smart man." She shoved him harder. "You going to stay there all night?"

He didn't move. "I can't believe she'd do that," he said softly.

"Don't think less of her. Please. She knew I'd just decided to break up with him. And she told me right away what happened, the very next morning. She cried harder than I did."

His hands found hers in the dark, took the flashlight from her. The sudden light blinded her. "You cried?"

She kicked him and took the flashlight. "I got over it." He was big, but she wedged her foot under his ribs to find the next step and climbed over him.

"Obviously," he said behind her. "That's why I found the chicken in the dishwasher."

To hell with what he thought. She jogged up the stairs to the house. The kitchen was a mess, even after she took the poultry out of the top rack of the Whirlpool. The basil could be saved, but the rest would go in the trash. Next time her ex-boyfriend came to woo her pregnant roommate, she'd order takeout.

Mark came up behind her, rinsed his plate in the sink.

After a couple minutes of silent, side-by-side dishwashing,

she said, "I just need to know why he's here so I know how I should react, how I should treat him, how I should feel."

He handed her a handful of rinsed silverware to put in the dishwasher.

"Is he here to tell Blair he's changed his mind?" she asked. "Or to start planning for shared custody? Single custody? Marriage?"

"Was it only that one, uh, time, or did they date?"

"They dated. There wasn't even a few days' breather."

"It's official—I don't understand women. How could you stand that?"

"It sounds worse than it was," she said. "He and I never got serious. We met at the gym, started working out at the same times, having a smoothie at the club afterward. One thing led to another and he ended up at my place. It was mostly a physical relationship. We never talked about the future, or even whether we were exclusive."

"And then he met Blair," Mark said.

"I introduced them, and now look at her. Half the time I feel like I should apologize to her."

He didn't laugh. "I don't think you should."

That was sweet. "Blair's never had any luck with guys. You'd think it would be the reverse, wouldn't you? Small and petite, not an ounce of fat on her... but no. She's always hidden herself behind a book, video games, the Internet, big sweatshirts, baseball caps, baggy jeans," Rose said. "She never dated in college. After graduation, it was just work and hiding herself away at home, never wanting to go out."

"Huh," he said.

"Yeah, I know. You can relate."

"Unfortunately."

He would've been perfect for Blair. Something else to feel bad about. She punched the button to start the dishwasher.

"Look, Mark, I'm obviously screwed up right now. The rest of the mess can wait until the morning. I think I need to be alone. Do you mind?"

He looked at her. His eyes were serious, grayish blue with long, curled lashes she would've killed for. "I'll bring a ladder over in the morning."

"No, don't worry about it," she said. "The list for the hardware store is getting ridiculous. I'll get one in the morning with everything else."

He picked up the duct tape where he'd placed it on the counter. "Don't forget this, though." Slipping the dish towel out of her hands, he replaced it with the roll of tape and folded her fingers over it. "You wouldn't want to buy more than you needed."

"Thanks, Mark. You're a nice guy." She walked him to the door, thinking someone so reclusive had to be eager to get out of the house, away from the social drama. The contagion of people.

"Lot more than you bargained for, aren't we?" she said, pulling the door open.

He turned back and studied her for a moment before smiling and walking away.

She figured that was the last she'd see of him.

MARK CONFRONTED HIS MOTHER IN THE UPSTAIRS bathroom while she was giving all three dogs a bath in the large spa tub. The jets kept them paddling furiously while the steam rose up around their pointy ears. His mother called it their aqua aerobics class.

"Funny thing," he said, leaning against the wall next to the tub and crossing his arms. "You never forget to tell me when the mailman dropped off a package, if the meter reader came by, if a bird bumped into the front window. Yet you forgot to tell me one of our next-door neighbors came by to cancel her dinner invitation."

She drizzled blue shampoo on Zeus's head and lathered his quivering body with both hands. He was the biggest one, dark brown with white feet, and not purebred Chihuahua or anything with its own rescue organization—which was why his mother kept him. Mark wasn't convinced Zeus was a dog. Perhaps a guinea pig with a long nose. Who barked like a baby with a chest infection.

"Mom," he said.

"You had a nice time, though, didn't you?"

"Sure. Until the man they're both in love with showed up."

She dropped Zeus and twisted around to look up at him. "Both of them?"

"It's a mess over there, trust me. Rose was doing me a favor in trying to keep me away."

"From looking at your room, I'd decided you liked a mess," she said.

"Very funny."

Done with the swim, Zeus scrambled up on the tile ledge around the tub, body shivering, nails clicking. Mark swiftly captured him in a towel before doggy reflexes shook the water all over the place. Cuddling him to his chest, Mark rubbed some warmth into him. He was an ugly dude, but sweet as hell. Too bad he couldn't keep that tongue in his mouth. Or open both eyes at the same time.

"I take it you're talking about Johnny, Ellen's boy," his mother said.

"Everyone calls him John."

"He finally came," she said. "That's good. Good for him."

"After months of silence, the guy just shows up, no warning, big smile, waves his dick around—and he gets a prize?"

"Watch your language, please."

He sighed, let Zeus lick his face. The only tongue action he'd had in a long time. "Sorry, but you're too forgiving. He left Blair here to face it all on her own. And now she's grateful—*grateful*—he's decided to man up."

"It's a tough situation. Hard to do the right thing."

Mark shot her a look. "You're defending him?"

"No. I'm defending her."

He rubbed Zeus between the ears. "She's sweet."

"I'm sure." She shot him a sympathetic look. "What did they cook for you? I bet it was good."

"Rose put the chicken in the dishwasher so we never got to eat it. And Blair went out with John."

"Oh…"

"Then Rose got drunk and told me she'd been dating John when he got Blair pregnant."

"Oh my." She reached down to pull the drain plug. The remaining two dogs, Luna and Europa, rubbed up against her arm, desperate to escape. They found the drain's slurping noise terrifying. She patted their backs, waiting for the water to drain, and in a moment the dogs were shaking and dancing in the empty tub with towels thrown over them.

"Yeah. So," he said. "Next time, would you please give me my messages?"

"What makes you think they're both in love with him?"

"I'm observant." Mark set Zeus on the floor. The dog tore away to race through the house, rub his ears on the carpets, break outside to replenish his stink. Good idea. "I'm going out for a run. I'll take Zeus with me."

"You never know what could happen. John has a lot of explaining to do." Holding Europa in her arms, she frowned at

Mark's frayed A's T-shirt. "Didn't you go shopping yesterday? Those shirts are *muy elegante*. Why aren't you wearing one of those? I bet the red is very flattering."

"You looked through the bags?"

"I hung it all up in your closet where it belongs. You left two thousand dollars' worth of gorgeous new clothes from Nordstrom's in a pile next to your laundry," she said. "You make me look bad. People will think I didn't raise you right."

He kissed her on the cheek, wondering if it was time to get his own place. "Please don't go through my things."

"I'm sorry, but it was a crime to leave it there on the floor. Really, a crime. I bet her eyes lit up, didn't they, when you went over for dinner? Quite a change from what you had on when you fixed the car."

"I didn't fix anything."

"Wait until she sees you without them, though. Then she'll really be impressed."

Face flooding with heat, he handed her the dog towel. "I need to get out of here."

His mother followed him out into the hall. "Wear the black shorts from Fite your brother gave you. They really show off your *you know what*."

"Thank you, Mother," he said through his teeth, ducking into his bedroom and locking the door. He didn't hesitate to choose his baggiest, grubbiest basketball shorts. When he got back, he'd start looking for a condo or something. Hell, maybe he could pick one out on his run; plenty of real estate on the market these days.

Her voice came through the crack in the doorway. "I meant your bottom, honey, not your penis."

That's it. I'm bringing my checkbook. I'll be in escrow by the time I'm back to shower.

6

ROUND NOON, BLAIR FINALLY CALLED Rose on her cell.

After scanning websites all morning for a job, Rose was sitting at the patio table on the rear deck, laptop and coffee in front of her, revising her résumé. Anything was better than reliving the night before in her mind. The way John looked at her over Blair's shoulder, guilty but smug. The shock in Mark's voice when he learned about their past. The bits of slimy poultry carcass still clinging to the silverware basket.

"I can't talk much right now," Blair said, "but I had to talk to you."

"When did you get in?" Rose had stayed up until one thirty, but that wasn't late enough.

"It was late. We had a lot to talk about."

"And you slipped out of here before I woke up this morning—"

"I didn't even sleep. Just took a shower and got on the train."

"God, you must be exhausted. Just give me the quick version."

Silence.

Rose tensed. "That bad?"

"No, it's good. For me. I mean, I hope it is. It is. But Rose…"

More silence. Rose ran a hand through her hair, twisted a strand at her temple. "If it's good for you, then that's good. Don't get upset."

"Look, I'll be home at six. We'll talk then."

"If you're that afraid of talking to me, you're either moving back to New York or he's moving in. Which is it?"

"I want you to know, no matter what happens, you can stay in the house. He and I agree on that. Absolutely. We both feel horrible about what happened."

As if it had been an act of God. *What happened.* Like a hurricane or cancer. *Whoops, that penis just fell right into the vagina, nothing we could do about it but ride it out.*

Rose scrolled over her résumé and deleted PEDIATRIC CARDIOLOGIST, 2003—PRESENT. Best not to put the big lies in print. "No matter what happens, don't feel sorry for me. Really, Blair, it just pisses me off," she said. "And anyway, I've got a job starting Monday." Given that it was only Wednesday, that gave her a few days to make it true.

"That's fantastic. Where?"

"Oh, no. You're tired. We can talk when you get home."

Blair let out a breathy laugh. "Touché. All right, that's fair. But like I said, don't worry. No matter what, you've got a place to live."

"Just tell me. Is he moving in?"

A long pause, then, "Yes."

"Soon?"

Blair's voice couldn't hide her happiness. "Yes. Soon. He's… oh, Rose, he groveled. He really did. He… he cried. He told me about his therapist, who helped him see how much his panic and withdrawal had to do with his mother, and how he doesn't know how I can forgive him but he's willing to wait. He's already reduced his hours at work so he can make the transition to California, and he has a business contact in Cupertino and Los Gatos or Los Mateo or, I don't remember exactly, and…"

Rose let her rattle on, tuning out the details of John's big revelation and plans for the future.

Damn it. Well, it was her own fault. She'd known when she moved out here there wouldn't be any guarantees. She'd just expected to have a bit more time. "I'll figure it out."

"I'm so sorry," Blair said.

"Not to be a bitch, but I'm getting sick of you saying that. You slept with my boyfriend. You got pregnant. Let's move on."

"I love him, Rose."

"Better you than me."

Blair squeaked out another apology and Rose hung up. Fighting the urge to hurl her laptop off the deck like a Frisbee, she walked inside, found the duct tape, the flashlight, and a chair, and went down into the basement.

John had looked good last night. Even better than usual, with his genial arrogance softened at the edges by the stress of the situation, his clothes worn from travel, his jaw shadowed with whiskers. He'd let his hair grow out past his ears and it suited him. The glasses were a nice touch, too; John Lennon the Venture Capitalist. Maybe he'd thought they would stop her from punching him in the face.

The chair under the duct wasn't going to get her high enough to fix it. The break went clear around, and she'd have to reach the top. Either she went next door to ask for a ladder, or she'd have to go to the store.

As she was going back upstairs, chair banging against the

wall, she stopped and glared into space. *What the hell am I doing? I'm moving out. Let them freeze.*

She dragged the chair back into the kitchen, and cursing her weakness as she dialed the number, called her mother.

"Well, it happened," Rose told her after a cursory hello. "He's here and they're going to make a go of it."

"Oh, baby," her mother said. "Baby, baby, baby."

"Yeah, that's probably why."

"I'm not going to tell you it's for the best."

"Good. Because that wouldn't help me feel better."

"Even if it is."

Rose took Blair's favorite yogurt out of the fridge, ate it straight from the container.

"And I'm not going to say you're welcome to come back home," her mother said.

"Even if I am."

"I'm not going to say that, because you're not. Phil and I decided a little push would be good for you."

Her stepfather, Phil the Slug, had been unemployed for the last two years and had moved into their house before they got married. Rose's house, where she'd lived with her mom since she was seven, just the two of them, after years of living with her grandparents.

Rose suddenly forgot she'd vowed to never move back home. "You're letting Phil talk you into kicking me out of the house? *Our* house? Who the hell does he think he is?"

"He's my husband, Rose, like it or not. And this is our home. It *was* yours, too, but you're an adult now, and it's really for the best if you set out on your own. Don't you think? Say, how's the weather out there in California? I bet it's lovely."

"You know what I think? I think a little push would be good for Phil. He's an adult now."

"I'm so glad you called, honey. I know you can't see it now, but it's all unfolding according to a cosmic plan, I'm sure of it." Her mother took a deep breath, which was a bad sign. "If your best friend weren't so attractive to John, he wouldn't have slept with her. And if Blair hadn't been so honest, she wouldn't have told you what happened the very next day, so you knew John wasn't the man for you and could put an end to it immediately. And because you'd given Blair that chest cold that led to her being on those nasty antibiotics, her pill didn't work, so she got pregnant, moved to California, and had to invite you to live with her rent-free, which is exactly what you need right now."

Rose closed her eyes and counted to ten. "I can't live here with them."

"Of course not, which is just the next step in the cosmic plan. Don't you see?"

"You know, pot is legal out here. I'm thinking about giving it a try."

"Surely you got that out of your system in college," her mother said.

"No, I mean professionally. Because if I'm going to afford my own apartment in San Francisco, I'm going to need some serious cash. Soon."

"You'll be fine. Just you wait and see."

"Sounds like you're the one waiting and seeing," Rose said, but she managed to stay polite as she said goodbye. It wasn't as if she'd planned on ever moving back into the house, not with Phil there.

Very interesting he was the one who didn't want her moving back in. He'd seemed rather fond of her presence in the house. So fond he'd developed a tendency to walk in on her when she was working out in the basement, getting dressed, taking a shower. For the first time in her life, she'd begun locking doors. He never said anything, never touched her. Maybe he feared that if she came back it was only a matter of time.

Time. She needed a job even sooner than she'd thought.

She called the temp agency again and assured them that yes, she was proficient with Adobe Illustrator, Photoshop, and Microsoft Excel, as well as being a talented speller and snappy dresser. They had a good-paying job starting next week, it turned out.

"Know any HTML?" the woman at the agency asked her.

"Sure. Tons."

"Fantastic. That's great. We were having trouble finding somebody for this assignment. I'll email you the address and person to see first thing Monday morning. It's in San Leandro. Will that commute be a problem?"

"Where's San—never mind, no, it's no problem. I've got a car."

"Fabulous."

Rose went to her laptop to see where the heck San Leandro was. "How long will they need me?"

"I'm afraid it's only for the week."

Rose's hope fell. "A week? They want me doing all that and it's only for a week?"

"That's what they say, but many companies, if they like you, ask you to stay longer. Sometimes permanently."

"All right. There's nothing else for a longer term? Or something the week after?"

"We'll be sure to let you know."

Right. Rose hung up and studied the map on her screen. Not far at all, just south of Oakland. All the towns out here sounded the same, San This and Santa That.

In five minutes she was walking across the driveway to bother Mark again. She'd planned to leave him alone, but this was an emergency. Trixie answered the door, smiling as usual, and practically dragged her inside.

"Just the person I needed," Trixie said. "Are you allergic to dogs?"

"No," Rose said, following her through the house to a porch off the kitchen. "Is Mark here by any chance?" She'd learned her lesson from yesterday; best not to depend on Trixie with any messages.

"He's working. We'll go interrupt him in a minute, I promise, but Zeus needs his drops, and Mark isn't tough enough to hold him properly. You look like a practical girl. You wouldn't mind giving me a hand, would you?"

"No problem." Rose frowned at the tiny, very ugly dog in Trixie's hands. His tongue was hanging out and one eye bugged out twice as large as the other. Tufts of hair stuck out of his upright, triangular ears. He was giving Rose an adoring smile, apparently not embittered by his own horrific appearance. "What do I need to do?"

"Just hold his head very still."

They'd never had pets when she was growing up, but she'd always wanted one. This particular creature wasn't what she'd dreamed of as a child, however. Hesitantly, Rose reached out for the dog, held its little thin torso in her hands, felt its heartbeat under her palms.

"Maybe you could sit down," Trixie said. "Hold Zeus's head in your hands. Just for a second. Don't be afraid to be firm." She took out a little bottle and began to shake it.

Laughing in surprise as Zeus climbed up her chest and licked her face, Rose sank down into a chair, got a hold of the little skull with the big tongue, and held him still. "Hey, buddy, easy with the toenails there. This is my favorite sweater."

"Great color. That periwinkle really brings out your eyes,"

Trixie said, wielding the dropper. "Hold him tighter, please. If I miss, we just have to do it again, and I'm going to run out of the medicine. I squirted the first dose into his ear, and that's not going to do any good, is it, little guy?" She made kissing noises and squeezed the clear contents of the dropper into the small eye.

"What's the matter with him?"

"Nothing serious. Just a little infection." She did the next eye. "There. All done."

Relieved, Rose released him. To her surprise, Zeus didn't jump onto the floor to make a run for it but turned back to lick her face some more. His claws dug into her right breast, above the bra line, using her cleavage as a step stool to her face. "He smells like shampoo."

"Two baths today. Mark let him play with a dead animal when they went running."

Rose pushed Zeus away and set him gently on the floor. "Yummy," she said. "So, is Mark here? I'm sorry to bother him again, but—"

"Of course you're not bothering him. He gets his work done before breakfast. He thinks I don't know that, but of course I do. Did you know Mark went to MIT when he was sixteen? He's always had more smarts than he knew what to do with."

"Which is why I'm living at home with my mother," Mark said, coming into the kitchen. "Did you show her my baby pictures? My chess trophy from third grade? My framed SATs?"

Beaming, Trixie slipped quickly across to the kitchen doorway and gave Mark a hug. "Rose was just helping me give Zeus his drops. You're too soft with him. It needed a woman's touch." She grinned at Rose. "Men are such babies."

To Rose's appreciative eye, Mark didn't bear any resemblance to an infant. It wasn't just the new clothes, the polo that hugged his biceps and broad shoulders, the jeans that emphasized his long legs. He had a confidence when he was on his own turf that was nothing like that stumbling, nervous man who'd sat with Blair in their living room.

"You just wanted an excuse to keep her here," Mark said. "Be careful, Rose. My mother adopts more than just dogs."

Rose surreptitiously wiped her hands, stained with doggy spit, on her jeans. "I'll tell my mom she's got some stiff competition out here."

"Well, I'll just leave you two alone," Trixie said. "The suppositories can wait until your next visit, Rose."

"Gotta draw the line there," Rose said. "I don't do doggy butts. Not even Zeus's."

Trixie laughed. "See? Tough. That's what I like. Not afraid to say what you mean." Hugging Zeus to her chest in one hand, she slapped Mark on the shoulder and left the kitchen.

"Now you've done it," Mark said, taking a pitcher of water from the fridge, pouring a glass. He handed it to her. "She's on the scent. No shaking her now."

Maybe it was her mom's belated declaration of apron-string cutting earlier that day, but right then it felt good to be adopted by Trixie Johnson. She sipped the water, tasted lemon and lime, took a deeper drink. "I need your help."

He slapped his forehead. "The ladder! I forgot. I'll go get it now."

"No, not that. Blair and John can get their own damn ladder."

He stared at her. "Ah."

"Yeah."

"He's staying."

"He will be."

"When?"

"Soon. Probably in about two weeks, maybe three. He's got to settle things back in New York, find a job here."

"Couldn't he have done that earlier?"

"I imagine he wanted to make sure she'd have him before he took any big steps," Rose said.

Mark took her glass and refilled it. "What are you going to do? Just pack up and move out? Where are you going to go?"

"Thanks for the indignation." Smiling, she patted him on his arm, reflecting that all the lifting in the world wouldn't give her definition like that. How hard did he have to work to keep in such great shape? Because from the look of those jeans, his muscles weren't limited to his biceps. "I'm certainly not living with them."

"Of course not." His expression turned from disgust to alarm. "Are you moving back home?"

"Absolutely not."

"Good."

"Worried about your mom missing me?"

"I'd miss you," he said. "You're the first woman I've been able to talk to since—well, for a long time. God knows how long it would take me to find another gay or pseudogay female to practice with me."

"I'm so flattered."

He grinned and his face came to life. All that charm, hiding, disguised. She stared at him, amazed by the trans-formation.

"You can take it," he said, putting the pitcher back in the fridge. "You're sexy and you know it."

Her face flooded with heat. That wasn't what she'd expected him to say. He wasn't too far off. She wasn't thin, she wasn't the modern ideal, but she'd been getting male attention since she was in seventh grade. Strangely, her suitors thought they were seeing something the others were missing, that she should be grateful, melt under their regard, when in fact she was constantly having to say no, no thank you, I'm not interested in you in that way.

"I've shocked you," he said.

"You're full of surprises, I'll say that."

He grinned again. "So, what do you need from me?" His smile fell. "Better not tell my mother you're about to be homeless. She'll put you in my sister's room."

"Not unless she has a gun," she said. "I just need you to teach me HTML. I've got a job starting Monday."

"HTML? Monday?"

"It's just for the week."

"That doesn't sound right." He shook his head. "Besides, I can't teach you HTML. That's not my thing. And three days isn't enough time to learn anything."

"I just need to know enough to fake it. I can fake anything for a week."

He laughed. "You're crazy."

"Look, learning a little code can't be that hard. I've known some pretty dumb web developers."

"It's not hard at all," he said. "At least not the code part."

"There you go."

"You'd have better luck with a book than with me."

"You're a professional teacher, right? You're perfect." She indulged in touching his arm again. What had he said? *The first girl I've been able to talk to since...*

Since who?

"All right," he said, "but don't blame me when they fire you."

AN HOUR LATER MARK SNUCK OUT OF THE HOUSE WITH A

couple of books and a laptop shoved in his backpack. He got in his car, hoping Rose would be quick. Within minutes, his mom would sense something was up and look out the window. If she saw Mark and Rose driving off together in his Jetta, she'd put fresh sheets on his bed and a fresh box of condoms on the pillow.

Rose popped open the door and climbed in. "Let's get out of here before Blair gets back from work. I don't want her getting the wrong idea."

He backed up into the road, careful not to spin the tires on the gravel, enjoying the adrenaline rush of the escape and then chiding himself for being thrilled to drive away from home at the age of twenty-nine in a late-model Volkswagen without getting in trouble with his mommy.

"I really need to get out more," he mumbled.

Her hand patted his thigh. "Workin' on it."

He thought about telling her it was all right to leave her hand where it was, but he didn't want her getting the wrong idea.

The right idea.

He glanced at her. What would she be like in bed?

No. Don't think about that. At least, not right now.

"Which café do you want to go to?" he asked.

"You're the native. Where can we work without being interrupted?"

"I don't know. I've never been the type to hang out in cafés."

He decided on College Avenue, close to the Berkeley campus. They managed to find a table in the middle of the crowded space, students already camped out in most of them with laptops, books, tablets, and drinks over every surface. Original art hung on the walls with immodest subject matter but modest price tags, mostly naked women, some men. Mark found it distracting, but was grateful none of the guys were full frontal. At least none in the main seating area.

"It's like being in college again," Rose said, peeking around them.

"Is that good?"

Her tongue darted out between glossy rosebud lips to lap at the foam on her cappuccino. Mark stared, mesmerized, as those lips curled into a smile. "Oh, yeah."

I went to the wrong college.

She took the book he had next to him and flipped through it. "Don't you have something a little more general? Like *Websites for Dumbshits* or something?"

"Nope. Maybe you should've asked a dumbshit to help you. I buy the books for smart people."

"Pfft. They're great for learning something new." She smiled at him over her cappuccino. A dab of foam clung to her upper lip. "I'll get you the one for social skills."

He reached over, swiped the foam away with a fingertip. "It wouldn't help. Book learnin' only goes so far."

She'd frozen in place when he touched her and now watched him with those big blue eyes. "Won't take you all the way, huh?"

"Something like that."

She flipped through the book, scanning the pages, sipping her drink. "I'll read this tonight. You got anything on Illustrator and Photoshop?"

"No, why?"

"They think I'm a graphic designer." She laughed.

"You're not?"

"Can't even draw a straight line."

He groaned into his cup.

"Don't look at me like that. I was desperate."

"Did you tell them anything that was true?"

She wiggled an eyebrow. "I'll make sure the direct deposit info is right." She propped an elbow on the table and leaned forward, flashing her cleavage. "How hard could it be?"

He fixed his gaze on her face. "Very. You're doomed."

"Oh, thank you very much, Mr. Positive."

"Why not tell them you're a biochemical engineer? Snag that higher hourly wage from the temp agency," he said. "Maybe even get some vacation time."

To his surprise, she didn't fire back a retort. Slumping over the table, she stared forlornly into her glass. "You're right, I *am* doomed."

"Now you're making me feel bad," he said.

"I do know a little Photoshop. And I've poked around a few websites. I thought it would be enough."

"I'm sure it is."

"Liar," she said.

"You're one to talk."

Smiling, she stood up. "I need to pee. Be right back."

He watched her weave through the crowded tables to the back of the café, her blonde hair flowing down her back in long, golden waves as she passed the artistic porn hanging on the walls.

Other eyes, male eyes, followed her. A guy wearing headphones big enough to DJ a dance club looked up from his laptop and tracked her, even craning around in his seat to check out her ass. Another man, sitting with a redhead glued to her smartphone, watched Rose out of the corner of his eye, scanning her head to toe, his gaze lingering at chest level. And the guy near the back, whose long legs were blocking her way, leaned back with a grin and said something to her, something that made her laugh and touch her hair as she stepped over him.

Guess she has a little something for everyone, Mark thought sourly, draining his cup. He was developing a little crush on her himself, if you could call nagging lust a crush.

Some people just had it. Sex appeal. Nicki Cameron, his high school's class president, had it, in such excess that three guys were willing to endure the others dating her at the same time. No matter that she was a sociopath, cruel and dismissive; she was *hot*.

Not that Rose was a sociopath, in spite of the lying. But he was looking for something more than sex, someone who made him feel a deeper wanting—primal, protective, profound. When he'd seen Blair the first time, he'd felt it, this masculine urge to step in and beat the world away with a club and cherish her forever.

Rose just made him want to tear her clothes off.

When she came out of the bathroom, the excessively extroverted, long-legged dude stood up and said something to her. She flushed pink, laughed, and shook her head, her gaze drifting over the tables to where Mark sat.

Long-legged dude looked over, saw Mark, and frowned, but then he said something to Rose and she laughed again. When she finally rejoined him at the table, Mark gave her a sour look and said, "You're popular."

"It's the hair. Next time I'll wear a hat."

He didn't think it was the hair. "What did that guy want?"

"To have sex with me," she said.

"He said that?"

She gave him a raised eyebrow.

"Fine," he said. "Don't let me stop you."

"I won't, sweetheart, but at the moment I need a job more than I need to get laid."

"I've got the opposite problem," he said, instantly regretting he'd said it out loud.

She smiled. "Let's get out of here. I can't concentrate and you're grumpy."

"I'm not grumpy, I'm mature." But he got up and bused the tables, giving Long Legs a hard look as he dumped the dishes in the bin. He didn't look old enough to drive. What made him think he could hit on a grown-up woman like Rose?

Encouragement. On their way out, while Mark watched in shock, Rose accepted a piece of paper from Long Legs and slipped it into her shoulder bag with a smile and a wave.

The night was unusually calm, almost balmy, and the moon was an orange globe at the horizon. Mark pulled her car door open. "Did you tell him I was your brother?"

"Nope."

"Just friends?"

"I didn't say anything about you," she said.

"And he just gave you his number anyway?"

"Sure. That's how it works, Mark. You can't wait for girls to fall in your lap."

"You can in some places." He started the engine. "It just costs a little extra."

"Whatever works for you," she said brightly, patting his knee. "It's great to get out, isn't it?"

"I'm sure your website skills are totally at professional levels now."

"Yeah. That *is* a problem. Thanks for reminding me of the carnage of my life. For a minute there I was almost feeling happy."

He pulled out into traffic, glanced at her. "Sorry."

"Yeah." Twisting around in the seat, she dumped something in the back with a thud, rearranged herself facing forward. "Shit."

"What was that?"

"Your book," she said. "You're right. I can't fake this one. I'll have to find something else."

Oddly disappointed she was giving up so easily, he said, "If anyone could fake it, you could."

"Thanks, I think."

"What did you study in college? Did you say you went to college?"

"Yeah, I went."

He waited. When she didn't elaborate, he said, "Even if it was underwater basket-weaving, there has to be some practical application. What was it, art history? English?"

She spoke so quietly, he barely heard her. "Biology."

"Really? That's great. There's tons of work in the medical field."

"Oh, yeah? Have you looked, Einstein?"

He braked hard enough at the stop sign to make her grab the dash. "Just because you're feeling sorry for yourself is no reason to yell at me."

He accelerated, passed a bike pulling a baby trailer covered with blinking yellow and orange lights. They passed under the BART train tracks into Rockridge.

"You're right," she said softly. "I'm sorry. You're great. I am feeling sorry for myself and I've got no right to."

"No, you should feel sorry for yourself. Your ex-boyfriend and your best friend are moving into your house together to have a baby, and you've got to move out but you don't have a job," he said. "Just be nice to me while you wallow."

"I will." She patted his thigh again. "I promise."

When her hands were back to her side of the car, he relaxed. Maybe he should ask her to stop doing that. "You want to stay here in the Bay Area, right? Or are you thinking about just going home?" He realized suddenly how badly he wanted her to stay.

"Not going home."

Good. "Okay. So, you were a bio major. Did you graduate?"

"Yes."

"Was it, pardon me for putting it this way, but you haven't bought me *Social Skills for Dumbshits* yet, so I might get offensive here," he said. "Was it a real school? One somebody out here might've heard of?"

"Those are two different questions," she said. "It was Cornell. Whether or not Californians have heard of it, who knows? You all have your heads up your ass about some pretty basic stuff."

"You have an Ivy League degree in biology," he said.

"Yes."

"You're right," he said. "It's hopeless. Shall I drive you to the homeless shelter?"

"You don't understand. I'm not a doctor or anything, I only have my bachelor's."

An idea was nagging at him, but it was risky, loaded with pitfalls, potentially embarrassing. Did he want to give up his peaceful, private, profitable gig to help a woman he'd met only a couple of days ago?

"I know a company that hires bio grads," he said with a sigh.

Her head turned.

"Mine," he said.

7

ROSE SKIPPED INTO THE HOUSE, her heart light.

Mark was sure he could get her an interview at his company. Why hadn't she ever asked him what kind of software he worked on? If she hadn't finally spilled about her biology degree, he might not have thought she'd be right for a popular health-and-wellness website.

To hell with pretending to be a graphic designer or webmaster for a week. She might actually find something *cool*. With benefits. A future.

"There you are!" Blair jumped up from the couch, dropping her box of Cheez-Its on the table. "Where have you been?"

Rose frowned at the box. "Is that really the best bite for your baby?"

"Shut up. I was hungry and you weren't here. Want to go out to dinner?"

"Where's John?"

Blair picked up the box. "He had to fly back."

"Already?"

"He didn't want to miss any more work. Don't give me that look, he's about to quit and he has tons of loose ends to deal with."

"Fine." Rose took a deep breath. "I'm glad. It's hard to have him here."

Mouth full of crackers, Blair gave her a sad look, chewing.

The grim contours of her life came back to her. "So. He's moving in," she said.

Blair nodded, swallowed. A smile crept across her face. "He's already got a job lined up. A startup in Silicon Valley."

"Isn't that a long commute?" Rose held up a hand. "Forget it. Not my problem. Good for him. Really. You'll need the health insurance for the kid, all the other benefits."

"Thank you, Rose, for everything. I want to buy you dinner somewhere. Anything."

"Aren't you tired? You didn't sleep last night."

"I had a nap."

"Not enough. You've got to take care of yourself."

Blair hugged her arms around herself. "That's what he kept saying."

"Sure. He wants you to do all the work."

"You're wrong. He's changed. He had some kind of… thing. He's really come around. He bought a dozen pregnancy and baby care books."

Rose wanted to believe it, she did, but it was too much, too soon. "Let's do dinner tomorrow night. Tonight you can get into bed and I'll work on my résumé."

"I thought you had something starting Monday."

"Yeah. Well. I think I've got something even better," Rose said. "Mark said he can get me an interview where he works."

"Oh, that's great!"

"They're always looking for people with medical backgrounds, he said, but an MD isn't necessary. In fact, they like people who aren't doctors. Something about the corporate culture—it's more patient oriented, a little alternative. I want to research it tonight, really get a handle on it before I go in." She looked down at her jeans and sweater. "I'll have to figure out what to wear. They're much more casual out here. He didn't think a suit was the right vibe, but my mother would roll over in her not-dead-yet grave if she found out I wore jeans to a job interview."

Smiling, Blair sank back onto the couch. "This is great. I knew you'd find something out here. Was it hard talking Mark into getting you the interview?"

"It was his idea." Rose took the box of crackers away from her and went into the kitchen. "How about we order a pizza?" she called out. "I'll make a salad while we wait."

Blair got up and followed her into the kitchen. "His idea. Interesting."

"We'll be getting married first, of course," Rose said, getting out the lettuce, carrots, and a bag of spinach. "Isn't that what you were going to suggest next?"

"Beat me to it."

Very carefully, Rose kept her voice light. "Speaking of marriage, will it be a double ceremony?"

After a small pause, Blair said, "We want to keep it small. Very small. Very, very small."

Rose had braced herself for the idea of John and Blair getting married, but it was still hard to accept. John had told her the first time they'd woken up in bed together that he couldn't imagine anything more beautiful than her naked body. He'd called her a goddess, made her feel worshipped, wanted.

That had ended quickly. Rose turned to Blair, saw the glow in her cheeks, the animation in her eyes that hadn't been there for weeks, and worried her happiness wouldn't last either.

Damn it, Rose would be as big as her bra size and hope it would. Forever and ever after, for the baby who deserved both parents, for her friend, even for John. "Will there be guests at this infinitesimal ceremony?"

"If they'll come," Blair said, putting an arm around her waist.

"I will," Rose said. "But… I won't be in the ceremony. I can't. Standing up with you guys…" She shook her head.

"I understand."

"It's not you. It's everyone knowing, watching, comparing us. I'm not a masochist."

"I know. I totally understand. I just want you to be there," Blair said. "We're thinking City Hall now and a party after the baby's here. I want to be able to really let loose at the reception, have champagne, all that."

Drinking. Now that's an excellent idea. Five minutes later, martini in hand, Rose was listening to Blair gush about John's plans to be at her next doctor's appointment, his ideas for the nursery, how he didn't want to know if they were having a boy or a girl, baby names.

"He's got some crazy ideas," Blair said. "I think it's because he hated his own name—John—growing up. He likes something more unique."

Not trusting herself to speak, since she had a few creative ideas of her own, Rose peeled the carrots into the sink, wondering why it didn't bother her to think about the baby, just John.

Their relationship had been so quick, a fling. On Monday they were talking about form in the weight room, and by Friday they were having sex in the backseat of his Explorer in the parking lot. Then all weekend long, all over the place, and every night the following week.

He loved having sex with her. He loved her body. He loved touching, kissing, smelling, tasting, watching her.

Going out with her? Not so much.

Being seen in public with a fat blonde with an affection for chunky jewelry, bright colors, broad gestures, and loud laughs?

Nope.

As much as he turned her on—and John still made her burn at night, remembering their times together—she'd been about to break it off with him because of his problem. And it was his problem, not hers, that he was embarrassed to be seen with her. You couldn't argue with attraction, and if he hadn't been attracted to her, she wouldn't blame him. She majored in biology—she respected it.

But to want her and be ashamed of it? That made him a spineless, shallow, insecure hypocrite.

And he was going to marry her best friend. It didn't matter that he loved to be seen with the petite, quiet Blair, and doted on her in a chivalrous way in public and in private, in ways he'd never shown to Rose. What if it didn't last? Blair might get fat. She'd certainly get old, God willing. And then what?

"Have you told his mother yet?" Rose asked. "She might not agree to the civil ceremony."

"He can stand up to her."

Rose had never seen him do it, except by running away. "I wouldn't mind driving to Reno, just so you know. If it comes to that. It's only a few hours from here." Earlier that day, desperate and reckless, Rose had researched the drive on the Internet, considering gambling as a possible way out of her financial limitations.

Sipping her martini, she reflected that it was best to adopt vices one at a time. More than that might be more than she could handle.

"She'd hate that," Blair said.

"Bonus."

"They do have a condo at Lake Tahoe. Right on the lake." Blair smiled, shaking her head. "We couldn't. She'd be so upset."

"Start as you mean to go on. If you let her walk over you now..."

"You're right. It would be fun, don't you think? Just us, Elvis, and the casinos? We could do something more formal next year when we have the reception. This would just be like a starter wedding."

"Sounds like a plan," Rose said.

"You'd do it? Make the drive?"

"Sure. And I bet your unborn child won't be the first baby to visit Nevada in utero. Maybe they sell baby tees for that."

Brighter than Rose had seen her in months, Blair grabbed the salad bowl, laughing. "I can't believe this is happening. I'd started to worry it was going to be just me and the Wicked Witch of the West."

"Thanks a lot," Rose said, draining her drink. "Now you're calling me names."

Blair squeezed her. "Let's order two pizzas. I'm starving. And if you ever question what I put in my mouth again, you're dead. I don't care how much I love you."

Rose saluted her with her drink, nodding. "Ditto."

Dinner was excellent. Blair ate enough for three, Rose drank enough for two; they sat, bundled in blankets on the deck, watching the San Francisco skyline disappear under a blurry gray fog across the bay. They had the happiest evening together they'd had since John had entered their life.

Knowing it might not last.

THE CUBICLES SPREAD OUT OVER A HUNDRED FEET IN each direction. On the perimeter, offices with tall, skinny windows surrounded the sea of gray carpeted dividers. The ceiling was white, the carpet was tan, the walls were beige.

It was like a maze of oatmeal, Mark thought.

"Have you seen our new building before, Mr. Johnson?" the woman escorting him down the corridor asked. As they walked, curious heads popped up like pocket gophers in a soccer field, checking him out.

At first he didn't realize she was talking to him. "Call me Mark," he said, his palms sweating.

Did they know who he was? Is that why they were staring like that? It was supposed to be a secret. Ancient history.

"Here's his office," the woman said. Bridget, her badge said. She was in her mid-twenties, short curly hair a nondescript sandy blonde—*more beige*, he thought—with glasses. Dressed like an administrative type, not technical, which is to say she was wearing a blouse and black pants instead of the jeans programmers liked to wear, male or female.

When she saw the room was empty, her eyes widened with alarm. "He should be back any second. I don't know what happened to him. Can I get you anything? Coffee? Red Bull? M&M's?"

"M&M's? Really?"

"If that's not okay, we've got Twizzlers, PowerBars, fresh fruit, and cashews. No peanuts, since Allen Buckworth is allergic. Like, fall-over-and-die-allergic." She looked at him expectantly.

"I'm fine." He made his way to a chair in front of the black desk and sat down.

"I'm sure he'll be here any minute."

He gave the most reassuring smile he could manage. "I'm fine. Really."

Nodding, she left. As he watched her go, he noticed a guy step out from behind a cubicle to whisper something to her. They looked back at him, saw he was watching, and quickly turned away.

They knew. Damn it.

The CEO of WellyNelly, Sylvester Minguez, burst into the office with his usual loud charm, striding right over to him and slapping him on the shoulder. "Mark! So awesome to see you, man!"

Though Mark had tried hard over the years, it was impossible not to like Sylvester Minguez. The CEO of a promising tech startup in the Bay Area who insisted people call him Sylly —pronounced "silly"—was determined to be liked, and what Sylly was determined to get, Sylly got.

Well, not with everyone. "Hi, Syl," Mark said.

Flashing him a mock frown, Sylly closed the door. "You've refused the M&M's. I can't believe it."

"I gave them up. Bad for my health."

"None of us are getting any younger, are we?" Sylly said, perching himself on the front of his desk next to Mark. His sharp brown eyes moved over him like the laser in a photocopier, taking in every inch, remembering everything. "You're looking good. New threads?"

Mark leaned back, crossed his legs, ankle on knee, and tapped his fingers on the arm of the chair. "You promised when I took the job you wouldn't tell anyone."

White teeth flashing in his confidently cheerful face, Sylly shrugged. "I didn't."

"They know. It's obvious."

"Word gets around."

"You could deny it."

"That wasn't part of our deal," Sylly said. "I can hardly

erase your name from the source code. Your fingerprints are everywhere."

"Tell them it's a different Mark Johnson. It's not like my name is Sylvester Minguez or something crazy like that. There are thousands of Mark Johnsons in the world. We're a dime a dozen."

"Not at WellyNelly. Not who seemed to know the source code on his first day as if he'd written it himself. You're a legend around here. Of course people guessed."

Mark rubbed his face with both palms. "I should've used an alias."

With another whack to Mark's shoulder, Sylly got up and sat behind his desk, grinning. "It's great to have you back. Admit it, you've got to be a little bit proud of yourself. Look around, you did this. Your acorn has grown into a very strong, very profitable tree. Why wouldn't you want to be a part of it?" He pointed a finger at him. "Openly. Not like some hermit taking wire transfers while he slums it with unappreciative children in Iowa."

"Wisconsin," Mark said. This was pointless. He hadn't come here to talk about his career, his ego, or lack of either. "I'm here to cash in on the referral bonus I know you've set up. The company website says we're eligible for five grand if we get somebody we know to work here."

"As if you need the money. You know how rich you'll get when we go public or sell?"

"You MBA types are always saying that. How many people in the Bay Area have gone broke over the last twenty years waiting for their stock options to be worth something?"

"You still can't believe your little hobby is more successful than you ever dreamed it could be," Sylly said.

"I never dreamed it because I didn't want it." Mark reached over to grab a Nerf ball on the desk. Squeezing the orange foam in his fist, he looked around for the hoop, found it over the dart board near the minifridge. "My dad was dying, Syl. I wanted to help my mother get through it. That's all."

"No, it's not all. You helped thousands—hell, we're pushing a million users now, Mark—get through the shitty tragedies of life." For the first time, Sylly looked genuinely frustrated. "I just don't understand why you're not proud of what you made. WellyNelly helps people. It's not spyware, it's not boring corporate evil shit, it's *nice*. We're the good guys. Why are you ashamed of that?"

"I'm not ashamed, I just don't want…" Mark threw the ball, missed the hoop. "I don't like all the attention."

Sylly held out his hands, palms up, looking around. "What attention? Who's bugging you? So the staff here is curious to see what you look like. Hiding for years makes people curious. It's not like people are chasing your car demanding autographs. Taking pictures of you clubbing." He grinned.

"They will if and when Welly goes public. You said yourself, imagine how rich I'll get."

"You won't be the only one, buddy," Sylly said, rubbing his palms together. "We can console one another. Misery loves company. And we're going to be very, very miserable."

Mark retrieved the ball, threw it at Sylly's smug head. "How's your mom?"

"Excellent. Thank you. She uses WellyNelly to manage her diabetes."

"I'm glad. Not about the diabetes. That sucks."

"And your creation helps her deal with it. As well as me, my sisters, her doctor, the pharmacy, and the insurance company. Just like you envisioned."

Mark sat down. The only way to win an argument with Sylly was to keep your mouth shut. "Anyway, about that job referral thing. I know somebody."

"Vegetable or mineral?"

He meant, was she technical. "I'm not sure. She's got a degree in biology from Cornell. Doesn't want to be a doctor but has a great personality, real smart, team player and all that bullshit. I thought you might find something for her."

Sylly's dark eyebrows were high on his forehead. "She?"

"It's nothing like that."

"Uh-huh."

He shrugged. "Really. I even assumed she was gay for a while."

Sylly tapped his fingers on his lips. "Now that you know she's not, however, here you are."

Mark leaned forward, trying not to lose his temper. "Look, she's my neighbor. She just moved here from New York and needs a job. We're practically family. Her best friend is about to marry this guy that's about to become my brother's cousin-in-law…" He trailed off, realizing that sounded ridiculous. "Anyway, I just want to help her out. She's fun. Has lots of energy. I wouldn't recommend her if I didn't think you'd like her."

"I'm thinking you wouldn't recommend her if *you* didn't like her," Sylly said.

"I do like her."

"And you want her to like you right back, don't you?"

Annoyed by an argument he hadn't expected, Mark felt his patience give way. "Not all of us use the workplace as our personal harem, Syl."

Sylly's eyebrows came down. Any hint of a smile vanished. The cold, hard steel that had made him CEO of a rising tech startup rose to the surface.

Mark stared back at him. WellyNelly had settled a sexual harassment claim the year before. One of the marketing guys had been sleeping with one of the admins, and it went sour—

or at least that was the guy's story. The subject was taboo and Mark had never learned the details. "Sorry," Mark said. "You know I'm not like that."

Sylly's hard look didn't waver. "You swear you're not just trying to get into her panties?"

Infinitesimal pause. "I swear."

"Because you're not just some low-level grunt around here, no matter what the paperwork says."

"I know."

"You're the prodigal programmer, the native son, the founder. The brains of the outfit. The big daddy—"

"Enough," Mark said, cringing. "My God, give it a rest."

"As you noticed, everyone here knows exactly who you are. If you bring in women you're trying to get naked, there are lawyers out there who'll jump on us like flies on shit."

"I'm not trying to bring in *women*, plural. It's *woman*, singular," Mark said. He thought of something. "Is this a speech you give all the men in the company? Because that means you're not allowing anyone to refer women to work here. Call me paranoid, but isn't that asking for trouble?"

Sylly looked down at his desk, fiddled with a pen.

"What's the ratio these days, male to female?" Mark went on, glancing toward the cubicles. "I'm seeing a sea of Y chromosomes out there. A case might be made WellyNelly is has a gender-based hiring problem, don't you think?"

The hard look in Sylly's eyes faded. He pursed his lips together.

That got him, Mark thought.

"This is important to you?" Sylly finally asked. "It's not just for show? You can't just get her an interview and you're off the hook?"

"No, I'd really like to get her a job."

"Well, then, that's going to cost you."

Mark let out his breath, ready to deal. "You can give her my salary, I was thinking. I don't really need it."

Sylly stared, then rolled his eyes. "You know, for a genius, you're full of some pretty stupid ideas."

"Thanks."

"Pay her your salary," he repeated. He threw his head back, threw a disgusted look at the ceiling. "I swear, you're impossible."

"It was just an idea."

"Even if she was a seventy-six-year-old lesbian without a vagina, there's no way you're opening yourself up to any possible claim that you were trying to compel her to have sex with you, you get my drift?"

Mark put his hand over his eyes. "Nice mental image. Thanks."

"Got it?"

He nodded. "You said it was going to cost me."

Sylly stood up and wandered over to the window, a smile creeping over his face. "It's something I've been thinking about for a while."

Mark stifled a groan. "This isn't going to be good."

Flashing a grin, Sylly slapped his hands together. "On the contrary, my geeky hermit friend. It's going to be excellent. For everyone."

8

"MARK'S AT THE DOOR!" BLAIR called from the top of the stairs.

Rose looked over from her new ladder, duct tape in hand. She was coated in sweat, hair glued to her forehead along with clumps of dust, dirt, desiccated insect carcasses, and less identifiable nastiness. After Blair bought the ladder and made her favorite stir-fry for dinner, Rose tackled the dirty work. "Tell him I'll be right there."

In a minute she heard Mark clomping down the stairs. Her heart lifted, hoping for news about the job. And she had to admit it was just good to see him.

"So much for letting them freeze to death," he said.

"This is all for me. I was dying last night. I thought California was supposed to be warm." One last strip and she decided she was done. "I used the whole roll, just in case."

"Who needs ducts when you have tape?"

"Exactly." She climbed down.

"Hey, you fixed the light." He looked around the dingy basement. "I think I liked it better before."

"I didn't want Blair tripping and falling if she ever came down here."

He put out a hand to help her at the last step. His fingers wrapped around her upper arm, his knuckles brushing her left breast. If it were any other guy, she would've thought it was intentional.

"Let's turn it on and see if it works," she said.

He plucked a wad of gray nastiness out of her hair. "Ew."

"Yeah. I wish I'd worn a hat. I can't wait to take a shower." She pulled the elastic band out of her hair, bent over and riffled her hands through the strands, shaking off as much of the dust as she could. "Okay, you're killing me. Do you have good news or bad?" She straightened and combed her fingers through the tangles while Mark stared, silent.

"I have good news," he said finally. "I think."

"I'll be grateful just to have an interview." She took a deep breath. "And for your sake, I'll try not to lie too much."

"You won't have to lie at all, except for the parts about me. You can embellish that all you like."

She caught his arm in hers and guided him to the stairs. "Tell me about it while I turn on the heat. Is there a time scheduled for an interview or do they need me to send a résumé?"

"Do you have your heart set on an interview?"

"They need a résumé first. Sure, of course. I've got a few versions, but it would help if I knew what kind of position they were considering me for. Or"—she turned and smiled at him following her up the stairs—"rather, *you* were considering me for."

"It's not that formal. You won't need a résumé."

"Oh." She fought disappointment. "Is it just an informational thing, then?" He looked uncomfortable, so she said quickly, "I don't mind. Really, I appreciate whatever you—"

"I thought you'd like to start Monday. Since you were going to do that temp job next week, I figured you could just try this instead, see if it works out." He strode away from her down the hall to the thermostat in the living room, flicked it on. "Let's see if that works. There might be other leaks in the ducts, but you should really let John deal with his mother and the pros for that one."

"I start Monday?"

"Is that good?"

"Are you serious?"

His face lit up with a big grin. "Would you rather start tomorrow?"

"You're shitting me. How could you possibly line it up that fast? I don't even know what I'll be doing."

"They've got a few positions and think you'll be perfect for one of them."

"That's crazy. They haven't even met me."

"Some random people were going to hire an unknown temp to do their web design, and you didn't question that," he said. "Here you've got me vouching for you and your degree from Cornell. That was true, right?"

She nodded, her mind whirling with potential. She could catch up on her college loan payments. Have her hair done. Get an apartment. "This is great. I don't know how you did it, but thank you." On impulse, she flung her arms around him and hugged him, wiggling and laughing.

Rigid at first, arms lifted in the air like a scarecrow, he slowly relaxed enough to pat her shoulders. Then he gently pushed her away. "You're welcome."

"Wait until I tell Blair."

"I heard," Blair said, coming into the room. "That's amazing. How long have you worked there, Mark?"

Rose saw a flicker of panic on his face. Unblinking, he stared at Blair. "Not very long, but they like my work."

An accomplished falsehood artist herself, Rose smelled something fishy. But he was always so nervous around Blair, it was hard to tell. Was that blush because Blair had addressed him or because he was hiding something?

"Stay for a drink," Blair said, hooking her arm in Rose's. "How about a beer? John bought a case of Anchor Steam and we'll never drink it. I'm pregnant and Rose likes the hard stuff."

Rose watched him trip over his own feet as Blair tried to guide him into the kitchen. "No, thank you, no, that's nice of you," he said, reaching out to the wall for balance. "Unless I'm doing you a favor or something, like you're afraid you might drink it yourself and it's bad for the baby. And my drinking it would be a heroic act."

Smiling, Blair looked up into his face, which was now flushed a rich rosy pink from the social exertion of his earlier speech. "It *would* be heroic," she said. "Glass or just the bottle?"

"Just the glass." He shook his head. "I mean bottle." His wild glance hit Rose, who wasn't finding his thing for Blair so cute anymore.

"Maybe it'll relax you," Rose said.

Humming to herself, Blair got the beer, opened it, and handed it to Mark with a smile. "I've got chips and guacamole, homemade, too. Interested? You'd be doing us another favor. The guac doesn't store well."

He was still staring at Blair. His eyeballs were frozen open like a corpse's. Rose's fingers itched to reach up and close them for him like the sensitive homicide cop in a TV show. Instead, she guided the beer to his lips and said, "Sit down, eat, drink. Let Blair lavish her domestic happiness on you while I take a shower. Then you can tell me everything you know about this company. Though it probably isn't much, since you never leave your house and you've only worked for them a little while, right?"

His gaze finally broke away from Blair. Gulping his beer, he looked off into the distance, then nodded and sat down at the kitchen table.

Something other than puppy love was going on inside that handsome skull of his, but she didn't know what. Feeling a creeping itch on her own skull, she remembered the urgency of her shower and left them there, hoping he didn't faint from the anxiety of being alone with Blair.

A job. Monday.

And she didn't even have to sleep with anyone to get it.

THE OFFICES FOR WELLYNELLY WERE IN AN INDUSTRIAL area of Berkeley, down near the bay in the patchwork of business parks, auto repair shops, restaurants, car dealerships, apartment buildings and semi-gentrified single-family homes.

Rose parked her car in the visitor spot of the company's marked parking lot as she was told in an email. Not surprisingly, Mark had stayed home, telling her it was probably better she made her first impression on her own.

And what an impression it would be, Rose decided, marching from her car to the front door. Without spending a dime, she'd outdone herself. Just a little flashy but not tacky, feminine but not slutty, professional but not stuffy. Though Mark had told her to just wear jeans and a T-shirt, she was well aware of the biased source of the advice and decided on fitted charcoal trousers and a black sweater adorned with her usual scarf, handmade jewelry, and smoky eye makeup.

The woman at the front desk jumped up when she came in. "Rose?"

Surprised by the immediate welcome, Rose paused in the doorway before holding out her hand and marching forward. "Nice to meet you," she said, smiling with a glance at the woman's badge. "Bridget?"

The woman came out from around the desk. She was young, had short hair, wore no makeup, and made lots of eye contact. "Did you have any trouble parking?" Her handshake was firm but her skin was cold. Probably because the air temperature inside the building was low enough to kill tropical plants.

Rose pointed at her car right outside the front door. "Is that the right place?"

"Oh, absolutely. You can park wherever you want."

"How does that work? It doesn't look like there are many spaces around here," Rose said.

"You don't have to worry about that. Now that I know which car is yours, you can just park in the visitor spots." She lowered her voice. "I'm the one who gets people ticketed. Or if they really piss me off, *towed.*"

"I'll be sure to stay on your good side, then."

She drew back, shook her head. "Not you, of course." She gestured down a carpeted hallway. "Please forget I said anything. Sylly's waiting for you."

Luckily, Mark had already told her about the big boss's nickname. She hadn't expected to meet him so soon, however. "Does the CEO always greet the new people first?"

"God, no," Bridget said. "Though he does like to meet them eventually."

More confused than ever, Rose followed Bridget through the colorless work space, past cubicles, the bathroom, a full kitchen, and conference rooms, to an office just like the others on the right side of the building.

"You must be Rose," the man inside said, coming over with his hand out. "Thanks for making sure she made it, Bridget."

"No problem," Bridget said, smiling at him as she closed the door.

Sylly was a good-looking man of medium height and indeterminate ethnicity. His name and warm complexion suggested he was Latino, but the shape of his brown eyes was Asian, possibly Indian. Or Chinese. African?

She gave up guessing. She imagined he'd put up with enough nosy questions during his lifetime; she wasn't going to add to them, especially since she was looking for a job and didn't want to annoy him.

"Thank you so much for..." She stopped herself. Having her? It made her sound like a houseguest. They were acting so odd, though, like she wasn't an employee or job supplicant at all. "Thank you for offering me a job. I can't wait to find out what it is."

He flashed a set of perfect teeth, but she noticed his eyes were sharp, checking her out, sizing her up. "Have a seat. I've got your résumé here. Mark was right, you're perfect for Welly-Nelly. I'm sure we'll find a way to make each other happy."

Her alarm bells' quiet buzzing at the front door rose to a steady *wah wah wah* in her head. Whatever was going on here, job or no, she had to understand it all.

She sat down and looked at him. "Why?"

This time she noticed he tried to stifle his smile. "I beg your pardon?" He continued his journey to a minifridge behind him, bent down with his back to her, popped back up with a bottle in his hand. "Mineral water?"

"What did Mark say to you guys to make you so happy to

see me? Because I'd hate to start on the wrong foot." A suspicion struck her. "This isn't all a joke, right?"

"No, I promise. No joke." He handed her the bottle.

"It didn't sound like Mark, but I don't know him very well."

His charming smile disappeared. "Really?"

Whoops. Mark had vouched for her; she shouldn't undermine him. "Not as well as I'd like to." Crap, that wasn't much better. Now Sylly thought she was barking up Mark's nerdy tree.

Eyes smiling, Sylly opened his mouth, closed it, then regarded her with his lips pinched together. After a moment, he said, "We like Mark a lot around here. If he says we should hire you, we get excited. We're growing so fast, we can't find enough good people. You were premed, he said. Ivy League."

"Yes, but that isn't very unusual."

He raised an eyebrow. "Sure it is," he said. "Why didn't you go to med school?"

That was the question she dreaded most. Admitting she'd simply changed her mind suggested she was fickle, indecisive, fun-loving, unreliable, lazy. It wouldn't be so bad if she'd jumped into another field and applied herself. For instance, if she'd gone to law school and clerked for the Supreme Court instead. Or if her undergrad years in bionanotechnology led to a stint on the International Space Station. That would be okay to talk about.

Too bad she'd promised not to make stuff up.

Why hadn't she gone to med school? She was still trying to figure that out herself. That first year after graduation was a recovery period. She'd been working so hard since she was ten, she didn't know who she was anymore. The fantasy of having no person or institution to please, only herself, had driven her to graduate with honors before her twentieth birthday.

And then… five years of aimless wandering. Retail. Selling used books on Amazon, garage sale finds on eBay, crafts on Etsy. Teaching SAT prep at the youth center. Learning German, Spanish, a little Thai.

Dating. A lot of dating. A lot of sex. John was only the last in a string of short-term flings she'd enjoyed since moving back home with her mother. That was a secondary advantage of having the occasional boyfriend: somewhere else to sleep.

Facing the sharp, successful man on the other side of that desk, answering for her unfulfilled life, was a nightmare that kept her up at night.

Why didn't you go to med school?

She settled for the simple truth. "I didn't want to be a doctor," she replied.

Beaming, he punched the air with his fist. "Awesome. Me neither." He held out his hand in a high five. "I was premed at Stanford. I didn't even graduate."

Fear dissipating, she reached up and slapped his palm.

"Mark's right. You're perfect for WellyNelly. The place is full of excellent people who rejected the easy, well-traveled path. You're going to love it here." Without getting up, he rolled his Aeron chair around to her side, reaching out to rotate the monitor as he moved. "Let's look at Welly in action. Then we'll talk about where you can help us out."

❧

Forehead pressed to his bedroom window, Mark watched the house next door, wondering if Rose was back yet. The living room lights were on, but that could be Blair.

Sylly had sent him an email around two: "Your 5K is on its way. See you in the morning, sucker. XOXO."

So they'd hired her. That was great. She'd help them

relaunch their women's health site, sadly neglected until now. Forums, drug and diagnoses encyclopedias, resource links, emotional support. Right now WellyNelly had a very male, utilitarian look, screen after screen of navy and white, every page branded the same way.

That's how he'd designed it when he was sixteen. The technology couldn't handle much back then, not while maintaining its performance. Sick people didn't have time to wait for the computer to load a photograph of flowers, animated babies, smiling healthy people. People wanted to find the best doctor, the best treatment, the best shoulder to cry on. As quickly as possible.

For themselves or somebody they loved. His dad never sat down and used WellyNelly himself, barely acknowledged it, but his mom had. Hours she'd spent, talking to other cancer patients and their families, survivors, and then widows.

Mark remembered the day he created the Widow Forum. The last time he'd worn a suit, the day he buried his father.

Until recently, that was the last work he ever did on the WellyNelly software. At college he vowed to do something wildly different from what everyone expected from the wunderkind: teach. Not at the college level, which would have required grad school, but earlier than that, with younger kids who didn't like math and science because they'd never had an enthusiastic introduction. Surely, he thought, if they could see how cool it all was, they'd be as excited as he'd always been.

Well, no. A better teacher could've done it, maybe, with some of the kids. Not him. Within five years he was as jaded as the alcoholic sixty-something precalculus teacher he'd had when he was in high school—but not as good.

And he was lonely. A girlfriend from Wisconsin had led him to Milwaukee for his accreditation and first job, but she hadn't lasted.

He pushed away from the window and strode over to the closet. Sucker. He had to find something to wear for tomorrow and every day of the week and every week after that, something that didn't have holes or smell bad or make him look like a crazed loser.

Because Sylly had named his price for hiring Rose. And he'd agreed.

At least he'd get to see her every day.

$\mathcal{H}$E WAS POURING HIMSELF A cup of coffee in the WellyNelly kitchen when Rose rushed over, smiling wildly, and squeezed his arm.

After a quick glance over her shoulder, she said quietly, eyes twinkling, "Howdy, neighbor."

No matter what she wore, even in black and gray work clothes and only a few necklaces, she blinded him. Blue eyes, pink cheeks, golden hair, all at once, pulsing with life.

"How's it going?" he asked, stirring cream into his mug. She even smelled good. No, not the word. Tasty. She smelled tasty.

Then again, maybe it was just the banana bread on the counter.

"Fantastic, thank you very much." She leaned across him to get a mug for herself out of the cabinet.

No, it was her. He inhaled, gritted his teeth.

"How am I going to pay you back for getting me this job?" she whispered. For once, she seemed oblivious to the joke potential. Innocent, happy, unguarded. "I still owe you a decent dinner. Maybe you and your mom could come over this week, before John comes back? Not Friday, since I'll want time to make something really good. Saturday?"

The coffee burned his tongue, but he swallowed it anyway. A hot woman asked him out… and included his mother. Didn't that just capture everything that was wrong with his life?

"I'm sure she'd love that. Just tell us when," he said, stepping away from her. She seemed to assume he wasn't affected by her like other men were, touching his arm, bumping his hip, smelling good around him.

"Are you really working in the office from now on?"

"A little," he said, meaning Monday through Friday, eight until six. "Trying to get out of the house more, remember?"

Another pat. This time her palm flattened against his back. He could feel her fingers splay out, press gently into muscle, electrify his spinal column.

"Good for you. If I weren't moving into my own apartment, I'd suggest we carpool."

"Maybe until then," he said.

She looked away. "Not yet, okay? It's obvious they hired me because of you, and I'd really like to establish myself on my own, you know?"

"I totally understand."

"Later. In a few months. Who knows? I'm looking at apartments in Berkeley. Maybe I'll be on your way. Of course, then I wouldn't be able to give you a ride, living way up in the hills."

"I wouldn't mind picking you up," he said.

She smiled, shook her head. "You're such a nice guy." For a moment she visibly struggled with something and then, suddenly, she went up on tiptoes and pressed her lips to his cheek.

Just as quickly, she was gone, out the door in a sweet-scented breeze.

Somewhere, Mark knew, he'd gone terribly wrong.

If only he knew where.

§

"THIS TIME I'M DOING IT ALL AHEAD OF TIME. No forgotten chickens," Rose said to Blair as they sprawled on the back deck in shorts and bikini tops, enjoying their first weekend as employed people since they'd moved to California. The high temperature for the day was supposed to hit ninety-two, a record for the last day of September. Mark and his mother were coming over for dinner that evening.

"Did you know some people cook fish in their dishwashers?" Blair asked.

"Lord," Rose said, turning her head to the other side. "You could cook one right here next to me here on this deck in a goldfish bowl. Like sun tea."

"I can't believe it's September. I could get used to living like this."

"I hope it's not too hot for lasagna," Rose said. "Should we make something colder?"

"I'll make ice cream!" Blair declared, all smiles. Now that Rose had a job, Blair let herself express how happy she was to have John back in her life. "I've been wanting to buy an ice cream maker. This is a great excuse."

"Sure, that's a practical purchase." Rose sipped her iced tea, rolled onto her back. She was glad Blair was happy but skeptical John would live up to her hopes. "Forget the baby stroller. Get the dessert appliances first."

"Be quiet. Pregnant women get whatever they want."

"God, I'm so glad I'm moving out," Rose said. "You're going to be impossible."

Blair poked her in the ribs. "I'll make strawberry."

Blair's homemade strawberry ice cream had halted more than one nervous breakdown over the years. "You don't have to make anything. I'll get it all at the store. Let's just keep it simple so we don't have to stress about anything."

"Why would having Mark and his mother come over be stressful?" Blair asked in a singsong, eyelid-batting way that made Rose clamber up to her feet.

"It's too damn hot out here. I'm going to the grocery store."

"He watches the house, you know," Blair said. "I've seen him."

"It's not me he's watching, babe." Rose stepped inside and slid the door shut.

The house was stuffy and warm, but not as hot as it would be when the sun set in the west, filling all the picture windows with late summer rays.

Maybe she'd make a Greek salad. Gazpacho. Shrimp cocktails. She'd hate to sit there sweating like a pig over the dinner table, dark circles under her armpits.

Not that Mark would notice. Like she'd said, he'd be too busy staring at Blair, trying not to swallow his own tongue.

The doorbell rang. Rose wiped the sweat off her forehead and laughed to herself. Mark. He was probably going to try to get out of dinner again, just like last time. Being in the office together all week had given him enough of her. Enough of humanity. He was probably eager to crawl into his cave for the weekend to recover.

She strode over, savoring how she'd tell him there was no way in hell he was getting out of dinner. He'd saved her ass with a fantastic job. If he tried to cancel, Rose would threaten to invite him—and his mother—every Saturday for a year.

Smiling, half-naked in her bikini top and cutoffs, she reached out just as the door opened by itself.

Standing on the front step were John, his mother, and a suitcase.

Three suitcases. As well as a duffel bag big enough to engulf the Toyota.

"Hi," John said, seeing Rose. His look was apologetic but determined. "Blair! I'm home!"

Ellen, John's mother, strode into the house, frowning at Rose's generously bare midriff and exposed legs. Her gaze lingered on the navel ring, then the blue butterfly tattoo on her upper left thigh, before rising up to her face. "Catch you at a bad time?"

Damn it, the bitch was going to see her blush. And she had plenty of skin, most of it on show at the moment, all of it rapidly turning pink.

John made himself busy hauling in the suitcases, piling them in the foyer, avoiding eye contact.

They'd met only once, but Ellen obviously disliked her. Somehow, months earlier, she'd interpreted her son's accelerated relationship with a big blonde weightlifter as evidence of the big blonde's loose character. No matter it had been John who seduced her in the gym parking lot, John who showed up unannounced at her apartment at all hours, John who cheated.

Sticking her chest out and sucking in her gut (a little), Rose gave her a huge smile. "Hot, isn't it?" To John, smile glued in place, she added, "Blair is out on the deck." No way was Rose going to let on that any of this made her uncomfortable.

"I'll go tell her I'm here," John said, walking away. Coward.

"I thought John had told Blair he was moving in," Ellen said.

"He also told Blair he didn't want anything to do with her or the baby, yet amazingly, here he is," Rose replied. Her cheeks were starting to cramp from smiling. "It's so hot. Can I get you something to drink?"

"Why are *you* here?"

Rose dropped the act. "Why are you?"

"I'll get my own drink." Ellen strode into the house like she owned it, which she almost did, while Rose clenched her hands into fists and went out to the deck.

Oh, please. Blair and John were making out on the towel like it was *From Here to Eternity* and the waves were crashing in. "Blair, can I talk to you for a minute?" she said loudly.

They broke apart and looked up at her in unison.

Then John turned back to Blair nestled in his arms. "Sorry, but my mother's here, too. Hide out here while I get you another drink and try to get rid of her." After a quick kiss on her forehead he got to his feet and walked into the house. Just as he passed Rose, he stopped, met her gaze. "She didn't know I was coming this morning. So don't blame her."

"I wasn't going to," Rose said through her teeth. "*She's* not the sneaky type."

His jaw twitching, he went inside.

Rose looked at Blair. "You're wearing makeup today. I thought you were just in a good mood."

Blair sat up taller. "I *am* in a good mood."

Rose closed the door to the house, squatted down next to her. "Did you know he was coming?" she asked in a low voice.

Blair drew back, eyes wide, hurt. "Of course not."

"Sorry. Of course not." Rose got up, feeling sweat pool between her breasts. "Better get packing." At least the hotel would be air-conditioned.

Blair climbed to her feet, grasped her wrist. "Don't go. We'll figure something out."

"As much as I'm sure he'd love a little hot three-way action, no." She wiped her forehead.

"Four if you count the baby," Blair said, then slapped a hand over her mouth.

Rose gaped at her, then burst out laughing.

Better than crying.

ENJOYING HIS SATURDAY AFTER A WEEK OF DRAGGING himself into the office, Mark didn't pull open his closet to get dressed until after two.

Frowning, he looked down at the floor where he usually threw his jeans.

Nothing.

Turning his gaze upward, he saw the weirdest thing: his Levi's, clipped to matching wood hangers, in a tidy little row of denim. The hems at the bottom were aligned in a perfectly straight line.

He groaned, rubbed his eyes.

When Trixie Johnson learned Mark was going to go into the WellyNelly offices every day, she started doing his laundry for the first time since he was sixteen. Using scented dryer sheets, folding everything, putting it away in his dresser, hanging up his shirts.

He pulled out what he thought was his favorite pair of jeans, though it was hard to tell. They were stiff, oddly flat.

He held them up and stared.

She ironed my jeans.

"The horror, the horror," he muttered, tugging them on. He'd have to have a talk with her. At first he'd thought she was just bored, or happy to get him out of the house. Soon she'd started asking about his coworkers. Female ones. Single, reproductive-aged female coworkers. How many there were, how smart, how interesting, how available, how lonely.

He couldn't believe it. She was worse than Sylly. Mind in the gutter, mind in the cradle, same difference.

Sighing, he went back to his computer, unhappy with the way the starched denim made him walk like C-3PO. He really should look for his own place. There was a ton of real estate to choose from, the market still suffering, everything on sale, and he was loaded.

Not even his mother knew the extent of the fortune he'd raked in from his assorted tech jobs over the years. Software companies besides WellyNelly had given him stock options when he was a teenager, companies that later made it big. Only his brother, Liam, knew he was sitting on more than five million dollars in cash, a fact he'd just shared very recently, when Liam's own business, Fite Fitness, was faltering.

"Keep it, little bro," Liam had said. "Bev is a marketing genius. We'll be fine. Though it sure would've come in handy earlier."

Until now, he hadn't been able to make himself look at places by himself. He imagined... more. Maybe now he couldn't wait, shouldn't wait. Maybe he was wrong to assume there was more to have.

Just as Mark began a search for Oakland real estate, the doorbell rang. Not trusting his mother, he went down the stairs three at a time and was short of breath when he flung the door open.

"How about I take you and your mom *out* to dinner?" Rose asked.

Her hair was pulled up on top of her head in a long, off-center ponytail like an 80s pop star. Big silver hoops dangled from her ears amid a few loose, golden strands.

Her T-shirt was tight, black, cut low at the neck in a *V*, and her faded cutoffs exposed her curves from upper thigh all the way on down.

Even her feet were sexy. On display in jewel-studded sandals, each toe carefully painted crimson with a pink polka dots, her second toe adorned with a ring, her shapely ankle highlighted with a thin gold chain.

With so much to look at, it took him a moment to notice she had tears in her eyes.

"What happened?"

She smiled, wiped at her face with the back of her hand. Her mascara ran down her cheek. "Nothing. I'm being silly. Everything's going great."

"Which is why you're crying," he said. "Is it WellyNelly? Because if you don't like it, don't worry about chucking it when you've got something else. I won't mind, really."

"No, the job is great. It's so exciting, I can't—oh, hey there, Zeus."

Yapping his odd, distorted yap, Zeus had run up from outside and was attempting to climb up Rose's legs. She bent down and lifted him up into her arms. As he licked her cheeks, his body shaking with joy, the forced smile on Rose's face became a real one.

"You must taste good," Mark said, then felt his face get warm. God. Even with Rose, he said the stupidest things.

"Is it my vanilla face cream, little dude?" she asked. "Do you think I'm an ice cream cone?"

Mark glanced past Rose's shoulder and saw his mother in the driveway, empty leash in one hand, the two better-behaved dogs tugging at the other. Before he could stop her, she pivoted on her heel and marched back out into the street the way she'd come.

Subtle, Mom. Very subtle. Now she'd have to keep carrying that plastic bag of dog shit around with her. Served her right.

"Come on in, tell me what's up," he said.

"No, I've got to find new digs first. I'll come back and drive us somewhere special. Where would you like to go? I hear the restaurant at the Claremont has a fantastic view."

"Get in here." He put an arm around her and tugged her over the threshold, willing himself to ignore how soft and warm and female she felt, the way his body responded to hers.

He released her the instant she was inside.

Like an elite mountain climber, Zeus had made it up the North Face of her chest and was rubbing his nose into her ear. Maybe because he was jealous, Mark captured the dog in his hands, and holding him like a football under his arm, gestured toward the kitchen.

"It's safe to talk," he said. "My mom's not here." *Probably won't be for hours. Crazy woman.*

She sat in the chair he held out to her at the kitchen table. "Will she mind going out to eat? I know it seems weird, like I've invited you to our house and then I'm trying to drive you somewhere."

"Understandable if it isn't your house anymore. How about staying at the Claremont?" The Claremont Hotel wasn't far from the house. Not far at all.

"Too expensive, are you crazy? But I was thinking we could go there for dinner. I'll find a cheap motel for sleeping." She reached out for Zeus.

"Tonight?"

"I've got a bag in the car. I'll have to get the rest later," she said. "I wish I'd just taken that first apartment I saw on

Wednesday, but I was holding out for something with a deck or a backyard. I put in an application for a perfect place in North Berkeley, a cute one-bedroom, very vintage, in a remodeled Victorian, but there were two dozen other people there. No guarantee I'll get it."

"All the students just moved in for the year. You might want to look farther from campus." He poured her a glass of iced tea. "So, what happened? Did John come back already?"

She leaned back, sighed, let Zeus kiss her face. "This afternoon. With Mommy Dearest."

"That guy needs to learn how to use one of our many forms of modern communications technology."

"No kidding."

"Maybe we can get him a cell phone as a wedding gift."

She looked up, pain in her eyes, and he swore inwardly. "Sorry. Social recluse strikes again."

Smiling weakly, she patted his arm. "She told me not to feel pressured to move. As if the thought I might have to listen to the two of them in bed together isn't enough pressure." Her voice cracked.

Sensing her need, Zeus accelerated the tongue assault. Mark resisted the same impulse.

"Does she know how you still feel about him?" he asked softly.

Beautiful watery blue eyes met his. She shook her head.

That didn't seem possible. Mark had only known her for a little over two weeks, and it was obvious to him. But people saw what they wanted to see.

"I guess you can't really tell her now," he said.

"They're getting married." She forced a laugh. "I'll be there to witness it. Isn't that beautiful?"

"I don't care for the guy, but I suppose he has his qualities."

"It's not just his looks. I know, you probably think I'm just in love with that face, but…" A flush rose up her neck. "Never mind. It wasn't meant to be. I'd already decided to break up with him, but sometimes…"

"Sometimes you can't help wanting it anyway."

She sighed. "Yeah."

Even smart, tough, spunky Rose couldn't help but fall for guys like that. Zeus suddenly jumped off her lap and trotted over to Mark. His good eye peered up at him while his tail wagged his butt wildly in each direction. With a whine, he rubbed his face against the ironed denim of Mark's leg.

Psychic little guy. "I'll get your dinner, Zeus. Back porch, come on, back porch." He hooked a finger through his collar and gently led him down the steps off the back of the kitchen.

After he'd refilled the dog bowls with water and chow, he turned on the fan, opened another window, and dropped the shades.

"It's freaky hot," Rose said, coming up behind him with her iced tea in her hand.

"Indian summer. My mother would say it's because you fixed the furnace. You tempted fate."

"Like washing the car makes it rain."

"Exactly."

They stood there silently, watching Zeus lap up water from his bowl. "Am I that obvious?" she said finally.

He knew what she meant. "No."

"What tipped you off?"

"Other than the chicken in the dishwasher?"

She sipped her drink. "Yeah. Other than that."

"You act differently when he's around. Nervous. More girly." He faked a giggle. "Like that."

"God. Thank you so much. That's disgusting."

"Be grateful you're not like that all the time," he said.

"You do the same thing with Blair, you know."

He sighed. "I know."

"We're pathetic."

"I am. You're fine. I'm that way with all women."

"Not with me," she said.

"You're different." He took her empty glass out of her hand and went back into the kitchen.

"You mean, I'm fat and obnoxious and you thought I was a lesbian." She had an edge to her voice. "You only get nervous around *real* women."

He turned. Met her angry gaze.

"Admit it," she said.

"You're a real woman."

She rolled her eyes. "As if you really feel that way."

"I feel that way," he said.

"The second Blair walks into your line of vision, you get all clumsy and sweaty and say stupid things. You watch the house, hoping to see her. If John hadn't shown up, you'd be biding your time, getting up the nerve to ask her out on a date. Because she's a real woman."

While she lashed out at him, he found himself moving closer to her until she was only inches away.

Her clear blue eyes flashed like sapphires. And that mouth, that mouth. He dreamed about it. Without thinking, he brushed a strand of hair off her forehead. Her skin was warm, peachy velvet.

She frowned. "What are you doing?"

He didn't know, but he was going to do it anyway.

10

HE SLIPPED HIS HAND DOWN her soft skin and cupped her cheek. Holding her gaze, he felt lust wash over him. "You've got plenty Blair doesn't have."

"Like an extra hundred pounds?"

She had a fantastic mouth, with full lips that were gently curved, glossy, red.

If only it didn't talk so much.

"Sex appeal," he said in a low voice. His thumb moved on its own to caress the moist fullness of her lower lip. He felt her shiver under his touch, which sent heated shock waves of desire through his body.

He leaned forward. Brushed his lips against hers. Gentle pressure, then a flick of his tongue to taste that gloss, see if it was as delicious as it looked.

It was.

She was motionless under his touch, not participating, not resisting. He turned her face with his hand, caressing her cheek with his thumb while he angled the kiss, licked the seam of her mouth. She made a little sound in the back of her throat, a delicate moan, and he felt fire at that small, involuntary response. He slid his tongue between her lips, past her teeth, and tasted her.

His hand slipped away from her face, down her smooth neck, over her shoulder. He pressed his palm into the hollow of her back. Her T-shirt was just a thin layer of cotton and he shoved it up to touch that perfect skin, slippery from the heat of the day, as hot as he was.

Then his hand moved lower, over her glorious ass, while his tongue found the ridge of the roof of her mouth and licked. Another sigh from her throat encouraged him to pull her hard against his pelvis. To show her, oh yeah, he felt that way.

It was Zeus who saved them both. Not appreciating the competition for Rose's affections, he attacked Mark's legs with his own, jumping and clawing at his calves, and when that did nothing, he went for Rose's bare legs.

She gasped and broke free from Mark, blinking and breathing hard. She stumbled backward until she was blocked by the kitchen counter.

They stared at each other.

"You kissed me," she said.

He nodded. God, he had. "You didn't believe me."

"You want Blair. You don't want me."

Uncomfortably aware of the tightness of his jeans, short of breath, he met her gaze, unblinking. "You need another demonstration?"

She looked down at his crotch. "All right, maybe part of you wants me."

What could he say to that?

"Just not the important parts," she added.

"I'm rather fond of that part."

She rubbed her temple, looked around. Her cheeks were flushed, her lips swollen. "I have to go."

The important organ in question was opposed to the idea, but now his mind was churning, processing, engaged.

This was wrong. This wasn't what he wanted. She wasn't what he wanted. Who he wanted. Not with the important parts above his shoulders.

His last girlfriend had taught him what kind of woman he definitely should *not* pursue. *You're like an old man*, Colleen told him right after he moved to Milwaukee to be with her. She'd gone to MIT with him, but right after graduation, went back home to be near her family. He'd followed, dumb as an ox, assuming he'd found his mate for life and could stop worrying about it.

She had different ideas. *I'm not ready to roll over and be old like you yet*, she said, as if life with him was as good as dying. An end to everything fun, exciting, lively. She wanted to go out every night, travel every weekend, join clubs, teams, party. What had been a fun experiment in college—being social—became an aggravating chore. He wanted to settle down, be social with her, not with the whole world.

She wanted more.

He'd always had a thing for outgoing girls. Obnoxious, funny, extroverted women who knew how to enjoy themselves, and therefore, how to make him enjoy himself.

Colleen had shown him how little he had to offer in return. What would a fun, lively woman want with him? He needed somebody quiet, subdued, solitary. Maybe even a woman who would look up to him. Admire him. Need him.

Blair was taken, but she was the type of woman he could be happy with. The type of woman he could make happy.

"I'm sorry," he said, looking down at his bare feet on the kitchen tile. Seeing her face just made him want to kiss her again. "I was just proving a point."

"That all men are driven by lust?"

He nodded, glanced up. "You were telling me I didn't think you were a real woman. I was showing you I do."

"Just proving a point." She wiped the back of her hand over her lips, then pushed it into her pocket.

He took a deep breath. Rubbed the back of his neck, sticky with sweat. "Damn, it's hot. Look, just forget about dinner. You've got enough to worry about."

She pushed away from the counter. "Like you proving another point."

"Don't worry, I won't do it again," he said. Was that anger in his voice? "But you were saying stupid things, insulting yourself."

"You felt sorry for me."

"No, you were pissing me off. Maybe I can't talk to Blair because I don't know her, that's all. And I probably never will."

Rose closed her eyes for a moment. "That's what's really going on here." She gave him a sad look. "They want each other, not us. That's why…" She waved her hand in the air between them.

That wasn't why he'd kissed her, but perhaps it was why she'd let him do it. Ego withdrawing into its cave, he grabbed the iced tea pitcher and refilled her glass. His body was returning to normal, chilled by the implication that her fixation was elsewhere.

"I wouldn't take him back, you know," she said softly. "Not even if he begged me."

"Because of Blair."

She shook her head. "Because he wouldn't make me happy." Lifting the iced tea, she tipped it to him, smiled tightly, and took a drink. He watched her lips curl around the glass, wishing it was him.

She put it down. Glanced at him. "Look, about dinner tonight—"

"Don't worry about it."

"Tell her how sorry I am. I look like such a flake."

"I'll explain. She'll understand." He gestured to the doorway to encourage her to make her escape. "Better make a run for it now. She'll be back any minute from walking the dogs."

Nodding, she walked slowly to the front of the house, turning to him only when she was outside and her foot was on the first step down to the driveway. "About what happened…" She raised a hand slightly, pointed in the general direction of the kitchen. "It's just—right now—John—Blair—my life—"

"Don't worry about it. It didn't mean anything."

She dropped her hand. Lips flattened together, she nodded again and walked down to the driveway where her car was packed and waiting.

MONDAY MORNING, ROSE GOT OUT OF HER CAR IN THE WellyNelly parking lot and tugged her sweater down over her rear.

Stupid low-rise pants. She hated to worry about her underwear showing, especially today, her first official day on the Women's Forum team.

Touching up her lip gloss, she walked up the sidewalk to the front door. Her foul mood began to lift. Soon she'd have an apartment of her own and wouldn't have to wake up on a stained mattress under a window covered with iron bars.

Her motel choice had been a poor one. Right after work she was going to visit another potential apartment and beg them, if necessary, to let her move in as soon as she got her first paycheck for the deposit.

Thank God she had a job. Last week she'd followed a few

people around, filled out paperwork, sat in on meetings, and played with the software to get a feel for it. Today she'd start working for real. Hopefully. It was still a little fuzzy what she'd be doing.

Sylly told her she'd be an important player in redesigning the women's health subforums, but in the twenty or so hours she'd spent since last Monday reading posts and articles, going back several years, she didn't see why they had such confidence in her abilities. The Women's Forum was popular already, though a little ugly. They had thousands of regular users, advertising, qualified health professionals giving general advice.

All she had was a bachelor's degree in biology and years working retail. What did she know about website design or software? Besides speed-reading a few pages of Mark's book in a coffee shop?

Mark. He'd kissed her. Really, really kissed her. She'd been too shocked to stop him. Shocked because it was Mark and shocked because...

Because he was so good at it.

Where did he learn how to kiss like that?

Her body had flared to life at his touch. It didn't know he was only making a *point*. It had felt strong hands and skilled tongue and said, *yes please*.

As if her life wasn't complicated enough. Seeing John had unbalanced her again. Just by showing up, looking good, and doting on Blair, he knocked down all her defenses. Any other time she could have pushed Mark away with a smile and a gentle explanation that it just wasn't a good idea. Blamed it on their new working relationship.

Instead...

Well, if it hadn't been for Zeus, she didn't think either one of them would've stopped what was sparked in that kitchen.

That would've been quite a *point*.

Would she see him at work today? He had his own office, and last week he kept the door closed, out of sight, hiding away. It was probably rough on him to adjust to being around so many people.

Then again, if he could kiss like that, maybe he was more sociable than she thought.

Bridget greeted her the moment she walked in the front door. "Happy Monday! Starbucks in the Game Room."

"I'm counting on it," Rose said, waving as she walked by. Bridget always smiled and spoke to her like she was just *so glad* to see her. At first it had creeped her out, but gradually she'd decided Bridget had been put at the front desk precisely because those bubbles came to her naturally. She was cheerful to everyone, especially the women, a distinct minority in the building.

Amit the hardware guy was in her cubicle. "I've set up your new monitor."

"I already had a monitor," she said.

"This one's better." He spun the chair around. Grinned. "See?"

She looked at it, suspecting she never would've noticed the switch. "It's great. Thanks."

Still grinning, he stood up, pulled the chair out for her. "Your new keyboard comes tomorrow."

"What's wrong with the one I have?"

"The one he ordered has excellent feel. I have one myself at home."

"The one *who* ordered?"

Amit glanced at the ceiling, wiggled his eyebrows. "You know."

"Sylly?"

"Yeah, right." He lowered his voice. "He's too cheap.

Candy, no problem. Two-hundred-dollar keyboards? *Fuhgedd-aboudit.*" He said this last with a really bad fake New York accent as he walked out of the cubicle.

She sat down. The keyboard was the same as any other keyboard. It had keys. They typed letters and numbers and other things. The monitor looked new, but so had the one on her desk the week before.

Sylly was too cheap to buy fancy hardware for the company.

Was it Mark? Was Hot Lips making another *point?*

At least her job was taking shape. She was going to be a team leader, ensuring that other people, mostly technical and a few in design, did their jobs on time. As she gained more experience, she could do more. More than just nagging, she hoped.

She spent the morning hours going through her email and sitting in on another meeting. After lunch she met with the Women's Forum team and tried to look useful, using the project calendar on her new tablet for the first time.

The three men and one woman were cheerful, competent, a bit goofy. One of the guys brought in a shopping bag filled with free samples from a tech conference—Intel bunny suit dolls, laser pointers, thumb drives, notepads, balls with blinking LEDs inside—and proceeded to play with them throughout the meeting. High pressure, it was not.

When it was over, she went to the kitchen (squeezing one of the LED balls in her hand) for a cold bottle of Pelegrino, her new favorite perk, and then, instead of going directly back to her desk, she wandered to Mark's office. She paused there, not sure if she was annoyed or relieved that his door was closed.

To her shame, her heart started pounding in her ears.
It's Mark. Just Mark.
She swallowed, took a breath, admitted the truth: the only

reason she'd detoured to the kitchen was because it would make her walk by his door.

"Isn't he answering?"

Sylly had walked up behind her as she stood paralyzed in the hallway.

She spun around. "I haven't knocked yet." Smiling, she made a big show of tapping on the wood.

"Maybe you could remind him about our open door policy," Sylly said. His eyes watched her in that sharp way of his, amused but observant. "How'd your first week go?"

"Great. Just ran my first meeting." She rolled her eyes. "Though they did most of the running."

"You'll whip them into shape in no time."

She smiled at him, uneasy. *How do you know?* she wanted to ask. *Why are you so sure about me?*

The door opened. Mark blinked, looked back and forth between the two of them. "Hello?"

"Well, I'll leave you two to it," Sylly said, walking on.

Mark looked at her. "Did you knock?"

"He told me to tell you there's an open door policy."

"It opens." He swung it back and forth. "See?"

"Did you—" she stopped herself. A tingly feeling came over her, like she was being watched. Sure enough, when she looked over her shoulder, she saw two sets of eyes peeking over the carpeted beige wall at them. Two of the programmers, guys she'd met earlier with names she hadn't memorized yet.

Mark took her arm and pulled her inside before gently breaking the open door policy again. "Did I what?"

"Why were they staring at me like that? Sometimes, I swear, I get the weirdest feeling around here."

"I totally know what you mean," he said feelingly.

"No wonder you liked working at home."

"I know, huh? We'll get used to it. The thrill has to wear off at some point."

She smiled weakly, again feeling like she wasn't quite getting the joke. "Sometimes I think you've understated your importance around here."

"It's not really my office. One of the architects moved back to India to telecommute. It had all the hardware I needed, so I use it when he's not here. Otherwise I'd be in a cubicle just like you."

"Sylly acts like you've known him a long time, though."

"Yes, that's it. That must be what you're feeling. He's known me since I was in high school."

She lowered her voice. "Is he gay? Not to freak you out, but… the way he talks about you, the way he just hired me like that with no experience… I think he's in love with you."

Mark's bark of laughter made her head snap back so fast her earrings rattled.

"Oh, oh, oh," he breathed, bending over his desk. "Oh my God."

"I'm serious. Either that or you saved his life in a war."

A dazzling grin on his face, Mark wiped the tears off his cheeks, nodded at her, took a deep breath. "That's more like it."

"So, he hired me because he owes you for something big."

The smile faded away. "Sort of." He shook his head. "No. He hired you because he thinks you'll be good for WellyNelly. Sylly doesn't have anyone around he doesn't like."

"Is that why you're not working from home anymore? Because he likes having you around?"

He stared at her. "Wow. You're good."

"That's it, isn't it? You just happened to start working in the office at the same time I did."

"What makes you think that's because of Sylly?" He

pushed a steel toy on his desk in motion, watched the balls tap each other. "I did throw myself on you in my kitchen the day before yesterday. Maybe *I'm* the one who likes being around *you*."

"If you did, why hide in here with your door shut?"

"I'm very shy?" He looked up at her, the hint of a smile in the corner of his mouth.

"Not with me you're not."

He was speechless for a moment. "That's true, isn't it?"

"Spill. Was having you work in the office a condition of them hiring me?"

Getting to his feet, he went over to the window and tilted the blinds, darkening the room. "I told you. I was determined to get out more. It's a short commute, just across town, and I can stay home whenever I really need to." He stroked his chest. "Though this way I get to wear all these new clothes. Makes my mom happy."

It was making her uncomfortably happy as well. Today's shirt was just a traditional long-sleeved dress shirt, but it was tailored perfectly to fit his muscled arms, broad shoulders, narrow waist. Even with the jeans—no, especially with the jeans—he was distractingly sexy.

She shoved her lust aside. "I owe you even more than I thought." Coming to see him had been a bad idea. Maybe her ego had wanted a little stroking. The thought of him wanting her, even if it was only raw biology at work, made her feel good. She liked feeling good. Good was good.

How badly did *he* like to feel good?

No. Casual sex was not on the menu. Fresh start, new life, et cetera, et cetera.

"You don't owe me anything," he said. "I haven't done anything I didn't want to do."

Shaking her head, she pulled the door open and went back

to her cubicle, realizing, hours later when she was in a meeting about the mammography subforum, she'd forgotten to thank him for the new monitor and keyboard.

And if she had the guts, she'd thank him for that kiss, too. Because ever since it had happened, she hadn't thought of John once.

But what if the cure was more dangerous than the disease?

AROUND 6:30 P.M., MARK WALKED PAST the cubicle farm outside his office, rubbing the crick in his neck, wondering if it would be tacky to order both him and Rose their own Aeron Miller chairs.

Probably. He'd have to order them for the whole company. Anonymously. And if that keyboard he got for Rose was good, he'd get a hundred of those, too. And talk to Sylly about having a massage therapist in the office during lunch hours for everyone. Working at a desk all day was really bad for the body. It was worth preventing permanent damage any way you could. They made their living helping people be healthy, after all. No sense getting sick while they did it.

Really, Sylly was such a cheapskate. The bowl of candy-covered chocolate drops in the conference room had been a store brand. *M&M's, my ass.* Not that they should have bowls of candy lying around anyway.

He stepped out into an evening blast of wind off the bay. It had finally cooled down. The parking lot was mostly empty, which was good; he'd been afraid WellyNelly would be overflowing with young workaholics wasting all of their waking hours on his little program instead of having a life.

Then he saw Rose in her Toyota, banging at the wheel.

His guts clenched. He began to sweat. His hands shook.

For God's sake, he thought, shaking his head. *Is this lust or food poisoning?*

Either way, finding a bed was very appealing.

No.

He went over and tapped on the window. She jumped, saw him, rolled down the window.

"Battery again?" he asked.

"No, there's a click. Hear it?" She turned the key and he heard a slight straining moan from under the hood. He started to move toward it, but she grabbed his sleeve. "Hold it, you've done enough fix-it work for me. I'll bring it to a mechanic. It needs a tune-up anyway."

"Do you have AAA to get it towed to a garage?"

She shook her head. "Damn it. I'll have to find somebody."

"It's late. I'll give you a ride to your motel and you can deal with it tomorrow."

"Yeah." She gave the steering wheel one last swipe and got out of the car. "Can you give me a ride in the morning, too?"

"Sure."

"I hate living like this." She walked around to the back and took out a backpack and a small rolling suitcase, both hot pink.

"Why do you have your bags with you?"

"I didn't like the idea of leaving them at my motel during the day. It's kind of sketchy." She looked around the lot, saw his VW. "Well, guess it won't make any difference to be a parasite one more time."

They went over to his car, put the bags in the back hatch,

got in. As she pulled the seat belt over her body, he sent up a silent prayer of gratitude that it was still warm enough for her to show some skin. Only two necklaces today, but both were long enough to fall between her breasts, nicely visible under her low-cut sweater.

Then he frowned, imagining all the guys at WellyNelly being able to see the same skin he did. Wasn't that sweater a little revealing for the office? And tight? He could see her nipples. If he looked closely.

She crossed her arms over her chest. "Shall we get going?"

Flushing, he backed up. "Sorry."

She was smiling. "There's that point again."

Yeah, and it was making his pants uncomfortable. He cleared his throat. "Where's your motel?"

"Turn right on San Pablo. It's about a mile."

"Down there? No wonder you didn't want to leave your bags."

She rolled her window all the way down, pulled the band out of her hair. The waves fell down around her shoulders and whipped around her face, a blonde cyclone. "I need a haircut. It's getting ridiculous."

"That's not the word," he mumbled.

"You like it, don't you?" She combed it with her fingers. Let the strands slide over her wrists. "Like peanut butter in a rat trap, that's what my grandmother says."

"That metaphor isn't very complimentary to any of the parties involved."

"My grandmother isn't very complimentary."

He didn't know what to say to that.

"She supported my mom when she was pregnant with me, though, so I can't complain," she said. "Though she can be a terror. Very critical. My mom has never really gotten over it."

"All of my grandparents died before I was in high school. I

barely remember any of them. I always felt a little cheated." They passed an abandoned car lot, a boarded-up Taco Bell with the signs removed, two hookers arguing with each other at the bus stop.

"My mother and I lived with her—my maternal grandmother—until I was seven," she said. "She was nothing like a cartoon granny with white hair and cookies. She's blonde and thin and perfect and insisted I be the same."

"She should be happy with two out of three." Realizing he'd said too much, he bit his lip, hard. He really needed to keep his mouth shut.

"She should've been happy about all kinds of things. Like we all should."

They drove on in silence, Mark increasingly uneasy with the location of her motel. When the light turned yellow, he floored it so he wouldn't have to stop.

"Slow down," she said. "It's right up here."

"You're shitting me."

"No, see? Right there."

The building was indeed visible. Hard to miss it with all the cop cars out front.

He didn't brake.

"Hey!"

"There's no way I'm going to drop you off in this neighborhood." He shifted up into third gear. "Way too many rats."

"Turn around right now. This is no time to get manly."

"To hell with that. I'm not manly enough to stop. Are you kidding me? Did you see those guys back there? They'd eat me for breakfast. And those were just the cops."

"It's not that bad."

"Why are you staying here? There's a huge range between this and the Claremont, price-wise. That place has, like, negative stars."

"I'm serious, Mark. Go back. It's only for another night or two. I'm looking at an apartment tonight—" She slapped her forehead. "I don't have a car. I had an appointment at seven. How can I find a place to live without a car?"

"I'll drive you. Unless it's around here." He shifted into fourth, took the next turn at forty miles an hour. "Where is this apartment?"

She sighed but pulled out her cell to read him the address.

"I'm not driving you there, either," he said. "You're not in New York anymore, Dorothy. From now on, run all the apartments you find by me, and I'll tell you if they're okay or not."

The light turned red in front of him and he had no choice but to stop. Grabbing her purse, Rose flung the door open, jumped out, and marched over to the sidewalk with her blonde hair flying behind her.

She looked up and down the street, then started walking in the direction of the motel.

"Rose! Come back here!"

Without even a glance back at him, she kicked off a tumbling sheet of newspaper that had caught on her leg and continued on her way.

The light turned green. "Shit!" He tried to get over into the right lane, but the cars behind him weren't stopping. One honked, then another. Muttering the same obscenities she had used back in the parking lot, Mark hit the gas, passed the asshole who was yelling at him, and pulled a U-turn at the next intersection while trying to keep Rose's bright, voluptuous body in sight.

He parked in a liquor store's loading zone and ran after her. "Rose!"

Without turning around, she pulled her hair into a knot on top of her head and pulled the hood of her sweater over it.

"That's not the only peanut butter you've got to worry about," he panted. "Damn it, will you stop?"

"Only if you promise to bring me back to my motel."

"You've got your suitcase in my car. There's no reason for you to go back there unless you've got a date there lined up to pay for it."

She gaped at him, outraged. "How dare you?"

How did he? he wondered.

"You need help, honey?" a woman asked. She had orange vinyl boots up to her crotch, a white lace bra, and not much else. Except for the tattoos.

"Yes, thank you. This guy is bothering me," Rose said, jerking her thumb at him.

The woman put her hand on her hip. "You only like blondes, Han Solo? I've got a few minutes."

"No. Thank you." He nodded to her, more furious than ever, and chased after Rose. "Get in my car or I'll have you fired," he said through his teeth.

Finally, she stopped. "You wouldn't."

"Try me." His heart was pounding in his ears. Adrenaline pulsed through him. He felt like Superman, like he could lift cars.

Or her. God, she was magnificent. Cheeks flushed, blue eyes flashing, chest heaving. He wanted to throw her over his shoulder and carry her to his cave.

"Fine." She started walking back to the car. "You'll pay for it."

I already am. He watched her hips as she marched away. The curve of her waist. The jiggles everywhere.

Then he ran past her to open the car door and waited until she was inside before he got behind the wheel, breathing heavily, so hot for her he thought he would explode.

Don't look at her. He'd never wanted any woman so badly,

not even Colleen, and he'd really, really wanted Colleen, enough to move to Milwaukee. Until now, he'd thought that had to be proof he'd achieved the pinnacle of desire.

"It wasn't as bad as it looked," she said.

He reached into his back pocket, pulled out his wallet. "There's a check in there that belongs to you. I've already endorsed it."

She gaped at him. "You're offering me *money?*"

"It's not from me. It's from WellyNelly." He waved the wallet. "Take it."

She didn't, so he threw it at her so he could shift gears. They passed a fast-food place that smelled so good his stomach growled, and he sped past, resenting her for his being hungry and angry and raging with lust.

It wasn't in his nature to be all stirred up. He hated stirring. All the muck at the bottom started floating around, muddying the waters, tasting bitter in his mouth.

"I'm not taking your money," she said.

"You just told me I had to pay for your hotel!"

"I was upset!" She huffed. "Fine. You can pay the difference between what I had and wherever you're taking me."

"I'm taking you to my house."

Her hand grabbed the car door handle again. "Like hell you are." It popped open.

The light was yellow, so he grabbed her thigh and floored it. "Hey!" she cried, hanging on the swinging door, gaping at him. "Are you insane?" She slammed it shut.

"Only since I met you."

"To hell with that. Let go of me."

His hand was stretched across the warm, rounded flesh of her upper thigh. Without looking at her, he increased the pressure of his fingers, gently, letting the car rock his hand higher between her legs. "I don't want to."

"You already made that point," she said tightly.

He glanced over. What was he doing? "I want you."

She pulled his hand out, pushed it away. "Join the club. Now drop me off somewhere your rich white boy sensitivities can handle, or I'm going to jump out at the light."

"That's it?"

Her eyes were wild with annoyance, not desire. "Bossing me around is not a turn-on. There are plenty of women who love it. Go find one of them." She slammed his wallet on the console between them. "Too bad Blair's taken."

"Yeah, too bad," he snapped.

She stared at him, picked the wallet up again, flipped it open. "This what you're talking about?" she asked, pulling out the check. He'd had to fold it three times to fit inside his old bifold. "Five thousand dollars. Not too shabby. That your weekly salary or what?"

"A bonus for referring you. Take it. You need it more than I do. Obviously."

"The last thing I need is for you to think I owe you anything." She crossed her arms under her breasts, scowling. "Obviously."

She was impossible. He nearly rammed the bus in front of them when it stopped, beeping and hissing at the curb. Through gritted teeth, he said, "Take it. If you stay a year, I get another ten."

"Ten thousand? *Dollars?*"

He pulled out into traffic and passed the bus. "So if you want to punish me, quit in eleven months and I'm out of luck. In the meantime, take the damn money, get a safe place to live, and I'll leave you alone."

"I can't believe they pay so well."

"Welcome to the high-tech bubble."

She dropped the wallet again but kept the check. "I'll pay you back."

"Whatever."

"You're so annoying." When she tucked the check between her breasts, he felt actual, physical pain. His plan had been to bring her up to the house so she could stay there, use their computer, borrow his mom's car, carpool with him into work for a few days. She'd be safe, his mother would have some company.

Now, however, it was obvious he was the one desperate for company.

Too desperate.

"I'll take you to the Holiday Inn," he said. She didn't protest.

❦

SHE PUSHED MARK'S OFFICE DOOR OPEN WITHOUT knocking and kicked it shut behind her.

"Since you're in charge of my life," she said, "tell me which of these apartments is in a good area." She flung a stack of printouts on his desk, enjoying the way he looked up from his computer with his mouth open.

She noticed he had a piece of toilet paper on his chin, a red dot in the center of it. His hair had dried funny, one side sticking up, and he had a pale shadow of dried milk on his upper lip.

Her heart softened. That was more like it, she thought, the nice guy she thought he was, not the macho bully from Monday evening.

He looked down at the papers. Frowned at the one on top. "Nope," he said. Picking up the stack, he leaned back in his chair to flip through the rest while Rose waited.

"Well?"

He shook his head. "You couldn't find anything up in the hills?"

"Please. Only rich people live up there. And I like to be more in the middle of things so I can walk places. Restaurants, shops, cafes, theaters—you know, where the people are."

"Huh." He nodded as though that had never occurred to him, looked back down at the papers in his hands. "These all suck." He dropped them on the desk.

"There were twenty apartments on that!"

"What about that place in North Berkeley you told me about? That sounded good."

"Gone."

"So, wait for another one."

"There aren't any." Though the Holiday Inn he'd inflicted on her was an improvement over the no-tell motel, she hated the street noise, the lack of privacy, not having a kitchen, being in limbo. She went over and picked up her printouts. "What's wrong with these? You barely looked at them."

"I can just tell."

"How?"

He shrugged, turned back to his computer monitor. "Just can."

For at least ten seconds she watched him in silence. When it was clear he wasn't going to elaborate, or even look at her, she said, "Busy?"

He nodded.

"Sorry to interrupt." She moved to the door. "I only showed you because you seemed determined to interfere. I won't bother you again."

He didn't look up as she moved into the hallway. Then he said, "Hey, how's your car?"

"It's fine now. I had it towed down the street."

"They fixed it?"

"For an arm and a leg and my firstborn son, yes."

He went back to his computer. "You should sign up for roadside assistance."

"I will. Thanks." She stared at him another second before closing the door.

What the hell? One minute he was chasing and kissing her, the next he couldn't even be bothered to look away from his computer.

Just as well. It was a mistake to get too close. Their early friendship had crossed a line, and there was no going back.

She'd find an apartment by herself. Why'd she asked him, anyway?

He obviously didn't care.

❧

MARK LET OUT THE BREATH HE WAS HOLDING.

Rubbing his face with both hands, trying to wipe away the image of her in a yellow sweater, this one long and loose but not loose enough to hide that body, he swore.

He never should've lent her the jumper cables. That's when it all began to go wrong. If only he could rewind. He'd be in his room, safe and quiet, watching Blair with twenty feet, two walls, and double-paned glass between them.

The door popped open, sending his pulse racing again, but it was only Sylly. "Hey. Got a minute?" Without waiting for a reply, he marched in and strode over to the desk. "You all right?"

"Yeah. Why?"

Sylly frowned. "You're kind of pink."

"I'm not feeling well."

He wrinkled his nose. "Maybe you should try leaving your door open like you're supposed to. Get some fresh air."

Mark nodded. "That's probably it."

"Maybe you're on social overload."

"That's definitely it. Can I go home, boss?"

Sylly raised an eyebrow. "You're backing out of our deal already? It's only her second week."

"You like her, though, right? You see why I recommended her."

"It's early to say yet, but the team likes her well enough. If Jake can keep his eyes above her neck, they'll be fine." Sitting on the edge of Mark's desk, Sylly studied his fingernails. "So, how do you think she'll feel about getting an MBA? Think she'd be up for that?"

"I have no idea. Why would you care if she had an MBA?"

"Not me. Our new corporate overlords." Jumping up, Sylly took over the computer and typed in a web address. "What do you think of these guys?"

Mark frowned at the homepage for a major drug company. "No way. That would suck."

"Don't be so sure. They're sharp, really sharp. I've had a few really interesting conversations with these guys."

"Big pharma? Buying WellyNelly? You're not serious."

"Not yet, but *they* are. They want to fold us into their operation. They were going to develop their own systems before they realized how hard it was. Now they're thinking we'd be a package deal, ready to go."

"You're kidding me."

"No, they really do."

"No, I mean, you can't really be considering this. They're a drug company. A business. They make money off of sick people."

"And we don't?"

Mark felt queasy. "That's different."

"It's America, buddy. I knew you'd be against it, but give it a few days. No rush. Really think it over."

"There's nothing to think about. This is *WellyNelly*. They'll push their own patented meds for every ailment, big and small—"

"They already do that, and it wasn't getting them the traffic they want. Migrating over to WellyNelly will give them access to customers without having to advertise so obviously. They like us as we are, Mark. Really. Warts and all."

Mark didn't demonize the pharmaceutical industry like some people, but any business with a product to sell would corrupt the site. All the advice, the forums, the photos, the links, the information—all of it would be filtered through a corporate committee. It would kill WellyNelly.

Mark stood up. "No. Never."

"Hey, relax. It's just an idea. Don't get upset," Sylly said, walking over to the door. "I wouldn't do anything you didn't think was right."

When he was gone, Mark slumped back into his chair.

Sylly wouldn't do anything he didn't think was right?

Mark didn't believe that for a second.

1 2

O N A SATURDAY MORNING TWO weeks later, Rose backed up behind Blair's car in the driveway and yanked on the parking brake.

Well, this is it, she thought, taking a deep breath. Time to move again.

It was Halloween. Next door, Trixie and Mark's big old house was decorated so wildly, it would stop traffic if it were on a busier street. Long strands of fake white cobwebs stretching from the front bushes to the gutters, and two dozen tarantulas, each at least five feet wide, crawled their way up the front of the house to the top-floor windows. One was already halfway inside, its fuzzy legs jutting out and its body crushed, as though a panicked human had slammed the window closed just in time.

With an appreciative shiver, Rose walked up to the house she'd fled a couple of weeks earlier to get the rest of her things. Her new landlord was letting her move in a day early, though she would've paid a full month's rent extra to avoid another night of polyester bedspreads and microwaved oatmeal.

Three pumpkins sat beside the front door. One big, one

medium, and a miniature one that would fit in the palm of her hand.

She had to stop and shake off the wave of pain that swept over her. She would be happy for them. It was good they were a family now. Babies needed families.

She reached for the doorknob but stopped, fingers hovering.

Should she knock?

Yes. Not my home. Not my family. Not—

The door swung open. "Hey! Why are you just standing out here?" Blair stepped outside and gave her a hug.

"I was just admiring the pumpkins," Rose said, "but you've got nothing on next door."

"Isn't that fantastic? John promises we'll go all out for Christmas."

They stared at each other, a gulf opening up between them, and Blair's smile became strained.

"I came for my stuff," Rose said. "Obviously."

"I know. I got your email. Well, you know where it is."

Rose went inside and made a beeline for the basement, then stopped short when she saw John standing in the living room, watching her. She'd assumed he would avoid her, and there was no car in the driveway to warn her she'd been wrong.

"Hi," Rose said.

"I hear you found a place," he said. He'd cut his hair short again, maybe for his new job, and he wore gym shorts and a muscle tank. He looked exactly the same as he had the day they met. "That's great."

"Yeah."

"You were welcome to stay here, you know. I could've stayed with my mother if you were uncomfortable. Or in a motel."

Rose just stared at him, not wanting to start a fight.

He stuck his hands in his pockets and looked over her shoulder.

"I made sure all your kitchen things got packed," Blair said from behind her. "Especially the knives. I know you paid a lot for those."

Rose turned, feeling odd to be sandwiched between them. "Thanks. I'm really looking forward to cooking again. The apartment has a great kitchen. Fantastic. Bigger than this one. It's twice the size of the bedroom."

"That's awesome," Blair said, frowning a little as if she didn't quite believe her.

Well, maybe that was understandable, given Rose's history of tall tales.

"I better get started." Rose managed to smile at Blair as she walked to the basement door, even though she found herself oddly enraged, then furious with herself for getting into such a mess.

"I'll help you," John said.

"That's not necessary. There isn't much."

He ignored her and followed her down the steps. "I would've carried it up for you, but I didn't want to look like we were in a hurry to get rid of you," he said.

Rose picked up the first thing in sight, a box of books, not prepared for how heavy it was. She staggered as she got up.

John put an arm around her to steady her. "Let me. Squats never were your best lift."

Her heart pounded. "Let go of me."

"Don't—fine." He let go. "I was just trying to help."

"I don't want your help."

He shook his head, scowled at her. "I told Blair this wasn't going to work."

The heavy box still in her arms, Rose shifted her weight

from foot to foot. "Here we go again. If you're going to leave her, you'd better get it over—"

"I'm not going anywhere." He made another move for the box, this time overpowering her, lifting it onto his shoulder with ease. "I mean *you*."

"What about me?"

"Nothing. Forget it."

"No, tell me. You owe me that. What were you going to say?"

"'Owe you.' See? That's what I told Blair. You're never going to forgive us."

She picked up a duffel bag and clutched it to her chest like a lumpy nylon breast plate. "You abandoned her, John. She faced everything, even your mother, on her own—"

"Before that. You and me, we had some hot times together, yes. But we knew it wasn't the real deal. We were just having some fun."

"Is that what you tell Blair?"

Exhaling with disgust, he dropped the box on the floor, pointed at her. "Blair doesn't believe me, but you are just as angry at her as you are at me."

"I'm not. I was hurt at first, but I got over it."

"Liar."

"She had the decency to tell me. She was honest."

"And you're not. You're pissed."

Rose glared at him, tightening her arms around the duffel bag. She wished she were angry. Anger would be easier than fear. Could Blair really be happy with this man? Would he betray her, too? "I'm not angry at Blair. You, yes. You're an asshole."

"You're angry because she has what you had. What we had was burning out, but you don't care, you want it back. You want *me* back."

"Actually, no," she said coldly. "I really don't."

"You wish I had stayed in New York. Because then you'd have a chance with me."

She realized she was staring at him with her mouth open. "You really believe that?"

"If you hadn't come out here to comfort Blair, she might've come back home, and we couldn't have that. Better get her settled out here with my mother where she'd be too trapped with the baby and everything to chase after me. You probably thought I wouldn't have the guts to come out here with you guarding over her." He wiggled his eyebrows at her. "I'm right, aren't I? You just can't let go of what we had together."

"Watch me," she said. "Thank you for carrying my bag to the car. I won't need any more of your help."

He stared. Uneasiness flickered in his eyes. "It was never meant to be, Rose. What I have here, well, I want it to work out."

"I'm so glad to hear that, but I think you could try a little harder." She picked up the box of books, barely feeling their weight this time, and marched past him up the stairs.

❧

LUCKILY THERE WASN'T MUCH TO HAUL UP THE STAIRS into her car. A few boxes, the duffel, a pair of stereo speakers, assorted camping gear, another suitcase. She hadn't planned to stay in California long, not very long at all, maybe a few months past a year. She'd temp and wait for the baby to arrive, help Blair, maybe, just maybe, apply to grad school.

It had nothing to do with scheming to get John back. Nothing. The only thing she wanted from him was to do right by Blair and the baby.

And she *had* forgiven Blair. Months ago.

She got behind the wheel and started up the engine. *Then why aren't you going in to hug her goodbye?*

She put the car in reverse.

All right, I'm still a little annoyed. So sue me.

Before she backed up, she couldn't help but look over at the house currently under attack by oversized spiders for a glimpse of Mark. They'd barely spoken in weeks. His office door, despite Sylly's policy, remained closed most of the time. He didn't seem to visit the kitchen at break time, and he didn't attend company meetings.

Fresh rumors were swirling around at work about a buyout, and she was as worried about the change as anyone. She still felt like a phony. Until she got some experience under her belt, she'd worry they only kept her around to keep their favorite programmer happy. He was obviously above the rules other employees lived by.

The way everyone tiptoed around him at the office was very strange. Eyes followed him when he walked past, male and female, and tech guys quoted him in meetings. He had the biggest office and a reserved parking space.

He must be a really, really good programmer.

She braked and stared at the house. He certainly was a really, really good kisser.

Her thoughts went back to the other house and the pair inside. It was unbearable that John thought she was pining over him. Blair must think the same.

Mark had seen it, too, and she'd even admitted it. But in the past few weeks, she'd scarcely thought of John.

Ever since that kiss.

She moved the car forward and killed the engine. Licking her lips, she eyed the spiders, imagining Mark up on a ladder. She smiled and got out of the car.

❧

MARK SHOOK HIS HAIR, WET FROM THE SHOWER, AND strode out of the bathroom toward his room. His head was in a problem at work, his mind running through lines of code, searching for a bug fix. He had one hand loosely gripping the towel at his hip when he looked up and saw Rose standing only a few steps away from him.

Her blue eyes were wide, her cheeks splotched with color. "Sorry," she said, a little breathlessly, "your mom sent me up."

"I bet she did," he muttered. His pulse tripped over itself as he realized how naked he was. "Hi."

"Hi." A slow grin spread across her face. "Bad time?"

He shrugged, tried to look casual. "Shower."

"I see that."

She didn't have to look so amused. It was his house, after all. Which reminded him of something. "Did you find a place?"

"I'm moving in today. That's why I'm here. I was wondering if you could give me a hand." Her gaze dropped down across his chest and back up. "Carrying stuff."

He swallowed and hoped she didn't look any lower. Why did she always wear such tight, provocative clothing? She was big, but half of America was bigger than her; she could find a baggier T-shirt if she wanted one. One that didn't let him see the outline of each full breast. One that was navy, maybe, not this bright orange one with black horizontal stripes that demanded he look below her chin. For a while.

"So, can you help?" she asked. "I'll buy you lunch afterward. And, well, I thought you might like to see where I ended up."

"I'd like that." He cleared his throat. "Give me a minute to get dressed."

163

Another grin. "Oh, all right. If you must."

He went into his room and locked the door. Then he wondered why he'd locked it, since his body would like nothing more than for her to come inside with him.

If I must?

Was she flirting with him?

Wildly scanning his closet for freshly ironed jeans and a dryer-sheet-scented polo shirt, Mark reminded himself of the couple next door. She must've just been over there, seen the lovebirds as she got her things. Blair was smiling a lot more, and John doted on her, always home, following her around.

Rose must've seen that, and then came straight over here.

To the guy with all those points to make.

He got dressed in his oldest jeans and a T-shirt from college and went out into the hallway. "Aren't you afraid I won't approve of your new home?"

She was studying the pictures on the walls. "Terrified." She turned. "Shall we go?"

If she was disappointed in his humble outfit, she didn't show it. He followed her down the stairs and out of the house. His mother, naturally, had disappeared.

The front seat was shoved all the way forward to make room for the cargo in the back. Mark had to fold his knees up to his chest and hold his breath to get the door closed.

She settled beside him, backed up into the street. "It's a short drive. Don't worry."

"I'm fine."

She patted his left kneecap, which was only inches away from his left ear, laughing. "You're flexible for such a big guy."

"Or highly tolerant of pain."

"Hang in there, it's only a few minutes."

Sure enough, while they were still up in the winding

streets of the hills, Rose took a left turn and went up, not down. "It's up here?"

"Shh." She was still smiling.

"I thought you liked the hustle and bustle of the flats. The great metropolis."

"The shopping," she said.

"Yeah. What happened to that?"

She shrugged. "Wait until you see it. You'll understand."

After about five minutes she slowed in front of a very modern house with a closed gate blocking the driveway. She pulled the visor down and hit the button on a remote clipped over the mirror. The gate glided open and she drove in.

He turned to her, the question in his eyes.

"I know, huh? Wait until you see the inside," she said.

The houses of this street were on a gentler slope than Mark's house was, each set far enough back from the street and each other to have front yards, flower beds, full driveways lined with lavender, rosemary, manzanita, and mounds of star jasmine.

"Will you be living in the servant quarters?" he asked. The houses on this street had to average in the millions.

She laughed and got out of the car. "Come on. Stretch those long legs of yours and see my palace."

He stumbled out, rubbing life into his limbs, and watched her hips sway as she strode across the flagstone pathway to the oversized red front door.

"Is this where you pick up the keys for your one-bedroom hovel off Telegraph Avenue?" he asked.

Without turning, she pushed the door open. "Come on, you haven't seen the best part."

He stomped his feet and followed. The house was modern, but warm, welcoming. Miles of wood trim, walls painted earthy colors, vaulted ceilings with stained glass skylights, a private deck with a panoramic view.

And furniture. Pillows, art on the walls, plants. Obviously, somebody already lived here.

"How long do you get to stay?" he asked.

"As long as I want."

He blinked at her. "Shall I call the authorities, or is your sexual servitude voluntary?"

"Thanks, Mark. That's the nicest thing anyone's said to me all day." She walked over to him, eyeing him suggestively.

He took a step back. "You were supposed to be offended. I just called you a prostitute."

"More like a kept woman."

He took another step back. "You're welcome, then."

Laughing, she put a hand on his arm and pulled him, reluctantly, deeper into the house. Its long, western-facing side was a wall of glass to drink in the view of the Golden Gate, San Francisco, Alcatraz on its rock in the middle of the bay, the soft golden hills of Marin.

Her warm, lush hip pressed up against his thigh. Although his body was responding cheerfully, he knew she was up to something he didn't trust. Digging his heels into the wide, distressed planks of the floor, he wiggled out of her grip and scowled at her. "What are you doing?"

"Showing you the spa. And not just the tub. You've got to see it."

"Why?"

Her smile fell slowly, some of the spark fading from her eyes. "It's cool. Or actually, hot." She folded her arms over her chest. He would *not* look at the cleavage, he wouldn't. "It's a sauna."

"Inside the house?"

"Right off the master bath." A fragment of her smile returned. "Want to see it?"

"I believe you." There was a sun porch off the hallway to their right, separate from the main living room, in a corner of the house that gave it two and a half walls of windows. Glossy-leaved tropical plants hung from the ceiling, and a mature, ten-foot ficus arched out from the corner. He stepped inside, observing and thinking, the facts falling into place. "You water the plants," he said.

"Among other things. There's an aquarium."

"When does the owner get back?"

"No owner. At least, not who lives here. They're looking for a buyer. I keep the place looking good while it's on the market."

"So you could be homeless again at any time?"

"I'd have at least a month warning if it goes into escrow. At least. And it's been on the market for over a year, so what's the chance of that?"

"Market's picking up. You could—"

"So? It beats the Holiday Inn. In the meantime I'll get to live here. Look at it. Isn't it gorgeous?" Her gaze dropped down over him, lower, back up. The interest in her eyes wasn't as playful as before, and he felt his temperature rise.

He'd been thinking about her for weeks. Not Blair—her. The feel of her, the smell of her, the sound of her voice. The taste of her in his mouth. His legendary productivity as a computer genius had taken a hit as he spent half of every hour imaging what almost had happened in the kitchen that day.

Even if he'd been thinking about her, why should he believe it was mutual? John, selfish prick though he was, also happened to be rich, tall, and good-looking, and she obviously still had a thing for him.

Mark was just the hired help, convenient for some ego stroking. Not the kind of stroking he had in mind.

He crossed his arms over his chest. "Did you see John when you went to the house?"

Her lips flattened. She nodded, looked away.

"Let's get your stuff," he said, and went out to the car. He lifted a backpack on his shoulder, hefted up a suitcase, and strode inside with them as she was walking out.

She glanced at him but said nothing.

He dropped the backpack in the hall, carrying the suitcase toward the master bedroom, but she strode past, pulled open a hall closet. "Just put that here for now."

"Why not the bedroom?"

"I'll probably end up sleeping on the sofa."

He snorted.

"Hey, it's my choice. The pillows need to be arranged just so every day in case there's a showing scheduled, and well, the master bedroom has a *lot* of pillows."

He peeked inside and choked. Red and gold squares and rectangles were arranged against the king-sized headboard in a mountain range of puffed satin, velvet, and tassels; big ones at the bottom, small ones on top. A cream blanket was folded across the foot of the bed; on top of that a silver tray with a teapot, cup, saucer, and vase with a single white rose.

"Holy crap," he said.

"They gave me photographs to help me remember how to put everything back, but I decided I'd rather sleep on the couch than deal with that every morning."

"It's like a movie set."

"Yeah." She closed the door, them out in the hallway, as if sealing the fantasy boudoir off from contamination. "That's why they call it staging."

"Do people really fall for that stuff?"

She grinned. "Not yet. Let's hope they don't for at least another six months."

He noticed then she had little silver broomsticks hanging from her ears. And a black cat with white feet dangling on a black ribbon around her throat. Very cute. He had an absurd love of Halloween and approved of her holiday spirit. Smiling into her eyes, he tried to remind himself she was using him but couldn't remember why he minded.

Smile fading away, she turned. "Let's get the rest, and I can get you back home."

"You make it sound like I'm out on parole," he said, following after. "Didn't you promise me lunch?"

"Yeah, sure. Absolutely. You're… interested in lunch?"

"I could be persuaded."

He saw her pause on the steps out to the driveway, continue without turning around. He took the opportunity to admire her ass. Enticing as always. The metallic studs on the rear pockets were flashy and eye-catching, drawing him out to the car like a lure on a nylon fishing line.

If she was offering a nibble, how could he not bite?

Just as he was reaching forward to lift a box out of her arms, not sure how he would segue into said nibbling, the gates opened and a familiar emerald green Audi pulled into the driveway.

Sylly's car.

What the hell is he doing here?

ROSE DROPPED THE BOX INTO Mark's arms and raised a hand, waving. "Hey, boss!"

She expected him.

Though Mark had been called a genius since he'd turned four, it took him a long, slow minute to figure out why Sylly was parking in Rose's new driveway on a Saturday afternoon, far from the office.

The first realization was instinctive. Male. The way Sylly studied Rose from head to toe when he got out of the car made Mark's hands curl into fists, his posture stiffen.

The other realization was rational, and therefore came last. "Why didn't you mention this was Syl's house?" he asked her.

"You were grumpy. I thought you might scold me."

So this was the place Sylly had been renting out to Welly-Nelly employees for years. Finding housing was so hard in the Bay Area, offering a discounted house was a great incentive to relocating the most desirable people. Mark had no idea it was this upscale, though. Or that Sylly had finally put it on the market.

Sylly joined them next to Rose's car, his handsome face

sporting one of his controlled, professional smiles that was meant to intimidate. "Surprised to see you here, Mark."

He shoved the box at him. "She asked me to help her move," he said. "I'm the neighbor, remember?"

"Not anymore." Eyes lingering on Rose, Sylly shifted the box to one side, held out his free hand. "What else? Load me up."

Oh, big strong guy, was he? Mark looked into the trunk. *Aha.* Keeping his face blank, he lifted the biggest dumbbell, an iron twenty-pounder, and held it out to him. "It's pretty heavy. Maybe you'd like to make two trips."

"I can handle it," Sylly said, but his jaw was tight. Mark enjoyed watching him stagger into the house.

"I LOVE HAVING MEN AROUND." ROSE PICKED UP THE sleeping bag and a black plastic bag filled with her pillows and followed Sylly through the front door.

She didn't understand why Mark was so unpredictable, watching her like a starving man one minute and turning cold the next, but she had a great house to live in and two strong, hot guys doing her bidding.

John was wrong. She wasn't angry. She could forgive him and Blair and herself, if not today, then soon. How could she not with that view to wake up to every morning? Money in the bank, a roof over her head, a Bay Area tech startup on her résumé.

Arguing with John had been a revelation. She felt light, free, happy. All these weeks, deep down, she'd been afraid he was right, that she was pining for him, that he'd damaged her. Having him throw it openly in her face, however, was like an antidote.

He was wrong. She didn't care about him at all. She should thank him for showing her that.

Biting back a smile, she eyed Mark.

Or thank somebody else.

"Love the earrings." Sylly had put her things down in the hallway and was staring at her ears. "Awesome holiday, Halloween."

She reached up to touch the dangling broomsticks. "I wonder if I'll get any trick-or-treaters up here."

"Not many, I don't think," Sylly said. His gaze drifted past her and sharpened. "What do you think, Mark? Will anyone come here looking for candy tonight?"

Rose looked between the two men, uneasy. Normally she would've said Sylly went out of his way to make Mark happy, but at this moment he looked hostile.

"Not if she locks the door and turns off the lights," Mark said, fists on his hips.

Were they fighting over her? She'd never gotten any flirtatious vibe from Sylly, not once. It had to be something else.

"Come on, boys, more work to be done." She escaped out to the car. The men followed, and five minutes later the three of them had piled up her things and were staring at the elaborate mountain of pillows in the master bedroom.

"How does it stay up?" Mark asked. "Are there wires under there? Scaffolding?"

"Annamarie is a sorceress," Sylly said. "She's the real estate agent's favorite stager. This place looked decent before, but then she came through here with her truck and her crew, and I thought twice about selling the place."

"Why did you buy it?" Mark asked.

"Buy low, sell high. I had the credit, some cash, thought I could flip it. Then the market dipped again, and well, here I am." Sylly shrugged, glancing between the two of them.

"She thinks she has to sleep on the couch," Mark said.

Sylly's frown was real. "No, don't do that. There are five beds in this house."

"She's afraid of the pillows," Mark added.

"I am not. I'm fine."

"I'll talk to Annamarie—" Sylly began.

"No! Mark, stay out of this. Where I sleep is my business." She pushed them both out into the hallway and shut the door. "So, lunch. How about I take both of you out?"

Sylly gave Mark another stony look. "I'd hate to crash your date."

All right, there was definitely something going on here. Had she been right earlier—Sylly wanted Mark? There was certainly something personal going on.

Whatever it was, it was a bad situation. Given Sylly was her boss and now her landlord, she couldn't afford to get between them.

She smiled brightly, determined to lighten the mood. "No date. Just my way of paying the movers."

"You can drop me off at my house on your way," Mark said suddenly, turning away. "I promised my mother I'd finish decorating the house."

"You're going to do more?" she asked, trying not to look hurt.

"I'll drive you, Mark," Sylly said. Then to Rose, "Sorry I can't make lunch, but thank you very much." Somehow he managed to usher them all out to the car. "Doing the light show again this year? Always putting your best talents to use."

"That's me," Mark said, opening the passenger door. "Mr. Talented."

When the two men drove away, Rose had to remind herself several times that she'd always wanted to live alone. She was happy to have the place to herself.

Very, very happy.

Damn it.

❧

"I STILL DON'T UNDERSTAND WHY YOU CAN'T GET A REAL telephone number," Rose's mother said that evening. "What if your phone is out of batteries and there's an emergency? How will I be able to reach you? Or you the police? Cell phones are awful with 911. I saw a show on TV about it."

Curled up on the couch, admiring the view, Rose moved her phone to her other ear. The sun had finally set, but the sky was still streaked with pale silver. She wondered if kids in the Bay Area waited until it was dark to go out trick-or-treating, if they went out at all. Just in case, she'd bought two bags of candy at the store with the rest of her groceries.

"It's not my house. I'm just staying here. In the unlikely event I forget to charge my phone, which you know I never do, then I'll run next door and use the neighbor's. Or drive to the hospital myself."

"What? Why would you need to go to the hospital?"

"I don't know. This is your nightmare. You tell me."

"Fine. Just promise me to plug it in every night. Do you have plenty of bars?"

"They're a bit of a drive, but it's nice you're thinking about my social life."

"Oh, be serious. Your phone. You have plenty of coverage?"

"I'm fine, Mom." Rose smiled and sipped her coffee, enjoying the return of her mother's maternal instincts. "Did you get many trick-or-treaters tonight?"

"Fourteen. You know how it is in this neighborhood; too many old people."

174

"Did you dress up?" Her mother's Elvira costume was legendary.

A long pause. "No, not this year."

"He didn't like it, did he?"

"This has nothing to do with him. It—" The line fell silent.

"He couldn't stand all the stodgy neighbors seeing you all hot and sexy, having some fun—"

"The dress didn't fit, all right? Now drop it."

Rose bit her lip. "Sorry."

"I've joined Weight Watchers again, and if I can just *stick* to it this time, I'll be the sexiest Elvira the world has ever seen. *Next* year."

"The world has already seen the sexiest Elvira ever," Rose said. "Every year at our house."

The only response was a delayed sniff.

"I love you, Mom," Rose said. "When are you going to come out and visit?"

"I told myself we'd visit when you had your own apartment."

"A whole house isn't good enough for you?"

"Your *own* place. With a lease. Not just another pit stop on the highway."

"This is way better than a pit stop. I'm sending you pictures. There's a bidet. A *bidet*. Have you ever seen one of those in real life?"

"I'd rather not think about you using your boss's bidet."

Rose laughed. "I invited him to lunch with me today," she teased.

"That's it. I take it all back. You should come back home. I just put a new comforter on your bed, bright red with yellow embroidery, little daisies. It goes perfectly with the carpet."

"Don't worry. I'm not going to sleep with him."

"I'm serious, Rose. I think you're in over your head."

"He's probably gay," Rose said. Though from the way she'd caught him peeking at her breasts while she carried boxes, she'd begun to revise that theory.

"Oh, God. Your gay boss's bidet. Are you in love with him?"

"Wildly."

"You're teasing me."

"Never."

"I've never liked your sarcasm, Rose. You should say what you mean."

"You wouldn't believe me. This way I get to have a little fun."

Her mother sighed. "I miss you. It's just not Halloween without you." Her voice got quiet. "I've got the album out."

Oh, no, Rose thought. Homesickness she'd been fighting all afternoon crept over her. "Don't. You're going to make me cry." Rose got up and padded into the kitchen. With the sun down, the house was getting dark, feeling bigger, emptier. The tile in the kitchen was icy underfoot.

"Your kindergarten costume is still my favorite," her mother continued. "I'm still angry with Miss Bullens about that. You were the cutest witch I've ever seen. All that blonde hair everywhere, the black dress, the tiny little black boots with the striped knee-highs…"

"The bitch made me take it all off."

"She *was* a bitch," her mother said feelingly.

Shocked, Rose laughed. "I don't think I've ever heard you use that word before." She frowned, tore open a tiny Twix bar. "Are you drinking?"

"I never drink when I'm depressed. You know that." She sighed. "Oh, look. Fifth grade. You're already starting to look like a little woman."

"You promised me you destroyed those."

"I had another set made from the negatives."

Rose popped the chocolate into her mouth. "That catsuit needed a built-in bra. I was so clueless. You should've told me."

"So cute. I love the way you sewed the white tummy panel on the front, just like Buster's." Buster had been her cat back then. Her mom sighed again. "Oh, now I'm thinking about Buster. Goldfish just aren't the same as a warm, furry animal, you know? Such a shame Phil is allergic."

"I looked like a penguin with breasts," Rose said.

"And whiskers," her mother sighed. "So cute."

Rose ate the rest of the candy and pushed the wrapper into the plastic bag she'd hung on a doorknob as a garbage can. Part of her agreement with Sylly and the real estate agent was making sure the house seemed *almost* lived in, but not yet. A fantasy. Every time she went out, she had to erase any hint of her existence, which meant she couldn't put her trash in a can under the sink, which might accumulate, emit odors, get forgotten.

"I have to go," Rose lied. "I think I hear the doorbell. I put out a pumpkin."

Her mom sighed and reminisced about her cuteness one more time before finally getting off the phone. Rose stared at the bag on the granite counter, wishing she hadn't bought any candy. She'd end up eating it all herself. No kids were going to walk down that street trick-or-treating; too dark, no sidewalks, gates on the driveways. Any kid brave enough to knock on her door was probably armed and dangerous.

She picked out one more snack-sized bundle of chewy processed corn syrup before heading for the front door to blow out the candle in the jack-o-lantern she'd carved an hour earlier. An early night would be good for her. She'd listen to music, catch up on her sleep.

When she pulled open the door and saw a full-sized vampire on her front porch, she gasped and started to slam the door.

Mark lowered the black cape he'd pulled up to his nose. "Rose, it's me."

She put a hand on her chest. "You scared the hell out of me."

He braced a hand on the door frame, leaned closer. His voice was low. "Trick or treat."

MARK DRANK IN THE SIGHT of her. Her cheeks were flushed, her eyes bright. "Oh," she said, seeming to regain a little composure. "Cool costume."

Hoping the cape and the gelled hair didn't ruin the effect of his elegant black suit, Mark let his eyes travel slowly over her pink T-shirt and tight jeans. "I like yours."

Her lips parted. After a long second, she said, "I was just about to give up on having any visitors."

"You're alone?"

She raised an eyebrow. Nodded.

"Your landlord and employer didn't find some urgent repair that suddenly needed doing? Pillows that needed arranging?"

"He got to that after the marathon of hot, sweaty sex."

He clenched his jaw. "Don't even joke about that."

She stepped past him, squatted down, blew out the candle inside the pumpkin. He became transfixed with the way her full lips puckered, the way her breasts moved as she bent over.

"Why not?" she asked. "He's awfully cute. Maybe I should let him know I'm interested."

"You don't know what a mistake that would be."

She had the nerve to pat him on the chest. "Oh, come on, Mark, lighten up. I was just kidding."

"I'm light," he said through his teeth.

"Sure you are," she said with a patronizing smirk before walking back into the house. "I'll go get you some candy."

That's not what I want. He strode into the house and planted himself in front of her. "Get your shoes on. I'm taking you to San Francisco."

She frowned, but interest sparked in her blue eyes. "San Francisco?"

"Big street party. Famous. Hundreds of thousands of people. Gets out of hand, like Mardi Gras. It's been canceled since 2006, but it's on for this year. This may be your only chance to see it."

Her face lit up. "Really? You want to go?"

"I love big crowds that get out of hand," he said. "Are you kidding?"

"I'd think you'd hate that sort of thing."

He despised them, but he'd get to be with her. "You might want to grab a jacket."

"I can do better than that." Beaming, she jogged away from him, leaving him alone in the foyer with nothing to admire but the flower arrangement on the hall table. It was perfect for the season, of course, rusty earth tones, black-eyed Susans, sunflowers, artfully arranged.

How could she live in this place? It was like a department store. He went over and messed up the flowers so they were off center and lopsided, then shook pollen onto the glossy mahogany table.

She still hadn't returned, so he went into the kitchen, found a bag of candy on the counter and helped himself. He had to admit it was an excellent kitchen. Huge with an island in the center, granite and marble and steel and warm wood, everything new and perfect.

Probably never used. Sylly had bought the place, fixed it up to sell without caring what he had, just eager to get what he could out of it.

Always the businessman. Mark tore open another candy bar.

He was chewing out his tension when Rose reappeared and took his breath away. Which meant he choked on the caramel and had to bend over to reopen his windpipe.

The tip of her red stiletto appeared in his teary vision. "Are you okay?" she asked, patting him on the back.

Fighting embarrassment, he stood up, hand over his mouth, and gazed at her. "You look great," he managed to say.

The dress was black and tight, the neckline a deep V that began at the shoulder and touched down between her breasts. No, below her breasts. The skirt, though nearly reaching her blood-red stilettos, was slit up both sides nearly to the hip, exposing long curvaceous legs in sheer black stockings. Thigh-highs, with lace at the tops.

Her hands slid down her hourglass body. "My mom gave me the idea. She said I was the cutest witch she'd ever seen."

He dragged his eyes up to her face. That mouth. She'd done something to it. Something naughty. The lips were full, red, and shiny, slightly parted. "Not the word."

Her eyelids fell. "Shall we go?"

No. Let's stay here. "Yeah." He turned away so he didn't embarrass himself. "Don't forget a sweater. It's cold in the city."

❧

THE CRUSH OF BODIES MADE A CHILL IMPOSSIBLE. ROSE

hadn't expected so many people: the press of strangers' elbows into her ribs, shoulders into her chin, stray hands on her ass.

People were everywhere, many in costume, many not, all mixed together in a slow, throbbing street party. She saw the pope, several Marie Antoinettes, roller-skating nuns, a giant baby smoking a cigar, conservative political figures in bondage wear, a giraffe. The other half of the crowd wore jeans and hooded sweatshirts, club wear, nothing at all. It was a circus and a Broadway show, a sporting event and a political rally, all in one, with the Victorian houses and storefronts looking down in aged, ornate resignation.

A few times Rose was separated from Mark. She was blindly pushed from body to body like a leaf in the choppy rapids of a colorful river, unable to see him, as tall as he was. So she clung to him, her fingers entwined in his, and let herself enjoy the rush of decadent mayhem.

"Can we get somewhere we can watch the parade?" she shouted to him.

"You are the parade, darlin'," a very tall Cleopatra told her.

Sure enough, they were walking down the middle of the street with hundreds of others decked out in costumes that filled her with alternating sensations of appreciation and alarm. Was that chain driven through that man's penis? Didn't it hurt when he flapped his wings?

Mark moved his mouth close to her ear. "I'm trying to get us over there. Less crowded."

She looked where he was pointing, a big intersection with cops lined up along the barricades. There was a small gap next to them, the party poopers.

"Okay," she agreed needlessly, since of course he couldn't hear her in the melee. They moved into an area with so many bodies, her average height wasn't enough to look anywhere but up. The wires from the electric city buses and streetcars dangled overhead like streamers. No, there were actual streamers, too, as well as silly string, lingerie, and glowing skull-shaped balloons. One young guy started to climb on top of the bus shelter before the cops called him down.

Rose and Mark finally broke through the densest crush and stumbled up onto the curb near the police.

Mark leaned down to her. "Do you want to leave?"

The feel of his breath on her ear sent sparks down her spine, into her belly. The throb of the music battling from multiple speakers around them, the bump of strange bodies against hers, not to mention Mark in that suit, dark and handsome—had her in a state of building, frustrated arousal.

Did she want to leave?

"It depends on where we go," she said, gazing up into his eyes. They weren't blue at the moment, but dark, almost black. Unreadable.

One of the mystery hands that had been groping her all night suddenly squeezed her left butt cheek. She slapped it away.

Mark frowned and looked between her and somebody behind her. "Did—excuse me, did you just touch her?" he demanded.

"Sorry." The voice was soft, young, female. Rose turned to see a girl with spiky white hair and a remarkable amount of rings through her eyebrows. "I couldn't resist."

"Well, maybe you should try harder," Mark said, scowling.

The girl grinned and slipped away.

"I'm sorry about that," Mark said.

"It's not your fault." Rose squeezed his hand.

"I brought you here."

"I love it," she said.

Sighing, he looked into her face. "I thought you might."

The crowd surged over them again, breaking the moment,

and they were forced to keep walking aimlessly, like cattle in a psychedelic dream.

As entertaining as it was, Rose began to tire of the crowd. Mark seemed to be holding her hand out of survival, not seduction. He was obviously miserable. Rigid-backed and serious, he pulled her along with him, a look on his face that a real vampire might've had: arrogant and ready to bite somebody.

Her own pleasure lessened. Then the hand cupped her ass again and she swung around to tell the girl to find a friend somewhere else—

Only to see the steroid-enhanced, tattooed chest of a blond man at least six and a half feet tall. He had a scar across his cheek and lust in his hungry blue eyes. If it weren't for his plastic Viking helmet, she might've been afraid.

"Did this guy touch you?" Mark growled in her ear.

"Yeah, but—" she began.

Mark pushed her behind him and said to the Viking, "Keep your fucking hands to yourself."

"Who the fuck are you?" said the Viking.

"The guy who's telling you to keep your fucking hands to yourself, asshole," Mark said.

The Viking rose up a few inches taller and planted his hands on his hips, his upper lip curling in a sneer. "Nobody calls me that," he said, voice gravely. He swayed slightly.

Oh God, he's drunk or high or something, Rose thought. She tried to pull Mark away, but they were wedged together in the crowd, and for some insane reason, Mark was solid as a lamppost.

"This your girlfriend?" the Viking sneered.

To her surprise, Mark answered, "No. And she's not yours, either."

The Viking leaned sideways to leer at her over Mark's shoulder. "Want to have a little fun, big girl?"

"No, thank you," she replied.

Suddenly the man was on top of her, one arm around her waist, one strong hand clasping her ass so hard, his fingers penetrated between her cheeks. She froze in shock, then reacted instinctively, drawing her knee back to crush his testicles.

Before her knee reached him, he fell to the ground. One second he was there, the next—prostrate at her feet, the Viking helmet knocked off.

With Mark kneeling on his chest, pressing an elbow into his throat. Stunned, drunken eyes gazed up in offended horror.

The crowd flowed around them, some looking down, smiling, as though it were all part of the show. Somebody in size-fifteen platform heels tripped over the plastic helmet; a moment later it disappeared into the forest of legs.

Mark said something Rose couldn't hear. At first the man's face twisted up in a sneer, but then Mark shifted his weight and the Viking's eyes bugged out.

"I'm sorry! I'm sorry!" the man cried, looking plaintively at Rose. "Help me!"

Mark said something else.

"I… swear. Just… let me… go," he gasped.

As graceful as a cat, Mark got to his feet. Rose watched in amazement as the blond giant rolled over, coughing, and staggered to his feet. He eyed Mark, confusion warring with anger and fear, rubbing his throat with both hands.

"Fucking vampires," he spat. Pointing a finger at Mark, he backed up into the crowd. "I am *so* fucking *sick* of vampires."

Rose let out her breath. The feel of that guy's hands on her body—almost inside her—had shaken her. Mark was brave, but he was smaller, and she presumed, nicer than the thug who'd groped her. If he'd fought back, Mark never would've survived.

Mark clasped her elbow. "I'm taking you home. It's not safe here for someone like you."

Or you, she thought, moving closer to him. She didn't want to risk him defending her again, no matter how hot it made her. "Okay."

He didn't say anything, just pulled her closer and started walking back toward the car. At least she thought it was in that direction. She looked up to catch his attention, not recognizing the hardness in his eyes, the tautness of his jaw. For a split second she wondered if she'd accidentally latched onto the wrong vampire in the throng, trading her mild-mannered neighbor in for this fierce, merciless stranger.

It took several minutes to reach the barrier around the crowd. Cars were backed up on the other side of the street, trying to get through, honking at revelers who spilled over the fence and staggered into the traffic. Mark maneuvered her around the corner onto an empty stretch of pavement in front of a car dealership.

Rotating her in his arms, he captured her shoulders in his hands and stared down at her. "Are you all right?"

The desire in his eyes made her breath catch. She nodded.

Cupping her cheek, he dropped his gaze to her mouth. While she felt her heart flutter into her throat, his thumb stroked her bottom lip.

"I wouldn't have let him hurt you." His voice was low and tense.

"Thanks." When she said the word, the tip of her tongue brushed his thumb.

And then he was kissing her, hard and deep, his fingers tunneling through her hair.

Not gently like before. This was furious, wild, hot.

Her defenses snapped under the sudden onslaught. She stretched up against him, her insides burning, melting, dripping, hot. Her knees wobbled and he slid a hand down her spine, pulled her firmly against his hips, supporting her, demanding her. She felt how hard he was.

"Rose," he growled in her ear, sucked the lobe into his mouth. "*Rose*." She felt his teeth.

Desire pooled between her legs.

She reached up to explore his chest, shoving under the suit jacket to feel the broad planes of muscle and bone. She kissed his jaw, fumbled with the tie, hungry for skin under her fingers.

His hands were hungry, too. She felt them slide down her back, over her hips, one slipping up her side to her breast. She pushed it into his hand. "Oh, yes," she whispered.

He dipped his head and kissed his way down.

Grabbing his head in her hands, she encouraged him lower, blocking out the sight of hundreds or thousands of people just a street away, even though some eyes were turned in their direction, openly drinking in the scene she and Mark were making with everything else raging that wild night.

Just as Mark's face was between her breasts, his breath hot and moist on her skin, he froze.

Hungry for him, she wiggled against him, but he broke free, gripped her shoulders, and held her away from him. "Not here," he said, voice husky.

"Right. Home."

"Yours," he said.

She smiled, thinking of the big bed. "Yes."

"We'll have to walk to the car. Can you make it?" His hands squeezed, loosened, stroked, squeezed.

She wasn't sure what he meant. She certainly didn't want

to wait, but they could hardly finish what they'd started pressed up against the glass window of the Ford showroom.

"Your shoes. You were limping," he explained.

His vampire hair was mussed. One floppy swath hung across his left eye, boyishly adorable, sexy. "I was?"

"Yeah." His gaze fell to her mouth again. He licked his lips.

Her feet could fall off and she wouldn't notice. "Let's hurry. Which way?"

He made a move to kiss her again, then stopped himself. "We'll never make it if I touch you again." He moved away and roughly took her hand in his, an arm's length of distance between them. "Let's go."

15

THE SLOW TRAFFIC OVER THE Bay Bridge only increased the tension between them. Mark had to drive but kept shooting hot glances at her that made her ache. One hand on the steering wheel, one on the stick shift, none on her. She rubbed her hands up and down her thighs and willed the cars in front of them to turn into pumpkins and roll out of the way.

Finally the car exited the freeway, crept through the city streets, headed up into the hills to the house. In minutes they would be alone, together, nothing stopping them.

She wouldn't worry about what would happen later. Wonder if this meant anything to either one of them. If this was going to be anything more than an easy, quick night of fun.

You swore to yourself you wouldn't do this again, she told herself.

Then she watched his long, lean fingers stroke the steering wheel as he pulled into her driveway. She shifted in her seat, restless to have those hands on her own wicked skin.

I don't care. I want him.

The Spanish-style mansion next door to her house was having a party; every light was on, music rolled over the fence, cars were parked in a long line along the narrow road. Mark pulled up in front of her garage and killed the engine. They sat in the car for a long second, not moving, not speaking, the muffled laughter and music from next door surrounding them like a blanket.

She turned her head and her chest tightened. He was staring at her, his eyes dark with desire. There was a ruthlessness there she'd never seen before, a hardness that made her breathless.

His voice was low, tight. "Have you changed your mind?"

Is that what he thought? Holding his gaze, she shook her head slowly from side to side, then turned and got out of the car. Her steps to the front door felt weightless. Vaguely, she tugged her skirt down, reached for the house key tucked in her purse.

When the driver's side door slammed, she looked over her shoulder to watch his familiar stride, suddenly undone at the sight of him. He looked different tonight. Taller. Older.

As she turned the key in the door, his hands slid around her waist, pulled her against him. He felt long and muscular against her back, her bottom, her thighs. Hardness everywhere.

"I want you," he said in her hair, making her shiver. She tilted her neck, and he pushed the hair aside to kiss her just where she wanted him to kiss her, below her ear, along her neck, there.

She exhaled, her knees weakening.

"Inside," he said. "Now." One hand tight around her waist so her ass was pressing against his erection, he reached past her to open the door. They stumbled in together, slammed it shut, turned into each other's arms.

His mouth came down on hers. She ran her fingers through his hair and tugged him closer. She was burning up, possessed with need. He tasted dangerous, familiar but foreign, her friend on fire.

To her dismay, he put a hand over her lips, lifted his head. His eyes were dark, unblinking. "Are you sure you want to do this?"

She stared at him, not sure what she was hearing.

He drew back another inch. "*All* of it?" he asked.

Rose felt suddenly uneasy. Was *he* having second thoughts?

She kicked off the heels, felt cold tile under her feet. Putting her hands on his chest, moving close, she backed him up against the door, satisfied to see the smolder came back into his eyes. *That's better.*

"Here's something you should know about me," she said softly. "I only have sex with guys who really, really want to have sex with me."

He closed his eyes for a second. Opened them, dropped his gaze to her mouth. "I'm really, really glad to hear that."

"Otherwise," she said, "I start to worry. Feel insecure."

His hands found her waist, slid up and down her hips, latched on there and pulled her close. "Here's something you should know about me," he said roughly. He lowered his head to her temple, his breath low and hot against her skin. "I've never wanted to have sex with anyone, ever, as much as I want it with you."

❧

HE KISSED HIS WAY DOWN HER NECK. SHE SMELLED SO good, even after the city and the groping Viking. The little hairs on her temple mesmerized him. The long hair down her back paralyzed him. He kissed and nuzzled, catching silky strands between his lips while his hands lightly brushed the undersides of the breasts he'd been fantasizing about for weeks. "Time to get naked," he growled.

She twisted around in his arms, smiling a little, looking him over. "You first."

"Me?" He reached for the zipper in the small of her back. "Forget that. I'm nothing special."

She batted his hands away. "I'll be the judge of that." Then, "No, not a judge. An appreciative audience."

"You're a much better performer than I am. I'm a hermit, remember?" He bent down and kissed her neck. She tasted even better than she looked. "You need to help me out of my shell." He captured a handful of her skirt and pulled it up, seeking skin. The lace band of her black stocking on her upper thigh captured his attention. He bent his knees, planning to pull it down with his teeth, when she escaped again.

"Look at you. What do you have to be nervous about?" She waved her hands up and down at him. "You're tall, you're male, you've got muscles in all the right places and nothing extra."

"Nothing?" He had to get her into the bedroom and show her about that. "All right. Me first. But not here." He captured her hand and dragged her down the dark hallway.

"No, not the master bedroom. I'll never get those pillows back up."

He kissed her hard on the lips before he went into the bedroom and strode over to the elaborate bed. First he got rid of the fake breakfast tray. Then, with an impatient yank, the comforter came off the bed, most of the tower of decor with it. He swiped the survivors to the floor and turned to face her, his hands at his collar. "Come here."

A faint smile wavered in the corner of those lush lips. "You're still dressed," she said.

He stared at her until she came over and sat on the edge of the bed. Seeing her there, lush and feminine, her knees slightly parted under the slinky fabric of that dress, knocked the air out of him. "You're so beautiful," he whispered.

With a sultry glance from under her lashes, she sank onto her back, reached her hands over her head, stretching like a cat.

The moon was nearly full, and the floor-to-ceiling windows let in the city lights; her fair skin glowed against the dark sheets.

"Take off your clothes, Mark."

Grinning, he lifted his hands to the shirt button at his throat. "I'm a little insecure."

She smiled, bit her lip. "I guessed."

His fingers worked their way down to the fourth button, stopped. "Is this enough or do you need to see more?"

"Please," she said derisively.

"Promise not to laugh?"

"Take it off before I do it for you."

He paused. "I'd like that," he said but added, "Maybe next time." He swiveled around, giving her his back as he continued. When the shirt was fully open, he peeked at her over his shoulder.

Smiling broadly now, she shimmied up the mattress, put her hands behind her gorgeous blonde head. The slit of her skirt gaped open, exposing the stockings again. He swallowed over the dryness in his throat and turned away.

His Nordstrom's trousers were too expensive to have a noisy zipper; they parted with a muffled metallic hum. He risked another glance over his shoulder and caught Rose's encouraging nod before he let the pants fall to the floor, pushed his underwear after them, faced her completely.

"Oh, my," she said, sitting up. She reached out both hands. "Come here."

His unbuttoned shirt still hung from his shoulders. "Would you be offended if I take the condom out of my pocket now?"

"I'd be more offended if you didn't."

Grinning, he squatted down to reach into his pants, threw off his gaping shirt, and crawled over to her, the foil packet between his teeth. Then he dropped it on the soft sheets in front of her like a Labrador with a tennis ball. "You don't have to worry about its expiration date."

She sank back, one arm reaching out along the bed, one in the air in welcome. "New?"

"Mm-hmm," he agreed. The day after she and her roommate had moved in, he'd had a deluded surge of optimism at the drugstore.

He'd deluded himself all right, thinking he could ever want Blair as much as he wanted Rose.

God, he wanted her. He'd wanted her from the first moment he'd seen her.

He hooked his finger over her bra, right between her breasts, pulled. "Your turn."

Still, she hesitated. He moved closer, took her in his arms, rolled her on top of him.

What began as a light and teasing kiss quickly turned dark and impatient. He pushed his tongue past her teeth and tangled it with hers, a moan escaping him at the knowledge he'd finally have her here, now, alone, for as long as he wanted. Her body was heavy on his, deliciously real, soft, erotic. While he distracted her with his mouth, his hands found the dress's zipper down her back and jerked it down. Then he slipped his hands inside, finding skin, glorious skin, velvety soft and warm.

She broke the kiss and wiggled around on top of him. Hands and knees braced on the bed, she sat up and straddled him, her hair a shining cloud falling around her shoulders. Full lips, ripe and parted. High cheekbones under those wide-set eyes that were looking at him the way he'd dreamed—awake and asleep—she'd look at him. With molten, eager desire.

Her fingers wrapped around him and squeezed. "You're huge," she said.

Jaw clenching, he arched his back, dug his fingers into her thighs.

She worked him harder, not afraid, gently demanding, perfect.

He wouldn't last if she kept doing that. Oh God. Just another minute, another second—

With a groan, he grabbed her wrists, flipped her onto her back. "Your turn." Stroking her shoulders, he explored her warm, inviting body; over her breasts, the gentle curves of her stomach, her hips, between her thighs. So hot. *God, finally.*

"You're good at that."

Seizing her mouth again with his, he pulled the stretchy fabric of her dress down over her shoulders, her chest, her stomach, her hips, and then, without stopping to admire the push-up bra or the crimson panties, he had the clasps unfastened and the elastic shoved out of the way and finally, Rose stretched out under him naked, gorgeous, and willing.

He left the stockings where they were. He liked those.

As he admired her, light-headed, hypertensive, he realized she'd said something. "Good at what?" he asked.

"Flipping people over."

He looked in her eyes, saw her smile. "Years of judo." He stretched out on top of her again, mouth against her mouth, then moved lower, determined to wipe that grin off her face. Too wild with raw, blinding need to make jokes.

She pushed her breasts together for him, an offering, and he gratefully sucked a silky pink nipple into his mouth and wondered just how long he was going to last this first time.

Once wouldn't be enough. There was too much of her for just once.

Her nipple pebbled in his mouth. He felt her arch, heard her moan. The sting of her nails raking his back made him suck harder. With the tips of his fingers, he traced the soft curve of her hip, then returned, finally, to the thatch of curls between her legs. He ventured deeper.

Moving his mouth to her other breast, he licked, blew, sucked. She cried out, driving her fingers through his hair to encourage him, then freezing under him when his fingers continued their exploration between her legs. He dipped a finger in an inch, then deeper, groaning with satisfaction to discover she was wet, slick, hot.

He let the nipple slide out of his mouth and kissed his way down her rounded belly, over the navel ring, the silky skin, and down between her legs to the fair curls.

❧

JUST IN TIME, ROSE REACHED FOR HIS FACE AND HELD IT between her palms. The roughness of his jaw felt so good against her fingers, almost as good as it did on her inner thighs.

She hoped he would understand. "Please don't," she said softly. "I don't like that."

With a laugh, he broke free from her grip and nuzzled his face between her legs again.

"Seriously, no." Squeezing her thighs together, she twisted to one side. "I really don't."

His head lifted. He stared at her. "I'm not just doing it to be polite. I really like it."

"Well, I don't." She put her hands over her breasts, turning further away, fighting a familiar feeling of inadequacy. Some people—some women—could open themselves up that way. She just couldn't. Never could.

"All right, sweetie." His hands curled around her hips, fingers digging under her bottom. "How about here?" He dropped little kisses on the tops of her thighs, right above the band of her stockings.

"That's—oh!"

Teeth.

She gasped. "That's fine."

Handsome backside up in the air, he worked his way down her legs, over her knees, his mouth and hands exploring every inch. Reassured his tongue wasn't going to attempt another go between her legs, she sank back, closed her eyes, let herself feel.

His light touch on her feet made her draw up her legs with a squeal. "That tickles."

He crawled back up her body, kissed her open-mouthed. "How about this? This okay?"

"Mmm," she replied, kissing him back.

His hand glided between her legs, cupping her but not going in. "This?"

She clutched his shoulders. "Yes," she whispered.

"I love that you're so wet," he said in her ear, penetrating her with his fingers, sliding in and out, more and more.

Not enough. "Now," she said, digging her nails into his skin.

"You first," he said, low and breathless. "I want this to be really good for you."

Her reply was to capture his penis in her hand while she sucked his tongue into her mouth.

He angled his mouth to kiss her deeper, then broke away to deal with the condom. She could hear him breathing, see the sheen of sweat on his bare shoulders.

He dropped a hand next to her head on the pillow, kissed her temple. "Next time will be better," he said roughly, shoving her legs apart with one knee.

"Now," she said, "I want—oh!"

He was inside her, hard and sudden. Then he withdrew, pushed into her again. "*Rose*," he gasped.

Her mouth fell open in a silent cry, stunned by the force of him. All her senses focused on the filling, breaking sensation deep inside her. He felt so good. Each thrust a caress, giving and taking.

She reached around him to help guide his hips, enjoying the feel of his slick skin, the taut muscles, straining and flexing as he pounded into her.

"*Mark*," she whispered, not believing it was him, that he could be the one doing this to her.

His rhythm increased, the force of each movement faster, harder. She lifted her knees, let her feet fall to either side, silently begging him to take all of her, go deeper, hit that spot inside her again, again, again.

His hand moved between their bodies. Rubbing her slowly at first, then faster as she moaned, he found the perfect pace and pressure to send her up into tight, perilous need.

His breath was ragged, matching hers. She felt his own building urgency and hoped he was enjoying it as much as she was, hoped he would stay a little while after they were done, and then she wasn't hoping for anything except that the blinding, shattering explosion of her climax would last forever.

16

THE SUN WOKE HER UP.

Mark's face was above hers. He'd been watching her sleep.

"Did you let John go down on you?" he asked.

She closed her eyes. "Good morning to you, too."

His fingers ticked her stomach, gently stroking, almost as distracting as his penis pressing into her thigh. They'd made love again after the first frenzied time, slow and drowsy. Even now, with his naked body stretched along hers in the bed, she found it hard to believe the confident, talented lover from the night before was her stumbling, shy, awkward, antisocial ex-neighbor.

She brushed a swath of light brown hair off his forehead. The morning sun made his eyes seem bluer than she'd realized, almost as blue as the midday sky.

Which was what she saw out the window. No fog, no haze —bright, midday light.

She started. "What time is it?"

Kissing her neck, he found her nipple and gently kneaded it between his fingers. "Who cares?"

"Seriously, what time is it?"

He drew back, his eyes narrowing. "Why, do you have a date?"

"More like an appointment. I have to get dressed." She rolled out of bed, found her phone mixed in the folds of last night's outfit. Shoot. Already 11:51. She hurried into the bra and panties, but she couldn't wear that dress without looking like a hungover, wrung-out Elvira.

He braced himself up on his elbow, the sheet tangled around his waist. He watched her as she struggled into her underwear.

He was incredibly hot. Not helping. "Can you please get up?" she asked. "I don't know how much time I've got before they get here."

He glanced down at himself. "I've been up for a while." Then he looked back up at her and frowned. "Before who gets here?"

"People are looking at the house today."

Grinning, he flopped onto his back. "I'd think you'd want to scare away potential buyers for as long as you can." He stretched out, wiggled his toes. "I think I should stay right where I am."

Her eyes fell on the chaos of bedding. "Oh, God. I've got to get that put back together."

He still wasn't getting out of bed. Where had she put her suitcase? The closet. Right. She jogged out into the hall and pulled it out, unzipped it, dug through for jeans and a T-shirt. Oh, clean underwear, too.

Shivering in the hallway, she wriggled out of last night's thong and pulled on something cotton and clean. Not sexy, but Mark would understand.

If they got together again later today…

No time to think about that right now.

Breathing a sigh of relief as she pulled the shirt over her head, Rose kicked the suitcase back into the closet. Then she realized they might look inside so she pulled it back out, zipped it up neatly, rolled it in next to the other bags, and closed the door.

There. Now if only Mark would get up, they could make the bed and go out for brunch somewhere. Luckily she hadn't made a mess in the kitchen. Or the bathroom. Which reminded her: she really, really had to brush her teeth.

"Mark, I hope you're getting up! Sylly will be here any minute with those friends of his!" she called out before she closed the bathroom door. Her toiletries were already neatly out of sight in the cabinet where she'd put them yesterday afternoon. After a quick pee, a teeth-brushing, a facial-cleansing wipe, a swipe of deodorant, a spritz of jasmine body spray, and a dab of lip gloss, she was ready. No, not quite. She had to compensate for the lack of a shower somehow. Another squirt of the jasmine and some eye shadow, a little powder on her nose.

There.

And then she wiped the sink with a paper towel and hid it under the sink.

Now she was ready—except for the bed. God, where had she put the binder of photographs the stager had given her? Hall table. She scurried down the hall, peeking into the master bedroom to make sure Mark wasn't snoozing with his sexy bare ass in the air.

She froze.

The bed was made, the pillows arranged. Just as ridiculously mountainous and symmetrical as before. Even the rose slanted in its vase at a perfect twenty-degree angle.

Mark was nowhere to be seen.

"Mark?"

The doorbell chimed. *Mozart*, she thought. It went on and on, *dum dum da dum, da de da de da dum dum...*

She raised her voice. "Mark?"

Then there was laughter and several voices coming from the front of the house.

"Rose? You here?" Sylly's booming voice, not Mark's.

Was he hiding in a closet somewhere?

Had he *left*?

"I'm here! Just leaving!" she called out.

She scanned the bedroom for her dress and stockings, used condoms or their wrappers, then gave up and went to greet Sylly and his potential homebuyers on her way out the door.

How can I not have her cell number? Mark thought. He scrolled through his contacts as though Rose's number would magically appear.

Any minute now his mom would realize he was parked in the driveway. She knew he'd gone out with Rose last night, had certainly noticed he hadn't come home.

Would she wag a finger at him for not calling? Or book the wedding chapel?

He needed an alibi before his mother got the wrong idea. Or got any ideas at all.

He called his sister, knowing it was early for the little party girl, but desperate.

"Mark, what the hell?" she groaned over the line after six rings. "It's practically still dark out."

"I need a favor," he said.

"What?" Her voice got muffled as she spoke away from the phone—to someone in her apartment, probably a boyfriend.

"Okay, Mark. Hello? Are you dying or something? Should I call 911?"

"Not yet. I need you to lie for me," he said, eyeing the house. The spiders weren't half as terrifying as the woman inside. "Back me up when I tell Mom I was at your place last night."

"What? Why…" she trailed off, then squealed. "Did you finally get laid?"

"Just tell her I was there, okay? I went to the city for Halloween but didn't want to deal with traffic on the way home, so I crashed on your couch."

"Where were you *really*?"

"Please. Just back me up."

"You have to tell me everything."

He snorted into the phone.

"That's my price," she said. "You're asking me to lie to the woman who gave me life."

"Can't you just do something nice for nothing for once?"

"How do I know it was nice?" she said. "You're not talking."

"April," he said through his teeth. "I can't tell you everything."

"Then I'm sure Mom can tell me."

He sank lower in his seat, eyes on the house. Any minute now she was going to come out and see everything in his eyes. His mother had always seen right through him.

"Fine," he spat out. "It's my neighbor. I'm not telling you any more."

"You slept with a pregnant chick? Dude, that's—"

"No. The other one. Her roommate. Well, not anymore. She moved out."

"And you followed, huh? What's her name?"

"Later. I have to go inside."

"Her name or I spill."

He squeezed the phone. "Rose."

Her smile was audible. "Excellent. I can't wait to meet her."

God forbid. "So, I arrived last night after midnight and left around eleven-thirty this morning."

"You should say we got shit-faced to explain why you look the way you do."

"How do you know how I look?"

"Please," she said. "As if I don't know what a dude looks like in the morning after he's been screwing all night."

He put a hand on his stomach, feeling queasy. "Right. Shit-faced."

April started to ask for their drink menu for the night before—"For realism's sake," she said—but he couldn't deal with his fun-loving sister any longer and got off the phone.

As he walked toward the house, he hoped Rose would forgive him for taking off like that.

But *Sylly…*

He couldn't find out either. *Will we be paying out a referral bonus every time you want to get laid, Mark?* he would ask, only pretending he thought it was funny.

He'd promised Sylly he wasn't interested in Rose. Now he'd put both of them on the spot. Mark was fine no matter what happened, but Rose…

She needed that job—probably more than she needed him.

Sylly was still dancing around that drug company. Mark needed to muster all the clout he had to talk him out of it, not show up embarrassed and defensive about starting an affair with the newest hire. One who was living in the boss's house.

Damn, if only he had her number.

Maybe she'd call him. His mother was in the book, had

been for years. He'd go in, shower, tell his mom to mind her own business, and—

Blair. Of course. He'd ask Blair for Rose's number.

He got out of the car and stopped himself from going straight over. He was wearing his vampire suit. Now that it was Sunday morning, his outfit had a religious air, perhaps in even a door-to-door sort of way, but he'd feel better if he changed.

His mom was sitting at the old upright piano in the living room and stopped playing when he flew in.

"Morning! Sorry I didn't call. I crashed at April's last night." He waved and ran up the stairs. "Can't talk!" In sixty seconds he was in jeans and a T-shirt, leaping back down the stairs and out the front door. "I'll get the paper!"

If his mother said anything, he was moving too fast to hear her.

He swept up the Sunday paper in the driveway and rapped on Blair's front door.

John answered, a phone at his ear. "Oh, Mark. Hi." His eyes were bloodshot, heavy-lidded, tired. "No, it's just the neighbor… I don't know, she's in bed… I hope so." He rubbed his hand over his face, glanced at Mark, eyebrows up, waiting.

Mark's own troubles faded away. "Sorry. This looks like a bad time." He took a step back but his worries overcame his manners. "Is everything all right?"

John closed his eyes for a moment, held up a finger, his attention back on the phone call. "She's in bed. We'll go in tomorrow to… induce." He rubbed his eyes. "They have to… she has to, you know…" His voice cracked.

Mark fell back another step, his stomach clenching. *Oh, God.*

John cleared his throat. "No, she wasn't bleeding. I thought she was worried over nothing."

Blood. The baby. Blair. The images struck Mark with such

graphic detail, his vision went sparkly around the edges. He put a hand on the side of the house for support. Sweat broke out on his forehead.

John continued talking into the phone. "She'd had a bad dream and kept insisting something was really wrong. Finally I took her to the ER, and they did an ultrasound." His hollow, red-rimmed eyes met Mark's. He listened for another moment then said, "No, please don't come over. I'll have to call you later. Really, I have to go." He hung up abruptly, shoved the phone in his pocket, looking at Mark.

"I'm so sorry," Mark said, trying to swallow over the dry lump in his throat. "Blair?"

John nodded, lips tight. Then he tilted his head, looked him up and down. "You all right? You look green."

After everything John had probably been through, the last thing he needed was his neighbor to faint on his doorstep. "I was just… bringing your paper. It was in the driveway." He held it out.

"Thanks," he said with a sigh, taking it. "You sure you're all right?"

"I'm fine." Unlike Blair. The baby. You. "Let us know if we can do anything."

"Thanks." Nodding, John stepped back into the house to close the door.

Mark sucked in fresh air and hurried back to his own house, his skull floating a foot off his shoulders, trying to focus his eyes on the agapanthus, the Meyer lemon tree, the blue sky streaked with a single gash of fog. Anything to wipe away the image of blood. Blair, baby, blood—

Just inside his front door, his ears roared and the world shrank to a pinprick before the lights went out completely.

ROSE GOT THE CALL WHEN SHE WAS WAITING FOR HER latte at Peet's Coffee and Tea. When she saw John's number on the screen, she went out onto the street, fearing the worst.

Why else but for an emergency would he call her, after all?

"She was asking for you," John said after he'd given her the news, sounding exhausted. Blair would have to go into the hospital the next morning to induce labor and delivery. She was already so far along—

It wasn't supposed to be like this.

"I'll be there in ten minutes," Rose said, her throat tight.

In fewer than seven she was pulling into the driveway. Frowning at Mark's VW next door, she strode up to the door and didn't bother knocking before she went in. "Hello? It's Rose." She dropped her keys and bag near a large box, then saw it was a baby car seat and felt her eyes fill with tears.

"Hello?" she called again, her voice wobbly.

John wandered over, hands in his pockets. He looked terrible: unshaven, limp. "She's on the sofa. Just fell asleep."

Rose put her hand over her mouth, cursing herself for shouting her arrival. "Poor Blair," she whispered. Then, perhaps belatedly, she put a hand on John's arm. "You, too. I'm so sorry."

He shrugged, looked away. "Yeah."

"Thanks for calling me."

"She asked."

Rose bit her lip. He'd been through a lot, he could be rude. "Can I do anything?"

"What can anyone do?" Shoving his hands deeper into his pockets, he walked away.

Rose followed him into the kitchen. "I can stay with her if you'd like to go out—"

"Go out? Where the hell am I going to go?"

She drew back, palms out. Took a deep breath. "I didn't mean that. I was thinking—I don't know. Forget it."

"You think I'm going to leave now, don't you? That I'm only here because of the baby?"

Rose glanced over her shoulder. "Please. You're going to wake her up."

"Everyone thinks I'm the bad guy. What the hell did I do? I'm here, aren't I?" He turned around, massaging the back of his neck. "I don't know how everything got so screwed up."

In a less friendly tone, she said, "Look, are you sure you don't want to get out just for a little while? Get some air. Walk around the block. I'll stay here with her."

"I was a happy, fun-loving guy, on top of the world. Now look at me."

He was feeling sorry for himself? After leaving Blair to face everything on her own for months? She wanted to slap him. "This is a lot harder for her than it is for you," she snapped. "She has to—" She cut herself off. *She has to deliver her baby tomorrow.*

It wasn't supposed to be this way.

He raised his bloodshot eyes. They were shining with tears.

She took a moment to control her own emotions. Whatever he said, whatever he'd done or not done, this was no time to judge him. Admittedly she *had* thought this would be it for him, that he might even be relieved. Not swamped with grief, shaken and weak and afraid.

So, maybe she was wrong about him.

She touched his arm, struggled for words. "I'll go to the store to get you some food. Fill up your freezer with easy meals. You probably won't be up for cooking for a while."

Deflating, he sank against the counter, face in his hands. "Food," he said, voice muffled. "As if either one of us is hungry."

"You will be." She left him and went into the living room.

Blair was stretched out on the couch, her slight form nearly invisible under a pink checkered comforter. Rose waited a moment to see if she stirred. Satisfied that she and John hadn't woken her up, she headed back out to her car.

Mark. She'd almost forgotten him. For a couple of minutes, lost in Blair and John's loss, she'd forgotten about the smoothie of happiness and fear churning in her stomach after their night together.

She stared at his car. He'd left without saying goodbye—but she'd told him they had to hurry.

Did he even have her cell number? She didn't have his. He could be sitting in there waiting for her to call the house. Or show up to work tomorrow. Or...

Rose put her car keys in her pocket and walked up to Mark and Trixie's front door. She'd make it quick, explain why, with Blair going into the hospital tomorrow, she wouldn't be able to see him for a few days, maybe longer. This was going to be a rough time for Blair and she had to be there for her. And perhaps even for John.

Trixie answered the door, her face unusually serious. "Oh! Hello." She had a towel over her shoulder and a dog in one hand. Not the bug-eyed, tongue-happy Zeus, but a sleek little Chihuahua in an orange sweatshirt.

Belatedly Rose realized she had no idea if Trixie knew Mark had been with her last night. She wasn't smiling in that giddy way she had earlier. Just polite. "Sorry to bother you," Rose said, her mind stumbling around for a neutral reason to be standing there. "I was wondering if Mark is home."

"He is, but..." Trixie glanced back into the house. She turned back to Rose, looking past her. "Is it your car? Do you need the cables again? I can get them for you."

"No, it's fine. I just..." Obviously he hadn't told her they'd spent the night together or she'd be dragging her inside, grinning at her, popping the champagne.

Wouldn't she?

"I just wanted to…" Rose tucked a strand of hair behind her ear. Well, this time she didn't have to lie to wiggle out of an uncomfortable situation. "I wanted to tell both of you that Blair has lost the baby," she finished, sighing deeply. "I thought you should know."

To her surprise, Trixie nodded solemnly. "Yes, Mark told me." Her mouth tightened. "It's awful. I'm about to cook a casserole for them. Pathetic, but at least they won't starve."

So, Mark knew already, but where was he? "I was just about to go to the store. I don't know what else to do."

"She's going into the hospital tomorrow?"

Rose nodded.

"Let us know if there's anything we can do. Anything. Even if it means trapping Ellen in the basement."

That surprised a smile out of her. "I will. Thanks." Rose hesitated, more confused than ever about Mark—*where is he?* —then said goodbye and went back to her car.

17

ROSE WENT TO WELLYNELLY MONDAY morning, wishing she were with Blair at the hospital, but she'd been asked to stay away.

"John and I need to be alone," Blair had said, and Rose had to respect that. Even if she and John didn't have a bad history together, it would be hard to have too many people around. She talked to John next, making him promise to call or text with any news, any requests, anything at all. They were starting the induction at nine, less than an hour from now.

When Rose got to her desk she found a yellow note on her keyboard folded into a tiny square. She unfolded it, some of her worry lifting as she read.

Come see me?

—The Count

Smiling, she tucked it into her purse, then touched up her lipstick. Glancing around the cubicles, nodding hello at the people she'd gotten to know, she walked to Mark's office. After all the pain with Blair losing the baby, it felt really good to have this life-affirming gift. A little fling, a little fun. She could handle it.

Mark was a decent guy. When she'd vowed not to have any more sex without a long-term relationship, she was imagining a guy like John. A user, a ladies' man, a mimbo. The kind of guy who would have sex all night and then pretend not to know you in front of his friends.

Mark wasn't like that.

She opened the door slowly without knocking, peeked around the corner.

"Rose." He stood up. "Hey."

"Hey."

He stared at her, glanced over her shoulder. "Got my note?"

"Count von Count, I presume?"

Smiling, he approached, sticking his hands in the pockets of his dark jeans. He wore a crisp white shirt, open at the throat, the sleeves pushed up.

Caught up in the vision of his muscled forearms, Rose stood in the doorway and stared. Every time she saw him, he got better looking. That Indiana Jones resemblance was no joke. Her heart was fluttering around in her chest like a trapped butterfly.

Hey, this is Mark. Just Mark.

"I was thinking Dracula, but *Sesame Street* is better," he said, moving closer. "I always related to that dude. Very OCD with the 'von, two, tree.'" He strode over and pushed the door closed behind her shoulder. He was only inches away.

She tilted her head back, moistening her lips, waiting for him to kiss her. It seemed longer than twenty-four hours since she'd touched him.

But he didn't kiss her. "Speaking of numbers, give me your phone number, woman," he said, pulling out his phone and walking back to his desk. "I had no way to reach you."

Rose watched his retreating back, let out a breath. She

went over and picked up a stress ball on his desk, trying to calm herself the heck down. Back to reality.

"Where were you on Sunday?" She tried to keep her voice casual. "I talked to your mom at the door but I didn't see you."

His annoyance was sudden and sincere. "You came to the house?"

"Yes. Just—I talked to your mom. I didn't know what to say about us, so I told her about Blair and left." She watched his face, more confused than ever by the emotions twisting his face. First he was angry, then… uncomfortable.

"She's at the hospital right now," Rose added when he didn't say anything.

"Poor Blair. I—we're next door if she needs anything. My mother's in touch." He ran his hand through his hair. "Sorry about Sunday, by the way. I don't know what happened. Maybe I was in the bathroom, and she didn't want to embarrass me."

Trixie hadn't shown herself to be discreet or sensitive thus far, Rose thought. Out loud she said, "I should be at the hospital with Blair. I keep thinking I should be there."

He gave her a sympathetic look. "John's with her, right?"

"He'd better be."

"She knows your number if she needs you." He held up his phone and looked at her expectantly, finger poised over the screen. "Unlike me."

She managed a smile. "So you can call me and then run away?"

"So I can call you when my boss is about to find me naked in his house and thus I'm speeding away from it as quickly as possible."

"I'm allowed to have guests," she said.

"Relationships between coworkers are always bad."

"I didn't get that impression from Sylly."

"Really?" His eyes narrowed. "What did he say to you?"

"Nothing. He seems like a fun, good-natured guy. I doubt he's going to get all pearl-clutchy about people sleeping together."

"Regular people, no problem. WellyNelly people, yes."

"Come on."

"Really."

Rose rolled her eyes. "Please. I've been here a month, and I already know about three office romances." She counted on her fingers. "Von, two, *tree* office romances. They aren't even sneaking around, either."

"Well, they should."

She didn't buy it. "Since when are you so uptight about the rules?"

"I'm very uptight. Look at me." He held out his arms. "Geek, remember?"

"Not about authority. For instance, you never leave your door open. We get an email every week about that."

"An exception."

"That proves the rule," she said.

He looked at the door again. Stepping close to her, he lowered his voice. "I never would've run out like that if it weren't for Sylly."

She looked into his eyes. "At least you put the pillows back together." She crossed her arms over her chest. "How did you manage that, by the way?"

"Strong visual memory," he said. "So… Rose…" He raised his eyebrows.

"Yes?"

"Have you forgiven me for taking off on Sunday? I swear, leaving you was the last thing I wanted to do."

He had such a sweet face. Gentle, soulful eyes. "There was a lot happening that day." She didn't want to be a pushover, but she didn't want to be unreasonable either. "Couldn't you have hacked my phone number from the WellyNelly database?"

"You only gave them the old house number. I checked."

She smiled. "Okay, okay." She went over to the desk and wrote down her cell number.

As she handed him the paper, he wrapped his hand around her fingers, gazed into her eyes. "Without my vampire suit, I'm not sure how to do this."

"Dial?" She stepped closer, lowered her voice. "It's all about finding the right buttons."

His jaw tightened. "I want to see you again."

"You do?"

"I do. How about tonight?"

Her skin tingled at the idea. She closed his eyes, let herself enjoy the way he was stroking the tender skin between her knuckles. Heat pooled between her thighs.

Then she remembered. Opening her eyes, she squeezed his hand and stepped back. "I'd like that, but we'll have to wait a few days. Blair, you know? I want to be there."

"Right. Of course."

"They might not want me around, but if she calls, I don't want to be, you know—"

"I understand." He stuck his hands in his pockets again. "Tomorrow?"

"That still might be too soon. I just don't know how it'll be for her. She might still be—"

"Sure, of course. I'm being selfish."

"It's sweet."

"It is?" He brightened.

"Yeah. Nice to be wanted, you know."

He shot her a smoldering look. "Oh, you are that."

She felt herself flush all over. Unbalanced, she couldn't think of a snappy reply.

"Will you—" He looked down at the floor, then back at her. "If you want to see me later, when you come to the house to see Blair, I'll be there. Just knock on the door."

"All right."

"Or wave. Sigh loudly. Glance in my direction. I'll be there, ready and waiting."

She had to smile. "Okay."

"And willing," he said, not smiling back.

God, she wanted him. Her mouth was dry. "Maybe we could have lunch together tomorrow," she offered.

"Here?"

"I thought we'd go out for a burrito or something," she said. "The taqueria down the street is popular. We could walk there."

"Let's wait until we can have dinner. Out of town, far away from this place. That would be better."

Better?

"When you feel okay about leaving Blair."

Out of town?

"All right. I'll let you know. Maybe this weekend."

"Right." He strode away to the door and pulled it open. "I hope Blair is all right. My mom really wants to do something to help. I've got her tied to her piano with duct tape, figuring they need some time without a crazy busybody neighbor lady butting her nose in."

"Good old duct tape."

His eyes met hers. "Yeah. Though she'll probably make them another casserole."

Too many emotions were spinning around inside her to deal with the way her chest squeezed when he looked at her like that. "Food is good." With a smile and a wave, she walked away, dwelling on how he hadn't wanted to have lunch together. Was she just being too sensitive because of what had happened with John?

Probably. One of the pitfalls of starting one relationship when you hadn't recovered from another.

If it was a relationship.

Too much to worry about right now. She went back to her desk to work and wait for news about her friend.

And to cool the hell off.

❧

"I'M FINE," BLAIR SAID.

It was early Saturday afternoon, one week after losing the baby. Blair had been in the hospital for almost two days but insisted she was fine: John took off work and was with her every second. They were closer than ever. She was fine, she said, over and over.

Rose hadn't been surprised at all when Blair called Friday afternoon, weeping. Rose's tentative plans with Mark to catch a movie—and each other afterward—were put on hold. She went over to the house and watched reality TV with Blair until one in the morning. If John minded her being there, he didn't let on, just made an extra batch of popcorn and kept quiet.

Rose did glance at the house next door on her way home, and again when she drove up that morning, but she didn't see Mark.

After sitting with Rose over a lunch she didn't eat, Blair was pouring potting soil into a recycled yogurt container at the kitchen sink. Her hair was pulled up into a high, sleek ponytail; her face pale but carefully made up with concealer, eyeliner, lipstick.

Rose didn't believe her for a second. "You don't have to be fine, you know."

"We named her Catherine," Blair said quietly, not meeting her eyes. "After my grandmother. Even though she was barely three months—" Her voice caught.

"It's a beautiful name," Rose said, feeling her own throat tighten.

"It was just one of those things, the doctor said. They don't know why she—she didn't—" Blair cleared her throat. "A huge percentage of pregnancies end in miscarriage. You just don't know about it because you don't even know you're pregnant."

But you did. "I've heard that." Rose put her hand on her back and stroked gently.

"So, you don't have to keep coming over here to make sure I'm all right," Blair said. "I'm totally fine." She patted the soil into the container, checked the drain holes she'd punched at the bottom, set it on a saucer to catch the water.

"Okay."

Blair turned to her. "You don't believe me."

"Sorry. No."

"What can I say to make you believe me?"

Rose looked at the pot. "What are you growing?"

"What?"

"In the pot."

Frowning, Blair looked down. "I don't know yet." Her lip quivered. She poked her finger into the soil.

Rose put an arm around her. "Let's get out of here. You've been stuck in this house long enough," she said. "We can drive down to College Avenue for coffee. Maybe stop into the bakery for that sourdough you love."

"I should be here when John gets back from the gym."

"Why?"

Blair frowned. "I just should."

"We'll leave a note."

Dropping her hands to her sides, dusting the floor with potting soil, Blair stared off into the foggy distance out the window. "I wonder if he'll leave me a note."

"When?"

"When *he* leaves."

Rose felt so powerless. "You don't know yet what's going to happen."

Blair turned to her. "Thank you."

"For what?"

"For not just saying, 'Of course he'll stay,' when you don't know either."

"This isn't all up to him, you know."

Blair turned on the faucet to wash her hands. Dark water with flecks of white pooled around the drain. "He's kind of a key player."

Rose watched her bring the soap to a lather. "Have you talked at all?"

"He says he loves me."

"That's good." Rose paused. "Right?"

"What else can he say?"

Nudging her in the arm, Rose, said, "I can imagine a lot worse." She turned off the water, handed Blair a towel. "'Yo bitch, get the hell out,' for instance."

Blair smiled. "That might be a relief."

"You're such an Eeyore. My goodness."

"His mother called this morning. She practically threatened to disinherit him if we break up."

"Really?" Rose shook her head. "She's one scary lady. I might still be with John if she'd been gunning for it. She's relentless."

"You'd—what do you mean?"

"Oh, Blair, I'm just kidding."

"Do you wish you were still with John?"

"Of course not." Rose hung the damp dish towel on the refrigerator handle, smiling because, for the first time, she knew it was absolutely true. Nothing like a long night of hot sex with somebody else to reset yourself.

"His mother says you do. She thinks I should refuse to let you in the house." Blair said this with a hint of a smile. "I told her to piss off."

Rose laughed. "Really?"

She nodded. "A few days ago."

"I wish I'd been here."

"John was. He made her leave. She calls but hasn't been back in person since."

"That's great."

"John says the best thing about it is we can blame it on the drugs," Blair said. "I was loaded up with painkillers."

Rose smiled. "I think maybe I've been too hard on him. He's not a bad guy." Then she saw the wrinkle form between Blair's eyebrows, and she wished she hadn't said anything. "Not that I want him for myself, because I don't."

Blair nodded, but looked unconvinced.

Because of the miscarriage, Rose hadn't told her about her night with Mark. Not knowing where that fling was headed, she wasn't sure she wanted to talk about it now, but she couldn't stand the idea of Blair—and John—thinking she was pining over him.

"I've moved on." Rose cleared her throat, smiling. "Get your shoes on and I'll tell you about it."

Blair's eyes lit up with the first real happiness she'd shown all week. "It's Mark, isn't it? Oh, I knew it!"

Rose walked away into the foyer and slipped on her jacket, wrapped a jade-green angora scarf around her neck. For some reason Blair's enthusiasm bothered her. Not just because she wasn't sure if there was any future with Mark, but because perversely, she felt bad for him: the woman he really wanted was thrilled he'd found someone else.

Maybe she shouldn't have told Blair anything. "Please don't read too much into it. It was just one night."

Blair followed her, smiling, and wriggled her feet into her Crocs. "When?"

"Halloween."

Face falling, she nodded. "Oh. When I was—"

"Yeah." Rose sighed.

"I'm so glad I didn't call you. I almost did."

"No, you should have. You're more important than… what I was doing."

"I bet Mark is going to be very important."

Rose rolled her eyes. "It would make things easier with John's mother."

"That's not why I'm saying it. He's sweet. You can help him out of his shell." Blair looked around, grabbed a black trench coat she'd had since their freshman year at Cornell.

"I'm taking you shopping," Rose said, wrinkling her nose at the faded, wrinkled garment. "That coat needs to be retired."

Blair tightened the belt with a jerk. "When did you decide you were interested in him?"

"I'm still not sure I am."

"Oh, poor guy. Don't say that." She opened the front door. "Let's go to that café near the Chinese place. You can tell me all about it."

"As if I ever tell you the really good parts."

They stepped outside. Blair locked the door, took in a deep breath, still smiling. "I'm so happy for you," she said. "And him. He seemed to relax around you."

"And get nervous around *you*."

"That doesn't mean anything. It's you he likes."

Just as they were walking to Rose's car, John's car pulled up on the side of the narrow road, his wheels crunching in the gravel shoulder.

Knowing Blair would want to talk to him, Rose bit back a sigh and stood next to her, waiting for her to change her mind.

"Still want to go out for coffee?" Rose asked.

Obviously unsure, Blair's gazed followed John as he strode over to them. He was still in his workout clothes. "I want to hear about Mark," she said finally.

"What about Mark?" John asked, glancing at the house next door. He bent down to kiss Blair on the cheek.

Rose groaned inwardly. She considered lying, but though *she* was skilled in the arts of prevarication, Blair was not.

So she said, "I slept with him," and pointed at the car. "Blair and I were just going out for coffee."

"Are you shitting me?"

"No, it's a popular beverage," Rose said.

Blair gave her an apologetic look, took John's arm. "How was your workout?"

He turned to her, his face softening. "Fine. You didn't answer my text."

"Sorry, I was talking to Rose."

"About Mark." He looked at Rose. "Seriously. What happened to Mark?"

"Seriously. I slept with him."

"Does he know this?" John asked, then laughed at his own joke.

"What's so funny?"

"Sorry, sorry." He held up a hand. "Stranger things have happened, I guess. Maybe I just needed a laugh."

"Why is that so funny?" Rose asked through her teeth.

"Please, guys. I'm sorry I said anything," Blair said.

"Maybe John and I are the ones who need to go out for coffee," Rose said. "Clear the air."

"I said I was sorry." He put an arm around Blair. "It's been a rough week."

"You don't need to apologize," Rose said in the calmest voice she could manage, "I just want you to explain why it's funny to you that I would sleep with Mark."

"More funny that Mark would sleep with you," he said, then quickly added, "with anyone, Rose. With anyone. God, obviously *I* can imagine why somebody would want to sleep with you." He looked down at Blair. "Maybe you should go inside for a minute."

"I think Mark is sweet," Blair said, not moving.

"Of course he's sweet." Sighing, John gazed heavenward. "But girls don't usually go for sweet."

"I happen to *love* sweet," Rose said.

He crossed his arms over his chest. "Since when?"

"You don't know me very well, John."

"I know—" he stopped, looked at Blair, softened his voice. "Please, I think it's best if Rose and I hash this out on our own."

Blair lifted her chin. "I'll wait in the car." She took out her keys, headed for her Toyota. "My car. I'm not some delicate princess, guys. I can listen to conversations and drive and everything."

Rose waited until she had the car door open. "Thanks, Blair."

"Yeah, thanks, sweetie," John added.

She slammed it.

Rose turned on John. "What do you know?"

He moved closer. "I know what turns you on," he said softly.

"Which is you and nobody else, I take it?"

"A guy *like* me, anyway. Mark's a great guy, but he's not your type."

"This is a fascinating analysis," she said. "Why would a great guy not be my type?"

He scoffed. "You had a problem with how *I* didn't want to go out together. That guy doesn't even like to go out by himself."

"We went out. To San Francisco for Halloween. It was his idea."

"There you go."

She clenched her jaw. "What the hell does that mean?"

"Even a hermit has to let loose once in a while. Good day for it. Easy to disappear."

"You don't know him."

"I know you. You need an alpha male. A top dog. A leader." He exhaled, looked back at his house. "Somebody who can go out into the world and take charge."

"I think you've got somebody else on your mind," she said. "I've never needed anyone—or wanted to need anyone—that way."

He seemed to mull that over. Then he shrugged. "It's just hard to believe that if I wasn't strong enough for you, Mark would be."

"I don't need superman, John. I just need a man who's willing—no, proud—to be seen with me."

His only answer was to roll his eyes and go back into the house.

Rose stood there, her own words reverberating in her head. *That's what I need.*

She glanced over at Mark's house. Interesting how he never came out to see her when she was obviously standing right there in his front yard. Her car had been there for hours. She and John had even made a scene.

Smoothing her hair back from her face, she slowly made her way over to the passenger side of Blair's car and got in. Slowly, giving him a chance to come out and say hello.

Not slowly enough, apparently.

Blair backed out into the road and they drove away.

18

ONDAY MORNING, MARK STARED OUT the window of his office, wondering how he was going to get into Rose's bed again. He understood why she'd canceled their date Friday night and didn't even try to call on Saturday when he saw her car next door.

Sunday was a series of missed connections; he had promised the neighbor kid a couple hours of math tutoring in the morning, and his mother needed a ride out to a nursery in Lafayette where he lifted approximately four tons of perennials, organic mulch, and a small thorny tree into her SUV. By the time he called Rose in the late afternoon, she said she was doing her laundry.

That didn't sound good. He thought he was being considerate, giving her space to deal with Blair, but somehow…

He'd screwed up.

His mother was worried about him, thinking he was torn up about Blair. That day he fainted in the living room had given her the entirely wrong idea.

His aversion to blood was well-known, but this was the first time he'd fainted at the mere thought of it. His mother, who had guessed earlier he'd been interested in Blair, now assumed he was having some kind of romantic, sexual, and ethical breakdown over her.

"Give it time," she told him. "Don't feel guilty for hoping this is your opportunity to be with her. Or even for hoping it would happen."

The more he protested, the more she believed he was in love.

He was certainly feeling preoccupied in that department, but it wasn't that, and not for Blair.

Friendly lust? Affectionate sexual obsession?

The thought of Rose was bright, colorful, hot, distracting, made him useless for anything. Last night she'd let his calls go to voice mail. He couldn't put anything in an email, not at work. And the cubicles were no place to have a private conversation, not with the legendary Mark Johnson.

Maybe he was just too stupid to realize she wasn't interested. He'd had his shot and blown it. Part of him thought, if only she'd let him use all his special skills and pleasure her properly, she'd be in his office right now, door locked, naked, sitting on his desk with her legs open.

He pressed his forehead onto the glass. He'd like that. A lot.

He couldn't just let her get away, not that easily. No, he'd have to throw himself at her in person. Going to her house seemed stalkerish, but the office was a fishbowl.

All he wanted was to be with her, yet somehow he'd managed to convey the opposite impression.

Maybe he should beg. Appeal to her conscience. She'd always tolerated him, even when he was mooning over her roommate—

Blair. Rose had been with her a lot this week. She was probably exhausted from all that giving, loving, and understanding; she didn't have the patience to deal with some dork who'd never been any good at casual dating.

He'd have to trick her.

Relieved to have a plan, he combed his hair back with his fingers and strode out into the hall, devising his scheme as he counted the cubicle openings—seven, eight, nine, turn right—scheme some more—one, two, three, four, *there*. On the left.

She was at her computer, her back to him. He took a moment to admire the way her bottom filled out the space between the backrest and the seat.

"I need to see you." He made his tone serious. Brusque.

She swiveled around, eyes wide. "Mark."

Frowning at her screen as though it contained the problem that was consuming him, he bent over her shoulder, inhaled the garden breeze she seemed to carry around with her, and braced his hands on either side of her keyboard. The one he'd bought for her. "No, yours isn't going to work. I'll have to show you on mine."

"Show me what?"

"I'm changing around the UI. Come into my office. I'll show you."

"Rick's doing the interface for the women's site. I just met with him this morning. It's going fine."

He shook his head, lips in a flat line, trying to look too brilliant to explain. "This is for later. Long-term stuff, but it's… important. I need the feedback from somebody on your team right away or I'll lose a month's work."

His serious tone finally caught her. She stood up. "Okay." *Yessss.*

Frowning hard so he didn't smile and do a little dance, Mark led her through the beige carpet labyrinth to his office. He shoved his hands into his pockets to stop himself from touching her.

He closed the door behind her. Finally. Now he had a chance to look commanding. He'd show her the software he was working on, talk shop, get her to remember how well they got along, gracefully maneuver her into accepting a dinner date.

She stood in the middle of his office, arms crossed, head down, cheeks pink.

That last detail was hopeful. He moved over to her, dipped his head to look into her face. "How are you doing, Rose? You've kind of had a rough weekend, haven't you?"

When her blue eyes looked up into his, his lungs exhaled a breath and refused to take another. Vivid memories of the taste, feel, and smell of her washed over him. The way she smiled. The soft moans she made when she came.

He hadn't intended to kiss her, he really hadn't, but his hands came up to capture her face, and his mouth was on hers, impatient, demanding, furious.

How could she ignore him after the night they'd had together? How could she?

At first she tensed, but then her lips parted for him and she sighed into his mouth, slid her hands around his neck.

This. This was what he wanted.

She was what he wanted. Not tonight or next week, not as a memory, *now*.

Holding her chin, he kissed his way up her nose, across her cheekbones, over to the pulse on her neck that made her shiver in his arms.

"I'm sorry about the weekend." He dragged his mouth over to her mouth again, nibbled her plump bottom lip. "I didn't want to bother you. Make demands."

"This kind of bothering," she said, arching into him, "is fine."

"Thank God." He slid a hand down from her shoulder,

stroked the underside of one delicious breast, kneaded the hardening nipple through her sweater.

Her mouth, hot and fearless, kissed its way over his jaw to his ear. His hands roamed over her body, reclaiming the curves he'd explored Halloween night. Now, here in one of her work sweaters and a long, stretchy skirt, her hair in a ponytail, her feet in the silver sneakers she liked to wear, she was even hotter. Hotter because she was herself.

It was his favorite sweater, too, the pink one with the belt that tied on the side like a present. His judo-trained fingers had the belt falling open in two seconds. There was another layer of something silky. He shoved it up, out of the way, found skin.

"On my desk," he said.

"Mark…" She shook her head, laughing like it was a joke.

He kissed her to show her there was nothing funny about her sexy body and what he was going to do with it. His tongue pushed between her teeth, swept into her mouth. She melted under him. He led her over to his desk, kept pushing, kissing her as their momentum forced her to sit on the edge.

It was her perfume. It reached inside him and flipped a switch. Nothing could stop him from what he was about to do.

"Does the door lock?" she asked vaguely, eyes never leaving him, as though it didn't really matter.

At first he wasn't going to answer. He pulled her skirt over her knees and slipped his hand between her thighs before some better part of himself made him reply. "No."

He trembled, heart pounding in his ears, waiting for her to give him permission to continue. Her leg was hot silk under his palm.

Then she spread her knees wider. "Be quick."

Hands shaking, he pulled a condom out of his pocket. "Not a problem."

"I'll do it." She watched him unzip his fly, then looked up at him, held his gaze. "I could go down on you."

He closed his eyes, clenched his jaw. "I'd like that, but not here." He shuddered as she slipped the latex over the tip, rolled it down. "I want to be inside you."

Nibbling his lower lip, she reached down between her legs. "I'm wearing boy shorts. They're loose. Just—yeah. Closer."

She was wearing boxers? No, they were stretchy, satiny, and oh God, she was wet. He felt her nails dig into his lower back. He pushed past the fabric into her, his knees already starting to shake.

He thrust inside of her, stifling a moan on her shoulder.

"Oh," she gasped. Then, more quietly, "*Oh. God.*"

He'd never believed his real life could be this good. Her legs lifted, hooked around his hips. Her arms wound around his shoulders. She moaned and gasped and was soft, responsive, tight.

He slid out, pushed in, went as fast as he wanted, not even remembering she'd asked him to be quick, just not able to do anything else. His body was in control, taking her, his famously powerful brains shut down long ago.

"Harder," she gasped.

Her voice destroyed any thread of rational control he'd maintained until then. Bending her over the desk, he slanted his mouth over hers, seconds from coming, ashamed he wouldn't be able to slow down just a little. Again and again, harder, deeper, each little noise in her throat making him go faster.

And then he came and he thought he would die, that he was dying, dead.

He couldn't see. His knees buckled, his heart hammered against his ribs. Another second before he could breathe.

"Someone's at the door!" she whispered furiously, shoving him away, rolling out from under him while she pulled her shirt down. "Sit behind your desk. Fast!"

He zipped up, barely able to manage the button, and did what he was told.

This time he heard the knock at the door.

The condom. He pushed to his feet and peered over his desk, afraid it was in a puddle on the floor.

Rose was sitting in a chair on the opposite corner of the room, legs crossed. "I took care of it."

The door opened and Sylly strode in, an open laptop balanced in one hand, his voice brusque. "Morning. So sorry to interrupt." He barely glanced at Rose before giving Mark a very bad look.

Rose got up, hurried to the door. Her sweater was tied but uneven, one belt hanging twice as low as the other.

Afraid to look at her because of what might show in his eyes, Mark rearranged his keyboard on his desk, knowing he should care about the suppressed fury on Sylly's face.

Instead of being so damn pleased with himself.

A LITTLE UNSTEADY ON HER FEET, ROSE MADE HER WAY to the women's restroom. She was furious with herself.

Was a quickie more important than her job?

Her reputation?

Anybody could've come in. Sylly almost did. How would she ever be able to face him if he walked in on her having sex in an unlocked office in the middle of the day? He'd be right to conclude she was disrespectful, irresponsible, and foolish to risk such a thing.

She yanked a handful of brown paper towels out of the dispenser near the sinks and wrapped the condom inside before dropping it in the trash can. Then she washed her hands and locked herself in the farthest stall.

Her underwear was bunched up around her hips. She smoothed it down, fixed her sweater, and admitted to herself how disappointed she was they'd had to stop.

But how could she have let them start?

It wasn't Mark's fault. She never said no, never pushed him away. He might have a job death wish, but she didn't. Being the programmer wonderboy might make him immune to criticism, but she was just a recently hired, entry-level wannabe. A nobody. As dispensable as that condom.

She stayed in the stall for another minute, lecturing herself, then washed her hands again and went back to her desk.

Well, at least he'd shown he was willing to be seen with her. She tried to laugh but couldn't.

She'd screwed up. She'd had flings, some in crazier places than this, but she'd never come close to risking her livelihood over it. How could she? For *Mark*?

Staring at the floating orbs of her screen saver, she considered the possibility that Mark was far more dangerous than she'd thought.

At the very least, she'd have to stay away from him at work. Where would they do it next—the massage table in the break room?

Her phone was ringing. She glanced at the screen before she picked up. An outside call.

"Oh, Rose! I'm so glad I found you," a cheerful woman's voice said. "I didn't know your last name, but the gal at the front desk said there was only one of you. Rose, I mean. Well, that's obvious."

Lord, it was his mother. Rose sat down, blushing as though Trixie could see her. "It's me. What can I do for you?"

"Well, I wish I could say, 'Nothing, it's what I'd like to do for you,' but I'll be honest and admit it's probably more for our pleasure than yours."

Rose wondered if it was even remotely possible that Trixie knew what she'd just been doing with her son. Her timing was just too perfect. "Yes?" she asked, trying to sound casual, not tense and slutty.

"Saturday afternoon we're having a special—no, not special, I don't want you to feel like it's intimate or anything, though it won't be big or anything like that—anyway, we're having a picnic." Trixie took a deep breath. "It'll be Mark, of course, and Liam and Bev, maybe April and her latest boyfriend. I was hoping you'd join us."

"Oh." Her mind raced through a list of potential excuses. She wasn't prepared to be with Mark and his family, not knowing what they knew about her, what they expected. Did Trixie know Mark had spent the night with her? She didn't seem to.

"I've invited your friend Blair, too, and John, of course, but given what they've been through this week, I hope they don't feel obligated to do anything they'd rather not do," Trixie said. "Please pass that message along to her, will you? It's only if she's feeling up to it. We'll have good food, drinks, and our favorite spot at the park. Nobody will bother her with nosy questions, not even me. I promise."

A vivid image of diverse, hours-long social discomfort flashed before Rose's eyes. Hoping she had something already on her calendar, she pulled it up on her phone and scrolled through the days. Blank, blank, blank. "A picnic, you said? But... it's November."

"Shoot, I was afraid of that. You don't want to come."

"No, no, I'm just—you caught me off guard."

"Without an excuse. No, I'm sorry. You don't have to think of one. I want you to know you can always be honest with me. I'm very thick-skinned. You never knew my late husband, but you'd realize I'd have to be to love him as dearly as I did." She hesitated. "Unfortunately for Mark, he was such a sweet boy, so brilliant, so sensitive—his father just didn't understand him. He was very critical, you see, didn't always show his love in the easiest ways. I think it's taken Mark a few extra years to grow up because of it."

In spite of her discomfort to be trusted with Mark's secrets, Rose hung on every word. "He doesn't talk about him much."

"I'm surprised he's mentioned him at all."

Sexually graphic memories flooded Rose's brain. "A little bit, I suppose," she said, dropping her head into her hand, biting her lip.

"Well. In case you change your mind, it's Saturday, two o'clock, at Redwood Park in Oakland, right off 13. We'll have a barbecue, a few picnic tables, the dogs, a ball or two. And the cake, of course."

As if she didn't feel guilty enough. "Cake? Is it someone's birthday?"

"Oh! Didn't I say? That's why I had to call you directly instead of having Mark invite you," she said. "He's been dreading it all year, I think. I wanted to make it as distracting as possible."

"It's Mark's birthday," Rose said, realizing it was hopeless, she was trapped. "A big one?"

"Let's just say it ends in a zero. Of course, he has no idea

I'm doing this. He'd never come if he *knew*." Her laughter bubbled over the line.

Rose pictured Mark's miserable face, thrown into the center of attention on a day he'd rather ignore.

Would make it a happy birthday for him to publicly acknowledge her as his romantic interest?

Or the opposite?

Time to find out, I suppose, she thought. "What should I bring?" she asked, typing the date into her calendar.

19

"THAT'S WHAT YOU'RE GOING TO wear?" Liam asked him.

Mark got into his brother's SUV and slammed the door. "I'm not a fashion designer like you, Liam. I don't need to look pretty to go hiking."

Liam didn't back out of the driveway. He kept scowling at Mark's sweatshirt. "Not only is it butt-ugly, stained, and too small, but it's *mine*. When did you steal it?"

"You *gave* it to me."

Liam stared, shook his head. "The last time I gave you any of my old clothes, you were in, like, elementary school."

"So? It's stretchy."

"It barely covers your elbows."

"Will you shut up and drive? What the hell do you care what I wear?"

Liam killed the engine, crossed his arms over his chest. "Do you let me buy inferior consumer electronics? Run lame software on my computer? Hell—you gave me a hard time about my new computer's *keyboard*."

"You love the new one I got you, admit it," Mark said.

"I only said that to get you to shut up."

"Fine. Give it back to me. I'll let Mom use it." Mark tightened the seat belt, looked straight ahead.

"My point is, you have professional standards and so do I," Liam said. "Change. Mom said you went shopping recently. Wear that. Something that doesn't make me embarrassed to be seen with you."

"We're *hiking*. Just because you were in the Olympics a million years ago doesn't mean photographers are still following you around."

"We'll still be in Oakland. I know people here. I've got a fitness wear company to represent, dude. Go get something else, or I'll put you in the latest Fite the Man compression tee." He jerked a thumb toward the backseat. "With matching pink compression shorts. I've got a box of samples with me."

Knowing his brother would never stop bitching about it, Mark gave up and went in to change, came back out in khaki shorts and a dark green polo shirt.

"I look like a retired golfer," he said, slamming the door.

Liam backed up into the street, grinning. "But a handsome one."

"Bite me."

His brother just laughed. Patted his knee. "And you *are* getting older," he crooned.

Mark scowled out at the bay, hazy blue and dotted with boats in the distance. "Next year I'm flying to Maui for my birthday."

"Lots of retired golfers there, too."

"Why did I agree to this?" Mark muttered. "Right. Because you said it would stop Mom from throwing me a party at the house."

"And to see if your leg muscles have atrophied completely, living your life glued to a computer. If I weren't much happier being with Bev, I'd be over here every weekend making you take that lazy ass for a run."

"Speaking of ass, I'm going to kick yours today. I may be getting older, but I'm not as bad as you, old man."

They continued with this loving brotherly banter all the way down the hills and onto the highway. Mark's defensive jabs were halfhearted. Most of his mental processing power was engaged with the mess he'd made of his relationship with Rose. And his job.

Sex in the office was fun for the three minutes it was happening, but he was still reeling from the ten minutes afterward during which his boss had ripped him a new one.

Mark had never seen Sylly so angry.

"Do you realize," Sylly had said, pacing in front of his desk, hands clasped behind his back, "if I hadn't just happened to walk over here a few minutes ago and seen—through the glass panel in the wall, Mark. You did know glass is transparent?—if I hadn't been the one to discover the little party in here, but instead, oh, Janice from HR—you do know Janice? The one with the forms and the lawyer on speed dial? And an enthusiasm for pursuing sexual harassment claims?—and if I hadn't distracted her with a rambling question about withholding taxes just a few yards away from your door, *if*—"

"*God.*" Mark braced his forehead against his fingertips. "Oh, God."

"I understand it's a new experience for you to find a woman willing to have sex with you," Sylly continued, "but if it ever happens again within this building—hell, within a hundred miles of this building, and that includes my house—I don't care if you're the founding genius or my old friend, your ass is grass."

Mark looked up. "You can't—I understand, right now, you're upset—"

He lowered his voice to a cold whisper. "Can't?"

"Nothing here, yeah, of course," Mark said, "but in our private lives—"

"Private? Where have you been? There's no such thing as 'private' anymore." Sylly rubbed his face with both hands. "I'd have to fire Rose, too. Don't you see? Every move we make is being audited and measured right now. We can't have a record of hiring our girlfriends or wannabe girlfriends. As much as I like her, as much as her team seems to think she's a good fit for WellyNelly, I'd escort her to the front door myself. Right after you. And I'd probably have to resign, too, since I'm up to my neck in personal ties to both of you."

"That wouldn't be right. I'm the one—"

"Exactly. So hands off. Got it?"

Mark didn't reply. Taking his silence as agreement, Sylly nodded. "I'll send her to that conference in Sunnyvale for the rest of the week. WellyNelly will pay for her hotel so she doesn't have to commute. Maybe that'll give you time to get a grip." He looked him up and down. "With your right hand if necessary."

Then he'd stormed off and Mark hadn't spoken to him since. Rose had left for the conference, and she and Mark had only exchanged one quick, shallow message on the phone about talking this weekend.

What was he going to do? All week he'd agonized over it. It wasn't right to make her choose between him and her job— she *needed* her job. And what made him think she'd even have to think twice about which was more important to her?

He'd almost gotten her fired. He was such an asshole.

He should quit. Then he'd have a chance with her. It wasn't like he needed the money.

He'd never be able to stop the sale of WellyNelly to Big Pharma if he left, however. Sylly acted angry now, but only because he'd had his own problems keeping his zipper up; he'd forgive Mark eventually. They'd laugh about it someday.

What if he jumped ship in mid-development? The new senior software architect, right before a release?

Sylly would never forgive him. He might even get violent or litigious or worse—hurt. In their own odd, geeky way, they were friends. Just last night around three a.m. Mark realized, in the dark, after hours staring at the ceiling, Sylly was the best friend he had.

Except for Rose, a voice inside him said.

No, she was something else—and he wanted to know what.

The limitations of his experience with the opposite sex had never bothered him as much as they did now. A date here and there in college, then the disastrous collapse of his relationship with Colleen. He just didn't have the data to proceed knowledgeably.

He thought about talking to Liam about his problems, but… looking at his soon-to-be-married, photogenic, Olympic-medalist older brother only made him feel more inadequate. And he figured Liam would mock him. That's how it always was between them.

It took them fifteen minutes to reach the park, and another five to pay for parking and drive through the valley to the lot near their favorite trailhead.

Mark frowned at the clock on the dash. Half past one and the sun was bright overhead. "I still don't understand why we didn't go out this morning. You usually like to hike early."

"Bev," Liam said.

"Ah."

Grinning, Liam elaborated. "Saturday mornings are reserved for a different kind of workout now."

Mark held up a hand. "Spare me the gory details."

"Feeling faint?"

"You never get tired of hearing yourself talk, do you? All that hot air could be harnessed as an alternative energy source."

They got out of the car. "How about you?" Liam asked, shoving a water bottle into his backpack. "Anyone special in your life? Other than Mom, of course."

Mark pulled his sunglasses down over his eyes, headed out of the parking lot to the dirt path that wandered along the creek. Their favorite hike began off to the left, a sharp switchback up into the redwoods.

"I don't want to talk about it." Or her.

Liam grinned, slapped him on the back. "Going that well, huh?"

"Why did I agree to this? It's like an anti-birthday present being with you."

"You know, it gets even funnier," Liam said. He looked excessively pleased as shit about something.

Mark stopped, suspicious. "What do you mean?"

"Nothing. Let's get going."

Taking a step back, Mark held out his hand, index finger pointing between his brother's eyes. "Tell me."

"It's nothing! Jeez. Forget it."

"Why are you smiling?"

"I tried to tell you, but you told me to spare you the gory details," Liam said.

Mark relaxed. "This is about Bev?"

"Maybe." With a shrug and a glance at the line of trees high up on the ridge, Liam's smile grew. "We were just talking about having a baby, that's all."

"Bev's pregnant?"

"Not yet," Liam said, "but we've decided not to wait." The two of them followed the trail away from the parking lot. The winter rains hadn't started yet, and the creek under the foot-bridge was low, almost rocky. "None of us is getting any younger."

"That's great. Really," Mark said. "Does Mom know?"

"No, and don't tell her. If you do, I'll tell her about some single girls I know. Whether or not she's already got her eye on somebody for you. I'm sure she'd be happy for runners-up."

"Calm down, I was only asking."

"I know, I know," Liam said. "Mom's been harassing me for years. I don't want her to stress Bev out. We're not even married yet, you know? First things first."

"How's the wedding planning going?"

"My advice? Elope."

"That bad?"

"The second after you pop the question is the moment to strike," Liam said. "I'd give my left nut to be done with this by now. I should've bundled her off to Reno. When she was all gooey and romantic and thought I was perfect."

"Now she knows better?" Mark asked.

"Exactly," Liam replied, walking past a fork in the trail.

"Hey, right here. Aren't we doing the French Trail?"

"Yeah, but let's do it the other direction this time. I'm not up for that climb first thing. I'd rather take it slow today, warm up gradually," Liam said.

"You *are* getting old."

"Not the only one," Liam said with a grin.

Two minutes later, on the way to the other end of the trail, they came out into a clearing with picnic tables, public barbe-cues, and familiar people gathered around them.

"You son of a bitch," Mark said under his breath.

His brother just laughed. "Happy birthday, little brother. Mom said she invited a friend of yours. That must be her in the pink sweater." Eyes narrowing, he studied her.

Mark's molars pressed together in the back of his mouth. Liam wasn't supposed to meet Rose yet. He'd ask questions, make jokes, tell embarrassing stories. "She invited both the neighbors. Looks like only one of them came."

The group had noticed them now and was standing up, waving and calling out. "She's just one of the neighbors?" Liam asked, still studying Rose.

Mark couldn't let his brother get involved. Whatever he'd started with Rose was too precarious. "She moved out. Now we just work together." Mark started to walk toward the group in resignation. "That's all."

"You sure?"

Mark waved at his mother, avoided Liam's eyes. "Definitely."

He'd explain everything to Rose later.

"LOOK AT HIS FACE," MARK'S SISTER SAID. "HE'S TRYING to decide if he can make a run for it."

Rose almost regretted participating in the surprise. The horror on Mark's face was too genuine. *I should've warned him at least,* she thought. Although she'd been grateful to get sent out of town for a few days, knowing she'd be unlikely to keep the secret face-to-face. And she'd had other good reasons for staying away, like keeping her job, her self-respect, her peace of mind.

And her heart. She'd thought it would be safer to have a fling with such a nice guy, that she could keep it fun, friendly.

But that scene in the office hadn't been fun and friendly. It had been…

Insane.

He looked adorably uncomfortable, deceptively harmless,

but all that niceness hid an intensity that scared her. A deep part of her responded to him, connected to him, and wanted more. More, she suspected, than he was looking for from her. Sex, yes. Obviously. Frequently. But beyond that?

Rose knew she wasn't the one who made him trip over his feet, turn red, look like an idiot. *Blair* did that to him. Those were the feelings that ran deep to his heart, the romantic, emotional craving she herself was beginning to feel for him.

Whatever he felt for her, it wasn't strong enough to make him nervous—whereas she suddenly was shaky just looking at him from fifty feet away.

Be careful, Rose.

"Happy birthday!" Trixie shouted, arms raised. "Don't let him get away, Liam. Hold on to him!"

Mark's brother was a staggeringly gorgeous blond with a lanky, athletic build and an arrogant grin. Blair had told her he was an Olympic gold medalist in swimming, and she believed it; he certainly had the physique.

"He's not going anywhere," Liam said, putting a second hand on Mark's shoulder; Mark flinched.

"Happy birthday, you geezer!" his sister called. April, a curly-haired brunette who looked about seventeen but apparently was much older, had one hand in the bag of corn chips and one in the rear pocket of her boyfriend's jeans.

"I think he needs a beer," Bev said. Rose had been surprised to find out the warm, voluptuous woman engaged to Liam was also the head of Fite Fitness, the apparel company where they both worked. Bev had just inherited it, Mark had said. She looked more like the preschool teacher she'd been until recently. A down-to-earth, maternal type in yoga pants and a hoodie.

Bev went over to the end of the table and got an Anchor Steam out of the cooler, popped the cap with the opener.

Rose reached out for it. "I'll administer it."

After a slight pause, Bev handed it to her, smiling. "Tell him there's more where that came from."

Rose walked over, eyes fixed on Mark's. She handed him the bottle.

"Hi," he said, then looked down. His jaw was tight.

Poor guy. This was torture. She resisted the urge to kiss him on the cheek and embarrass him further. "Happy birthday," she said, settling for widening her grin.

"Thanks." He turned red and stepped away.

"Hi, I'm Liam." The blond Adonis cut in, held out his hand.

"Rose Devlin. Nice to meet you."

He had a firm handshake and held it a little extra, sizing her up. He had a hard, confident way about him, very unlike his brother. "You work at WellyNelly?"

"Just started," she said.

Liam raised an eyebrow. "How did my mother know to call you?"

Rose waited a moment for Mark to explain. Then another. She finally said, "I was living next door. Mark got me the job."

"Of course." Liam regarded her steadily. "Now I remember. Your friend is engaged to Ellen's son."

"Yes."

Suddenly joining them, Bev wrapped an arm around Liam's waist, pointed at the table. "I just put out the chips. We'll have steak and salad a little later." Then in a lower voice to Mark and Rose, "You should get some of the guacamole now before April and her boyfriend eat it all."

"I'll do that," Mark said, striding away.

Rose watched him go, her hand tightening over the beer bottle.

With his fiancée at his side, Liam seemed to lose interest in

Rose. "Always feeding people, aren't you?" He turned into Bev's arms, lifted her a few inches off the ground.

"Can't let the kids get cranky," she said, laughing.

"I'm a grown man. We need beer. Beer and women." He put Bev down and glanced at Rose. "Don't let Bev shove food at you. She's relentless. The more sugar the better."

"I don't force you to eat anything," Bev said.

"You would if you were strong enough, but all that crap has made you weak."

"Pfft," Bev said, rolling her eyes.

Liam turned to Rose. "Seriously, watch out for her. You'll end up eating way more than you should."

Rose's smile was no longer coming naturally. She hadn't liked the way he'd grilled her like a steak for the barbecue, and she really didn't like any comment, however oblique, about what she should eat.

And Mark had barely looked at her.

With a wave, she escaped from Liam and Bev and joined Mark at the table with his mother, sister, and her boyfriend. Mark wasn't talking to them, either, so she may have misjudged him; he was just on social overload, shoving chips into his mouth to ease the pain.

"Happy birthday," Trixie said, getting up to hug him. "Don't be cross. I had to do something."

Mouth full of avocado mash, he stared bleakly at her.

"I tried to invite Blair, too," she added in a stage whisper, patting his back. "She's just not ready yet."

"Of course she's not," he said, frowning.

She leaned in closer, patting him again. "Give her time." Then she stood up straight, smiled around at the group, obviously pleased with the party, and strode over to the grill with a wire brush in her hand.

Rose took another swig of her beer. Then another.

Blair. His mother thought he was pining over Blair.

She tried to meet his gaze, but he was making love to the guacamole.

His sister kept giving her looks, though. *She* knew.

"I like her, Mark," April said suddenly.

Mouth around the lip of the beer bottle again, Rose realized she was talking about her.

"Way to make her feel at ease," her boyfriend said. He was bald and dark-skinned, with a round, youthful face and a gold hoop in one ear. If it weren't for the North Face jacket, he'd look like a baby pirate.

"Why wouldn't it? It's not like I said I didn't like her," April said.

Mark stalked around the picnic table and said something in April's ear. She rolled her eyes at Rose and made a zipper motion across her lips.

"We haven't met," Mark said to April's boyfriend, sticking his hand back into the chip bag. "I'm Mark."

"This is Samuel, but don't bother getting to know him. We just broke up," April said.

Mark hesitated, then held up his chip to him in a salute. "Congratulations on your narrow escape."

"Hey," April said.

Samuel, who had been scowling at April, raised a bottle. "Yeah, thanks. Sorry to put a bummer on your day."

"It's all right. I was already depressed."

"The big three-oh?"

Mark nodded solemnly, drained his beer. Rose watched him look around, find the cooler, his eyes lighting up.

He returned with two beers, set them both on the table. "One for you," he said to Rose.

The first thing he'd said to her all day. "Thanks so much."

"For the record, *I* dumped *him*," April said.

"You wanted to wait until tomorrow," Samuel said. "It was my idea to go ahead and end it now."

April stole the beer out of his hand, took a sip. "What's the big hurry? We've been miserable for weeks. What's one more day?"

Samuel reached over and reclaimed his drink. "I'm not your bitch."

"That is so offensive," April said. "I can't believe I ever slept with a guy so sexist."

"Yeah? Sexist?" Samuel stood up, leaning over her, and stroked his fleece-lined chest. "'Sexy,' more like. You want one more night because you can't bear the thought of living the rest of your life without one more taste of all this, baby."

Trixie returned, dropping a bag of charcoal in the middle of the picnic table with a mushy thud. "Who wants to start the fire? I'm starving."

April popped up. "I would *love* to set something on fire."

"That'll be a first," Samuel said.

She spun to face him, eyes flashing. "I can't believe I ever had sex with you."

"Because you still can't believe you could be so lucky," Samuel replied in a low voice, moving closer to her.

"You are so full of yourself."

"You like it."

April's mouth dropped open. The rest of the group watched silently, shooting sideways glances at each other. A bowl of spiced almonds on the table caught Rose's eye; she sat down, scooped up a handful, and settled in for the rest of the show.

Mark strode away from the table to help his mother with some folding chairs. Rose stared at his long legs, remembering how they felt under her hands, strong and solid, how they flexed when he took a few minutes to bang her on his desk.

Did that really happen? Nothing in Mark's demeanor suggested it had.

She shoved another handful of almonds in her mouth, washed it down with a mouthful of beer, struggling to hide the building pain—no, *rage*, she was just enraged—inside her.

Trixie slapped her forehead. "I forgot the lighter fluid in the car. April, could you please get it for me?"

After a second, April broke her unblinking gaze on her pirate baby ex-boyfriend. "What?"

"The lighter fluid. In the Volvo. Could you get it, please?"

April looked around the table, saw they were all staring, sighed. "Fine. Yeah, I get it. I mean, I'll get it." She leaned under the table for her shoes, then gave Samuel a dark look as she put them on. "You might as well help me."

"Oh, I will," he said.

The two of them marched off in single file, April leading as fast as her rubber platform flip-flops would take her.

Mark sat down at the opposite end of the table. "I hope the presents aren't in the car. We won't be seeing them again."

"Who says we got you presents?" Liam asked.

"What he wants can't be wrapped," Trixie said.

Mark abruptly stood up. "I'll get the lighter fluid," he said. "At the store."

"Oh, what do you know?" Trixie pulled a reusable shopping bag out from under the table. "Here it is."

Mark grabbed it. "I'll get to work."

"It's your birthday," Trixie said. "You don't have to do that."

"I'd rather keep busy." Charcoal on his hip, he strode over to the barbecue.

He never looked at Rose, not once.

20

"ROSE! WAIT UP!" MARK HURRIED down the path to the parking lot, pulling the family's wheeled cooler behind him. Rose was disappearing up the path, much more sober than he was. She was hardly weaving at all, whereas he found the gentle undulation of the dirt trail underfoot to take enormous concentration.

Not even sparing a glance over her shoulder, Rose walked faster.

All right, it didn't take a high emotional IQ to see she was upset.

"Rose, please." He picked up his pace, ignored the way the cooler wobbled sideways off its wheels and dragged on the ground. "Rose!"

She did stop then but didn't turn. Her shoulders were rigid, her hands balled into fists.

Taken aback, he stopped several feet away, let the handle to the cooler slip out of his fingers.

Had Liam said something to her? He'd agonized during the picnic about taking her aside to warn her about his over-protective brother but figured her cheerful ignorance was a better smokescreen. He'd been relieved when she seemed to take his cue and not act overtly familiar with him in front of his family.

"Rose," he said, catching his breath. "I need to talk to you."

She spun around, eyes flashing like blue LEDs. "*Now* you want to talk."

"Yeah, I need to explain…"

Her hands went to her hips. Her lips pressed together.

He ran his hand through is hair. "Why I was ignoring you," he finished. The picnic was breaking up; others were certain to come down the path any minute. But she looked too angry to wait.

"Oh?" she said.

"Yes."

"You can explain?"

"Yes," he said.

Crossing her arms over her chest, she gave him a look that said, *I doubt that very much, you ugly loser.*

He glanced over his shoulder. "Let's get out of here so we can talk privately."

She shook her head and marched away. This time he didn't catch her until she was almost at her car—the car he hadn't recognized in the parking lot earlier when he'd arrived because it was so similar to half the other sedans on the road.

She slammed herself inside and started the engine.

Cursing himself for that last and second-to-last beer, Mark jogged over and put his hand on the hood of her car. She wouldn't really run over him, right? "You're overreacting!"

The look she gave him through the windshield caused him physical pain. He felt an urge to hide behind the hood to avoid the hostile rays. "I take it back," he said hastily. "You're not overreacting. I'm an idiot. Please listen to me."

She wasn't listening. When the car started to back up, he scrambled around the hood and jerked the passenger door open, thanking his luck her car was too cheap to have auto door locks as he threw himself inside.

She pushed his knee. "Hey!"

"It's just like our first date." He jerked the door shut and reached for the seat belt, breathing heavily.

Rose shoved him harder. "I don't care if it's your birthday," she said between her teeth. "Get out."

"I need a ride."

"Your mommy can drive you."

"Are you upset about the picnic?" He snapped the belt into the buckle. "Or because of what happened at the office?"

Her mouth fell open. "What *happened* at the *office?*"

He was wrong, very wrong, but not sure how to get it right again. "So," he ventured, "it's because I was kind of aloof today?"

The dam broke. "You didn't even talk to me! You were too busy having a carb binge."

"That *is* it." He let out a long breath. "I can explain."

"Sure you can, buddy." She laughed mirthlessly. "You lost me at *no hello*, you understand? You could've made small talk, smiled, anything—" She shook her head, stared straight ahead, scowling.

He put a hand on her leg, her face. "Rose, I'm so sorry. I should've called you earlier this week, but I wanted to see you in person—"

"Alone?" Her voice was low.

"Yes. Definitely."

"God forbid there be people around."

"In this case, yes," he said.

She pushed his hand off her leg. "You left the cooler on the path."

"My mom will see it."

"Go ahead and get it." She shifted the car into reverse. "You can put it in my trunk."

He wiggled his ass into the seat. "I'm not going anywhere, are you kidding? You'll drive away."

"I promise to wait for you."

He snorted. "You'd be lying."

After a moment, the corner of her mouth twitched. "Yeah, I would be." She slapped the wheel with her palms. "Fine. I'll drive you home, but only because it's your birthday and God forbid I *embarrass* you." And then she backed up and the Toyota was rattling over the broken concrete to the road ahead.

He rubbed his eyes, more relieved than he'd ever been in his life.

Oh, God. He had to tell her about Sylly. What he'd seen, what he'd threatened.

He took a deep breath, rubbed his damp palms over his thighs. "Thank you."

She braked for a speed bump. He watched her lovely profile, cheeks brightly flushed, chin up, and took the plunge.

"I was trying to protect you," he said. "My brother saw you and assumed—well, it wasn't any of his business. He jumped to all kinds of wrong conclusions, assuming he knows what's best for me. He still thinks I'm twelve years old."

"Then maybe you should stop acting like it."

He swallowed. She didn't understand. It was more than Mark, it was his mother, the people at work, all that attention when he didn't even know what she wanted from him, where they were going. "I didn't want to make a big deal about us—"

"Big deal? You didn't even thank me for my birthday present."

A case of duct tape. In assorted colors and prints, including pink zebra stripe. "Thank you. It was great."

"That's why you thanked me on behalf of your *mother*? As though it had been a gift for *her*?"

He flinched. "I'm so sorry. I saw the way she was looking at me and—believe me, the last thing you want is my mother gunning for you to... be with me. If Blair weren't already living with another man, she'd be at her door every day, nagging, leaving gifts, teasing, hinting..."

"So you like the way things are, is that it?"

He looked at her. Didn't she? "There's more," he said. "I didn't know if you'd want to keep seeing me when I told you."

A humorless laugh escaped her. "How ironic."

"It's Sylly. He told me if I ever touch you again"—he stopped, swallowed down the cotton in his throat—"I'm fired. And so are you."

She braked so hard he almost hit his head on the dashboard. "What?"

The seat belt, as alarmed as he was, locked itself and sliced into his neck. He popped open the buckle to readjust it, reminding himself not to talk to her while she was driving. "At work," he said. "At *work*."

With a loud exhalation, she drove on. They exited the park, joined the main road west. "Oh."

He had to tell her everything. "And at his house."

Her mouth fell open another inch. "God."

"He's paranoid about sexual harassment claims, doesn't want to be connected in any way." He hoped that would be the end of it.

She sped through the curves winding under the canopy of trees. Another minute went by. "But... how does he know...

you said if you ever touched me again at work, which means he knows you did…"

Mark drummed his fingers on his thigh, said nothing.

Her face showed it was sinking in. "Does that mean… Nobody saw… He didn't…"

"Yes, it does mean," Mark said softly. "Somebody did."

"Oh, oh, oh. God." Her hands nervously patted the steering wheel. "Who?"

"Him."

She gaped at him, then turned back to the road.

He watched her carefully, alarmed how quickly her angry flush had drained out of her face. Now she was almost as pale as her hair. "I have to pull over," she said quietly. At the next turnout, a semicircle of gravel in the forest, she swerved to the edge, put the car in park before dropping her face into her hands.

"It's okay," Mark said, reaching out to lightly touch her shoulder. He should've waited until they got to the house, but he was afraid she'd find some way to eject him out of the car before he could explain. "I'm sure he was exaggerating. He was just upset."

"Upset." She brushed his hand off her shoulder.

"At least he's got plenty of incentive to keep it to himself. Unlike an HR person or somebody."

She closed her eyes.

"I almost didn't tell you," he admitted.

"You almost didn't tell me," she repeated.

"I can't make any decisions for you. Or for us, whatever it is." He looked down at his hands, back up into her face.

"So if Sylly finds out we're—whatever it is—I'm fired."

"Both of us," he said.

She rolled her eyes. "He's not going to fire you. You'd have to kill puppies on YouTube before he fired you, and even then he'd suggest therapy first."

"He'd fire me. Believe it. Nobody's indispensable, nobody."

"Damn," she said, shaking her head, lost in her own thoughts. "Damn."

"I'm sorry. I never should've—I've put you in this position."

Finally she turned to face him. "You're giving yourself too much credit. I didn't do a thing to slow it down." She shook her head slowly. "Neither time."

He'd expected her to be upset, but not this much. "Whatever you want to do, I understand," he said.

"You'd love it if we kept sneaking around, wouldn't you?"

He suspected yes was the wrong answer to that question. "I don't want to do anything you don't want to do."

"Oh, sure. Well, news flash. I don't sneak around with anybody."

His stomach sank so deep, it was practically touching the gravel under the car. "I can understand that," he managed to say.

"Not at work," she said, narrowing her eyes, "and not around your family."

For a moment he drifted out of his body and looked down at himself—helpless, fumbling, speechless in the passenger seat, wanting to say the perfect thing that would bring the warmth back into her eyes. Instead all he said was "Right."

"You didn't tell your family about me," she continued, "but it had nothing to do with Sylly or work, did it? You still wouldn't want to tell them about me."

He closed his eyes. Shook his head.

"That's what I thought." Pivoting away from him, she twisted the steering wheel back toward the road, looked over her shoulder, and hit the gas, sending gravel spinning back behind them into the redwoods.

$$\text{\textnormal{\&}}$$

HE CALLED THAT NIGHT. ROSE STARED AT HIS NAME ON her screen. She let it go to voice mail, then waited for the message to show up.

"Hi," Mark's recorded voice said. Then a long pause. "It's me. I was kind of hoping you would talk to me." Another pause. "But you aren't. Unless you're talking to me in your mind and I just can't hear you. God, that sounds stupid. If this were an email I'd delete that part. No, I'd cancel it and start over. Which is one more reason email is a technological improvement over phone mail." He sighed. "I'm really doomed now, aren't I? Right. Well. Call me or answer my next call. Of course you could be in the bathroom or something and you— forget I said that. Delete delete delete. In case you don't recognize my voice, this is, uh, John." Then he hung up.

I liked this guy, dammit, she thought, staring at the phone. She bit her lip, fought back tears. Why couldn't he be just a little bit… more?

The house was quiet, dark, empty. She'd always dreamed about living alone. Growing up without any privacy, always living with family and classmates and friends, she'd thought it would be delicious. But now—

It had been two weeks since Blair lost the baby. She said she was fine, that she didn't need Rose to keep her company anymore. There wasn't any harm in checking in, however.

Blair picked up on the second ring. "I was calling to see how you're feeling," Rose said.

"You've been listening to me for weeks. It's your turn," Blair replied. "How was the birthday party? I was hoping you might call tomorrow, if you know what I mean. Because you'd be too busy tonight."

Rose swallowed, determined not to lose her grip. "It didn't really work out."

"Oh," Blair said. "Look, he's shy. You might have to make the first move."

"That's not it. As long as other people aren't around, he's all over me."

Blair knew all about how John had treated her. "Oh," she said again.

"Yeah. I've got alarm bells going off."

"You've always got alarm bells going off—usually around the third date," Blair said.

"I do not."

Blair was quiet.

"I do not," Rose repeated.

She still didn't say anything.

"Fine," Rose said. "I have high standards."

"Unlike me?" Blair asked.

Rose went into the bathroom, looked at herself in the mirror. Pretty eyes, pretty lips, pretty hair, blah blah blah. She'd heard a lot about her pretty face growing up, not so much about the rest of her, even from men she slept with. John had been one of the few to appear satisfyingly worshipful.

Was that what she needed? Worship?

"I've watched my mother put herself down my whole life, settling for losers, never thinking she deserved better," Rose said. "I refuse to make the same mistake."

The line was silent for a moment. "I think you're over-thinking this," Blair said. "He's not a loser, and you're not marrying him or anything. Just give him a chance. See where it goes."

Rose bent over the vintage pedestal sink until her forehead bumped the mirror. Her ego was still recovering from the damage John had done, and she liked Mark as a person a lot more than she'd liked John. Way too much. "He wants to keep everything a secret. We have to be sneaky at work—that's another story—but in private, too. Everywhere." She paused. "He lets his mother think he's in love with you."

"Jeez," Blair said, finally sounding indignant. "That's bad. Do you think he just needs a little time?"

"That's what his mother says about you."

"Oh, Jesus."

What if he was thinking the same thing? Rose closed her eyes. "I refuse to waste another minute on a man who only loves me when the lights are out," she said quietly, her breath fogging the mirror.

"Oh, Rose."

"I thought I was beyond all this. I'm twenty-six, not sixteen. I accept myself. I love myself. All of me." She stepped back, scanned her figure in the mirror. "So why do I feel so scared all of a sudden?"

"Maybe because this is a man who could really mean something to you."

Rose stared into her own eyes, not sure she liked the sound of that.

A long silence ensued. "What are you going to do?" Blair asked.

Rose had been asking herself that for hours. "I've been underemployed for a really long time. I can't tell you how incredible it is to be proud of my job. Having a job at all. Good health insurance, bonus programs, stock options." She ran her hand through her hair. "My tenth high school reunion is coming up. Now I might be able to go. I was this smart chick who graduated at sixteen, voted most likely to succeed. But then I went nowhere."

"It's not just you, it's everybody. The economy has been terrible."

"Sure, but can I throw my first real opportunity away on a guy who hasn't even had the guts to smile at me in front his mother?"

Blair's silence was answer enough.

21

FOR THE NEXT WEEK AND a half, until Thanksgiving break forced her to stay away, Rose arrived at the WellyNelly offices before eight in the morning and went home after seven in the evening.

She discovered she wasn't the only ambitious employee at WellyNelly; although most of the staff worked more modest hours, there were a few young men and women who seemed to have nothing except their workstations, the software, the forums, the online community, and vast quantities of imbibed stimulants, most of them legal.

Rose joined their ranks with a psychic sigh of relief, anything to stop herself from thinking and feeling too much about her personal life.

She'd worried about seeing Mark around the office but shouldn't have. He hadn't been into the office since his birthday.

"Back to working from home," Jared, one of the programmers, told her as they refilled their coffee mugs in the break room. "He gets more done there. In November his productivity totally tanked. What used to take him a day was taking him forever. Now he's back, true to form, saving my ass."

"Yours?" Mark and Jared, so far as she knew, were in totally different departments. "How does he do that?"

"I have no idea," Jared said, misunderstanding her. "Some people are just insanely brilliant, you know? He doesn't even care if I pass off his work as my own. In fact, he encourages it." Smiling, he sipped his coffee and walked away.

Rose heard similar tales from others around the office, even from Bridget at the front desk.

"He set up a camera for me so I can snap a quick picture of everyone who comes through the door, label it with their name, study it later. That's how I learned everyone's name so fast." She grinned. "Sylly's promoting me next month because he says that's what management needs, more people people. Instead of just geeks."

Rose forced a smile, her heart squeezing. "You'll do great, Bridget. Really great. Congratulations."

Just because he was Mr. Wonderful with everyone else didn't mean he was wonderful for her.

So she went back to her desk, threw herself into her work. Most of her extra hours were spent studying the revenue stream, a creatively unobtrusive array of advertising.

The numbers—and the opportunity for growth—fascinated her. Her group, the Women's Forum, had the same kinds of ads as the rest of the site, which she felt was a major problem. Not that she wanted flashing tampon ads all over it, but WellyNelly was neglecting a lot to keep the site strictly non-gendered and medical. Vitamins were great, but why not put in a little fun? Moisturizers, aromatherapy, yoga-themed spa vacations... she began creating a spreadsheet of hundreds of companies and services she thought would be excellent sponsors of their vibrant, growing network.

One evening, as she was eating a sandwich for dinner at her desk, she scrolled over the open positions within the company, curious to see what other people, who didn't have Mark recommend them, had on their résumés. She enjoyed the planning work on her team, but she felt like she was missing out on a lot, had so much to learn.

The list of qualifications for existing openings at the company made her put down her sandwich.

MBA. MA. PhD. Ten years' experience. Computer Science. Economics. Marketing. Electrical Engineering.

Stanford, Berkeley, Harvard, Yale, MIT.

She'd expected at least one position similar to her own, some entry-level biology graduate-type thing, but no.

Mr. Wonderful had pulled more than strings, he'd pulled ropes. Massive cabling. Enough to suspend the Golden Gate Bridge.

She scanned the jobs again, swallowing the food in her mouth that had turned into a hard, dry lump, then logged off her computer.

Maybe she was just tired from the long hours and the sleepless nights, but at that moment, Rose felt as if she'd been fooling herself. Just as if she'd tried to pass herself off as a web developer or pediatric cardiologist.

Except this time, she'd lied to herself.

&

THE JOHNSONS ALWAYS HAD THANKSGIVING DINNER AT their house. Every year, even if Liam was competing around the world, or Mark was on the other side of the country, or even if April was backpacking with another dopey boyfriend in Central America, they all made the journey home to gorge on roasted oversized poultry and hug their mother. This year was no different.

Well, it was a little different. Liam had Bev at his side, and she wasn't at all thankful for the Johnson family's traditional low-carb, protein-powder pie crust—so she baked three pies of her own. Each of them, she declared, placing them on the kitchen table, was half butter and half sugar.

Nobody complained, not even Liam.

And April was alone—no sulky, body-pierced lover in tow; another first. She'd been inviting boyfriends to their Thanksgiving dinner since eighth grade, but this year she showed up in her own car, sober, not wearing her usual black eyeliner, and set about making a salad without insulting anyone.

Mark assumed he looked the same as he always did: alone, quiet, slightly miserable. He snuck pieces of Bev's pie crust into his mouth while he stringed green beans next to the sink, lost in thoughts of soft, creamy skin, smiling blue eyes, and deep feminine laughter.

Liam poked him in the ribs. "What's the matter with you?" He offered a glass of wine.

"What do you mean?"

Liam rolled his eyes. "You're sighing so loud, I could hear you over April's awful music."

"She dumped him," April said, reaching across Mark's chest, claiming the glass for herself.

"Ah," Liam said knowingly.

Mark flung a green bean into the bowl. "What's that supposed to mean?"

"I didn't say anything," Liam said.

"*Ah*," Mark mimicked. "Like you've got me all figured out."

Liam shifted his gaze to April. They stared at each other.

"Forget it." Mark dropped a handful of beans and strode

out of the kitchen to the back porch. The winter rains had started, making a satisfying march out into the peace and quiet of the great outdoors unavailable, so he paced back and forth between the doggie beds.

Zeus joined him a few minutes later, looking as miserable as Mark felt. Some sadist had put the dog in a miniature reindeer suit, complete with antlers and sleigh bells. Never had Mark seen such disgust on the loving, patient animal's face. The bug eyes and lolling tongue suddenly captured the indignant rage poor Zeus was unable to express verbally. *Look at this shit*, he was saying. *Can you believe what I have to put up with?*

Mark squatted down. Unfastening the antlers, he gently rubbed Zeus's tiny, bony skull. "Who did this to you, dude?"

Grateful, Zeus applied his tongue to the side of Mark's face like the chamois in a touchless car wash.

Liam stepped out onto the porch and closed the door to the kitchen. "Looks like this is where the men hang out."

Not interested in conversation, Mark lowered himself all the way to the floor, legs crossed, and captured Zeus in his arms without a word.

His brother joined him on the floor. "I told her the antlers were too much."

"Who?"

"Kate. Bev's sister. She's designing the Fite Dog line. I was just showing everyone how hideous it is."

"I knew I didn't like that woman."

Liam stifled a snort.

"Shut up," Mark said. Kate was just one more of the women Mark had the misfortune to dream about. Very briefly in her case, thank God; Bev was a lot nicer than her sister.

"Sorry." Liam held out another goblet. "I got you a fresh glass."

Shaking his head, Mark nuzzled Zeus, remembering the look on Rose's face when the dog climbed up her chest.

God, he missed her.

"You might as well tell me. I'll keep harassing you until you do," Liam said.

"You wouldn't understand."

"What're you, fourteen?"

Holding Zeus to his chest, Mark shifted his weight to get up. Liam stopped him with that grip of death of his, with one of the enormous hands that used to paddle through the water at sixty miles an hour and was now clamped on Mark's arm. "Sorry," Liam said. "I didn't mean to be an asshole."

Mark stared at him. His brother had always had it so easy. His looks, his talents, his confidence.

And Dad had loved him best.

Realizing how ridiculously low he'd sunk, Mark dipped his head, laughed softly to himself.

Liam relaxed his grip, smiling a little. "What?"

"Just now I was feeling sorry for myself about how Dad gave you all the attention."

Liam lifted his wine glass off the floor, gulped down a large mouthful. "Yeah, lucky me. Years of my life wasted on a sport I didn't even like," he said. "For a man who'd never be satisfied."

"You must've liked swimming a little bit. You lived in the pool for, like, twenty years."

"Sure, I loved it when I was, like, five. After that—" Liam shook his head. "Anyway. I don't think this is about Dad, is it?"

Mark reached over, claimed the glass Liam had brought, wondering if his misery did have some roots in their father's cold, driven, critical personality. That bone-deep sense that Mark would never be good enough; that he was so inadequate, his own father gave up on him. Now that he was older, Mark could see, intellectually, that his father was a sporty, competitive guy who just didn't understand math, engineering, chess, chemistry, computers. Putting Mark down was a way of holding himself up.

Not a good quality in a father. And hardly Mark's fault.

"It *is* Rose," Mark said finally, lifting the wine to his lips. "And don't say 'Ah.'"

"What happened?"

Mark looked at his brother, scanning his face for any hint of mockery, amusement, criticism, boredom.

There was none.

Fortifying himself with the rest of the wine, Mark told him everything, from the day he lent her the jumper cables to the afternoon of the picnic.

Well, not everything. Some parts were too good to share.

When he was done talking, Liam was silent for a full minute, and the two brothers sat together with the appreciative, ugly dog, staring off into the rainy November night.

"You haven't spoken since?" Liam asked.

"She won't answer my calls."

"How about at work?"

"Oh, I'm working from home again. With Sylly threatening to fire her because of me," Mark said, "it seemed like the least I could do."

"It definitely is."

"What's that supposed to mean?"

Liam whacked him on the back, not quite hard enough to hurt. Not quite. "You screwed up. Time to stop moping around and fix it."

"How the hell do I do that? By getting her fired? That job is the one thing she's got going for her right now. She's great at it. They love her there. It's the perfect place for her." Mark put

Zeus on the floor and climbed to his feet. "I'm not going to screw it up."

Liam stood up next to him. "So find another way."

"How?"

His brother whacked him on the back again. "You're the genius. You figure it out."

$\mathscr{T}$HE WELLYNELLY HOLIDAY PARTY WAS held the afternoon before Christmas Eve in a trendy bar and bistro a few blocks from the office. Since the entire company would be closed until after New Year's, the atmosphere at the party was especially festive—and given the long hours that everyone had been working to allow them to shut down for ten days, particularly alcohol soaked.

Rose was an exception. Although Mark hadn't shown up at the party, she didn't want to risk losing a shred of her self-control around her coworkers ever again. Her tonic and lime was boring but safe.

That's me, she thought. *Boring and safe. Safe and boring.*

Perhaps because the other employees hadn't nearly been caught screwing at the office, they seemed not to be under the same constraints. The bistro was in a converted warehouse, and they'd opened up the interior to give them room to dance, jump on pogo sticks (provided), attack each other with inflatable bats, compete at carnival arcade games, get their faces painted, and generally let loose in geeky, immature abandon. The bar was open and free, and everyone took advantage.

Sipping her water, Rose watched as Jared, in his usual Levi's and gray T-shirt, slow-danced with Bridget under the climbing wall, hands drifting lower with each beat of the imaginary music only he could hear. Well, Bridget seemed to hear it, too. She seemed to be leading the steps, her happy face even happier than usual.

Rose dropped her gaze to the ice in her glass. She'd intentionally stood with her back to the door so she wouldn't be tempted to watch for him, but it hadn't worked, not at all. Her eyes might've been on Jared and Bridget, but her thoughts, as they were most of the time, were on Mark.

Who wasn't there.

It had been a month; she should've been over him by now. Or at least, the ache should've faded, the bruise healed.

Instead, she hurt more, felt damaged, incomplete. Like a bone that had been fractured and never set properly.

Screw it, she thought, heading for the bar. *I'm getting a martini.*

The crowd around the free booze had thickened since she'd gotten her earlier drink, and she was forced to wait in a long line that snaked past an alcove filled with antique arcade games. The sounds of Pac-Man and Space Invaders tangled with those of vintage Atari and Nintendo consoles, plugged into a 1980s-era TV with rabbit ears.

The guys inside were gathered, backs facing her, around the Atari, the young ones laughing with disgust at the primitive graphics, the older ones gleefully reliving their youth. The room was dim, crowded, lit only by the glow of the old screens.

Smiling, Rose watched them play Asteroids, considered joining them. One of the guys, Rob, was on her team, an engineer who'd been with WellyNelly for years and wasn't thrilled, she suspected, with her lack of experience.

Maybe it was time for a charm offensive. Giving up on the martini, she took a step into the room.

"And then he disappears again," Rob was saying, "and she's still here."

Another engineer, also one of the old guard, shoved him, laughing, and grabbed the joystick out of his hands. "No accounting for taste."

"I'd hit it," Amit said, kicking back a beer.

"Careful she doesn't roll over on you afterward."

Rose felt the blood drain out of her face. She stopped in the shadows of the doorway, tightened her grip on her drink.

Amit shook his head. "You're just jealous, Dennis. I've seen the way you watch her."

"She's so big, what else can I watch?" Dennis said. "Blocks out the view."

"Guess MaJo had the same problem. He didn't get shit done after he got her hired," Rob said. "Double-whammy having her here. First we have to carry her weight"—the others laughed—"and then MaJo is too horny to carry ours." Shaking his head, he changed the cartridge on the Atari.

"Hope we don't get a newbie overlord each time he wants to get laid," Dennis said.

"Don't think we will," Rob said. "Sylly's learned his lesson. When the deal's done, MaJo's toast."

"That's not what I heard. Big shit's going down," Dennis said. "He's always been the heart of this place, everyone knows it."

"Just because he was here at the beginning doesn't mean he should be here at the end," Rob said.

"Sure wasn't here in the middle," Dennis said.

"I'd like to be in *her* middle," Amit said. "I wonder if he's done with her."

"Fap on, Amit," Rob said. "Unless you founded a few tech

companies in secret and have millions in the bank, she won't give your skinny ass a glance."

Amit snatched the joystick out of Dennis' hands. "She's not like that. She doesn't even know who he is."

"Yeah, right," Dennis said.

"Who'd tell her? We're not even supposed to know."

"You can't keep a secret like that, give me a break. It's like people at Apple not knowing who Steve Wozniak is."

"I'm telling you, she doesn't know." Amit hit a button on the Atari, and Space Invaders started up.

"She's dumb enough," Dennis said.

"Take it easy, Dennis," Rob said. "You're just annoyed she pointed out you're two months late on your QA testing."

"And that she turned down his generous offer to suck his dick," Amit said.

To Rose's immense satisfaction, Dennis turned bright red. "Chick doesn't have a sense of humor."

"Then why was she laughing so hard?" Amit asked.

The men, except for Dennis, burst out into guffaws.

Rose braced a hand on the door frame, willed herself to start breathing again. She swallowed hard, grateful she hadn't had a sip of anything but citrus-flavored water, because anything stronger would've ended up on her shoes.

She pushed away from the wall, took a step into the room.

Their shoes. Because she was going to have a little *word* with these assholes.

"Happy holidays, guys," she said, striding forward with a broad, fake smile. "Playing with yourselves?"

Dennis spun around first. "Shit," he muttered.

"Happy holidays," Amit said nervously, eyes darting around.

Rob closed his eyes for a moment. "You heard us, I take it?"

She stretched her smile another centimeter. "It was very educational. Until now I liked you guys." She let her gaze drift over to Dennis. "Well, most of you."

Amit froze, stared at the floor. Dennis shifted his weight from side to side, licked his lips.

"It's been a rough couple of weeks," Rob said. "They're just letting off a little steam. Maybe had a little too much to drink. Nothing to take seriously."

She batted her eyes at him. "Me?" Pressing a hand to her heart, she sighed. "I'm too fat and stupid to realize I'm being insulted by a few—pardon me, Amit—a couple of pencil-dicked, misogynistic losers playing video games."

Amit shrank into himself. Dennis's jaw went slack. Rob flinched, glanced over her shoulder to see if she'd been overheard.

"After New Year's, when you guys have had a little time to sober up, we'll have to have a meeting to discuss this unpleasant conversation," she said casually. "Look for it on the calendar."

Never dropping her smile, she turned on her new crimson patent leather heels and sashayed out of the room.

In the hallway, she made her way through the line of people still waiting at the bar, unsteady on her feet, heart pounding, hands shaking. She placed her glass on an abandoned drink tray near the kitchen and focused on the front door of the restaurant.

Get me out of here before I lose it.

She had to dredge up a smile for a couple of people who greeted her, people whose names she'd suddenly forgotten. Never slowing, she wove right and left through tables and waiters and coworkers until her palm was flat against the glass door and she was pushing it outward.

"Need a cab?" a young woman in a royal-blue WellyNelly bomber jacket asked her on the sidewalk.

"No thanks." Rose reached for her keys, turned left to the side street where she'd parked her car.

"You sure? Company's paying."

She waved without turning, giving thanks she'd stayed cold sober tonight. God knows what she'd do right now if she had even one drink in her. Her keys, clutched inside her fist, bit into the skin of her palm. She was so angry, so itching to punch somebody.

Unfortunately, flattening Dennis wouldn't help her in the long run.

Pieces fell into place, clues she'd ignored for weeks. Mark Johnson. Hired only a month before her, yet treated as a prince. Getting a random acquaintance a job without a résumé, interview, education, or experience. His familiar but tense relationship with the CEO.

The bastard should've told her.

Millions in the bank, founded a few tech companies…

She tripped over a tree root that had broken through the sidewalk, fell onto her hands and knees. The sharp pain sparked tears she'd held back until then; biting her lip, blinking furiously, she regained her feet and staggered on.

It was always too good to be true. She was just a body, lots of it. Tits and ass and blonde, blonde hair.

I'd hit it.

She jerked her car door open and climbed inside, vaguely aware of the dampness on her palms. They stung where she'd fallen.

Why didn't he tell me? Couldn't he have trusted me with that?

She kicked off her shoes and dug around in her purse for a tissue to wipe the blood off her hands and knees.

It was *always* too good to be true.

She drove home in a daze, barely seeing the road or feeling the cold on her bare arms. She'd worn a sweater to the party, but it was thin, low-cut, frilly. Two days before Christmas, even in California, that wasn't nearly enough. When she parked her car in the driveway of her house—Sylly's house—her hands were numb, in part because she'd been too distracted to turn on the heat.

The house was dark, not what she expected. The real estate agent had come by with the stager the day after Thanksgiving and strung up pale yellow Christmas lights all over the gate and front windows.

As Rose got out of her car, not bothering to put on her shoes, she wiped a stray tear off her cheek and squinted through the darkness. The lights were gone. Not just turned off; gone.

For a split second she wondered if, in her upset, she'd pulled into the wrong driveway. But it was a custom house. And the number was right. It was Sylly's house.

Then she noticed the key box that used to hang from the front door was missing, and for the second time that night, she felt the blood drain out of her.

Fumbling with the key, she unlocked the front door and went in, bracing herself for what she was afraid she'd find.

There wasn't anything to find.

No hall table, no flowers, no decorative ceramic elephant. No furniture.

The house was empty.

Not even a note or phone message. She dropped her purse on the floor and flinched at the tinny echo it made in the bare, vaulted space.

Merry fucking Christmas.

Sylly had sold the house and hadn't bothered to tell her.

She'd call him right now—to hell with her job, to hell with it—but he was at the party.

The tropical plants in the windowed sunroom were gone, only dead leaves and potting soil remained on the shelves and tile.

Dirt. They'd left the dirt.

She went into the kitchen, the bedrooms, the living room, the bathrooms.

The closet.

She jerked open the door and stared at the bare shelves, bar, carpeting.

They'd taken her suitcase.

Her *clothes*.

So enraged her jaw was starting to ache, Rose punched Sylly's number into her phone.

He didn't answer right away, and when he did, he had to yell. "Rose?" She could hear the hum of the party behind him.

"You sold the house!"

For a moment she heard only the sounds of the party. Laughter, screeching, pop music.

"I'll have to call you back." He hung up on her.

"No!" She yelled at her phone, glared at it, set it down on the kitchen counter so she wouldn't throw it out the window.

She paced around the marble-topped kitchen island. Fine, he sold the house; it was for sale. But it was two days before Christmas, and he hadn't said a word when he must've known for days, at least. The stager knew, the stager's semi and moving crew knew. One phone call, that's all she would've needed.

The bastards took her *clothes*.

Her phone vibrated on the counter; she picked it up, breath tight.

"Rose?" It was quiet. He must've left the party.

"Yeah."

"You heard about the house?" Sylly asked.

"Heard? They took my clothes!"

"Who took what?"

"I knew it wasn't going to last forever, but you should've told me because I've got to find a new place to live, and it's the holidays and *they took my clothes*." She pinched the bridge of her nose. "All I have is the dress I wore to the party." She had a doomed job and no clothes.

"Hold on a minute, try to calm down. Something about your clothes?"

A fresh realization hit her; her eyes popped open. "And my *shoes*, Sylly. You need to call somebody and find out—tonight —what they did with my shoes." Her voice had dropped to a growl.

"Call whose shoes?" Sylly asked. "Hold on. I can't call anybody, I'm on the phone with you. Why is that? Shouldn't you be here?"

Frowning, she pulled the phone away from her ear, stared at it, put it back. "Are you *drunk*?"

"Of course I'm not drunk. What kind of CEO would get drunk at the company Christmas party?"

She gritted her teeth. He was wasted. "When do I have to move out, Sylly? Not that I have much to transport, *since they took everything*, but I'd like to know how long I have a roof over my head, if you don't mind."

"Well, this is awkward, isn't it? I'm not really sure. I'll have to get back to you."

"You're not sure? I don't even have—"

He hung up.

She didn't even have a toothbrush.

❧

"I'M GLAD YOU ACCEPTED SYLLY'S OFFER," MARK SAID into the phone. Instead of attending the WellyNelly holiday party, he'd worked late from his desk at home, three computers whirring around him.

Gloria laughed. "Oh, I didn't accept his offer, but he accepted mine. After a little back and forth."

"Good. You deserve whatever you asked for."

"That's what I told him," Gloria said. "I start the day the office reopens after the holidays. We'll announce the change then, but Sylly will stay for a transition period."

"Shovanna Wise and Helen Shih start a week later. They need a little more time to relocate. Finding a house in the Bay Area isn't easy." On his middle monitor, he opened the window for the Sport Injuries Forum. As they had for the past three weeks, all over the WellyNelly site, users were protesting the rumor that a large drug company might swallow up their beloved social network.

Mark smiled, counted the vast number of views, comments, links. He'd been busy the last few weeks stirring up trouble, and it was all paying off. "Did Sylly give you a hard time about your plans? All your do-gooder nonprofit stuff? He seemed set on the Big Pharma deal."

"He didn't say anything about that. I got the impression he was looking forward to something else he's got going on. Whatever's made him decide it was time to step aside as CEO, just be the owner." Gloria chuckled softly. "I'm sure you have no idea what that might be."

"Me?" Mark asked.

"Right. Whatever it is, Sylly's lucky you're including him in it. You've got a golden touch, Mark. Makes me terribly jealous."

"Yeah, you're a real slacker," he told her. Gloria had an MD, an MBA, and a decade's experience as a clinical psychologist. Now in her sixties, she was just hitting her professional stride. She'd be a great CEO. "Well, like I said, glad it worked out. WellyNelly is kind of important to me. I'm glad it'll stay private for a little longer."

"Private or no, we'll honor your dream, Mark."

He laughed uneasily. His dream was probably quite different from what she was imagining. "Listen, if the touchy-feely path isn't working out, don't fire people to stay afloat. Do whatever you can to keep people working. Even if you have to sell to the big guys, go public, anything."

"Don't insult me," Gloria said. "If anyone can do touchy-feely and profitable, it's me. That's why you brought me in."

"You're absolutely right. Forgive me."

"And your girlfriends from MIT should help turn around some of that boy-club trouble you were telling me about."

He groaned. "Don't ever let them hear you call them my girlfriends," he said. "They'll quit on the spot. Neither one of them would go out with me."

She made a sympathetic noise. "I'm not sure I want to hire women with such poor taste."

"In the interests of full disclosure, you should know I never got up the guts to ask them."

Gloria laughed. "Good to know. I'll withhold judgment. How long will you be staying with the company—on a daily basis, I mean?"

"I'm not sure. I promised to give Sylly my full attention by the end of the March. He's eager to get started." He closed the window for the Sport Injury forum, moved over to Women's Health. "I'll let you know as soon—hold on, I've got another call coming in."

"I'll let you go. Happy holidays."

She hung up and Mark looked at his phone, saw Sylly's name. "Aren't you at the party?" Mark asked him.

"Don't get pissed, but there's been a little snag."

Mark sat up straight. "What happened?"

"Crossed wires somewhere. Quite a few people get involved in a real estate deal, you know?"

"Spit it out, Syl."

"Somehow Annamarie didn't get the message it was a special situation. When she saw the sale was pending, she went in with her crew and cleaned the place out. Guess she wanted to get it done before the holidays."

Mark stood up, sending the chair shooting out behind him. Rose would assume she had to move out, might do something drastic before all of his plans were in place. "Damn."

"It's worse. They even took Rose's clothes. Actually, she seemed most worried about her shoes," Sylly said. "Women."

"This is bad."

"Suddenly those pillows aren't sounding so bad, are they?"

Mark paced across the floor of his bedroom. "What are you doing about it?"

"I can't do anything right now. Nobody's picking up the phone—tomorrow's Christmas Eve."

"I'm not ready yet," Mark said.

"Well, whatever you've got planned, just push it to eleven." Sylly's smile was audible over the line. "I'll try to get the stuff put back tomorrow, but she'll want an explanation."

Mark went to the window, pressed his forehead to the glass. "I'm not ready."

"Yeah, you are," Sylly said. "And it's about time."

Mark hung up, found himself staring at the house next door. John had stuck around, which surprised him a little. He and Blair seemed to be a couple, often side by side as they came and went, talking, holding hands, stringing Christmas lights together.

A fantasy struck him, as it had been striking him lately with increasing frequency.

Maybe if his neighbors were happy, they'd want to spread some of that around.

Maybe they'd help him.

23

THE DOORBELL RANG, SENDING WOLFGANG'S tune echoing throughout the empty house.

Groaning, Rose rolled over in her sleeping bag, slapping the floor, feeling for her phone. Her new pillow had slipped away from her head; her neck was cramped.

7:03 a.m., her phone said, December 24.

Who the hell would come to the door so early on Christmas Eve?

Her mind woke more fully. Maybe Sylly had found her things and sent the real estate people to return them. Thank God. She'd driven to Target the night before—with eight and a half million other people—and bought a few basics, but she wouldn't survive happily without her own clothes.

She crawled out of the sleeping bag onto her hands and knees, got to her feet wearing her Doorbuster flannel pajama set ("Perfect for Mom!") and went to the door.

It was John, not Sylly, who stood on her doorstep. A storm had come in late the night before and the rain was still pouring down.

She crossed her arms over her braless chest, shivering, and stared in drowsy confusion.

"Hi." Not wearing a jacket, John huddled close to the house to get out of the rain. He looked as terrible as she felt—tired eyes, hair uncombed, dressed in only sweatpants and a T-shirt. "Sorry to bother you."

She glanced past him at the gate, realizing she'd forgotten to close it. She and John had barely spoken since their conversation in the driveway about Mark. When she'd realized the tension between her and John was adding to Blair's stress, she began limiting her visits to the phone or away from the house. "Why are you here?"

"It's kind of raining out here, did you notice?"

Pausing slightly, Rose stepped aside so he could come inside. And see the vast emptiness.

"Where's all the furniture?" he asked, frowning.

"I'm going minimalist."

He gave her a look. She returned it.

With a sigh, he wiped the water off his arms, strode into the house. "Nice place."

"Yeah, but it looks like I won't be staying."

He was wandering from room to room, checking everything out. "You never do, do you?" he asked casually.

"What's that supposed to mean?"

He turned, raised a hand. "Sorry. I didn't come here to pick a fight. It's about Blair."

She started. "What happened?"

"Nothing like that." He ran his hand over a built-in bookshelf, now empty, littered with dust. "No accident or anything. And she's healthy. Physically, I mean."

Physically. "She seemed pretty happy the other day when we went out to the movies."

"She's good at hiding things from you." John walked away to the kitchen. "How about coffee or something?"

Embarrassed she didn't have a single mug, let alone a coffeemaker—and annoyed that she cared what he thought—Rose called after him. "I'm not the Starbucks drive-through. Just tell me what you came to say."

Slowly, he came back into the hall. "You never were a morning person."

"What do you think she's hiding from me?"

He strode into the living room, eyebrow raised at the bare floors, finally sat on the floor, leaning against the wall with the western-facing windows at his back. "I'll just sit here." He stretched out his legs. "As her best friend, I thought you should know she's going through a rough time."

Rose frowned. John was acting very strangely. "Yeah. She lost a baby."

He gave her a hard look. "I'm aware of that."

"She needs time to recover. I'm no expert, but I looked it up online, read about how hard it can be to move on, especially since she was already in the second trimester."

"It's more than that."

"Isn't losing a baby enough?"

"She hasn't gone back to work yet, even though the doctor said she could anytime."

"It was just a temp job. Is it you're tired of her living off of you? Because I can help out with money if that's the problem." Though she was homeless and in an untenable work situation, he didn't need to know that.

"I don't want your money. Jesus, Rose."

"You just said you want her to go back to work."

He crossed his arms over his chest. "You think it's better she's playing games on her phone all day?"

That got Rose's attention. After a moment's pause, she sat

cross-legged on the floor across from him. "She's hooked on those again?" Blair had nearly dropped out of school sophomore year because of her obsessive online gaming.

"Oh, yeah. Every second of every day."

"Have you talked to her about it?"

"Who am I to tell her she can't play a few games if that's what makes her feel better?"

"That's just it, isn't it?" Rose asked. "Who are you?"

He pushed to his feet, turned to the window. "I feel like I have to wait for her to figure that out."

"Maybe you do." The last time they'd talked, he'd been furious at the suggestion he was going to leave. But if he came to her for help, he couldn't get too upset if she shared her opinions.

"Maybe you don't know yourself what you want," she said softly.

He spun around. "Could you please stop blaming me for this?"

"I'm not—"

"I'm here because I thought you should know she's not doing too great. Forget about me for a minute." He made a sour face. "Yeah, I know, it's hard. But pretend. If I weren't here and Blair was playing games all day, never taking a shower, not eating, letting her job fall by the wayside, what would you do?"

"She's not taking her morning shower?" That was a bad sign. Blair was usually obsessive about her personal hygiene.

"She never takes off her pajamas."

Rose got to her feet. "She needs to go back to the doctor. Or see a therapist."

"Would you like to be the one to suggest that to her?"

"John, this is what I mean about who you are to her. If you're still—" She wasn't sure how to go on.

"If we're still getting married?" he asked, his voice danger-ously low. "Even though we don't 'have' to?"

She met his cold gaze, held it. "Yes."

"I'm not going to leave her now. I told you that."

For the first time, Rose wondered if Blair might *want* him to leave. Getting pregnant had confused things. Maybe now she was having second thoughts. "I'll go see her right now. Is she up?"

"I had something else in mind. That's why I'm here so early." He crossed his arms over his chest. "But I don't know if you'll do it, given your history."

That again. He'd never believe she didn't want him back, how completely she'd moved on. "What happened between us—"

"Not you and me. You and *him*. Mark."

The air went out of her. "What?"

"I know how you are with old boyfriends. Though I still have a hard time believing he came close to that."

"How does Mark have anything to do with helping Blair?"

"His mother invited us to Lake Tahoe for Christmas. They've got a big cabin up there, not far from my mom's place, though she'll be in LA this year with my aunt, cele-brating their new sisterly devotion to one another after years of hating each other's guts." He ran his finger along the windowsill. "I thought we'd join my mom at my aunt's, but given how Blair's feeling, I didn't think that would be such a great idea."

Rose fought down the toxic jealousy that struck her at the thought of Mark's family reaching out to Blair. "Trixie invited you guys to join them for Christmas?"

"Not *me*." He snorted. "Though the crazy hippie had to include me when we reminded her I exist."

So, Mark's mom was still trying to set him up with Blair.

Rose studied her recent manicure so John couldn't see the pain in her eyes.

Trixie was a kind woman, sweet and nurturing. Rose wouldn't be insulted she'd never turned her matchmaking eyes in *her* direction; if Mark had given any clue, she would have.

"You should go," Rose said finally. "She needs to get out of the house, be with people on Christmas. It sounds beautiful up there."

"She won't go. Not for herself." He crossed his arms over his chest, raised an eyebrow. "But she will for you."

Her throat constricted. "I'm not invited."

"It's a casual thing, Trixie said. 'The more the merrier.'"

"But why—why would Blair go if I go?"

"She's worried about you being alone. And she wants to get you back together with Mark. She has this wild idea you two are meant for each other."

Turning, she closed her eyes. A cabin in the mountains, Christmas, family, him. "I can't."

She heard him exhale. "Yeah, that's what I thought," he said.

"You don't know anything."

"I know a little bit."

"Look around, John. I've suddenly lost the roof over my head. Again. And I just found out my job isn't as great as I thought it was." She tightened the drawstring of her red pajama pants. "I've got a lot to take care of."

"Sure. Because Christmas is such a great time to find a house and a job." He strode toward the door. "It's got nothing to do with you being a commitment-phobe."

"You don't know—"

He held up his hands, waved away her words. "Had that third date, no reason to have a fourth. I get it."

"You got that from Blair. I've gone on lots of fourth dates. With you, for instance."

He turned, held up his fingers. "We had *exactly* three dates. I counted them. We spent a few weekends in bed, but if you count the times we actually went out together, it comes up to three. I went back and checked my calendar." He grinned, eyes narrowed. "Blair's right. You act all tough on the outside, but inside you're just as soft as the rest of us, terrified of getting hurt."

"We had three dates because you never wanted to be seen with me and then slept with my best friend," she spat out.

"I seduced your best friend because I knew you were about to dump me." He shrugged. "And I liked her more."

Rose ground her molars together, desperately fighting the urge to deck him.

She couldn't abandon Blair—to her depression, to the company of this selfish, arrogant toad.

"I would be happy to join the Johnsons for Christmas if I thought it would help Blair," she said through her teeth.

"You sure you can handle the ghosts of boyfriends past?"

"I have no problem seeing Mark or even you, no matter how many or how few dates I had the misfortune of experiencing."

John smiled. "I'm glad to hear that." He pulled out his phone, touched the screen. "I'll tell Trixie to expect us around six."

A FEW MINUTES AFTER JOHN DROVE AWAY, JUST AS ROSE was cursing at herself for forgetting to buy shampoo the night before, the doorbell rang again.

Now what did he want? She threw down the bag from the

store and marched to the door, thinking she should just go to their house to shower. If the three of them were going to spend the next few days together in some mountain cabin anyway, there was no point avoiding them now. She rubbed her scalp, dreaming of her favorite salon back in New York. She hadn't even looked for a place to get her hair done here in California yet.

Should she bother?

She stopped with her hand on the black wrought-iron door handle, surprised by how vivid the image was of her hopping into her Toyota and flooring it eastward for two thousand miles.

She could live in her old bedroom rent-free, go back to school. Then she'd be prepared to rejoin the workforce with the ammunition to deal with pricks like Dennis and Rob. Sure, living at home meant she'd have to deal with Slug, but he was no worse than the guys she fought off in public. Well, maybe a little worse, since her mother seemed to love him.

And would put up with unbelievable amounts of crap from him because she was afraid of being alone.

She exhaled, opened her eyes.

No. I won't go home. I won't run away again, even if I have to start over.

She pulled open the door.

Earlier that morning, she'd expected Sylly but got John. Now it was the reverse.

Her red stilettos dangled from his extended fingers.

"You got my stuff!" She surged forward and gave Sylly a hug, not caring he'd caused her all kinds of trouble. She saw her suitcases, boxes, and kitchen gear stacked up next to him on the steps.

He patted her shoulder. "You won't be so happy when you

find out the truck won't be back with all the furniture until next week."

She stepped back, reclaimed the shoes, air-kissed them. "The furniture's coming back? You don't have to do that. I just needed my stuff. And a heads-up," she said. "You said you'd give me at least a month's warning." Her suitcase was heavy, which made her happy, imagining all her precious sweaters and scarves and underwear and bras—oh, thank God she wouldn't have to wear that scratchy, ill-fitting torture device she got last night—

"You don't have to move out at all. It was just a screw-up."

"A screw-up?"

Sylly squatted down, lifted a box. "Let's get this all inside before it starts raining again."

He was right; the sky was still heavy and dark, the handle of the suitcase already damp from the misty air. "Right." She dragged the suitcase over the threshold into the foyer, fighting the urge to unzip it right there and fondle her belongings.

"I wouldn't have put anything down on the wet driveway," he said, dropping the box and going back out for more, "but I wanted to make a big impression."

It wasn't much, but it was all she had, and when it was stacked up in the empty foyer along the blank wall, she felt renewed hope. "Thank you." She tucked her hair behind her ear. It was all a mistake, he'd said, which was great, but now she knew she couldn't live this way, at the whim of others, no future she could count on.

"Annamarie is very sorry," Sylly said. "She'd already noticed your things and had them separated out."

"I thought I'd have to wait until after Christmas."

"I'd be some kind of shit Santa if I let that happen." A smug grin on his face, he nudged one of the boxes with his toe. "Now I'm wondering if I should give you your other present."

She straightened from where she'd been peeking into her duffel of shoes.

He laughed. "Don't look so worried."

She was afraid to guess. The relief of getting her things back began to fade, a strong memory rising up in her mind of the guys from work playing video games. "I should probably talk to you later about this, but as long as you're here"—taking a deep breath, she turned, perched on the edge of her suitcase —"I know about Mark, about him founding the company, why you hired me—why he did—and I've decided that I just can't stay. I'm a phony. The others have noticed, and it's not right."

"But you can't—"

"Yes, I can." She looked into his eyes. It was the right thing to do, it had to be. She was tired of pretending. "Sylly, I quit."

"HOLD ON, HOLD ON, LET'S sit down and talk this over." Sylly looked around. "God, they didn't leave a damn thing, did they?"

Rose shook her head.

He exhaled through his nose and squatted on the floor in front of her. "All right. Let's back up. You found out about Mark, you said, so you're running away." He ran his hand through his dark, wavy hair, looking amused. "Was it his vast stockpiles of wealth that turned you off? Or the annoyingly large brains?"

"People know I was hired because Mark wanted to have sex with me. I'm not qualified."

"First, nobody knows anything. Second, you're doing fine. It's only been a couple of months."

"'*Fine.*' I'm a glorified secretary. I monitor the calendar and tell other people what to do. I don't have any actual skills of my own."

"Welcome to management," he said, grinning again.

"I want more." She stood up. "I think I should go back to school."

He tilted his head. "Great. Keep working at WellyNelly, do night school. The company will subsidize your classes."

"What?"

"Not many deals like that will fall into your lap, will they?"

She paused, knowing the answer, but the favors had to stop if she was going to retain her self-respect. "I can't—just because Mark and I—"

"It's open to everyone after their first year."

"I didn't see that anywhere in the benefits package. HR gave me a big packet."

He rolled his eyes. "Not my idea. Gloria insisted on a new subsidized training program when I hired her to take over." With a grin, he added, "You'll like her. She'll need women like you on the team to help her beat the men into submission— no, I shouldn't say that, very sexist—into shape."

Rose rubbed her eyes. It was too early for all this. "Who's Gloria?"

"Top secret, so just between you and me," he said, "Gloria is taking over as CEO right after the first of the year. I'm stepping aside, for the most part. I've got a new venture I'm going to launch. I'm really more of a startup kind of guy. Other people can keep the old ball rolling while I move on to something new."

"Wow." She liked Sylly, had hoped to work with him more, but…

If he wasn't the landlord or the boss anymore, he wouldn't care about what she and Mark—

No, that was old news.

"What were you thinking about, degree-wise?" he asked. "Decide to go for the MD?"

"No. MBA."

He laughed.

"See? You think that's funny. This is why I need to prove myself on my own."

"It's only funny because I asked Mark when we hired you if you'd be willing to get one."

She blinked at him. "You did?"

"Yeah, your résumé was a bit thin. We usually only hire bachelor's degrees when they're in engineering. But we're growing exponentially, Mark vouched for you, you seemed capable and eager"—he shrugged—"I only had one concern."

Hope we don't get a newbie overlord each time he wants to get laid. She felt her face get hot. "I'd think you'd be glad to get me out of the company, given—what you—what happened."

His ducked his head, hiding a smile. After a moment he shifted his weight and stood up. He studied her, his expression growing more serious. "I told him I'd fire you both if it happened again."

She nodded.

"Is that when you broke up with him?" Sylly continued. "When he told you?"

"It's when, but not why."

"Why then?"

"I'm not sure it's any of your business, Sylly."

"Not as your boss. As Mark's friend. I need to know."

"Why?"

"Please. Humor me. I won't tell a soul, not even smarty-pants."

She had to smile. "Okay. Although I was upset when I found out you'd, you know, seen us, and I didn't want to lose my job because of it, I wouldn't have…"

"Wouldn't…?"

"Wouldn't have let some power-tripping boss guy tell me who I could sleep with in my own home," she finished. "Even if it happened to belong to him."

He nodded, apparently pleased with something. "So why'd you dump him, then? No good in the sack?"

Rose stared at him. Why the hell did he want to know?

"Only good on the desk?" he continued.

Enough. She turned, grabbed a mug out of the kitchen box, strode to the kitchen.

"There's something I want to tell you, but I need to be sure of how you feel about him," Sylly said, right behind her. "Otherwise I'd be an asshole to say anything."

She turned. "Just tell me."

He shook his head.

"It's about Mark?" she asked.

He nodded. Waited, eyebrows up.

"Fine," she said, putting the empty mug down on the marble countertop. She might as well tell him. As his business partner and friend, he'd probably sympathize. "He didn't want anyone to know about me. Not even his family."

"That was a big problem for you?"

She lifted her chin. "I can't be with a man who's ashamed to be seen with me."

"Ah. And you think he is?"

Her head hurt. She rubbed her temples, suddenly overwhelmed by the thought she had a long, awkward weekend to endure and too little sleep to get her through it.

At least she had her clothes, underwear, shoes. It would be a lot easier to face Mark, and his family that didn't know she'd ever been anything to him, if she looked like hot shit.

Memories of his mother, brother, sister rose up in her mind. How Trixie had called her at work, not knowing her last name, just to invite her. How she'd always been warm and welcoming, never got too personal or made her uncomfortable in any way.

There was also that time she didn't tell Mark not to come

over, and the way she got Rose into the house to help with the dogs on the slightest pretense.

And how she'd always disappeared so quickly whenever Rose was with Mark.

Not sure of anything anymore, Rose picked up her mug, filled it with water from the fridge dispenser, stared outside the kitchen window at the rain. "I felt that way. Combined with your threat, it seemed best to cool it."

"And you're happy with how things turned out?" He walked around to face her. "Or are you all torn up with regret now that you know he's secretly rich and powerful?"

She looked down into her mug. "I don't care about that."

"Too bad for him." With a sigh, Sylly turned away. "I wish I knew what to do here. He'd probably kill me if he knew I was talking to you like this."

She'd never seen Sylly flustered, emotional. As uncomfortable as she was with his questions, she was touched by his concern. "Your friendship means a lot to him," she said, "not that he's probably ever told you that."

"Scarcity drives value," Sylly said, the corner of his mouth curling up. Then he touched her shoulder, smiled more broadly. "What the hell. Here goes."

"Look, if you're breaking a confidence—"

"No, we need to talk about MaJo. His social nerditude, is, I'm sure, many offenses to your pride," he began. "Do you think he's ashamed of the fact he became a millionaire before he graduated from college?"

"I have no idea."

"Take it from me, he's not. He's damn proud of himself."

"He should be."

"I agree," Sylly said. "So. Why do you think he keeps it a secret? Even with the woman he's desperately eager to… to…"

She raised her eyebrow. "Get laid with?"

"Aha!" He pointed his finger at her. "If that's what he wanted, why not tell you right away? Why do all the elaborate, unreliable shenanigans with the job instead of flashing around a little of that precocious financial success?"

"Because he doesn't think I'm a prostitute?" she asked sweetly.

"Yes, yes, but more than that. He didn't tell you because he likes his privacy. He's just a private guy. And, this is important, so pay attention—he wanted more than just sex." He saw her expression, continued more enthusiastically. "More than wanting to impress you, he wanted you to *like* him. For himself. Because he likes you."

Her heart went thump, squeeze, thump. It was hard talking about Mark, not being with him. "What's your point?"

"You're hearing it. You just don't want to admit it." He jumped up onto the counter, swung up his legs, and bracing his wet Keens on the marble, stood up to retrieve something from the space above the cabinets.

"You're getting mud on the counter."

"Got it." He leaped down, chestnut-brown bottle in hand. "It's a little early, but what the hell. I put this up there when I bought the place. Little tradition of mine." He reached for her mug.

"It's nine in the morning."

"So?" he asked. "Fine. I'll drink alone."

With a shrug, she poured the water in the sink, let him have the mug.

He poured an inch and knocked it back. "Yep," he said tightly. "Good shit."

Frowning, she watched him pour a second shot, tilt his head back and drink it with his eyes closed. "Mark never mentioned this side of you," she said.

Licking his lips, he splashed out another and held it out to her. "You sure?"

"Very," she said. "Why are you doing that?"

After a salute, he downed it. Coughing but smiling, he gasped out, "I'm celebrating."

The booze had been hidden in the house he had on the market. *His little tradition.* "You *did* sell the house."

Smiling, mug at his lips, he nodded.

Exasperated, she pulled the mug out of his hands, put it in the sink. "Whatever. I'm moving out either way."

His posture less regal than it had been, he leaned back against the counter. "Today?" he asked, then burped, laughed into his hand. "Sorry."

"How long until the new owners take over?"

"If everything goes well, we close in mid-January." He lifted the bottle, sighed, smiled at it. "I've waited a long time to drink this. Didn't expect the damn economy to collapse."

She could find an apartment by then if she was willing to commute, give up the perks, share a place. If she stuck it out with the assholes at work—and why should she let them drive her away?—she could afford a decent place of her own, even while she was going to school. "Why did you say I don't have to move out?"

He opened his eyes wide. "Weren't you listening to me?" Hugging the bottle to his chest with one hand, he patted her shoulder with the other. "Because your new landlord's in love with you, that's why."

Her heart began to pound. "What?" she whispered.

Sylly was already striding out of the kitchen, cell in his hand. "I better call a cab. Don't worry about the car, I'll get it later. I'm sure Mark won't mind."

"Mark?" Her voice was almost inaudible.

"So nice to do business with a friend," he said. "Don't you think? Especially one who pays in cash."

&

"Easy, little guys," Mark said to the dogs in the backseat of his VW. "We're just stopping for a minute. Calm down."

Good advice for himself. He hadn't slept well, fearing this was his last chance with Rose. Nothing solid was keeping her in California; even WellyNelly was just a job, and everything there would be changing very soon. For her benefit, and hopefully his own, but it was too early to say.

And she'd had the scare about the house. Hopefully he—Sylly—could explain the new owner was in no hurry to move in and liked having somebody there.

That had been phase 1.

If only he'd had more time for phase 2, but he couldn't risk another day, especially when that day was a holiday famous for making people homesick and the object of his affections had her own form of impulsive transportation.

And so, ready or not, phase 1 was underway.

At precisely 11:59 a.m., he parked his car in Rose's driveway, waiting for the dash clock to hit noon before he got out and rang the doorbell.

His driveway, his door, his bell.

Trapped inside the car, the three dogs yapped and danced on the seats, pawed at the windows. Zeus was especially animated, probably because he sensed Rose was near.

I know how you feel. When Rose opened the door, Mark felt his heart expand under his ribs like a balloon in an undersized box.

Beautiful, yes. Wavy golden hair, shining in the daylight.

The lush rosebud mouth. Her dramatically shapely figure, all curves, breasts, hips, so feminine, alluringly displayed under a snug royal-blue sweater, long black leggings tucked into knee-high black boots.

But it was how her brilliant blue eyes studied him as if maybe, just maybe, she was glad to see him again, that made his pulse leap like the dogs in the car.

"What are you doing here?" she asked, looking past him into the driveway. "I thought Bev and Liam were going to pick me up in their truck."

He cleared his throat. That was a lucky development. The storm had hit the Sierra and was dumping the first big snow of the year, multiple powdery feet of it, making her old sedan with the bald tires an unsuitable mode of transportation. "Change of plans," he said. "My mom doesn't like to drive in snow, so we rearranged everyone a little bit."

"But your car—it's no bigger than mine."

"I've got chains," he said. "And I've driven up there dozens of times, in all kinds of weather."

Her expression shuttered; she took a step back into the house, pushed the door shut.

Mark's nervous system went into high alert. He tapped on the door, raised his voice. "And I need help with the dogs. Please, Rose, don't make me drive up there alone with them."

She reappeared, backpack slung over her shoulder. "I was just getting my stuff."

He stepped back, commanded his heart to shift into a lower gear. "Sorry. I thought you were still too angry to be with me."

She gave him the funniest look—curious, worried, something else. Then she dropped her gaze to the ground and strode past him to the car.

"Don't you want to lock up?" he asked.

"Can't you do that?" she asked, then busied herself greeting the dogs. "Hello, little ones. Especially you, Zeus. Oh, I missed you."

Couldn't *he* do it? Surely she didn't know—

He looked at the door, back at her. "I'll need the key."

Holding Zeus in one hand while the dog licked her face, she leaned back against the door, eyes on Mark. "Oh, right." She lifted her hand, wiggled a set of keys, lobbed them at him. "You haven't closed yet."

He caught the keys, barely, and squeezed them between his fingers.

She knows.

25

HE HADN'T PLANNED ON TELLING her, not for a while. He'd had a plan, a cover story. One that he couldn't use now.

While his mind raced, she turned and got into the passenger seat.

She knew, but she was putting on her seat belt.

She was going to come anyway.

After a deep breath, he used her keys to lock the front door—his door—and made his way back to the car somewhat unsteady on his feet.

Not helpfully, he asked himself what his father would do. Lie? Bluster and evade? Charm and distract her sexually?

He opened the car door, as disappointed as always in his father's example. Nudging Europa out of the driver's seat, he got in, handed Rose the house keys, and backed out into the road without a word.

"Don't you want to close the gate?" she asked as he started to drive away. "All that lovely furniture in there, the ceramic elephant, all those beautiful, beautiful pillows. We wouldn't want anything to *disappear* while I'm gone."

He looked at her. So, she wanted him to say it; she wanted him to confess.

"I don't have the remote control," he said.

She slapped her forehead, nodded. "Silly me. Or should I say, Sylly Minguez. *He* has one."

She was so damned adorable. He almost laughed. "Would you like to get it out of your car?" he asked. "So you don't have to worry?"

"Nah. Not my problem." She nuzzled Zeus, let him lick her forehead. "Everything I need is right here."

His foot pressed down on the gas pedal, but he told himself to calm down, she was just playing around, laughing with the dog.

Everything I need...

"How long is the drive?" she asked.

"Depends. Traffic, weather. It might take us the rest of the day, unfortunately."

Hopefully. He didn't know how much time alone he'd get to spend with her at the cabin. This way she was all his, whether she liked it or not, at least for the next four to ten hours. It all depended on forces outside of his control.

He hated outside forces.

Maybe they'd get stuck in a snowbank. He'd seduce her, convince her he was wildly in love with her and wanted everything big and small she was willing to throw his way, and then they could skip the whole Christmas gathering thing with family and spend the next two weeks in a remote mountain chalet. Naked.

Just as he was imagining stripping off all her clothes so they could survive the night in the snowed-in car with skin-to-skin contact, Rose asked, "So, why'd you do it?"

"Do what?"

"Come on."

He'd done a few things. He'd bought Sylly's house; fomented an online rebellion, ruining a multi-million-dollar deal; recruited a new CEO for WellyNelly; started a new company with this new little thing he'd coded up in his spare time…

"I'm not staying, you know," she added.

His stomach clenched. "Excuse me?"

"I'll get my own place. With an actual lease. I can't afford to buy any property of my own, of course, not yet, but I need a place to live that isn't under the control of other people." She poked him in the leg. "Get it?"

She was staying in California. He looked over his shoulder, checking his blind spot as he merged, slowly, into the lanes to Sacramento. The traffic was bad, over a dozen lanes across of stop-and-go traffic in all directions, everyone trying to get out of town or into it. The rain made everything worse, slick and dangerous, and he'd already seen three cars pulled over, hazards on, fenders smashed.

There were some things you just couldn't hurry.

"I'm sorry," he said finally. "I was just trying to help."

"Who? You or me?" She set Zeus down in the back. "You own WellyNelly and now my house. Maybe you think I'm part of the package. Because I'll be so grateful."

God, she knew more, or thought she knew, but her voice was so soft, so controlled, not angry at all. What was she thinking? Feeling?

"I don't own WellyNelly," he said carefully. "Only a part of it."

"It was all your idea. You created it when you were, like, in diapers."

"Don't mock. It's not easy going to high school in Depends, believe me."

She didn't laugh. "Why didn't you tell me?"

He signaled, moved into the far left lane. Maybe he didn't want this ride to last as long as he'd thought. He hadn't trapped her; she'd trapped *him*. "I don't know," he said quietly.

"I was starting to feel like maybe I'd been too quick to, you know, give up on what we'd started—"

He swerved to avoid rear-ending the pickup in front of him. Heart in his mouth, he glanced at her.

"But then I find out you didn't trust me with huge parts of your life. And mine. You left me out to dry, Mark. At work. I should've known what I was walking into."

"You're right. I'm sorry."

"Why not tell me?" She addressed her hands, the side of the road, Zeus, who'd climbed back into her lap—she talked to everything but him. "Early on, okay, we were practically strangers, but later…"

"I should've. It was one of those things that changed over time. My reasons changed."

"Hmm," she said, still not looking at him. "You know why I'm here today? What my reasons are?"

He gripped the wheel. "What?"

"I'm trying to help Blair." Rubbing Zeus behind the ears, cuddling him to her chest, she added, "We'll see if any of my reasons change over time."

If the minivan in front of him hadn't changed lanes suddenly, he would've plowed right into it.

﹖

ROSE AWOKE JUST AS THE SUN WAS SETTING. THE SNOW was falling so thick and fast, she could hardly see five feet in front of the car, even in the remaining daylight.

"How long was I out?" Disoriented, she rubbed her eyes.

Last thing she remembered, they were driving through Sacramento. If she hadn't been so sleep deprived, she never would've lost consciousness for hours so close to Mark—only inches from those eyes, that profile, those arms and chest and long, muscular thighs.

She hoped she hadn't drooled in her sleep.

"A few hours," he said, offering her a gentle smile. "You must've been exhausted. You barely stirred when I got out to put on the chains."

Vaguely she remembered a stop, cold wind blowing in, dogs yapping. "You put me in chains?"

His smile turned wolfish.

What am I saying? She reminded herself the dream she'd been having about him wasn't real; they weren't on those terms anymore. Kissing and licking terms. He was tempting as always, but not enough had changed; when they were alone, he'd always been charming, sexy, talkative, engaged, lovable—

When they were alone.

"Sorry I didn't help out with the dogs," she said. Zeus was huddled under the heating vent at her feet, gazing up at her adoringly. "Did they get a bathroom break?"

"Yeah. I thought for a minute I'd lost Europa in a snowdrift, but she'd already jumped back in the car." They'd left the freeway and were now passing through the business district of a small lakeside town. King's Beach, the sign said.

She pulled out her phone, looked at the map. They were on the North Shore of Lake Tahoe, heading southwest. The lake was just to their left, though too whited out by snowfall to see much of it.

"I really didn't expect so much snow," she said. Hardly the beaches and sunshine she'd imagined when Blair told her she was moving to California.

"Forecast is for two feet overnight," he said.

She broke her gaze away from his profile and focused on the white road, white trees, white sky. "Are we going to get stuck up here?"

The car turned right into a development rising up above the lake. He was busy maneuvering around a snowdrift as high as the car, but she saw him bite back a grin. "Like the Donner Party, you mean? We passed the highway marker for them when you were asleep. I was tempted to wake you up."

"When your brother offered me a ride, I told him I'd like to make it back by Monday."

"Why?"

Mouth open, she hesitated. Being with John and Blair in the same house could be uncomfortable, and being with Mark, even more so.

"The office *is* closed for the week," he added, giving her an intense look that made her insides flutter.

Was she really in such a hurry? Last night she'd been sure she had to leave her job, but Sylly's words had changed everything. New management, a chance to pursue an advanced degree…

Oh, and this little idea that Mark was in love with her.

She shook her head. Mark throwing around his money and influence—which he had in excess—didn't mean that much. He probably needed an investment opportunity anyway, and why not buy a friend's property—beautiful, luxurious, close to home?

"Your brother can drive me if you don't want to," she said.

"I'll drive you wherever and whenever you'd like."

The car crept through the snow.

"So, you bought Sylly's house," she said, giving him an opening. He hadn't taken any of her hints so far.

He shifted into low gear. The chains on the tires rattled and crunched with each inch they traveled. "You weren't supposed to know."

"Oh, really?" She laughed. "How was that going to work? You didn't think I'd notice?"

He came to a stop, squinting out at the A-framed houses lining the winding road. "Why, look—here we are. Can you see any numbers? We want 405."

Zeus's ears were silky under her fingers. "Were you going to set up fake showings with a fake real estate agent?" She leaned back, tilting her head toward him, and let herself get into the spirit of the game. "Or was he going to say it was purchased by an investor who was deeply involved in business out of town—no, out of the country, for a long, intractable period. Europe, maybe—no, more remote. Kazakhstan. Bad roads, poor infrastructure, organized crime, very hard just to hop on a plane or the Internet and deal with a new house. Better to have a tenant there keeping things safe and cozy until he gets back. Which could be a really, really long time. In fact, he bought the house precisely *because* I'm living in it. I can't leave. He'll offer to *pay* me to stay."

He stared at her, awe and amusement in his eyes.

She grinned. "I'm good, aren't I?"

Rolling down the window, he stuck his head out into the thickly falling snow. "This is it! We're the first ones here." When he pulled his head back in and shut the window, clumps of snow scattered around him in the car. "Our place has orange reflectors along the top windows, but it's not dark enough yet to light them up." With a forced, bright grin, he hit his turn signal, checked over his shoulder, checked his mirrors, and slowly edged the car into a driveway.

"Mark."

He still didn't look at her. "It looks like it was plowed about ten minutes ago. This whole development pays for it privately. We'd never get near the house otherwise." He pulled the car just in front of the support posts of a deck wrapping around the second floor. The windows were dark, the sharply slanted roof blanketed with white powder.

"We'll have to shovel the steps," he continued, "our punishment for getting here first."

Smiling, Rose dipped her head to nuzzle Luna, the smallest dog, who'd climbed into her lap next to Zeus. She trembled with excitement, even with the heat turned up.

She'd have to pry more out of Mark once they were inside. "Will the house be warm? The dogs aren't exactly Siberian huskies."

"Hope so." He killed the engine, then looked at her and the dog and turned it back on, the heat blasting out of the vents. "Stay here. I'll kick a path up the stairs, make sure the furnace is on before you go in."

"I'm fine, it's just the little guys," she said.

"Of course. A tough New Yorker like yourself can handle a little weather."

"Exactly."

He stared at her for a moment before getting out. Slipping his hands into gloves, he climbed over a snowdrift in front of the bottom stairs, kicked away some ice, and made his way slowly up to the door.

"Our evasive hero," Rose whispered in Luna's oversized, pointy ear.

A minute later he was back outside wielding a broom. He brushed the handrail, then the steps, his movements powerful, graceful, and assured.

"Funny how he's so different when he's alone," she told Luna.

No, not just alone. With her.

She remembered the day they'd met, how he thought she was a lesbian. And then the way he tripped over himself whenever Blair was around. For the first time, Rose wondered if she should be flattered, not jealous, that he found her so comfortable to be with.

But she admitted to herself, she *was* jealous. What if he was pursuing her because she seemed easy? Not promiscuous —though she'd been that—but convenient? Practical? Not the love of his life, not a great passion, but… good enough. Comfortable. Like a well-padded sofa. The kind of girl you'd settle for when you were ready to settle down.

Luna yelped and she realized she'd squeezed her. "Sorry, girl. Your daddy's cleared the way, so let's get you inside."

Maybe she was wrong to want more passion, more need, just *more*, than that.

But why should she be the only one to suffer?

She pulled on the only gloves she had, rainbow-striped acrylic with pink fake-fur trim at the wrist, and gingerly stepped out into the snow.

Her foot sank down. And down and down and down. By the time she stopped moving the snow had swallowed her leg all the way up to her right thigh.

One hand still on the door handle, she struggled back up into the truck, short of breath, half of her body caked with white, dry powder.

Mark had been able to walk right over to the stairs. Was she that much heavier than he was?

He pulled open the driver's side door. "Come out over here. There's a drop-off on that side. Sorry I didn't warn you."

Relieved, she crawled over the center console. "I was feeling very heavy just then."

He got a silly grin on his face. "Like gold."

The dogs wiggled their way over to the steering wheel but stayed in the truck, big eyes on the big, cold, white outdoors. Trying to ignore how Mark took hold of her arm, she put her left foot out, then her right. "Thank God I didn't sink to the center of the earth again."

He looked down at her right pant leg. "Those boots are made for city walking."

"Yeah, well, they're all I've got."

"I'm not complaining. They're sexy."

She looked up into his face.

"I'm not going to apologize," he said. "That's not a come-on, it's a fact."

Ducking her head to hide her flushing cheeks—honestly, they were turning snow into steam—she scooped Luna up into her arms and went up the stairs, wrapping her into her jacket to shield her from the wind.

He reached out and touched her back. "Careful, it's icy. I'll get the salt out here in a minute, after the dogs are in."

Luna seemed to know where she was. As soon as Rose crossed the threshold, the dog wriggled out of her jacket onto the floor and immediately trotted down the wood-paneled hall, bottom wagging happily.

Mark came up behind her with the other two dogs. "You stay here. I'll get the stuff."

The dogs' toenails clicked on the floor as they trotted after their friend.

"That's not fair, I can help."

"Let me feel manly," he said. "So seldom do I get to enjoy the sensation."

Smiling, she wiped some snow off her shoulder. "Oh, all right. You can be manly."

His eyes were hot on hers. "Thanks."

"Mark…"

"Don't say anything. I know." He turned. "I'll get the rest of the stuff. You can pick out whatever room you want. That's part of the tradition, first come first serve." He stepped outside, shutting the door hard behind him.

All right, so he didn't look at her as though she were a comfortable sofa. Those sharp, hungry, smoldering eyes were not those of a man who wanted to lie down, roll over, and take a nap.

Breathing unsteadily, she bent over and unzipped her boots, knocking away the snow as best she could. She hung up her jacket on one of the brass hooks sticking out of a snowshoe bolted to the paneled wall.

If only they'd come up here together earlier, just the two of them, before—

No. She couldn't think like that. Two people couldn't live in a bubble; they had to fit in the world together, too. She was no hermit. Couldn't be.

There was a long hallway that stretched straight ahead, doors on either side, the walls decorated with vintage ski resort posters, more antique snowshoes, a pair of thin wood skis hung in an X. The floors, walls, and ceiling were honey-colored wood, glossy and warm. Colorful Native American and Mexican area rugs dotted the floor.

Very welcoming. Maybe she could live *here*.

The door opened behind her, bringing Mark hauling their luggage and a blast of cold air.

"You come up to this place every year?" she asked.

He piled the bags up near the door, stomped his feet on the rug, nodded. "Have you picked a room yet?"

"Any recommendations?"

"The left one on the end is a good choice. It usually goes first."

"I'll go check it out." She tiptoed over the clumps of snow

to her bag, lifted it over her shoulder, her eyes on his face. He turned, disappeared into a closet.

All of the bedrooms were similarly decorated: lots of wood, colorful quilts, fluffy down comforters, wool blankets—floor-to-ceiling mountain chic.

Even the last bedroom on the left. She went in, dropping her bag and looking around. It was nice, but she didn't see why he would suggest it. The decor was the same, and it seemed a little smaller than the others, perhaps because the four-poster king-sized bed took up most of the floor space.

He'd followed her, stood in the doorway, watching her with a serious look she couldn't read.

"It's fine," she said, sitting on the bed, bouncing a little. It was firm, high off the ground, didn't creak at all. Her grandparents had a bed like it, joked they'd have it forever because it was heavier than the house itself and couldn't be moved.

He continued to stare.

"What?" she asked.

He walked across the room until he was standing a few feet from the bed. His eyes darkened as he gazed down at her. "You should know this," he said in a low voice. "I'll do everything and anything to join you in that bed before you go back home."

His words floated down her spine like kisses. She wished she hadn't sat down, that she could meet him eye to eye. Then again, it was good she wasn't standing; she suddenly felt weak all over. "Consider me warned."

He tilted his head, letting his gaze rake over her, then left without another word.

She counted to ten before letting herself fall onto her back, her heart pounding. The ceiling was decorated with more antique snowshoes, one modified with a light bulb.

His voice surprised her from the doorway. "By the way, my family refers to this as 'Mark's room,'" he said, a slow grin forming on his face, "but I'm happy to share."

And then he was gone again.

26

AFTER MARK PUT AWAY THE groceries in the kitchen, he poured himself a beer and got busy making lasagna. They'd have a big holiday dinner on Christmas, but people tonight would be arriving in waves, needing to eat. While he gathered the ingredients, he thought about Rose downstairs in his bedroom. And smiled.

Because of the deep winter snows every year, the house was designed with the bedrooms on the ground level and the kitchen, deck, great room—and second entrance—on the top floor. There were thousands of similar cabins all around the lake, but this one was special. When Mark was in eighth grade, his father had taken him up here, just the two of them, not to pressure him to win chess matches or become an Olympian like his brother, but just to hang out. It was the only time Mark could remember the two of them being together without a competition and some prize dangling at the end of it.

He filled a pot with water for the pasta, let the bittersweet memories wash over him. His father had been domineering, unyielding, competitive, tough, and often a bully, especially to

Mark, but during those few days in February years ago, he'd just been a dad.

Mark had known then what kind of man he wanted to be. The kind of man his father had been on that trip—loving, patient, *nice*—not the one he'd lived with at home.

That man, however, didn't win over the ladies. Acting like his father, like he'd just done downstairs, apparently did. Rose had given him a look he could get used to, a potent combination of desire and respect.

Lust washed over him. If the macho posturing didn't do the job, he'd fall back on being a sensitive provider. With the bedroom skills only an obsessive engineer with access to unlimited porn could hone to perfection.

A commotion downstairs told him others were arriving. In a couple of minutes Rose, Blair, and John appeared, all three of them looking around the vaulted family room with appreciation.

"We just got here ourselves," Rose was saying. "I haven't even been up here yet."

"Nice," John said.

Blair was silent, her eyes downcast.

John threw an arm around her shoulders. "Don't you think so?"

She nodded, smiled tightly.

"We took the room with the snowshoes on the walls," John said. "Is that okay?"

"They all have snowshoes on the walls." Rose squeezed Blair's arm. "Did you notice?"

Blair let out a loud, breathy sigh, kept her eyes on the floor.

Mark frowned, hoping Blair didn't overdo it. She was biting her lip as though trying not to cry, when he knew she was fighting the giggles. The entire scheme to get Rose up here had been her idea—though John had jumped at the chance to participate.

"Getting her hitched would finally get my mother off my ass," he'd said the night before, when Mark had gone over to ask for help.

"You're just saying that. You want her to be happy," Blair said.

"Why would I want that?" he asked. "She hates my guts."

"Because you're secretly a wonderful man?" Blair asked.

John looked at Mark. "Can you believe this woman? Nobody's ever accused me of being wonderful in my entire life. I'm cruel and selfish, just like my mom raised me." He bent down and kissed Blair on the neck. "Don't you forget it."

While John nuzzled her, Blair smiled at Mark. "She's been rescuing me for years. Now it's my turn. I totally know how to get her up there."

And she'd been right; Rose had come. Now she was watching Blair with worry in her eyes, glancing at John, who, with a straight face, nodded sadly.

For God's sake. Mark stabbed the mozzarella with a paring knife. Rose was going to be furious when she figured out what they were doing.

And Mark would get the blame.

"You might rather sleep in the loft up here," Mark said, opening a jar of tomato sauce. The less Rose saw of Blair, the less likely she'd spot the ruse. He pointed at the staircase that rose up behind the entertainment console. "It's small, but cozy."

Blair wandered away from the group, looking up at the narrow hideaway. It was only about eight by twelve feet, just enough for a full daybed, lots of pillows, and a reading lamp.

Blair turned to Mark. "Nobody else wants it?"

"Take it. It's all yours."

"The bed's right under the skylights," John said. "You won't be able to sleep in."

Blair gave him a pointed look. "You keep telling me I sleep too much. *Remember?*"

John bit his lip, flushed. He, too, was on the verge of smiling. "If that's what you want, honey, I'll move your stuff up there for you."

Glancing at Rose, Blair sighed, turned it into a yawn, covered her mouth. "I think I'll lie down for a little while," she said in a listless voice, "if that's okay. Don't bother to wake me."

"How about we hang out a little? Have a drink? Tea? Talk?" Rose asked.

Blair sighed again. "No, I'm just not up for it."

Mark thought she if she kept this up, Rose would catch on before dinner. "Could you wait, Blair? I haven't put the sheets on that bed yet." He held her gaze. "Come sit at the counter, I'll get you a drink."

Blair got his hint and came over.

John walked into the kitchen, biting back a grin. "Bit over the top, isn't she?" he muttered in Mark's ear.

They were having way too much fun with this. As if Mark's life wasn't on the line. "There's beer in the fridge," he said, pounding the garlic with the flat edge of the knife.

John chose a bottle of Lagunitas, took the opener Mark handed him. "You want anything, Rose?"

"She likes martinis," Mark said.

"That's right." John grinned at her. "How could I forget?"

The blush that bloomed on Rose's face made Mark white-knuckle the garlic press.

"A beer is fine," she said.

"No, no," John said, striding over to her. "I'll make you a martini. Where—"

Mark pointed at the small standalone bar along the wall. "It should be stocked. Olives in the fridge."

"I can make it," Rose said. "It's not like I've got anything to do."

John caught her in his arms and guided her to the sofa, a move that brought a growl to the back of Mark's throat.

"Sit," John said, still holding her. "Enjoy yourself. That's what I always liked about you. You're a woman who always knows how to have a good time."

The knife slipped, lopped a sliver of skin off of Mark's index finger.

Cool it. Stay calm.

"What can I get you, Blair?" he said tightly, eyeing his finger for signs of blood. "How about wine? Red or white?" He remembered the way she'd watched him drink his wine months ago when she was pregnant and couldn't have any.

"Whatever's open is fine." Eyes downcast, she climbed up on a bar stool at the kitchen counter across from him. Sighed again.

Mark opened both bottles and set them in front of her with a glass. "Your pick."

She looked up, glanced behind her again, smiled mischievously. "Thanks."

He finished making the sauce, mixed the spinach, egg, and ricotta with his hands, then got out the lasagna pan.

"I can tell you're a good cook," Blair said, sipping her wine.

"Hardly. I only know how to make this because they print the recipe right on the box. If the store had stopped carrying this brand of pasta, we'd be eating Cheerios tonight."

"It's more than that. You made the sauce from scratch."

"I just added a little extra garlic."

"Improvisation is the sign of a born chef." She saluted him with her glass.

"Do you cook?"

"I love to cook."

He nodded, glanced over at Rose and John, laughing with each other.

Now he was the depressed one.

"I used to think about going to culinary school," Blair said.

"Used to?" He wondered if Rose had ever told John to take it slow. The bastard—what was he doing now? Sitting right next to her when there was a perfectly good chair on the other side of the coffee table?

"Yeah, you know, before," Blair said.

Mark stared, confused for a moment because he'd forgotten what they were talking about. "Before," he repeated.

"Getting pregnant, moving out here, everything."

"There are lots of cooking schools around San Francisco. Not that I'm an expert, but I've enjoyed eating at them. So they can't totally suck, assuming they cooked the food I ate." He wiped his hands and slipped the lasagna into the oven, wishing he'd just ordered a pizza. Because of his jealous distraction, he had half the ricotta left over and the pan was overflowing with tomato sauce; who knows what else he'd screwed up while John cozied up to Rose.

Blair sighed. "Do you think I could ever—forget it. I don't have any experience. It's a crazy idea."

He leaned against the counter, picked up his beer. "I'd never be able to work in a restaurant myself—too many people yelling at each other."

"I don't mind yelling. Or people." She smiled.

"Then you should look into it."

"Thanks. I will." She put down her glass, climbed off of

the stool. "God, it's great to come up here. I was totally dreading—" Seeming to remember how depressed she was supposed to be, she slapped her hand over her mouth, peeked over her shoulder.

The chatty, sociable couple was still having a great time together on the couch. Two extroverts, well-dressed and fun-loving, strident, confident. John said something that made Rose throw her head back and laugh, her blonde hair flying. Grinning, John waited, watching her, then said something else that set her off again.

Now Mark was the one to sigh.

Apparently sensing something was amiss, Rose broke away from her handsome, amusing companion and came back over to the breakfast counter. "Everything okay?"

Blair sipped her wine, offered her a weak smile. "You know, it is. I'm so glad I came."

Rose beamed.

"When's chowtime?" John asked, rejoining them. As though he couldn't bear to be left out for a second. And did he have to stand so close to Rose?

"About a half hour. Unless it's really bad, in which case you'll have to add on the time for the pizza to get here," Mark said.

The dogs began barking furiously. Zeus in front, they tore across the living room floor and clattered down the stairs. Exclaiming so loudly her voice carried upstairs, his mother sounded as thrilled with the reunion as her dogs.

Now it was really time for the show to begin.

ROSE WATCHED MARK TENSE UP as the sounds of his family arriving filtered up the stairs.

What had he and Blair been talking about? *She'd* certainly perked up. And until the dogs had started barking, Mark had been talking to her without stammering, blushing, tripping, or gawking.

She studied the olive at the bottom of her martini. How nice for them they could be so happy together.

Very, very nice.

She opened the top button of her sweater, tugged the neckline down another inch, and downed the rest of her drink.

Liam was the first to appear, his cheeks flushed from the cold, a grocery bag in his arms. "Mark said he made dinner. I don't believe it."

"It looks really good," Blair said. Mark smiled at her.

Rose tugged her sweater a little lower. Leaned forward, propped her elbows on the counter.

Mark glanced over, smile freezing in place. His eyelids dropped. She saw the motion of his throat as he swallowed, watching her.

"We brought some bread and sandwich fixings in case it's inedible," Liam said.

Mark barely glanced at him, not seeming to register what he'd said.

Bev walked up from behind Liam, her straight black hair hanging loose around her face. Like her fiancé's, her cheeks were splotched with color. "Oh, my God, I'm freezing. Did you guys get caught in the storm? I lost my hat in the driveway. Look—my fingers are like little popsicles." She held them out.

"'Freezing.' I used to swim in water colder than this," Liam said.

"And look how strong it made you," Bev said, patting his chest. Then she saw Blair sitting behind the counter and her smile faltered. "Blair. It's good to see you again."

Rose forced herself to look away from Mark, fearing an outpouring a pity that would make Blair uncomfortable; but Bev only offered her hand for a quick shake before muttering something about coffee as she dug into the cabinets.

Trixie arrived, still wearing her coat, leading to more hugs among the family. Rose stepped back to watch. Though Bev and John were first cousins, she didn't see much resemblance, and their body language suggested they weren't very close.

"Where's April?" Mark asked.

"Not coming until tomorrow," Liam said. "She said she had to work today, didn't want to drive in the dark with all the snow."

Mark frowned. "She had to work?"

With a shrug, Liam got himself a beer. "I know, huh?"

"Doing what?"

"Drawing or something. I have no idea," Liam said. "I thought she was just shacking up with some guy, but apparently she's devoting herself to the arts. Or something."

"Huh. I didn't know she had any devoting in her," Mark said.

"Be quiet, you two. She's just a late bloomer, that's all," Trixie said. "I'm going to take the dogs out for a walk. I'll try to find your hat, Bev, but if my little guys get to it first, you might want to save up for a new one. They love peeing on new things."

"Isn't it too cold to go out?" Bev asked.

Liam snorted, caught Rose's eye. "Southern California girls are such wimps."

Trixie poked him in the shoulder. "She's absolutely right. They need to wear their new outfits." She pulled a miniature orange sweatshirt out of her coat pocket and held it up, a big grin on her face. "The latest and greatest from Fite Fitness!"

Liam groaned and turned away.

"Is that reflective piping?" Rose asked, studying the tiny garment. A silver FITE FITNESS logo filled one short sleeve.

"Safety first," Trixie said. With a wave, she left them, passing Mark at the top of the stairs.

Bev smiled at Rose. "Fite Dog hits stores next fall. Isn't that great?"

"The things we do for love," Liam said, kissing Bev on the lips.

Mark snaked around them, checked his creation inside the oven, then scowled at the crowd in his kitchen. "Why is everyone in here when there's a perfectly usable living room right over there?"

Liam bumped him roughly as he got a bag of corn chips out of the cupboard. "Parties always end up where the food is. You should've bought a house with a bigger kitchen."

He should've? Rose frowned at the brothers. "I thought your family had been coming up here since you were kids."

"I was already working at Fite, I think, the first time I was here," Liam said. "Hard to remember, we rented different ones over the years, all around the lake. What year was it you bought this place, Mark?"

Not even Blair looked surprised at the news that the house belonged to Mark and not his mother. Rose stared at him, amazed to see him turn an odd, mottled red color.

"I—I—a while ago," he said, unblinking eyes on her.

"You'd just turned twenty-one, right? That second dotcom went public, and you didn't even tell us how much money you got," Liam said, then frowned at Bev when she elbowed him in the ribs. "What?"

"Maybe he likes to keep that sort of thing private," Bev said, hooking her arm through his. "Come on, let's give the chef some room. Let us know if you want us to help with anything, like a salad or whatever."

"As if you know how to make a salad," Liam said. "Bacon salad, maybe."

Bev dragged him past the kitchen counter into the large living area. "You say that like it's a bad thing."

"I didn't realize you'd caught the IPO wave, buddy," John said. "What company was it?"

Mark stuck his head in the oven, mumbling something.

Glancing at Rose, Blair slid off her stool. "I better put my things in the loft before somebody else claims it." She staggered a little, caught herself, and bent down to lift the bag.

Tabling his question for Mark, John strode over. "I'll do it." He kissed her on the cheek. "That bed better have room for two."

Rose watched them walk across the room and up to the loft before turning back to Mark. "Why didn't you tell me this was your place?"

He stared at her. "Didn't I?"

Rose snorted.

The timer went off. He grabbed the oven mitts and got out the lasagna, avoiding her eyes.

"What else are you hiding?"

"Rose, this cabin, WellyNelly, some money—all come from the same period in my life. I'd done some coding for some guys—like Sylly—who I met at the hobby shop, never expecting anything to come out of it. They wanted to compensate me, I said I didn't care. I ended up with stock options." He slipped off the oven mitts and, staring down at them, arranged them on the counter in a straight line. "I didn't really deserve the money. It was crazy back then. Millionaires springing up overnight."

He really didn't think it was a big deal. It *embarrassed* him. "That's why you didn't tell me? Because you thought you didn't deserve it?"

He moved the oven mitts around until they were standing upright, leaning on each other like a house of cards. "I *didn't* deserve it. Chris and Ben did the architecture, I just helped out when they had questions. They were stupid to give some random teenager such a big piece of the pie."

Stupid. He was worse than she was.

She went over to him, close enough to rest her hand on his arm. "I doubt you were just some random teenager, or that they were stupid," she said quietly.

He gazed down at her. Something in his face shifted, opened, warmed. "You do?"

"They paid you what they thought you were worth." Suddenly she was aware she was touching him, that he'd ducked his head closer to hers. His eyes were dark, gray-blue pools, deep, inviting. "Why are you so convinced they were wrong?" she asked.

He reached up to her cheek, traced the tender skin under her eye. "Why are you so convinced they weren't?"

Her throat went dry. He was always throwing her off balance. Strong one minute, sweet the next. "I just am."

"Maybe you're biased." His hand glided down her cheek to her chin, caressing.

"Maybe I am," she whispered.

He smiled slowly and abruptly stepped away. "Do *you* know how to make a bacon salad? It's almost showtime."

Deep breath. Hand on the counter. "I'm more of a lettuce type."

"That'll do."

Still unsteady, she walked slowly over to the fridge. "Just don't say, 'That'll do, Pig.' You know, like from *Babe*."

"Why would I?"

She grabbed the romaine, glanced at him over her shoulder. He looked genuinely stumped.

"Because I'm a plus-sized woman." She waved the lettuce at him to lighten the mood. "Do you have a salad spinner in this vacation home of yours?"

Frowning, he squatted down, dug around and held out a colander. "That's all I've got." He leaned against the counter and watched her tear the leaves, rinse them under the water. Finally he said, "I still don't get it."

She hit the tap, wishing she hadn't said anything. "Nothing. It's nothing."

"Please. I know I'm an idiot. You have to explain. I'm obsessive like that. I'll be up half the night trying to figure it out." His gaze dropped to her mouth, then lower, slow, deliberately suggestive. "Of course, I hope I'll be up half the night doing other things."

It was amazing how he could make her shivery and heated at the same time. "Your mother tried to put John in a room downstairs. By himself. I think that was for your benefit."

"You're trying to change the subject. Why would I say, 'That'll do, Pig'?"

She crossed her arms over her chest. "Have you seen *Babe*?"

"Yeah. Talking animal movie. Heartwarming. Evil cat."

She shook the colander, turning away. "You're teasing me."

"I swear I'm not." His fingers wrapped around her shoulders, turned her firmly to face him. "There was a little, hairless, sheepherding farm animal. Or is it something to do with the wife? Because she was *hot*."

Rose jerked away. "Now I know you're teasing me." She reached up to open a cabinet. "Is there a bowl for the salad?"

He captured her in his arms, facing him, his hips pinning her to the counter. "I want you to say it."

Her heart pounded. "That I'm a pig?"

He pressed his body harder against her, not hiding his arousal. "That you're not." His hands came up, cupped her face. He dipped his head but his lips didn't touch hers, just hovered close enough to feel his breath blend with hers.

"I'm not," she whispered.

Shaking his head slowly, he sank a millimeter closer.

The dogs chose that moment to tear up the stairs, Trixie shouting behind them to wait. "You'll get snow all over Mark's perfect house!"

Right. People. Everywhere. She started to pull away, but he held her.

Trixie's voice was right behind them. "I'll get them, Mark, don't wor—" Her voice cut off as if sliced with a knife.

Rose had her hands on the counter, a smile on her face, ready to joke about not even liking *wool*, let alone *sheep*—

When he kissed her.

Oh.

He was tender, his lips brushing hers gently but thoroughly. No hurry, just steady pressure, fully covering her mouth with his while his hand caressed her waist.

Slow, luxurious kisses. She forgot everything but the careful, controlled movements of his lips, the feel of his breath, the pressure of his hand—no, his hands, because the other one was sliding around her back and up between her shoulder blades to tangle in her hair, stroke the back of her neck where the skin was soft and particularly sensitive to his touch.

Her knees buckled. He pressed closer, holding her up.

It was too slow, too soft. Tension wound tighter inside her belly, between her legs, her heart. She opened her mouth and invited him inside.

Which is when he broke away. Holding her at arm's length, eyes obsidian black, he seemed to be struggling for breath like she was, and gradually the noises of the five other people in the house broke through the haze of her desire.

He released her, a faint, wicked smile in the corner of his mouth. She looked past him, expecting to see his mother watching them, wide-eyed, horrified, but she was sitting with her back to them on the sofa with Liam and Bev. Someone had turned on a football game.

"She saw us, you know," she said.

Mark leaned against the counter next to her, hands on either side, staring at her sideways. A lock of his hair had fallen over one eyebrow. Her fingers itched to brush it back, but if she touched him again right now, she'd never stop.

"I should probably serve the dinner," Mark said, pushing away from the counter. "Such as it is."

She took a breath, honest enough to admit she was disappointed. They could've run downstairs for a few minutes—

Everybody was right there. His brother, Bev, John, Blair, Trixie.

Nobody said anything.

"I'll finish the salad," she said shakily.

♨

So far, Mark thought, phase 2 appeared to be working. Play her hot and cold, keep her guessing. His initial plan had been to make his big move after Christmas dinner, right when she'd be all soft, sentimental, vulnerable—but that was over twenty-four hours away and he wasn't sure the wait was necessary. She'd melted when he kissed her in the kitchen, not even scolding him afterward.

Though his mother had. "You don't want to embarrass her, honey," she'd said quietly as they cleared the table after dinner. "She's the skittish type."

But Mark had finally figured out how badly Rose wanted the public display. How much she needed it. Standing in the kitchen, he glanced at Rose still sitting at the table. "Just don't act surprised, whatever I do. I want her to think you've been in on this all along."

His mother patted him on the shoulder. "Oh, honey. I've been in on it longer than you have."

To Mark's disappointment, Rose said good night to everyone, retiring to her room, as soon as the plates were in the dishwasher. John and Blair dressed up to hit the casinos on the Nevada side of the lake, leaving Mark, Liam, Bev, and his mother to sit together in the living room.

While they watched TV, Mark tried to distract himself with websites and playing games on his phone, determined to leave Rose alone for at least an hour. Apparently bored with the sports coverage, Liam turned off the TV, threw the remote into Mark's lap. "Edible lasagna," he said, kicking him in the leg. "Even though you had to eat it with a spoon."

Bev, curled under his arm, switched the TV back on, flipped through the channels. "Leave him alone. It was great."

"I never realized how good lasagna could be without all that cheese," his mother said.

It wasn't Mark's culinary prowess that he cared about tonight. "What are you guys doing tomorrow before dinner?" He hoped to have the cabin alone with Rose after they opened the small pile of presents under the tree. Not everything he did with her had to be publicly displayed.

Liam scowled. "Aren't we skiing?"

"I'm not," Bev said.

"Yes, you are."

She laughed. "Nice try. I trip over myself as it is. Can you imagine if my feet were suddenly six feet long?" She snorted. "Forget it. I'm not asking for trouble."

"How can you come to Tahoe and not ski?"

Bev looked up at him, raised an eyebrow. "That's all you can think of?"

Liam grinned, then glanced at his mother and made a face. "Hey. Not in front of the parent."

"I am a little jealous, I admit," Trixie said wistfully. "I'm a spare wheel around here."

Mark stood up. It was hard enough discussing his love life, let alone his mother's. He looked at his phone. Fifty-seven minutes since Rose had gone downstairs. What was she doing down there? He stepped around the sofa, his heart starting to beat faster. "I think I'm going to see what Rose is up to."

"It's not quite an hour yet," his brother said.

Mark turned. "What?"

"Since she went downstairs," Liam said, batting his eyes.

"Bev, I really don't understand what you see in that arrogant prick." Mark strode to the stairs while his brother broke out laughing.

When he was out of sight, Mark jumped down the stairs two at a time, reaching her door short of breath, heart racing, ready. He squared his shoulders, combed his hair with his fingers.

As he lifted his hand to knock on the door, he hesitated.

What if she rejected him tonight? They'd just arrived. Tomorrow was Christmas. She'd feel awkward, uncomfortable. Everyone would notice. She might even ask to leave—though he had thoughtfully ensured her lack of a vehicle.

Even if she did sleep with him, how could he assume she wouldn't regret it like she had before?

Closing his eyes, he slowly, agonizingly, lowered his arm. No. She had to come to him this time. He'd act like the smitten lover in public, touch her every chance he had, display every lustful thought on his face so she could never accuse him of being ashamed of wanting her, be seen wanting her.

Loving her.

He walked away and, treading heavily on the creaky wood floorboards, went into the room next to hers.

To wait.

It wasn't sugarplums that danced in his dreams.

2 8

JUST AFTER NOON, ROSE SANK into the couch with her coffee and stared out at the snow. Christmas Day was white, blue, bright, and lovely. Zeus jumped up onto the cushion next to her, dancing with joy, and licked her on the elbow, the highest spot he could reach.

At least somebody wants me, she thought, sipping her coffee.

Stupid. Mark was playing by her rules, and she was complaining.

She'd gone to bed early, then slept late. She'd turned down the offer to join him and the family when they went out to the slopes a few hours earlier. All of this a month after she'd broken up with him.

Whoops.

She'd been blind, willfully blind. His mother had seen that kiss and walked away without a word. April had known since the beginning. And just that morning, right before they left for the slopes, Liam came by her room to extend his own welcome.

"Mind if I go through Mark's bookshelf?" Liam had asked.

"My mother put some old photo albums in here I wanted to share with Bev."

Rose, still in her pajamas, half-asleep, let him in. "Come on in."

He walked past Rose, the hint of a smile on his face, and squatted down at the squat oak bookcase in the corner under the window. He rose, a dusty album in his arms. "This looks like a good old one." He grinned. "Want to see?"

Intimate pictures of Mark growing up? Hell yeah. "Sure," she said with a shrug.

His grin deepened. "No pressure."

"No, I don't mind. Really."

To her surprise, Liam sat on the bed, patted the mattress next to him, and started to open the book. Rose sat next to him, wishing she'd been nosy enough to find it on her own when she was alone.

Liam frowned. "Oh, this is just one of Mark's scrapbooks. He started making these in junior high." He shut it with a loud *thwap* and started to get up.

"Wait!" She thrust out her hand.

He turned his head, eyebrow raised as he looked at her. A hint of a smile twitched in the corner of his mouth. "You'd like to see it?"

She should've kept quiet and looked at it after he'd gone. "Sure. Why not?" She kept her voice light.

"Right. Why not." Liam opened the book again. The first page was a yellowed newspaper clipping. In the photo, four lean, muscular, bare-chested men stood at the edge of a swimming pool, big grins on their faces. One of the men was circled with a ballpoint pen.

"You?" Rose asked.

"Yup," Liam said, and turned the page. Here there were more newspaper clippings, mostly text. A color snapshot of

Liam with a Stanford towel tied around his waist took up most of the right side of the page; the ballpoint pen had drawn zigzags and lines around it, like a frame.

Rose felt a twinge in her chest. "He was a fan."

"My biggest." Liam turned the next page. "See how he never put in any pictures of himself?"

More photos—these candid, slightly blurry, obviously unprofessional—all of Liam. Some were cut out with scissors and arranged horizontally at the bottom of the page, overrun with hand-drawn blue, wiggly waves.

"How old was he?" Rose asked, her voice catching.

"This book, he made when he was about eleven."

"*This* book? There's another?"

He turned several more pages without pausing. Each one was filled with pictures of Liam—swimming, jogging, winning medals, lifting weights, posing at landmarks all over the world. "Look at the shelf over there."

Biting her lip, Rose turned her gaze to the bookcase in the corner. There were at least ten more books with bindings like the one in Liam's lap. "Oh, my."

"I didn't know about these until a few years ago," he said. "My mother boxed them up in the attic. I found them when I was looking for my camping gear."

"She never showed you? Never even hinted about them?"

Liam cleared his throat. "She knew I wouldn't like it."

"It's so sweet." She reached out and took the scrapbook from him. "Look at all that love. Wow."

"I wanted to throw them away, but my mother stashed them here for safekeeping."

"Throw them away?" Her jaw dropped. "How could you do such a thing? Look at the hours he must've spent making these. The days."

"Exactly."

They stared at each other. She saw sorrow in his eyes. "You don't like being idolized," she said.

"I liked it as much as anybody would, but not from my own brother." He reached across her and turned more pages, finally stopping at one with a photo of a teenaged Liam. The photo had been carefully cropped to trace his entire torso, though part of his arm had been cut off like the Venus de Milo. The real Liam sitting next to her tapped the blank part of the page to his right. "Guess who was here?"

Rose shook her head. "He seems to cut out everybody else."

"Not everyone. He usually left my teammates." She stared at the chopped photo until Liam answered his own question. "It was our father. He devoted his life to getting me to the Olympics. Mark and April were afterthoughts. Which I used to think was lucky for them, but… it messed with Mark's head, a son being neglected like that."

She pulled the book closer. "I don't think his head is messed up at all."

Smiling at her, Liam let her have the book. "He tends to put himself last. Like he thinks he's not worth as much as somebody else."

"He cares about people, that's all."

"Most of them can't see that, given how much time he spends avoiding them," he said.

"He's got to protect himself," she said. "The world's full of phonies and users. He's the real deal."

Liam's gaze sharpened, staring at her. "It can be hard to have somebody love you so completely, with no regard to himself."

"Please. He was your little brother. Of course he loves you," she said. "You should be grateful to have him in your life." She hugged the book to her chest, looked at him. "It's not a burden, it's a gift. Just love him back."

"Just like that?"

"Yes." She frowned, getting to her feet. "He's easy to lo—" She fell silent.

Liam was grinning at her. "Yes?"

She lifted her chin. "He's easy to love."

They stared at each other, any hint of mockery in Liam's smile fading. He stood up. "Are you going skiing with us?" he asked, reaching out to touch her arm.

Her mind spun. Had she just told Liam—

"No, I—I'm going to call my mom," she stammered. What had she done? "Maybe go for a walk."

"Maybe you'll join us tomorrow, then," Liam said as he headed for the hallway. He paused there, met her gaze. "I hope you do."

Nodding, Rose closed the door after him in a daze.

They were all in on it, always had been.

She needed to think. She crawled back into bed and stared at the ceiling, imagining Mark's boyish fingers drawing blue waves around his strong, famous older brother's body. Those little stars and frames around the pictures.

An hour later, after the whole gang had left to go skiing—even Trixie—Rose went upstairs to the empty kitchen. Sitting with her coffee and the dogs, she flipped through another one of the scrapbooks. Finally, in the third one, she found a picture of a young Mark in a *Return of the Jedi* sweatshirt. He stood next to Liam, trying to give him bunny ears but only reaching as high as his shoulder. His shaggy hair was light, almost blond, and the silver braces in his mouth glittered.

Her heart squeezed.

He could've become a hard, bitter person and hated his brother. He could've blamed him for taking all the oxygen in the room, all the love in his father's stingy heart—but he didn't. He made scrapbooks, designed software, taught school. He built a life of his own, quietly, never wanting the spotlight for himself—no matter how much he deserved it.

It would be hours before he came back. Suddenly feeling unbearably restless, Rose slapped the album shut. "Want to go outside, Zeus?"

At the mention of his fondest wish, the dog's little body quivered and jumped with such delight, he fell off the couch. Rose got up, smiling, put her coffee down and headed downstairs. She got on her sexy boots—*he said they were sexy*—and her coat, then remembered the dogs had outfits as well. She found them on one of the snowshoe hooks, and after a chase and a struggle, she finally got all three dogs in their little Fite Dog sweaters and their collars hooked to a bright yellow high-tech leash.

Out she went into the sunny, blinding day. Not windy, not too cold, just below freezing. The snow crunched under her boots, and patches of ice that had escaped the salt slowed her progress down the stairs.

Off to the right between the trees, Lake Tahoe glimmered as blue as the vintage tourism posters inside the house. She stared, surprised by its color, bluer than any body of water she'd ever seen.

Invigorated by the view and the snappy, fresh air, she gave the dogs a little more slack on the leash and stepped gingerly out into the road. Kids from the neighboring cabins were sledding down driveway snowdrifts and behind the houses, where a slope led to a creek.

She looked around for an adult, nervous to see freezing water at the end of the sled trail they'd made, but the child in head-to-toe Pepto-Bismol pink and her older brother in all black seemed to be alone.

The dogs, attracted to the children, tugged at the leash in that direction. Rose looked down at her boots and sighed. They weren't designed for deep snow, but they weren't expensive, either.

He said they were sexy.

Nevertheless, she took a deep breath and stepped off the paved road into the footprint-trampled snow between the houses, not surprised when she sank a foot lower than any of the children's feet had done.

The dogs rollicked over the snow, trotting gracefully through the footprints, not sinking at all.

Feeling like a good citizen for appointing herself lifeguard to the unattended sledders, she watched with dismay as the children suddenly waved at the house, grabbed their pink and red plastic sleds, and jogged up the hill—and disappeared.

Now Rose stood up to her shins in snow halfway between the house and the creek. The dogs had the leashes taut, pulling her like a metronome from side to side as they moved as a pack. With her feet pinned in the snow, any moment now she was going to go down like a tree under a chainsaw.

"I should've taken *one* dog. One I could handle," she muttered.

She decided to reel them in to reduce the torque. At first it worked—they were tiny animals, after all—but then Zeus slipped his narrow, odd-shaped head through his collar altogether and made a dash for the creek.

"Zeus!" Rose looked back at the house to see if anyone had returned, but no. "Bugger."

With long, laborious strides, she staggered forward down the hill. She couldn't let him fall in the water or get caught in a mini avalanche. Besides not wanting to tarnish her reputation with Trixie, she liked the dog too much to abandon him.

Seeing they were following their leader, Luna and Europa

pulled ahead, stopping where the trampled snow ended. They looked back and up at her, tongues lolling. Zeus hadn't been so intimidated; he had scrambled up the snow bank and was now paddling through the fresh powder's surface toward an enormous cedar.

"You crazy dog," Rose said. It was like he was swimming in snow. "Zeus! Where are you going?"

Finally, Zeus reached the tree. He sniffed it, then lifted his tiny leg.

Rose scoffed and looked at the sky. "Can you believe that guy?" she asked Luna and Europa. She waited, then called him again. No sign of him. What would she lure him with?

All she had was herself. She made kissing noises, made her voice soft and high-pitched as she repeated his name, but he kicked up the snow and turned away.

He was far too close to the water for her comfort. She dropped the nice act and made long strides into the snow. This time, Luna and Europa stayed behind her; she had to let out the slack in the leash to chase after Zeus.

He was rolling around on top of the snowbank as if it were a dead skunk and he'd just had a bath. More than a little tired of the game, Rose increased her stride, arms outstretched and ready for capture. Just as she was about to grab his bony little dog body between her hands, he rolled away, and feet up in the air, suddenly vanished into the hungry snow.

MARK SLAMMED THE CAR DOOR AND EYED THE HOUSE. IT had taken superhuman powers not to stay at the house with her today. Just the two of them—

He'd glimpsed her in her nightgown as he passed her door. Peachy, silky, transparent—

He'd given up around three. Who was he kidding? He'd never played hard to get in his life. He might as well pretend to be a kangaroo.

"Phew!" his mother said, getting out of the car with a smile on her face. "I feel like I've been run over by a truck. Every year I can feel my age creeping up on me more."

Mark snorted. After snowshoeing for two hours, he'd been the one to ask for a break. "You kicked my butt, young lady."

"You're just distracted. Next time we'll make it a threesome." Eyes growing wide, she covered her mouth, laughing. "Snowshoeing, I mean. I wonder if she had a nice time here with my little guys. I bet she's glad you're back, though. Don't worry, I'm going to change into some sweats and curl up with a book. And I'll wear my earphones and close the door, so don't worry about making any noise, though I did notice you chose the remote bedroom for her. You could set off a bomb in there and nobody would hear it."

He glanced at the house. It had seemed so big when he bought it. Was it too late to buy another one before Christmas?

They hauled the gear up the stairs and into the house. The door was unlocked.

"We're home!" his mother called.

Mark bent over to unlace his boots, visions of peach satin flashing before his eyes. He hoped she'd just gone back to bed without getting dressed. Maybe she was curled up under the covers right this minute, soft, warm, sleepy.

"She must be out with the dogs," his mother said. "You should go look for her."

"The door was unlocked."

"My little guys would be down here already to say hello if they were here. And their outfits are missing."

He straightened, one boot off, one on. "You're right." He

shoved his foot back inside the other boot and laced them as he hopped toward the door. "I'll go keep her company."

"I know you will, hon. Like I said, I'll be dead to the world, so just pretend I'm not here."

Shaking his head, he went back outside, scanning the road for a sign of a big, beautiful snow bunny with sexy boots and three well-dressed rats on a string.

The holiday weekend had attracted half of the San Francisco Bay Area up to the lake; most of the driveways were filled with SUVs, pickups, sedans, the banks littered with kids' plastic sleds set upright in the snow like a rainbow of tombstones.

Then he heard the yapping. Luna's familiar pop-star soprano, *ya ya ya ya ya ya ya*, filtered up from the left, down by the creek.

Uneasiness pricked the back of his neck; he turned to stride away from the driveway into the snow, finding the footprints, children's, dogs', and one—much deeper—adult's.

He saw her just as her head cleared the snowbank. One arm clawed at the powder, digging with the leash handle; her other arm hugged close to her body, not helping her at all to climb out of the hole she was in.

Later Mark wouldn't remember how he got from the driveway to the creek's snowbank, only that he was so damn slow. He saw the two dogs—Luna yapping, Europa whimpering—and then, finally, he was striding through the snow, only a body length away.

"Stop!" Rose cried. "Not safe. It's an overhang. The water's just below us."

His heart was pounding so hard in his ears, he barely heard her. "Hold still. I'll get a rope."

"I'm almost there. Just… get the dogs," she gasped.

He called them over, caught the woven string between his fingers. "Let go of the leash. I've got them."

Sighing with relief, she flung it at him across the snow, dug herself out another few feet, and then, while Mark forced himself to wait, she lifted her legs free.

To his surprise, instead of pulling herself along on her stomach, she rolled onto her back and kicked herself toward him. Her head disappeared into the powder, yet she continued to snowplow herself along on her back, away from the creek, until he was able to reach her and help haul her completely to safety.

"Careful!" Panting for breath, she pushed his hands away from her body. "Zeus is under my coat. Dude needs his… toenails… clipped. *Damn.*"

She was caked with snow, head to foot. Even her eyelashes were spotted with white clumps.

He'd ask what happened later. "We need to get you inside."

"Yeah. He's shivering really bad."

"I mean you." He helped her to her feet, slung one of her arms over his shoulder. Luna and Europa were running around them, tangling their legs together with the leash. He bent down to unhook them. "These two need to go."

"No! After what I did to save this one? Pick them up."

He pulled her closer. "You need help."

"I'm fine. It was Zeus." She shook her head, dislodging a clump of snow from her hair onto her shoulder. "Please, just pick them up."

He did as he was told and she unhooked the leashes.

"You first," he said, hoping she wouldn't be so bossy if she were hypothermic. "But if you fall, I'm dumping these rats and carrying you."

She didn't say anything, just shook her head, plodded past

him. Slowly, they tromped through the snow up to the house. He could see her knees buckle when they reached the clear, open surface of the driveway, but she waved him away when she tried to help.

"We need to get Zeus warmed up. He's shaking really badly," she said, but at the top of the stairs, she hesitated. "I'm covered with snow."

He reached past her and shoved the door open. "No shit. You're like the abominable girlfriend."

That earned him a glance.

He stared, breathless. Blue, blue eyes. He'd never seen a color so beautiful.

"It's your house," she said softly, and went in.

Luna and Europa leaped out of his arms onto the floor and immediately jumped up to paw at her legs. He pushed them aside and bent down to unzip her boots. Her skin was so cold. He reached up for her jacket. "We've got to get you out of these clothes."

"One-track mind," she muttered, then gasped in pain.

"You okay?"

She let out a breath, readjusting Zeus. "I'll be okay. It's just his claws are kind of sharp. Man, being a hero sucks."

She let him tear off the jacket while her arms took turns holding the bundle under her shirt. "Is your mom here? Zeus really needs some help, but I don't know what. He's wet."

Her own hands were shaking, her lips blue and trembling.

"Mother!" he shouted.

Luna and Europa gave up on Rose and scurried over to scratch at his mother's bedroom door. Mark followed them and rapped harder.

No answer. With a sigh, he rattled the doorknob before sticking his head in.

True to her word, his mother, eyes closed, tucked under

the covers up to her chin, had her black Dr. Dre headphones over her ears.

"Mom!"

She opened them, a half smile on her lips, then bolted upright when she sensed trouble. She tore the headphones off. "What happened?"

"Zeus fell in the creek. Rose got him."

"Oh!" She jumped out of bed. "Where?"

"Here," Rose said, slowly entering the room.

His mother's eyes grew more alarmed. She rushed over and caught Rose's face between her hands, glanced at Mark. "She's frozen."

"I know. You deal with Zeus, I'll help her."

Nodding, she stepped back to let Rose lift her sweater with shaking hands. Zeus, big-eyed, passive, and trembling, fell into his mother's arms. His stumpy tail began to wiggle.

"You silly little man," his mother said, clucking and cooing. "You're not a St. Bernard." Then she gave Mark a serious look. "Get her out of those clothes."

"Really, what k-kind of… f-family is th-this?" Rose asked, attempting a smile.

He put his arm around her, marched her to the bathroom. Too bad his house didn't have a sauna. He'd install one next week. Right now he'd get her in a hot shower, get some hot liquids in her.

To his credit, it took him another two seconds to think of what hot liquid he most wanted to put inside her.

He turned the water valve as hot as it would go to steam up the room, then turned his attention to getting her naked. Her head was lowered, her fingers fumbling with her jeans button. He took over and pushed the denim down, alarmed at the icy feel of her skin. Her socks were damp; he rolled those off, careful not to unbalance her. When she pulled up her sweater and T-shirt over her head, the breath went out of him. Her skin, her perfect skin, was scratched raw. Ragged red stripes from Zeus's panicked toenails covered her stomach, hips, chest.

"I'm going to kill that dog," he said through his teeth.

"Don't you d-dare." She reached behind her to unfasten her bra, but he got there first.

She was so cold. He caressed her back, her shoulders, her arms, willing her to warm up, massaging his own heat into her.

She wriggled out of the bra straps, gave him an amused look, and reached into the shower to test the water. "Are you trying to cook me? J-jeez. I'm not a l-lobster."

"At least he didn't get—all of you," he said, staring at her breasts. They were islands of creamy perfection in an angry red sea.

"No time to take off the bra. I knew skin-to-skin contact was the best way to warm him up." She turned the valve down a little, stepped in the stall, gasped.

He was already tearing off his own clothes to apply a little skin-to-skin therapy himself.

29

THE HOT WATER STUNG THE scratches on her torso, but she didn't care. It felt so damn good to be warm.

She remembered something about the danger of sending cold blood to her heart, but she hadn't been outside that long, and unlike Zeus, she had plenty of natural insulation.

Her boots were ruined, though. She'd fallen into the creek. It was shallow, but wet was wet. Her toes tingled under the hot water, which she hoped was a good sign. To hell with her boots—she couldn't buy new feet. Suddenly remembering the climbers on Mt. Everest with black toes, she bent over and massaged them while the water poured over her head.

The shower door opened; Mark's foot appeared next to hers.

Not entirely surprised—okay, not surprised at all—she stood up, admiring him on the way up.

"Hi," she said.

Eyes searching hers, he wrapped an arm around her waist and pulled her against his long, hard body. He tilted her so the water fell on her back and shoulders, stroking his hands along her bottom, up her spine. "We need to get you warm."

"Mmm." She wriggled closer, put her cheek on his chest.

"Are you warm?"

She laughed against his chest hair. "Getting there."

"When you are, let me know."

"Yeah?"

"Yeah. I want to chew you out for risking your life for my mother's stray mutant."

"Ah, honey, don't put yourself down like that," she said.

Growling, he caught her ass in both hands and ground closer. "I'm serious," he said in her ear. "You're too important."

Important? "The creek's about six inches deep."

"Under ten feet of ice and snow. There are rocks. You could've hit your head."

She reached up and touched his temple. "I think you already did."

Gazing at her, he moved back, pulling her eyes out of the spray of the water. "Yeah. Maybe I did."

The feel of his erection on her belly began to appeal to her more than the hot water. "I think I'm okay now."

Frowning, he captured her hand, lifted it to his mouth. "Frostbite is serious." One by one he sucked her fingers into his mouth. Around her thumb, he said, "I wouldn't want to lose any of you. Not even an inch."

Speechless, her muscles giving way to the massaging heat, the desire building inside her, she swayed against him.

He bent his head to her ear. "I want to get you in bed, but I'm afraid you might get cold again." His voice was low, rough. He kissed his way across her forehead to the other side. "I'll have to make sure I keep you warm." He sucked the earlobe into his mouth. "Hot."

Her hand found the water valve at her back, shut it off.

He grabbed a towel he must've hung over the glass wall of the shower and draped it over her shoulders. Patting her skin, he stopped when he reached her chest, his eyes getting serious. "You need some first aid."

"You need a towel." She traced the water droplets on his muscled shoulder, over his collar bone. "You're shivering."

Shaking his head, he tightened her towel around her and stroked her hair. Water dripped down her back. "We'll have to deal with your hair. You shouldn't have a wet head."

"I'm fine, Mark."

"Look at this." He frowned at her throat, his touch feather light on one of the scratches. "And this. I always hated that dog." He leaned back, gently touching other marks, his jaw tight.

"He's awesome, and worth a few scratches." She pushed open the shower door, tugged free of his concerned grip to reach for another towel on the hook. She handed it to him, but he squatted down and dried her legs with it.

"I'll get you some hot tea, coffee, chocolate, everything," he said.

Smiling, she watched him, naked and dripping wet himself, dab at her toes one by one with the thick, dark-green towel. She waited until he seemed satisfied before stepping away to finally get him a towel of his own.

He pushed it away. "You need one for that hair. It's dripping. You'll get cold again."

"I'm getting cold looking at you." She flung the towel around his shoulders and pulled it tight, smiling up at him, letting her own towel gape open in front.

He stood still, gazing down at her. His throat moved as he swallowed hard. "I'm having warring impulses." His eyes dropped down to her breasts, further, between her legs. Then he pulled the edges of her towel together, covering her, and turned away to dry himself with quick, efficient strokes. "There's a hair dryer under the sink. I'll get the first aid kit in the car."

Smiling, she rolled her eyes, reached out to squeeze his right butt cheek. "I'm fine."

He spun around, drawing the towel around him like a bullfighter with a cape, and scowled at her chest. "You're— you're—*bleeding*. God knows what Zeus had under his toenails."

"Snow, I imagine," she said, but she saw that he was right; some of the scratches were deep.

"I'll be right back." Towel tight around his waist, he pushed his hair back with his hand before he reached for the doorknob.

Rose forgot about her injuries and stared. "You are so gorgeous," she breathed.

He turned, held her gaze. "Dry your hair," he said in a low voice, then was gone.

ঔ

He'd never been so aroused and so close to fainting at the same time.

Blood.

He braced a hand on the doorway as he went into his room to get dressed. She probably thought he was a hero for insisting on the bandages before getting in bed with her.

Some hero.

He dragged on his jeans commando, pulled a sweatshirt over his head, marched to the front door and shoved his feet into his wet boots.

The first aid box was buried in the hatch under the snow-shoes, but at least it was there. By the time he stomped back into the house, his head was clear. Maybe he wouldn't make a fool of himself after all.

He kicked off his boots and went to knock on the bathroom door, forcing himself to think of her blue eyes, the blonde curls between her legs, anything but the—red—

He sucked in a breath through his nose, stared at the ceiling.

"Hey," she said, opening the door with a hairdryer pointed at her head. She plucked at his sweatshirt, lips in a mock pout. "You got dressed." She'd tied the towel around her waist, exposing her breasts, which were lovely, but uncovering the scratches, too, which—

He focused on her lips. That was the good kind of red. Really, really good. Full, sensual, rosy, glossy. He stepped inside, slamming the door behind him, and bent down to taste her.

God, he wanted her. He kissed her hard, driving his tongue into her mouth, everything else forgotten.

She stepped into his arms, kissing him back, but she still held the hair dryer in her hand. When she looked aside to turn it off, he turned his attention to the graceful curves of her ear, her silky neck, the long strands of her damp hair.

Still damp.

"Sorry." He stepped back, rubbing his mouth. "You keep doing that. I'll—I'll play doctor."

Grinning, she leaned her bottom against the sink, facing him, and lifted the dryer to her head again. Arching to her back, she gave her breasts a little shake and said, "Yes, Doctor."

Mouth dry, he tore open the ointment, wishing his lightheadedness were because of the hard pink nipples and the large, perfect breasts bouncing in front of him, and not because of any squeamishness.

The scratches weren't that bad, he told himself. Red but

shallow, most of them, and her breasts—oh, right there—had been spared.

With a pinkie fingertip, he dabbed antibiotic ointment on the deepest scratch first, ignoring the droplets of blood. He ripped open a half dozen bandages and lined them up on the counter, but Rose stopped him.

"Only on the really bad ones," she said. "The adhesive in those will hurt me more than the cuts. I've got really sensitive skin."

He frowned, nodding, gently stroking an uninjured patch. "Just this one, then. The one that's… bleeding." Swallowing hard, he dabbed away the drips, put the ointment directly on the bandage, and carefully covered it.

She watched him, a small smile on her lips, the dryer's high-pitched whine loud in the small room. Her hair was getting lighter and blonder each minute as it dried, fluffing up around her face in a pale gold cloud, and her cheeks were pink, flushed, warm.

He finished what he could do with her injuries, pushed the box to the floor, stood up. He took the hair dryer out of her hands and turned it off. "You're not chilled anymore."

Eyes dark as midnight, she wrapped her arms around his neck. "I've never been so hot in my life."

❧

A KNOCK SOUNDED ON THE DOOR. "KIDS?" IT WAS Trixie. "I'm so sorry to bother you, but I need a few more towels."

Rose stifled a groan. "We'll be right out!" she called, trying to step out of Mark's embrace.

He was immovable. Well, most of him.

Trixie knocked again. "I promise not to look."

Rose finally got the strength to break free. Breathing shallowly, she wrapped herself in a towel and waited for Mark, slowly, his eyes never leaving her face, to do the same before opening the door.

Zeus was bundled in Trixie's arms. "All better?" She was smiling.

Damn her fair complexion. Rose couldn't say anything, just nodded, knowing her face was as pink as bubble gum.

"How's the mongrel?" Mark asked, scowling.

Rose was surprised by his icy tone. "Don't tell me you're still holding a grudge."

"You should see her," he said to his mother, nodding his head at Rose as he waved his hand over his chest. "All torn up."

Trixie's eyebrows went up. "Torn up?"

"Just some scratches." Rose tightened the towel.

"Nothing that broke the skin?" Trixie glanced at Mark.

"Nothing serious," Rose said.

"Oh." She didn't sound convinced.

"It's really nothing." Rose reached out to pat Zeus's head buried inside the blanket. "Glad you're okay, honey."

"He needs his fingernails trimmed," Mark growled. "With a chainsaw."

"So you *were* bleeding," Trixie said.

"Just a little. Really, it's understandable. I shoved him under my sweater. There wasn't much room in there, and I probably squeezed him pretty hard trying to climb over the snow." One of Zeus's eyelids lifted for a moment before sinking back down. "It was probably more traumatic than falling in the water."

Trixie thrust the dog into Mark's arms, almost breaking his grip on the towel around his waist, then grabbed Rose's bare arm and ushered her off to the side. "If there aren't any bandages under the sink," she whispered, "I have a first aid box in the car."

"Mark got it for me. It's cool." Figuring a picture was worth a thousand words, she pulled back the towel to flash her well-bandaged midsection. "See?"

Trixie's face widened with alarm. Then she gaped at Mark.

"I'm fine too, Mom," he said, looking embarrassed.

"Why wouldn't you be?" Rose asked.

After an awkward silence, Mark reached forward and patted Zeus—gently, no hint of any hard feelings. "I usually faint at the sight of blood."

Trixie cleared her throat. "Always, I would've said."

"Only one cut bled enough to need a second bandage, but I just mopped it up with some toilet paper and—" Rose stopped when she saw how Mark had turned white.

"Just the thought of it can bowl him over." Trixie shook her head. "His father was the same way. Very embarrassed about it."

"I'm used to it," Mark said tightly.

Trixie patted his bare chest. "No, I meant your father. He was dreadfully ashamed of it."

"It's more of an inconvenience than anything else," he said.

"Worse than that, Mark. It can be dangerous, passing out here and there." Trixie looked at Rose. "Just last month I found him on the floor of the living room. Luckily he didn't hit his head on anything on the way down."

"I hit my head on *something*," he said. "The floor. It's not like we've got wall-to-wall shag. Oh no, you need hardwoods."

Trixie ignored him. "He'd just found out about Blair. I guess the thought of, you know…" She sighed, nuzzled Zeus.

That had been the day after they'd spent the night together, after Rose had visited Blair, when Mark hadn't come to the door.

Trixie had tried to get rid of Rose to protect her son from embarrassment. And he hadn't rushed out to see her because he'd just passed out.

"I'd appreciate an end to this conversation," he said. "Unless you'd like a demo."

Rose pulled the towel tighter. "You didn't say anything." Suddenly his alarm over the scratches made more sense. There'd been plenty of blood to gross out a squeamish person. "You should've said something. I could've handled it."

His hot gaze raked over her. "What fun would that be?"

Trixie jogged forward and reclaimed the bundled dog. "It's okay if you want to kiss now. I'll get the towels and go."

"Not necessary." Stepping forward, Mark hooked his arms around Rose and lowered his mouth to hers.

30

MARK DIDN'T KISS LIKE A man afraid of being seen. If Rose hadn't frantically ushered him into the bedroom, God knows how far he would've taken it in the hallway.

He tore the towel off her when the door was still open.

She gasped. "Your mom—"

He kicked the door shut, threw aside his own towel. His eyelids fell as he gazed at her. "No more talk. Only do."

She stepped backward until she bumped the bed. The late afternoon sun was pouring clear winter light onto the bed, onto her naked body.

Illuminating the welts on her stomach, her ribs, her collarbone. When she saw the way Mark flinched when his gaze raked over her, she reached for a burgundy throw blanket.

"Do you trust me?" he asked.

"I just didn't want you to, you know, feel bad." She draped the blanket over her chest.

He moved closer, captured her face in his hands. "You don't trust me." Kissing her forehead, he gently pushed her down onto the bed. "But you will."

Smiling at the erection now in front of her face, she wrapped her fingers around him, squeezed, stroked. Then, with a naughty glance up at him, she licked.

His jaw tightened. Encouraged, aroused with power, she slipped her mouth over the head and sucked him deeper. He was hard, velvety, thick. She felt herself get wet. Hungry for him.

"You like that?" he said through his teeth.

Nodding, she sucked him harder. Her left hand glided around his muscled thigh to his ass, pulled him closer.

To her dismay, he put his hand on her cheek and pushed her away. "I like it too."

"Then why do you want me to stop?"

He sat down on the bed next to her and kissed her. As he sank onto his back, he pulled her on top of him. They both kicked their way up the bed, tongues tangling, hands exploring each other, the playfulness erased in a wave of hot, sudden need.

"I want you so bad," she gasped. "I've always wanted you."

"You've got me." He licked the underside of her chin, the corner of her mouth, kissed her eyelids one after the other.

"Touch me," she said. "Touch me everywhere."

"Promise?" His hand reached between her legs, stroked the curls, but didn't push into the wetness.

"Oh, yeah." She was on top of him, knowing she should worry about crushing him, knowing she shouldn't. She spread her knees, inviting his hand deeper. He was hard, poking her stomach; she reached down, fisted him, pumped him up and down as she licked his face.

His fingertip teased her. Up and down, just a tiny, maddening stroke.

"Please," she said, but his fingers stayed agonizingly distant. To encourage him, she kissed her way down his neck and then followed the hair down his chest and navel. Lower. While her hand squeezed, her mouth slipped over him, took him deep. She bit him with her lips, so turned on by the way he got harder and bigger in her mouth.

He groaned, plainly enjoying her efforts, but again he put his hand on her mouth and moved her face away.

Confused, she pushed herself up to look at him. "Why not?"

"Exactly," he said softly. His face was flushed, strained, but he managed to raise a mocking eyebrow.

Suddenly understanding, she exhaled, annoyed. "That's—but—"

"What?"

"That's different."

"Why?"

"All guys like blow jobs," she said.

He smiled slowly. "And some girls like giving them."

"How do you know I'm not just trying to make you happy?"

"I can tell."

She licked her lips. "All right. So?"

"You may suck me," he said, arching his back, shifting his hips upward, "as long as you're facing the other direction."

Her temperature rose another few degrees. "You want to look at me?"

He sat up, took hold of her, rotated her torso away from him. Fingers splayed, his hands caressed her ass, pushed up her spine to bend her over.

Now she was facing away from him, her bottom up in the air, her elbows digging into the mattress, her face next to his knee.

One of his fingers slid to the cleft of her ass, glided down. Again, he only teased the folds, not entering. "Closer."

Gladly, she crawled backward, willing him to slip those fingers inside where she was wet and aching for him. He was hard, twitching with his own arousal; she wrapped her fingers around him again and bent down to suck him.

He gripped her left knee and lifted it over his body, spreading her wide so she was straddling his shoulders.

She ached, how she ached. She moved over so her left hand was on the other side of his hip and began sucking him in earnest, deeper and harder, afraid and not wanting and so, so desperate for him to—

His powerful arms pulled her down onto his face. She cried out, eyes closing, his erection sliding up her cheek as his tongue swept deep into her.

For a long moment, a paralyzing minute, every one of her senses was fixated on the feel of his mouth kissing her. He lapped at her, deep, hard. His fingers separated her folds and then, while she cried out again, his tongue flicked over her, over and over, around and around. Blinding pleasure shot through her. A shrinking voice inside her reminded her she didn't allow this, she didn't like this, and then it faded into silence.

He pulled her lower, dug his fingers into her thighs. The sounds were sexual, kinky, so hot; she wanted more. More of him. She let the pleasure travel up her body to her mouth, and sharing it with him, taking more for herself, she sucked him deep into her throat, tasting the saltiness of him.

Pleasure spiraled low in her belly. Her knees trembled. Yet he continued to suckle and tease her, and she him. Mindless, happy, loving, sexual, it went on and on until she was so high and tight inside, she simply couldn't support herself any longer. Her forehead fell to his thigh—and he, seeming to sense she was at her peak, touched her in just the way she wanted and needed and then she was over, exploding, *there.*

"*Oh,*" she cried, letting her hips fall to the bed.

He sat up and climbed on top of her. When he kissed her on the neck, she smelled herself on him. She wondered vaguely if she should mind, because she didn't.

He settled himself between her legs, breathing heavily, and kissed her deeply. Then with a slow, steady thrust, he pushed into her. A groan ripped from his throat. She sighed, closed her eyes, and shifted her hips to meet him.

Scattering kisses along her neck, face, and throat, he built up a steady rhythm that was gentler than their other times together. The moves were slower, more graceful, deliberate. She felt like he was touching her everywhere, inside and out, always keeping his torso lifted from hers in the middle, protecting the soreness there.

After a little while his movements lost their luxurious, lazy pace. With building speed, he pounded harder, his breath coming ragged, and she tightened around him, encouraging him, her own pleasure building again.

She dug her nails into his shoulders and he came with a shout. Throwing his head back, he moved roughly inside her one more time, twice, and then he collapsed on top of her. Then quickly to the side. He dipped his head against her temple, breathing heavily, and closed his eyes.

She smiled and watched him. When his breath slowed back to normal, the long eyelashes fluttered upward, and eyes like the ocean, not quite green or blue, regarded her.

After his breath had gone back to normal, he propped himself up on an elbow, brushed the hair out of her eyes. "I love you, Rose," he said. Serious, not smiling at all.

Her breath didn't come for a moment. "I love you, too, Mark," she whispered.

Frowning, he shook his head. "You don't have to say it just because I did."

"I know."

"I should've waited. I've really put you on the spot."

"Fine. Tell me later." She played with the lock of hair that had fallen over his eyes again. She wondered if it got blond streaks in the summer, cheerfully confident she'd find out.

"I will," he said.

"I know."

"THERE'S SOMETHING ELSE I SHOULD tell you," Mark said.

"Oh, God," Rose said. "What now?"

"It's nothing bad. At least, I think you'll understand."

"Let me guess—you own Google." She shifted onto her side to face him. "No. A cable news network."

He closed his eyes, laughing softly.

She tweaked his nose. "A small island in the Pacific?"

"Nothing like that." His hand slid up her thigh and around her hip to caress her bottom. "It's just—I had a little help getting you here today."

A few odd moments fell into place. She sorted through them in her mind. "Blair's not really that depressed."

He nodded.

"That bitch," she said affectionately. "I didn't know she had it in her."

"She'd been depressed, but John helped her through it. She's got a therapist, and John's promised—he begged her, apparently—to stay at her side," he said. "In fact, using Blair to get you up here was John's idea."

She thought back to his arrival at the house, the way he provoked her into joining them at the cabin. "That bastard," she said, less warmly. "Not that I'm surprised he could be a sneak."

"He's really not that bad." The sun outside was setting, and pale warm light slanted across his smiling eyes. "I kind of like him."

She sat up, dislodging his hand. "*That's* why he was coming on to me last night. I thought he was trying to make Blair jealous—you know, snap her out of her cloud of doom—but—" She laughed. "He was working on *you*."

With a scowl, Mark pulled her back down on top of him. "You didn't seem to mind."

She smiled coyly. "Were you jealous?"

"If I'd had a chicken, I would've put it in the dishwasher." He took her face in his hands, kissed her roughly. "I take it back. I hate that guy."

After a little more heavy petting and giggling, they reluctantly got out of bed to wash up and pull on fresh clothes to prepare for a sociable Christmas dinner.

Just as they were in the hallway, ready to head upstairs, Mark slipped one hand into her rear jeans pocket and another over her breast. She stumbled, unable to move, and he laughed into her ear. "Oh, I beg your pardon," he said, groping and squeezing. "I seem to have slipped."

She tried to push his hands away, unsuccessfully. "Let's see if Zeus is okay. Help out with the dinner."

"I can't decide." His hand roamed over to her other breast.

She managed to grab the banister at the stairs. "Decide?"

He hopped in front of her, ran his hands down to her ass, pulled her against him. "Which part I like best—the T or the A."

They were still kissing on the lowest stair when John and Blair came through the front door.

"I can't believe you pushed me!" Blair said, stomping her boots on the rug. "What kind of boyfriend are you? I was on the bunny hill because I *don't know how to ski.*"

"You weren't moving. I thought you needed help," John replied.

"You were laughing!"

"Not as hard as you were," John said.

The bubbly sound of Blair's giggles filled the cabin. "At least I got even, dude, when you were flapping your arms like —" She cut herself off. They must've noticed Mark and Rose. "Oh!" Blair squeaked, then let out a loud sigh.

"Get a room, you two," John said.

Blair shushed him. "We'll just tiptoe by—"

Smiling against Mark's lips, Rose turned her head, waved a few fingers at them. "Welcome back."

Blair's eyes were bright and happy, her cheeks pink. Clasping her hands at her chest, she looked between the two of them with her head slightly tilted to the side, smiling.

John clapped his hands together, strode up the hallway, Blair hooked under his arm. "I'm starving. You guys cool with a seven-o'clock dinner? I'd hoped for six, but we were having too much fun out there today to come back earlier."

"Eight would be a little better, I think," Mark said. "It'll give everyone else time to get here."

"Everyone else?" Blair asked. "Oh, right. Your sister."

"*You're* cooking?" Rose asked John.

"Blair cooks, I help," he said.

"We practiced the day before yesterday," Blair said, beaming.

"I've never had anything that tasted so good in my life as that roast beef, babe," John said.

Rose couldn't believe what she was hearing. "Like, from a cow?"

"Dropped the vegan thing. I'm more paleo now—you know, caveman-style." John lifted Blair off the ground with one arm. "Blair's got me into gourmet cooking. I was thinking about taking classes with her. Maybe—it's a long shot, but"—he smiled down at her—"I can totally see us owning a restaurant together. I've got the capital, she's got the talent…"

Blair's face lit up like an energy-inefficient halogen light bulb. She met Rose's gaze and nodded enthusiastically.

Just then Liam and Bev blew into the cabin, brushing snow off their hair, talking and laughing.

"April's right behind us in the driveway," Liam said.

Zeus bounded down the stairs and tore across the floor to greet the newcomers, Europa and Luna at his heels.

"He'll obviously need a long recovery period," Mark said dryly in Rose's ear. He kissed her cheek, nuzzled her neck. "I've got one more surprise for you," he whispered.

His tongue tickled the nerves of her neck, making her shiver. "I don't know if I can take any more surprises," she said.

"You'll like this one," he said.

Rose sensed from the way the others had fallen silent, staring at each other with smiles on their faces, that they were all in on it.

Whatever *it* was.

She brushed away any curiosity about their smug secret with the mellowness only profound happiness can bring. If they wanted to play their games, whatever; her soul was bursting with contentment, rosy with peace. *Let them have their little crumb of joy,* she told herself, turning to go upstairs and get to know Trixie a little better. Though she had the impression she'd have years to do so.

And then the door popped open and her own mother walked in. Big and beautiful, a royal-blue velvet cape over her shoulders, Kim Devlin threw back her hood and shook out her long, blonde hair.

"I made it!" she cried, snow cascading around her head. After tossing a bright smile at Rose, she turned to April, who'd come in behind her, stomping her feet on the mat. "That's Mark, right?"

"Not quite the same guy he was a few months ago, but pretty close," April said.

Overwhelmed, happy, shocked, thrilled, Rose ran down the hall and threw her arms around her mother's waist. "Mom!" Then she buried her face in her snowy hair, not caring about the tears pouring out of her. "Oh, Mom."

Her mother hugged her right back, laughing, then pushed her gently aside. "Merry Christmas, sweetie." She hooked her arm in Rose's, turned to Mark. "Well, I didn't need to be told who you are."

"Mom, this is Mark. The guy I'm totally in love with. And he loves me right back."

"Of course he does, baby," her mother said. She held out her hand, twinkling at him. "That's why I let him put me on a plane at six in the morning Christmas Day."

He did this for her? Rose turned her head to look at him, reeling again. It was so much.

He came over and kissed her mother on the cheek, a lopsided grin on his face. "Rose didn't tell me she had a little sister."

Eyebrows flying up, her mother laughed, kissed him right back. "Oh, you are a keeper."

That's the plan, Rose thought.

Slowly they all made their way upstairs, talking over one another, trying not to trip over the dogs. Zeus had taken a particular interest in her mom, and she'd picked him up for a cuddle.

It was all good. All wonderful. Even if her stepfather joined them, she wouldn't mind, she'd learn to get along, work it out. Even use his real name.

She reached around her mom's arm to scratch Zeus behind the ears. "Is Phil getting the suitcases?"

Pausing on the stairs, her mom sighed. "It's just me, I'm afraid," she said. "I couldn't get him to brave the plane."

Rose bit back a laugh, looked away. Mark helped her hide her relief by kissing her again, pinning her against the wall while their families left them alone.

It really was a happy ending.

NOT QUITE PERFECT (OAKLAND HILLS #3)

Serial temp worker April Johnson is nothing like her wildly successful brothers. She doesn't have an Olympic gold medal. She doesn't have millions in the bank from a tech company she founded as a teenager. She doesn't even have a place to live, not since her boyfriend sneaked off in the middle of the night —skipping out on the rent, his three-legged dog, and her. Now forced to move back home with her mother and grovel for a job from one of her brothers, April decides it's past time she got serious about her life.

Zack Fain, on the other hand, has been too serious for years. After losing his wife to cancer at the age of twenty-six, he's done nothing but work on his consulting business. But when he meets April at a new job, he forgets he's a humorless suit who never gets emotionally involved. She makes him laugh, she turns him on, and he begins to wonder if it's time he broke a few rules.

Although April refuses to get stuck in yet another dead-end relationship, Zack isn't like any of the guys she's dated before. This could be the real deal. This could be *serious*.

But is either of them ready for the kind of serious that lasts a lifetime?

BOOKS BY GRETCHEN GALWAY

OAKLAND HILLS SERIES

Love Handles (Oakland Hills #1)

This Time Next Door (Oakland Hills #2)

Not Quite Perfect (Oakland Hills #3)

This Changes Everything (Oakland Hills #4)

Quick Takes (Oakland Hills Stories Boxed Set)

Going For Broke (Oakland Hills #5)

Going Wild (Oakland Hills #6)

Oakland Hills Romantic Comedy Boxed Set (Books 1-3)

RESORT TO LOVE SERIES

The Supermodel's Best Friend (Resort to Love #1)

Diving In (Resort to Love #2)

ABOUT THE AUTHOR

GRETCHEN GALWAY is a *USA Today* bestselling author who writes romantic comedies because love is too painful to survive without laughing. Raised in the American Midwest, she now lives in California with her family.

To get an email alert about sales and new releases, please sign up for my newsletter at www.gretchengalway.com.

Happy reading!

facebook.com/AuthorGretchenGalway